P9-CDK-516

BAD, BAD SEYMOUR BROWN

Also by Susan Isaacs

Compromising Positions

Close Relations

Almost Paradise

Shining Through

Magic Hour

After All These Years

Lily White

Red, White and Blue

Brave Dames and Wimpettes

Long Time No See

Any Place I Hang My Hat

Past Perfect

As Husbands Go

Goldberg Variations

A Hint of Strangeness

Takes One to Know One

BAD, BAD SEYMOUR BROWN

A Corie Geller Novel

SUSAN ISAACS

Atlantic Monthly Press
New York

Copyright © 2023 by Susan Isaacs

All rights reserved. No part of this book may be reproduced in any form or by any electronic or mechanical means, including information storage and retrieval systems, without permission in writing from the publisher, except by a reviewer, who may quote brief passages in a review. Scanning, uploading, and electronic distribution of this book or the facilitation of such without the permission of the publisher is prohibited. Please purchase only authorized electronic editions, and do not participate in or encourage electronic piracy of copyrighted materials. Your support of the author's rights is appreciated. Any member of educational institutions wishing to photocopy part or all of the work for classroom use, or anthology, should send inquiries to Grove Atlantic, 154 West 14th Street, New York, NY 10011 or permissions@groveatlantic.com.

FIRST EDITION

Published simultaneously in Canada
Printed in the United States of America

This book was set in 12-pt. Arno by Alpha Design & Composition of Pittsfield, NH.

First Grove Atlantic hardcover edition: May 2023

Library of Congress Cataloging-in-Publication data is available for this title.

ISBN 978-0-8021-5906-9
eISBN 978-0-8021-5907-6

Atlantic Monthly Press
an imprint of Grove Atlantic
154 West 14th Street
New York, NY 10011

Distributed by Publishers Group West

groveatlantic.com

23 24 25 26 10 9 8 7 6 5 4 3 2 1

To my daughter, Elizabeth Picciuto,

my mentor and maven,

with gratitude and love

CHAPTER ONE

In the universe of 1990s Brooklyn bad guys, Seymour Brown, CPA, had risen way above most of the goons and gangsters. Not to the pinnacle, but close. He probably would have moved up even further, but he and his wife, Kim, were killed when their house was burned to the ground. Unquestionably arson, unquestionably murder—but the crime remained unsolved. For my dad, who was assigned to the investigation back when he was a second-grade NYPD detective, it was the coldest of his cold cases.

When Seymour and Kim Brown—along with their surviving daughter, April—came roaring back into my dad's life and mine, my parents were living with us. During Covid, they had moved in and never left: a mutually agreeable decision. That night, we were having an early dinner in the backyard, around six thirty, that lovely half-hour hiatus between flies and mosquitoes. My parents were gathered with my husband, Josh Geller, our sixteen-year-old daughter, Eliza, and me at one end of an enormous picnic table.

Oh, the table: it had been purchased by Dawn, Eliza's first mother and Josh's first wife. Perhaps she anticipated delightful Tuscan-style lunches al fresco, with twenty friends, all the women wearing gauzy white blouses and laughing as they raised overfilled glasses of Brunello. But before she could complete her set of Italian ceramic plates and bowls by finding a truly wondrous soup tureen, she died suddenly from an undiagnosed cardiovascular quirk during Pilates class. Eliza was only five when it happened. Devastating. I adopted Eliza five years later, soon after I'd married Josh.

Our meal, though, wasn't Tuscan as much as pan-Mediterranean-via-Long Island: shish kebab that Josh had grilled with scientific precision, as well as Turkish roasted veggies and an orzo salad I'd made. A family meal, not an idyllic, wine-drenched salut to la dolce vita. My mom was busy sneaking bits of shish kebab to our dog, Lulu; my dad was brushing his ear with the back of his hand in a failed attempt to discourage a bee from assessing his aftershave. I spilled about a quarter of my wine making a grand gesture as I opined on *Criminal Minds* post–Mandy Patinkin; Eliza gazed longingly at her phone, which we had insisted she place facedown during the meal even as it vibrated with near-constant notifications; and there was no way to stop Josh from explicating on his new, foolproof method of slow-roasting the kebabs.

Having my parents live at our house was more comforting than I would have thought. Blessedly, Josh's parents had been fine during the pandemic in their own oversize place; (also blessedly) they had inherited enough money to stay put. They were attended by a housekeeper named Roswitha; though reluctant to disturb any dust, she was a whiz at turning out strudel. My in-laws were totally content with their daily routine, which began with fresh-squeezed orange juice and ended with half a bottle of Rémy Martin cognac.

My mom and dad, however, were neither rolling in money nor catered to by a live-in strudelmeister. Their place in Forest Hills—the same apartment in which I'd grown up—was nice enough by city standards. Two bedrooms, so my dad, fifteen years into his retirement, could lean back on the giant recliner in his den (my ex-bedroom), watch his ginormous TV, and critique cop shows. He missed work so much that the cops on Netflix and Amazon Prime became his buddies. My mom said the only time he wasn't listless was when he was worrying about his favorite characters: Would hefty Andri Ólafsson have a heart attack trudging through the snow after killers in Siglufjörður and Reykjavík? Would Bosch deliberately walk into a bullet?

Pre-pandemic, my mom had spent many of her days auditioning, seeing her theater friends, going to shows, now and then acting in a commercial or uttering two weepy lines on *Law and Order*. Earlier in her career she'd played Mrs. Alving in *Ghosts* off-off-Broadway and Tinsley Bancroft for half a season on *Days of Our Lives*. But as the virus spread, she told me in her entre nous voice that if it weren't for her iPad (alternating between reading e-books and watching free Shakespeare on YouTube), she would have gone "utterly mad."

When the lockdowns began, Josh, Eliza, and I had held a family conference around pizza at the kitchen table about whether we should invite them to join us in our house. The discussion didn't take long. By the time Eliza nabbed the last bit of mozzarella from the bottom of the pizza box, the notion of my parents staying with us had moved from suggestion to strong agreement. Well, they were the Most Popular Older Couple in our lives, though that was hardly a contest.

There was plenty of room for all of us to have our own space, since our house was larger than even the average Long Island McMansion—unfortunately, it was also just as stylish. Josh had clearly found many qualities to adore in Dawn, but exquisite selection of home furnishings couldn't have been one of them. The grand entrance foyer had pinkish-white marble floors, the living room and our bedroom were dominated by grand, rosy mantels, and several of the bathrooms looked as if they'd been made from the same slab of blush marble with unfortunate red spider veins.

My parents moved into the guest suite—a massive bedroom along with a reading nook the size of the average studio apartment. My dad claimed half the nook for a recliner and his dream TV and ceded the other half to my mom as her library. He sweetened the deal by buying Bluetooth headphones so he could watch *Luther* while she read the latest definitive biography of Andy Warhol.

Before Covid, I'd primarily worked as a freelance literary scout. My specialty was seeking out contemporary fiction—and occasional nonfiction as well—that could be translated from Arabic and appeal to English-speaking readers. But during the pandemic the demand for books in my niche of Arabic fiction shrank to the size of an olive pit. That left me without the job I admittedly didn't want.

I hadn't always been such a homebody. Before I married Josh and adopted Eliza, I had spent more than a decade as a special agent in the FBI. Even now I still did some contract work for them—mostly interrogating Arabic speakers unlucky enough to have attracted the attention of the Bureau. (Back at Queens College, the class in Russian that I'd wanted was closed, so I took Arabic and wound up majoring in it. I sometimes wondered what would have happened if someone who was enrolled in that Russian class had dropped the course right before I went to register. I might not have followed my father's and grandfather's footsteps into law enforcement—nor met Josh.)

Lately I had been reluctant to take on more than the occasional FBI contract job. I still had PTSD symptoms from the last case I investigated, in which a killer, who realized I was onto him, kidnapped me. I was held for three days, tied up in a pitch-black attic, before I could escape—all while he described in grisly detail how my imminent death would go down. I finally got out, injured but able to move, by drawing him close enough to upend him with a couple of Krav Maga moves, then smashing his head against the floor, which stopped him just long enough. I'd been practicing Krav Maga, the Israeli martial art, since I was a kid, and at this crucial moment its aggressive street fighting techniques had saved my life.

Even after we were all vaccinated, I didn't want my parents to go back home. Having them in the house comforted me in the way the presence of mommy and daddy soothes a distressed little girl. Ironic, as I'd probably lost a millimeter of enamel during adolescence by grinding my teeth whenever they spoke.

But having them around meant I was less isolated. I had yet to become part of any scintillating group of friends in our Long Island town of Shorehaven. Or even a non-scintillating group. Well, I did meet up with a Wednesday lunch crew of locals who worked from home; it was a chance to get out of the house. I hadn't exactly reveled in discussions of wireless mesh networks, but during lockdown I missed their congenial blandness.

Only after my parents came to stay did it hit me how lonely I still was in the suburbs. Sure, I'd gotten to know a couple of great people in town, but I still felt I didn't belong in this land of lawns and money. With my mom and dad around, conversation brightened. Maybe it was because they brought some Queens to Nassau County.

Their stay in our house wasn't officially permanent. They still had their apartment. But when they'd begun dropping remarks like "We should probably think about getting back to our place," Josh astounded me one morning by replying to them, "Why not think about staying?" In a family that felt free to offer contrary opinions on the most minor subject, there were only nods and smiles of agreement.

I was refilling my wineglass and urging some orzo salad on my mom when my dad's phone chimed. Unlike Eliza, he received texts infrequently enough so that he didn't mute his notifications for meals. He read, his brow creasing.

"Excuse me. Got to make a quick call," he said, getting up and walking about twenty feet away under a sycamore—or maybe it was an elm, I still hadn't lived in the suburbs long enough to remember the difference. My mom and I kept sneaking glances at his end of an inaudible conversation. When he spotted me trying to read his lips, he turned so that all I got was his back. I guessed he wasn't actually hearing something supersecret, but wanted to preserve the opportunity to present the information to us in his own way.

He ended the call and walked back far more briskly than was lately his style, which rarely rated above a "meander."

"You'll never guess who that was!" he proudly announced.

"Who?" my mom breathed, leaning forward, hand on her chest. Compassion, curiosity: I could see how my dad, who generally had zero tolerance for anything that even vaguely resembled bullshit, had fallen in love with—and stayed in love with—her drama.

"Gabriel Salazar. He's a kid I knew from the precinct. Hell, he's not a kid anymore. Must be over forty by now. Heard he's done well. Anyway, he said that they got a call from the New Brunswick PD. They told him

April Brown is trying to get in touch with me. Apparently she wound up in Jersey. I told him fine, go ahead and give her my cell."

"Who's April Brown?" I asked.

"Do you remember the case—I must have told you about it—Seymour Brown, who laundered money for the Russian mob? He and his wife were asleep one night and someone set their house on fire. Ultimately barely anything left, of them or the house. Some bone fragments here and there, a diamond from her engagement ring, which was in perfect shape. The fire was so hot, though, that the gold band melted and then actually evaporated. But the couple's little girl—she was only five years old—managed to jump out of her window. Barely a scratch on her. That's April."

I did remember.

"It looked like everyone there was . . . not shocked, but surprised. Definitely expected a better class of funeral," my dad had explained to my mom and teenage me over a far, far smaller dinner table in our kitchen in Queens the night of Seymour and Kim's service, more than two decades earlier. His unit had just been assigned to investigate the double murder. "Mob-wise," he went on, "the top bosses get very high-class send-offs. A Mass with a monsignor swinging that gold thing with the incense."

"Catholics have a deep understanding of stagecraft," my mom observed, offering one of her highest compliments.

"And for Nicky Clark's eulogy, they got what they call a presiding elder of the AME Church. That's a very big deal. And I once saw—at Big Max Pinsky's funeral—the family had this woman rabbi flown in from LA. A beauty, I have to say. She had strawberry blonde hair. And a reputation as a serious scholar. Anyway, she sang the Twenty-Third Psalm and I swear, I felt like God was right next to me."

"Marvelous how God shows up for strawberry blondes," my mom murmured.

My dad seemed irritated by the digression even though he'd started it. He refocused. "The main thing is, Seymour Brown's funeral wasn't like any of those. Nothing fancy. Not even quiet simplicity, with big shots paying their respects. Just a sad half hour. Not boo-hoo sad. Crappy sad."

He went on: The ceremony had been held in a small nondenominational funeral home in Flatlands, a Brooklyn neighborhood that, ever since 1680, had been called "not as bad as it once was." No ornate coffins. Plain metal urns at the front of the room held the few remaining bits of Seymour and Kim. He'd overheard an attendee whisper that in the ladies' rooms, the paper hand towel dispensers were unfilled. Not just that, the memorial service was awkwardly brief. "No one from either of their families there—and him being such a successful accountant?" my dad added. "If he'd been alive, he would have died of embarrassment. The whole thing . . . pathetic. Especially considering he should have at least gotten a few curiosity seekers who show up for a funeral after a horrible murder."

My mom shuddered, then nodded and turned her attention back to her plate. She carefully cut a single string bean into three parts, then spent a few seconds deciding which to choose. Since I'd gotten to my mid-teens, her slo-mo eating stopped being an innocuous quirk and started driving me insane.

When teenage me wasn't loathing both my parents, I found their eagerness to converse in front of me pathetic; they seemed in the grip of an irrational belief that their lives were compelling. "Dinner table conversation," they called their talking, as if it were less stultifying than what they said to each other at breakfast.

My dad resumed. "Seymour Brown wasn't in the mob, not technically. But he was definitely involved with them—laundering money for the worst of the worst. He was supposed to be brilliant at it. But beyond financial fraud, there were at least a couple of felony assaults on his sheet. Vicious stuff. Charges dropped, so obviously he knew someone who knew someone." He shook his head. "Sickening."

"I've never heard of a violent accountant before," my mom observed. "At worst, they're a little pissy."

"When you looked at him, Seymour didn't come off like a scumbag. He'd wear these understated custom suits. I heard he had a Swiss watch that cost a fortune. He looked like he was enjoying life, being important in his world. The refined Mr. Seymour Brown—except when he beat the crap out of some maître d' who gave away his table. Guy spent weeks in the hospital. Seymour was a big shot in life. But in death"—he waved his hand as if to indicate the near-empty funeral—"no one gave a shit. He had no family, no friends, just a schlocky funeral home with plug-in air fresheners."

"What was the wife like?" my mom prompted. In her right hand, she still held her fork with its inch of string bean, but she used her left to fluff back the deliberately uneven bangs of her new, pixieish hairstyle, which she thought, correctly, made her look both adorable and brainy.

"No one really knew the wife," he said. "When we did our prelim house-to-house, a few people said she was either quiet or shy. But polite. She was from out of town. Basically, neighbors said she was nice. The closest thing to a negative we heard was the manager of the supermarket where she went. He said, 'Dumb as a rock.'"

"Attractive?"

My dad shrugged. "We're working on figuring out what she looked like. Family pictures would have gone up in flames. The perpetrator used a high-temp accelerant." My dad disdained the cop slang that had made it into the common culture, so "perp" was a rarity. "The neighbors said she was pretty. Beautiful eyes, good figure. The rest sounded okay. Light brown or dark blond hair, a lot of makeup even when she went to pick up a dozen eggs. All we have is a blurry headshot on file at the DMV from her license."

My mom nodded. "The DMV isn't known for its luminous photography." She pronounced the word "lyuuu-minous." If I hadn't had baked potato in my mouth, I might have retched. "Did they have children?"

"One. A little girl. Five years old. Her bedroom was on the first floor, and she managed to open her window and jump out! Amazing," my dad said. "Hardly even a scratch, just a burn where her hand touched the hot doorknob when she tried to leave her room through the door." He glanced at me for an instant, and then I understood why this case had apparently made a more vivid impression on him than the usual homicide. Like me, the daughter was an only child. Like me also, presumably strong-minded and practical. But unlike me, she was a little kid who had lost everything.

It made an impression on me too. I was more intrigued by my dad's case than I ever would have admitted, even to myself.

My mom changed the subject, lifting a finger to acknowledge the frivolity of interrupting a sad story of the orphaned little girl, but to set the scene in her mind, she needed to know how big the audience at the funeral home was.

"Thirty, tops," he told her.

As he was trying to get back on his train of thought, I spoke: "If this Seymour guy's job was hiding his clients' dirty money . . ." It was my first contribution to the dinnertime discussion. My parents both turned to me eagerly, shocked but thrilled to find me willingly participating in dinner table conversation. "And if his clients were mainly Russian mob guys, they'd stay away from his funeral, not come out in public to say goodbye. The whole point of money laundering is hiding stuff from the cops or Feds. Right? So why would a criminal show up?" My dad stabbed his finger in my direction: *You earned yourself a point there, kiddo.*

In the years since, I hadn't thought much about the sad, empty double funeral of the outwardly successful but ultimately isolated Russian Mafiya–affiliated CPA and his wife with too much makeup. Not even about the orphaned little girl. But my dad had mentioned them regretfully a few times over the years, and I understood that while some cold cases die from neglect, he couldn't let go of this particular unsolved homicide.

"No offense, but I'm surprised she remembers you," I commented. "How old was she when that happened?"

"She was only five." He took an ill-timed bite of shish kebab, sequestered it in his cheek, and continued talking. "We bonded, I guess, when I interviewed her. She really didn't have anyone. We finally tracked down a relative in Kentucky who took her in. But there was no one in New York, so I sent her holiday and birthday cards, just so she'd know someone cared about that part of her life." He swallowed, smiling fondly. "She reminded me of you. She always sent me a Christmas card, too, even as a little kid. It was something! The first time, she couldn't even write yet, so she drew a butterfly. Someone in the family addressed the envelope. After that, every so often she'd send me an update on her life, a letter to the precinct. She did well. Became a professor, I think."

"What's money laundering?" Eliza asked, far less contemptuous than I'd been at her age. She liked listening to my dad's NYPD stories and often got teary when he talked about his partner, Mickey Soong, who was killed on 9/11. Even though she'd joined the high school drama club, Eliza was less enamored of my mom's Delightful Show Business Anecdotes. She was herself a good enough performer, though, to make my mom feel as charming and witty as she believed herself to be.

"Money laundering doesn't involve detergent." My dad laughed and started to explain. I felt Josh wanting to jump in and give a more scholarly explanation from his perspective as a federal judge, but I put my hand on his arm to keep him quiet.

My dad had started a slide into depression on 9/11, and it only accelerated after he retired. He'd come out of it somewhat when he helped me investigate my own case two years earlier, although my getting kidnapped probably hadn't been a boon to his mental state any more than it had been to mine. Now, as he talked to Eliza about crime, he was more animated than I'd seen him in a while. I wanted him to have his moment.

"If you get a lot of money from committing a crime," he explained, "you can't just put it in the bank. Or start buying really expensive stuff. People will ask questions, and they might know you committed a crime. A money launderer moves the money from place to place until it's so far removed from the crime that criminal earnings look like legal money." Eliza nodded thoughtfully with furrowed brow.

Later, over blueberry pie, I noticed Josh looking over at me, his head tilted forward with concern. It was only then I realized that I'd pulled out the tiny LED flashlight I always wore as a pendant—or really, an amulet—on a chain long enough so that most of the time it was hidden in my cleavage. *Click-click, click-click.* My fear of the dark hadn't diminished since the kidnapping.

The flashlight was the suggestion of Dr. Greenblatt, the cognitive-behavioral therapist I was consulting for PTSD. I'd been initially offended at the suggestion that I get some help. After all, I'd survived. What had happened to me warranted praise, not therapy. "But you were genuinely tortured," Dr. Greenblatt assured me with unnerving earnestness. Besides therapy and medication, he gave me assorted tips and tricks to begin resuming the life I had chosen over the FBI: underemployed suburban wife and mother.

The little flashlight was meant to put me in control; I got to choose whether I was in the light or the dark. It wound up being more something I could fiddle with—and I clearly needed to fiddle.

My dad's text notification sound went off again. He peered at his phone. "It's April," he said. "She wants to know if I'd have a Zoom call with her."

"Does she say why?" I asked, raising my eyebrows.

He read aloud: "Hi Detective Schottland. This is April Brown. I'm glad I could reach you. I want to set up a time to meet with you over Zoom, if that's okay. I've gotten a little involved in a criminal matter, and I'd love to talk to someone who knows about police procedure, someone I'm sure I can trust."

"A little involved in a criminal matter?" Josh repeated, more curious than suspicious.

My dad shrugged. "You know what I know," he told him. "I'm guessing she means she's a victim, not a perpetrator, or the New Brunswick police would have been the ones to contact me." He caught my eye. He was mostly worried, but perhaps a tiny bit thrilled.

CHAPTER TWO

My parents were still in the kitchen when Josh and I came in hauling the dinner leftovers and plates. Dad was at the kitchen table with Lulu on his lap. He was mindlessly scratching her chest while she gazed up at him with poignant devotion that dissipated the instant Eliza emerged with her leash, ready for their evening walk. My mom was putting food away, at that moment swaddling three individual spears of asparagus, each in its own blanket of Saran Wrap. She was usually aware of environmental impact, at least for a Boomer, but she had always seemed possessed by some Leftovers Incubus that compelled her to seal up all food in an impenetrable vault, then throw it out two days later anyway since she was sure it had gone bad.

Josh had his own kitchen demons. His system of dishwasher loading had rigorous rules apparent only to him. I sometimes found him correcting my loading after I'd done it, though the dishes seemed to come out no cleaner.

In the first few months of our marriage, it didn't hit me that he was mildly nuts. Mostly what I did was gaze at him, whatever he was doing, in an awestruck way. How did such a wonder of a man choose me? Or why? It wasn't a low opinion of myself as much as an exaltation of him. He had the academic distinctions, the decency, the devotion to his daughter. And who could ignore his OMG looks? Golden skin, dark brown hair, and green eyes—not emerald, which would have been too showy, but a subtler jade.

Fifteen minutes earlier, while we were the only two left outside cleaning up, Josh had pressed up against me and whispered what he'd like to do to me, and I'd run my hand down his side and replied huskily, "Soon," even though we'd done an extended director's cut version the night before. Now I turned away before any spark of lust could be extinguished by watching him scrape off dishes with his beloved wide yellow spatula—discolored from years of marinara sauce and curry—that he'd dedicated solely to his preloading sacrament.

My dad and I were more alike: methodical when it came to investigatory work, but looser when it came to the rest of life. "Looser" meant anything from indifferent to chaotic. Each of us was content to defer to a spouse who had intense feelings about how to clean sink drain covers.

I sat down next to my dad. "Was it a total shock to you, hearing from April after all these years?" I asked.

He tilted his head and gave it a couple of seconds of thought. "Yes. And no," he finally said. "Like I said, we weren't completely out of touch."

"They found some relatives who took her in?" I rested my chin on the backs of my hands and leaned in, the way I sometimes did when I conducted FBI interviews and the moment came when there was a chance I'd finally hear the whole story. I just had to pause long enough so the witness would want to fill the empty space. And sometimes they did, a terabyte of random observations spilling out. (Although a hardened few just let the silence expand until part of me wanted to cover my ears to deny how overpowering it was.) My dad would have been a tough interviewee. He had no problem letting awkward silences grow.

"So April had relatives . . ." I prodded.

"She did. It took two or three months, but they were able to find Kim Brown's family—Kim was April's mother—in Fort Mitchell, a part of Northern Kentucky that's basically suburban Cincinnati. Never found anyone, not even a fourth cousin, for Seymour. But these people were shocked to see how Kim turned out. She'd run away from home when she was seventeen."

"Troubled kid?"

His head moved down to his left shoulder, then to his right—repeat, and add a shrug, a Jewish New York cop's way of saying *not really*. "No arrests. Mostly a loner, so no gang, bad crowd. She liked older guys with a few bucks who could show her a good time."

"Any signs of any abuse at home?"

"No. We checked. She was just a kid who was a little on the wild side. Sounded like she was born into the wrong family—they were Mass-every-day Irish Catholics, straightlaced. Nice enough people. Lucky we found them. Otherwise they'd have had to put April up for adoption or into foster care."

I decided to pitch in with the cleanup, but all that was left was the trash. I got up, and as I started to tie the bag handles, I heard my mom telling Josh, ". . . *The Tempest,* and Helen Mirren played Prospera with such authority," and he responded with "She was great in *Prime Suspect.*"

I called out to my dad, "Are you going to reply to her text?"

He walked through the garage with me to the bins outside and lifted the lid. "I did. I mean, how could I not? I'm hoping we can set something up for tomorrow." Back inside, he leaned against the pantry door and looked up at the ceiling, as if trying to jog his memory. "I just wish I had the case files with me so I could look at them before talking to her."

My mom, of course, overheard him. "Could that young detective—" she began.

"Gabriel Salazar," he interrupted.

"Right, Gabriel Salazar. Could he get you the files tomorrow?"

"Possibly," he answered, then paused to look at his phone, which had just made its loud text noise. "But it looks like I'm talking to her tomorrow. Eleven a.m. Won't have time to get them from Gabriel." Josh shot my dad a sympathetic *Yeesh, that's too bad* look before turning back to the dishes. My dad added cautiously, "I do have copies of some stuff from cold case files back in the apartment."

"Really? You're allowed to bring that stuff home?" I asked.

"Sure!" he answered a bit too buoyantly.

My own training and the skeptical look that passed over Josh's face—Josh, a federal judge and former prosecutor, could easily spot an iffy law enforcement move from across a kitchen—told me otherwise, but

I decided not to push it. My dad seemed to be hinting for a ride to his apartment to pick up the files. Though he had never said it directly, he'd clearly been reluctant to drive at night for a while now. I couldn't even remember the last time he wanted to do something after dinner other than fall asleep watching TV.

"I could take you over to your place tonight, if you want. That way, you could tell me what you do remember about the case."

My dad lit up.

I gave Josh a sheepish glance at the implicit cancellation of our evening plans. He pushed off from the center island with a vague air of regret. However, by the time he passed the microwave, I could see his shoulders square, his spirits start to soar—probably he recalled that the treatise on public utility regulation he'd ordered from the Harvard Coop Law School Bookstore had finally arrived.

My mom tilted her head with a small smile, taking the measure of my dad and me. I could tell she was glad to see him excited about something again. Then it hit me that she was also gratified to see *me* excited about something again, and I wondered just how apparent my PTSD was to everyone around me. With that glance of hers, relieved and benevolent, I understood: very apparent.

Well, we all had lived a three-day nightmare. I'd been terrorized. My family at the time knew something terrible had happened to me, but not what it was. To them, I was just gone.

When I first joined that weekly lunch group of people who worked from home, I told myself, *Hey, fun for someone other than me to make my lunch*, and while I was at it, I could get to know some of my fellow suburbanites. They were all freelancers, like me: garden planner, political speechwriter, product designer, photo retoucher. We were all looking for professional—and social—connection. But after many tedious salades Niçoises at the local French bistro, La Cuisine Délicieuse, one of the members piqued my curiosity. Something wasn't right about him. *Check it out? Why not?* I'd knock back any antidote to boredom. So I investigated him. He found me out and kidnapped me, tying me to a post in a blackened space. He was my captor, and I had to listen to him tell me in harrowing detail about my upcoming death and decomposition. I managed to escape. He wound up behind bars, I wound up with PTSD and a flashlight necklace.

"Corie, if you have an extra moment while you're there, could you please bring back some books? There are some I've been aching to read."

I waited impatiently as my mom wrote the titles down as if she were doing the calligraphy for a royal wedding invitation.

When we got into the car, my dad turned on the radio. I mentally crossed my fingers, hoping he would be focused on the Mets for the next twenty-five minutes. Unfortunately, he wasn't. He had never been great at being a passenger. He pointed out tractor trailers and offered advice on my route until we finally merged onto the Grand Central Parkway, which took us close to his apartment. Only then did he sit back and let me drive.

"So, yeah," he said suddenly after five solid minutes of silence, as we drove past the border from Nassau County into Queens. "Burnt to a crisp." Homicide cops weren't famed for their delicacy of expression. "Even the springs in their mattress melted. Believe me, the Bureau of Fire Investigation, a couple of techs from the ME's office, and our people all sifted through the rubble. Just a diamond and some bone fragments. No DNA could even be extracted."

"Do you think they could get any if they looked at it now?"

"Almost definitely not. When a fire burns intensely and for a long time, it can even destroy any detectable DNA. There will be nothing to test, even in bones and teeth. You remember that was an issue in 9/11, where they couldn't identify a good number of the remains? And that horrible fire in London—that apartment building, just a few years ago. What was it called again?"

"Grenfell Tower," I answered, and he pointed at me, as if to say, *That's the one.* "So how did you know Seymour and Kim were both killed? Because they weren't there anymore?"

"Yes, and April—the little girl—told us that both her parents were home. Her parents kissed her good night. She heard them going upstairs."

"It's technically possible that one or both of them escaped, then."

"Yeah, technically, though if the wife escaped, there was no reason for her not to come forward. Even if she were scared that someone would try again to hurt her, she'd be at least as worried about her daughter and would want to claim her. We considered whether Seymour faked his own death. But he not only left his kid—and everyone we spoke to said he really loved her—he left behind a good chunk of money and jewelry in a safe-deposit box. It would have been easy enough for him to withdraw it and set it up for a new life, if that's what he was doing. A guy like him doesn't leave millions for no reason."

I nodded. A minute later I asked, "Who did you suspect, then?" (Yes, I knew it was "whom," but self-consciously proper grammar was a class issue for my dad, a nudge by the uppers to remind him not to inhale too much of their purified air.)

"Well, you know. Seymour was mobbed up. He wasn't officially in the Russian Mafiya—the Vory, that's what they call themselves. Sometimes Bratva."

"Vory," I repeated. I'd heard that term during my FBI days, though I hadn't dealt with them directly.

"He was, well, a professional. A CPA. The kind of guy you keep on retainer or consult," he said. "A freelancer."

"Like me!" I said cheerfully.

"Slightly different," he said with a rueful sideways grin.

"He would have fit right in at our Wednesday freelancers' lunch. Criminal background was no obstacle."

My dad's face darkened a bit. "As much of a putz as Seymour Brown was—and he was absolutely a putz—he doesn't compare to the asshole who hurt you." As if on cue, my leg started to hurt. I'd injured it during the kidnapping and had gotten a nasty infection. Skin grafts and plastic surgery helped. At this point, a year later, the pain was less frequent, although my prospects as a catcher in the majors were fucked, as was my sleek-skinned allure in a bathing suit.

We drove on, both quiet for a while. "Anyway," I said to get him back on track.

"Anyway," he repeated, trying to refocus.

"He worked for the Russians, right? Not the Colombians or the Italians."

"Mostly just Russians, who had really come into their own in the US at that point. Especially in Brooklyn."

"Did he do any legitimate work?" I asked.

"He hadn't in a while. Working for the Russians got him a nice life, nice house, nice part of Brooklyn. Everything was nice. Or it seemed that way until someone decided he had to be killed. And, you know, if they wanted to, they could have just given him a clean shot to the medulla. But this was no ordinary hit. Someone wanted him to die horribly, and he did. Fucking arson. They didn't even care that his wife and child would go. Maybe they were collateral damage. Or possibly a part of a message: *Screw us over and not only are you dead, but so is your family.*"

"Were the killers definitely aware of Kim's and April's existence?"

"No way to know for sure," he said.

I leaned back against the headrest, then glanced over at my dad. He'd closed his eyes as if he were falling asleep, but then he opened them. "I remember checking with the Brooklyn Department of Buildings to see if anyone had come in and asked about the architectural plans for that address. I first asked them to look up the name, but it turns out the house wasn't even in their name—it was bought by a shell company. It was an old place, built in the twenties. Before they moved in, they had some construction done. Totally rewired, new oil burner. Made a master bathroom, bedroom, walk-in closets upstairs—that wasn't so common back then. The plans showed the kid's room downstairs, but like lawyers say, it was moot. Nobody had asked to see the plans since they were filed."

"You said his name was Brown. Doesn't sound Russian."

"Who knows what he was. It was like he came out of nowhere. We never found any relatives, where he grew up, where he went to school—anything. Used to tell people his motto was 'obscurity is security.' But it's not like he followed that to the letter. Once, when a driver leaned on a car horn too long, Seymour got out of his own car, reached through the other guy's open window, and smashed his head against the steering wheel. Why? There was no money in it. No power, cracking some nobody's head." My dad rubbed his temples. "Another time he got arrested. They found this young guy naked and crying near one of the offices Seymour used. The guy swore up and down that Seymour had falsely accused him of sneaking into the office and had stripped him and beat the shit out of him. But the grand jury declined to indict."

I gave him a side-eye to indicate *Are you fucking kidding me?* and he said, "I know, I know. Anyway, not Mr. Good Guy. 'A total piece of shit, but a great dresser.' That's what one of his clients said in an interview."

"So you suspected the Mafiya? The Vory?"

"How could we not? They're vicious, and he was one of the major guys in charge of hiding their money. So we suspected them from the get-go. Even though we never came up with solid evidence against any of the clients, we could never rule any of these bastards out completely."

I was no Vory expert, though I'd come across some US Russian mobsters selling weapons to Jemaah Islamiyah, al-Shabaab, and al-Qaeda in the Arabian Peninsula. Guys in the Russian mob were beyond vicious: they'd think burning down someone's home with them in it should be classified as a misdemeanor. The Russians weren't like the Italian Mafia, structured around families, and not like Colombian and Mexican gangs. They were more individual entrepreneurs, each with a small pack of employees. They'd hook up with others for a big job but then go their own way. Some terror cells I'd investigated in my years at the FBI operated on the same model.

"In the end, they weren't our primary suspects," my dad said. "There was a good amount of money the Vory couldn't get back, because Seymour had it hidden in all these shell companies or whatever. Fortunes were lost by him dying. I heard they even changed their accounting procedures to make sure it couldn't happen again."

"Like any responsible enterprise," I muttered.

"Well, yeah," my dad agreed. "It's not like they aren't sophisticated businessmen. Our main suspect was Seymour's assistant, or partner, or whatever he was. Guy named Hosea Williams. Very smart guy, no education, came from Appalachia or something. West Virginia? Lots of mountains, no money. But he taught himself everything. Taught himself Spanish when he was living in Chicago so he could deal with the Mexican cartels; then, when he got to New York, he learned Russian—which Seymour never managed to do. Seymour taught him accounting, and it seemed like he picked it up real quick."

Pointing out the window, he said, "Oho! Look at that!" as if he'd just won the lottery. There was, miraculously, an open parking space directly in front of my parents' building. I parallel parked, and he grinned rapturously at the thought that he wouldn't have to walk an extra couple of blocks. As we walked to the front door, he started patting his pockets, looking for his keys. I was ready to strangle him if it turned out that he left them at home, but he victoriously fished them out of his shirt pocket and jingled them in front of me. As he let us in the building, I asked, "So why did you suspect this guy? The language guy?"

"Hosea," my dad answered, jabbing at the elevator button. "Apparently he'd made a big scene in a restaurant not long before the murder. He was screaming at Seymour, saying that he was hiding money and not giving Hosea his fair cut. It was a fancy place. People had their wives with them. That just isn't done, even in those circles. Hosea told us that he and Seymour had made up, though who knows if that's true. We never found anything else in the way of actual evidence."

"If Seymour was hiding money from Hosea, he might have been hiding money from the Vory, too," I observed.

"Yeah, that's one reason we never entirely ruled out the Vory," he said.

As we stepped into the elevator together with one big simultaneous stride, the same way we always had since I was a kid, I asked, "Anyone else?"

He hummed and screwed up his face a bit. "Trying to remember." I was already impressed with his recall of the case, which was better than mine for cases I'd worked on only a few years earlier. "There was a chauffeur, a driver, whatever. He'd stopped showing up for work a few days before the murders. So that was weird. But I think he had an alibi."

As we entered the apartment, I was relieved that my mother had decided to stay back. There was a funky smell—if you gave it a couple more weeks, it would be a stench. Dad and I wouldn't have been able to leave until she'd scrubbed the entire place with bleach. But I wasn't even sure my dad noticed. I made a mental note to call for a cleaning service to visit. Meanwhile, as we walked around the place, I hoped my father wouldn't get homesick and decide he needed to move back.

Having my parents live with us had given Josh something important, too. He'd grown up in a family that believed geniality was a pleasing quality and enjoyed watching others laugh. Josh never doubted that his parents loved him. But they believed "I love you" should be saved for birthdays and ICU visits. Effusive Jews like my parents embarrassed them. Also, those whose pretentions were a tad too obvious made their skin crawl. I noted my mother-in-law's poorly suppressed wince when my mom said "I cahn't abide . . ." Josh found himself enjoying being part of a more gregarious and affectionate family, even if half the time he watched us like we were a spectator sport.

And Eliza, who had lost her mom so young, was buttressed by the support system my parents provided. She listened with surprising patience to my mom's Naughty Anecdotes about "the Woody Harrelson I knew." The two of them also continued the collaboration they'd started during the pandemic, baking two recipes a week from a cookbook called *Pastry Love*. Eliza and my dad bonded when they spent days in the garage sawing off, sanding, and restaining the posts on her bed and making a new headboard.

Other than the mustiness, my parents' apartment looked as lovely as it always had, and I was taken aback by the pang of wistfulness I felt. Though on a budget, my mother had scoured flea markets and estate sales to make this small apartment in Forest Hills a beautiful home. She intuited the appeal of clean mid-century modern well before every millennial couple on home redecorating shows avowed their love for the look, but she'd managed to give it a homey appeal as well. In our Long Island house I had no neighbors blasting TV late at night, more closet space than I knew what to do with, a yard, a kitchen stove with six burners. I didn't have to collect quarters and go to the basement to do my laundry. I had not only a master suite, but a living room separate from the TV room. Josh and I each had our own office. Yet part of me yearned for the old apartment in Queens, even for the radiators that clanged like sledgehammers every couple of hours; that sound meant *a cold winter night* as much as icicles sparkling on tree branches in Shorehaven.

While my dad looked for the files, I started searching for my mom's books. It took forever, as she had a ton of them, and though they were neatly placed on the shelves, they were in no discernible order. "Fuck!" I heard my dad yell from the front hall, and I popped my head around to see him precariously balanced on a step stool, trying to pull down a large, heavy-looking banker's box directly overhead.

"Here, let me . . ." I said, stepping into the closet, but he shooed me away. I saw him glance toward an ancient Bonwit Teller hatbox on the shelf near the banker's box. He didn't seem to have a clue, but I had known since I was thirteen that inside the hatbox was a locked metal box, and my mom had admitted, after much badgering, that it contained a gun. Despite the smallness of the apartment, I never did find where he kept the ammo.

"I'm fine, I'm fine!" he said, but to his annoyance, I stayed watching him until he had gotten the banker's box down safely. It was labeled 1990 2001. He slipped off the top and almost immediately pulled out a hanging file labeled BROWN, SEYMOUR AND KIM.

He opened it, saying, “It doesn’t have everything, just a few items I wanted to remember in case I ever decided to reexamine the case.” I saw him flip through some floor plans, photos that looked like they’d been printed out from a computer on regular paper, a folder labeled INTERVIEW WITH HOSEA WILLIAMS. He pulled out another folder, INTERVIEW WITH APRIL BROWN.

“This is what I wanted to read before I talk to her tomorrow.”

The musty smell of the apartment was getting to me. Plus it was past my dad’s usual bedtime. “Okay,” I said. “Let’s take it home and we’ll read it first thing in the morning.” We gathered the books, the banker’s box, and the hanging file and went out into the night.

CHAPTER THREE

My dad handed me the transcript of his interview with April Brown. To my immediate regret, I inhaled that very instant. Then I said "ugh," though possibly "blech," and handed it back.

"You got a problem?" he asked me.

"The paper smells sour," I told him. "Like old library books."

"It's been on the top shelf in the front hall closet for over twenty years. What the hell do you expect? French perfume?" He and I were going over the transcript together—he, feet up, on the leather recliner in my office and I on the desk chair I'd rolled over to sit beside him. Slowly, he turned back to the top page. We started to read. He slid his finger along the left margin so we could keep our reading to the same pace.

INTERVIEW OF APRIL BROWN
INCIDENT #1997-418385

October 14, 1997
8:21 a.m.
Detective Bureau Brooklyn North
Schottland = Det. Daniel Schottland
Pagano = Dr. Laura Pagano
Brown = April Brown

SCHOTTLAND: Hello, April. My name is Dan Schottland. I'm a police detective. You can call me Detective Dan. Just for the record, today is Tuesday, October 14, 1997. It's 8:21 a.m. The lady over there is Dr. Laura Pagano. She's a doctor whose job is to work with children.

PAGANO: Hello. I'm glad to meet you, April.

BROWN: [waves]

PAGANO: Detective Dan will be asking you most of the questions, but I might ask you a few, too. [pause] See over there, up on the wall? That's a camera. And right here on the table, we have microphones. We use them to record our conversation. That's so Detective Dan and I can remember everything you tell us. Sometimes one of us might forget things. The recording lets us listen to you without having to write everything down.

"My God, that Pagano woman drove me insane. In another case, too." Apparently my dad couldn't wait to get to the actual interview before he started to complain.

"Why? This introduction was fine. That's what I'd say to a child in an interview." I had never actually interviewed a five-year-old. The youngest person I had ever interviewed was ten, the nephew of a Jersey City pharmacist who had donated suspiciously regular and large amounts of money to Hamas. The protocols for interviewing a five-year-old and a ten-year-old weren't that different, though.

"It was really her attitude. She was just so goddamn sure she was right about everything. She made it clear that she believed any detective would barrel through an interview and retraumatize the child. Like for the hell of it or something." He shifted in his seat and emitted a mild *harumph*.

SCHOTTLAND: April, part of my job is to talk to children about things that have happened to them. I meet with lots of children. I talk to them, and they can tell me the truth about what's happened. Before we begin, though, I want to make sure you understand the difference between the things that are true and things that are not true. Okay?

BROWN: [nods]

SCHOTTLAND: If I say the walls in this room are red, is that true or not true?

BROWN: Not true.

SCHOTTLAND: Right, that's—

PAGANO: April, this can be very hard for children. Sometimes when something scary has happened—

BROWN: A fire.

PAGANO: Yes, like a fire. Children want to talk very quietly. But we need to make sure the tape recorder can hear you. Do you think you could talk a little louder? Not yelling or anything. Just a tiny bit.

BROWN: [nods]

SCHOTTLAND: April, you were exactly right. "Red walls" would not be true, because the walls are really blue. And if I tell you I'm sitting down right now, what would you say? True or not true?

BROWN: True.

SCHOTTLAND: Right. It would be true because you can see I am sitting down. That tells me you understand what telling the truth means. It's very important that you only tell the truth today. [pause] Another thing, April. If I ask a question you don't understand, it's fine to say "I don't understand." Okay?

BROWN: Okay. [pause] Sometimes my daddy says, "I don't get it." It means "I don't understand."

SCHOTTLAND: Exactly. It's another good way of saying it.

BROWN: Do you know where my mommy and daddy are?

SCHOTTLAND: Right now, I can't be completely sure. Part of my job as a detective is to try to find out what happened to your mommy and daddy. I'm going to talk to a lot of people, including you, to find out everything I can about them. I know this is a scary time for you, and I promise you I will work as hard as I can.

BROWN: Our house got burned down in a fire last night. There were firemen and trucks.

PAGANO: You can talk about the fire, April.

BROWN: Everything got in the fire. They said I can't go get them anymore. Chloe Bear. [cries] All my stuffed animals and my Lego castle.

PAGANO: You lost some important things.

BROWN: My Lion King socks.

"See what I mean?" My dad smacked the pages with the back of his hand. "I'm trying to set the guidelines of the interview, build some rapport by talking about safe topics before I get to the upsetting stuff. And she doesn't steer her away from the most upsetting topic. Everyone involved in the case told her, 'This is not therapy—before and after the interrogation, definitely, the kid is going to need all the help she can get, but right now this is a police inquiry. Take a back seat and be reassuring unless the detective is heading someplace that could agitate the kid.' But she kept interrupting. Cutting off the flow, the rapport. Egomaniacal fuck."

His cheeks flushed until the red spread across his face and deepened to mauve. This wasn't a new look for him. Whenever he got past annoyance, his complexion—from the underside of his chin to the far edge of his bald spot—darkened from pink until his head resembled an eggplant.

Far from unsettling me, this conniption fit was a comfort. My dad's purpling was part of the theme colors of my childhood. (The *temps perdu* rushes I kept getting from living with my parents were an antidote to my PTSD. They brought me back to what I now viewed as sweet times. Like a few days after my parents moved in with us, my mom made one of her *spécialités* from my childhood for dessert, My-T-Fine pudding with Oreo crumbles, served in a juice glass. I inhaled that fake vanilla scent and held back tears of joy.)

PAGANO: It seems like there's something else you want to say about the fire, April?

BROWN: The house kept burning even though they kept putting water on it. The firemen. Two ladies came and took me to a special house for kids who have fires and no more houses. A police lady and Maya. Maya got me hot chocolate with baby marshmallows. And she gave me this. [shows stuffed animal] She told me I could keep it. He's soft, so I called him Softy.

SCHOTTLAND: [to BROWN] That's a really nice penguin. He does look soft. [to PAGANO] Maya's the social worker from the Admin for Children's Services who's been assigned. [to BROWN] I would like to say a couple more things about this talk we're having. If I ask a question and you don't know the answer, just tell me, "I don't know." Like if I asked you, what's the name of my favorite stuffed animal, what would you say?

BROWN: I don't know.

SCHOTTLAND: Right. You don't know because you've just met me. I can see you've got it. When you don't know the answer, you don't guess. You just say that you don't know. Now, one last thing. If I make a mistake, if I have the wrong idea about something, what would you tell me?

BROWN: [pause] Could I say, "That's not right"?

SCHOTTLAND: Absolutely. If I have the wrong idea about something or the wrong information, it would be a big help if you could tell me "That's not right." And then tell me what really happened, or where I got it wrong. So if I said Softy was a bear, what would you say?

BROWN: That's not right.

SCHOTTLAND: Exactly. Now I'd like to get to know you a bit better. Tell me some things you like to do.

BROWN: Subways. The brake sounds don't bother me anymore.

SCHOTTLAND: You like to ride subways?

BROWN: Yes, and bikes.

SCHOTTLAND: Tell me more about riding bikes.

BROWN: My daddy raised the training wheels two inches on each side. He says soon he can take them off.

SCHOTTLAND: Sounds like you're good at bike riding.

BROWN: Yes, very.

SCHOTTLAND: This is helping me learn more about you and the things you do. A few weeks ago must have been your first day of school. Kindergarten?

BROWN: [nods]

My dad started flipping ahead several pages.

"Hey, wait," I said.

"You really need all the details of her first day of school?"

I shook my head, and he settled on a new page.

I was impressed with his interviewing. He had accompanied me and helped interview some witnesses in an unofficial capacity in the last case I worked on, but I had never seen him in action when he was a cop. He did a great job with the standard law enforcement technique of establishing rapport with a witness. But it's that much harder when the witness is a young child. He had also gotten April to feel comfortable answering detailed questions about her life on ordinary days so she could start to answer questions about the day that turned terrifying.

An interviewer of trauma victims, especially children, needs to come across as calm and benevolent—but also must subtly make the case that it is vital that the victim talks. April Brown, five years old, had lost everything—her parents, her home, Chloe Bear. And she might have the key piece of evidence.

There was no one to give the kid any comfort that night beyond a couple of neighbors and eventually a social worker. My dad told me they had to wake the principal of PS 195, where April was in kindergarten, who got the Browns' emergency contact from her records. The contact was Carly Campisi, who was Seymour's secretary, but the phone number was for Seymour's office. When they finally located the secretary at home—it must have been at four a.m.—she was upset but refused to give any information over the phone, saying, "How do I know you're really the cops and you're telling the truth?"

SCHOTTLAND: We do need to know as much as you can tell us about the fire last night. But before you do that, can you tell me what happened that day, from the time you woke up in the morning until you left with Maya and the policewoman?

BROWN: I woke up. [pause]

SCHOTTLAND: Then what happened?

BROWN: I looked for my school clothes, but I didn't leave them out.

SCHOTTLAND: Because it was Columbus Day, right?

BROWN: Right. No school.

SCHOTTLAND: Then what happened?

From the transcript, it was clear that for a kid, April was an unusually good witness. She had a sharp memory, an eye for detail, and a willingness to share her thoughts. It took four pages to get from brushing her teeth to a breakfast of oatmeal with brown sugar to her deciding on jeans with her new orange T-shirt with pumpkins because Halloween was coming up. Her mom said it would be cool even after Halloween. April had her doubts.

"I just let her go on as much as she wanted to," my dad said. "Let her talk about normal stuff. Eventually we'd get where we needed to be."

"Except with a talkative kid, you can tire them out before they get to where you want to be."

My dad rubbed his chin. "I think she wanted someone else to know all about the day."

On page eleven, she was recounting Seymour's letting her have milk in a paper container with a plastic stirrer while he was finishing his coffee.

SCHOTTLAND: April, you said your dad was wearing a suit and tie. Was he going to work?

BROWN: Yes. I said it's a holiday, but he said he has different holidays.

SCHOTTLAND: And then what happened?

BROWN: He went to the bathroom. Then he came back and kissed me and Mommy and went out to Toddy.

SCHOTTLAND: Who is Toddy?

BROWN: He's Daddy's driver. He's in the car in the driveway. That's where he waits.

SCHOTTLAND. Tell me about Toddy.

BROWN: He's nice. He wants to get a dog, but he can't because he lives in the Bronx.

SCHOTTLAND: Can't people in the Bronx get dogs?

BROWN: Because he's away all day and sometimes night, and dogs have to get walked or they'll poop on the carpet. That's gross. And the Bronx is too far away for Toddy to go and walk a dog. Mommy says he can come in the house.

SCHOTTLAND: The dog?

BROWN: No, Toddy. He watches TV in the basement, but I can't watch with him because it's a grown-up cartoon. It's called *Ren and Stimpy.*

SCHOTTLAND: When does he drive?

BROWN: He drives Daddy to work. Sometimes he comes back and picks up Mommy for a restaurant. She gets all dressed up, with earrings. And sometimes I go. Just Mommy, Daddy, and me in a restaurant.

SCHOTTLAND: Do you know what Toddy's last name is?

BROWN: No. His name is Toddy.

SCHOTTLAND: Does your dad ever talk about Toddy?

BROWN: [shrugs]

PAGANO: Do you know if your dad likes the way Toddy does his work?

BROWN: He says he's very . . . some word. He's always on time.

SCHOTTLAND: Let's get back to breakfast. Was your mommy with you?

As I swiveled a little in my desk chair and looked down at the transcript my dad was holding, I was struck by the absolute normality of that day for April Brown. She'd had a playdate with her friend Brittany. They had a snack of string cheese and red grapes and played Monopoly Junior. She watched 2 *Stupid Dogs* before dinner, and her dad surprised her by bringing home Chinese food and an extra bag of crispy noodles because her mom loved them so much. That night had been horrific, but the day sounded like a fine one in Brooklyn.

April had a mom who put after-school snacks on a doily whenever she had a friend over. Her dad took her to the movies every Saturday. In response to Dr. Pagano's questions, she said that yes, sometimes her mom and dad did yell at each other, but they went upstairs and didn't fight in front of her. One time she heard her mom yell that she was sick of restaurants in Brooklyn with the same people. Her dad yelled that she spent too much money and she should shut up about him working, because it was all for her and April. But most of the time they didn't fight.

SCHOTTLAND: While you were home yesterday, were there any other people in your house? Maybe someone your mom or dad knew, or someone delivering a package?

BROWN: Brittany was there.

SCHOTTLAND: That's right. Any grown-ups?

BROWN: Her babysitter came, but she didn't come inside. Mommy put Brittany's sweater on and helped her with her backpack.

SCHOTTLAND: Anyone else at your house? Maybe someone helping with the cleaning, or a deliveryman? Anyone who just stopped by, not an actual visitor?

BROWN: No.

SCHOTTLAND: Were there any phone calls, April? It could be a regular phone call, or maybe something that upset your mom or dad.

BROWN: [shrugs]

SCHOTTLAND: Okay, we can move on now. Now that I know you a little better, let's talk again about what happened last night. You told me about going to bed. Your mom was upstairs, and your dad read a story and tucked you and Chloe Bear in and kissed you and Chloe good night. Then he said, "Good night. Sleep tight."

BROWN: He says that every night.

SCHOTTLAND: Right. Now tell me everything that happened from the time your dad left the room. Big things and the little things. They're all important. I understand that this is a very tough time for you, but we need all the information . . . all the stuff you can remember so we can figure out what happened. So after your dad said "Sleep tight," what was next?

BROWN: I went to sleep.

SCHOTTLAND: Did you fall asleep right away or did it take some time?

BROWN: There's nothing to do and there's no light besides my night-light. It looks like a lit-up seashell.

SCHOTTLAND: Did you hear anybody talking inside the house? Your mom or dad?

BROWN: [shakes head no]

SCHOTTLAND: Anybody else's voice inside the house?

BROWN: No.

SCHOTTLAND: So another thing. Your room is on the first floor, right? Did you hear any voices from outside?

BROWN: No.

SCHOTTLAND: People sometimes make sounds besides talking. Sneezing, coughing, blowing their nose, humming a song . . .

BROWN: No, none of that. They can make noise with their feet, too. You know, footsteps, it's called.

SCHOTTLAND: Good point. Did you hear any footsteps?

BROWN: My daddy's.

SCHOTTLAND: You heard your daddy's footsteps outside?

BROWN: No, on the stairs.

SCHOTTLAND: Just going upstairs?

BROWN: Yes.

SCHOTTLAND: Only once, right after he said good night?

BROWN: [nods]

SCHOTTLAND: Okay, you're doing a good job, April. Dr. Laura and I appreciate your cooperating with us. But we still have more questions. So would you like to take a little break now? I could get you some juice, a snack from the machine down the hall. And if you want, you could go to the ladies' room with Maya or the policewoman.

BROWN: Chocolate milk and maybe animal crackers?

SCHOTTLAND: Sure. You know what? There's a little store down the block that has very good chocolate milk, so I'll get it for you there.

[INTERVIEW PAUSES 9:34 a.m.]

"Hey, you are good with kids," I said to my dad.

"You're surprised? It's not like I didn't have my own little girl. Though you were older then. And a pain in the ass," he said. He caught himself starting to grin, so he sped up his talking. "She was starting to move around in her chair, so I figured she was getting antsy or had to pee. Also, if I walked over to the bodega with the shrink, I'd get a chance to ask whether she thought there was any evidence that April could be a fire setter."

I wasn't shocked, but I confess that my jaw dropped slightly. "Someone that young . . ."

"It can happen. I didn't think so, but I wanted to make sure. I'd dealt with older kids a couple of times, arson that winds up as felony murder. But this . . . The Fire Department investigators were pretty sure, right from the start, that the accelerant was gasoline. But of course they had to do all sorts of examinations at the site and tests, though they couldn't imagine a little girl like April, five years old, schlepping five- or ten-gallon gasoline cans to the crime scene. And it wouldn't have been just one can. The fire was so intense, there would have been a fair number of cans. Plus she was on the small side even for a five-year-old. It would have been a stretch to imagine her being strong enough even to strike a match."

"What did the psychologist say?"

"That April definitely did not fit the profile."

[INTERVIEW RESUMES 11:08 a.m.]

SCHOTTLAND: You've told me a lot that really helps. But I need more information on last night. I want to make sure I understand, so can you please start at the beginning? Then we can go through it until the end.

BROWN: [nods]

SCHOTTLAND: Listen, though. If all of a sudden you remember something you hadn't said before, don't hold it back. Okay? Just jump right in there and tell me, "Hey, I forgot to say this."

BROWN: My daddy says I shouldn't say hey. He says, "Hay is what cows eat." That's a joke, but I still shouldn't say it.

SCHOTTLAND: I can understand that. So if you remember something you didn't tell me, just say something like "Excuse me, I forgot to tell you this." That's more polite . . . All right, after your dad kissed you good night, you said he left your bedroom. By the way, do you remember if he closed your door?

BROWN: Yes. [pause] Sometimes they stay downstairs. They could have drinks or watch TV, and that could wake me up.

SCHOTTLAND: All right, so he closed your door, and then what happened?

BROWN: I hugged Chloe.

PAGANO: You're doing great, April.

SCHOTTLAND: You are. What happened next?

BROWN: I woke up.

SCHOTTLAND: Do you know what made you wake up, April?

BROWN: Maybe the alarm. It went off, and it was so loud. Even if you put your whole hand over your ears, it's still so loud. My daddy told me it's for burglars and if there's a fire, so it has to be loud. Once, I opened the window by accident at night and I cried. It's scary—to scare burglars so they won't steal the stereo.

SCHOTTLAND: And the fire part of it?

BROWN: To wake up if there's a fire. But excuse me, I forgot to tell you something, okay?

SCHOTTLAND: Sure, please tell me.

BROWN: There was smoke too. Not going up, like chimney smoke. There was big, fat smoke in my room. It didn't move. It smelled so bad. And it made my eyes cry. I coughed a lot. And lights. Part of the alarm is giant lights. They go on and off, on and off.

SCHOTTLAND: What happened next?

BROWN: [pause] I wanted my daddy and mommy. The alarm made so much noise, so I didn't hear them maybe. So I tried to open the door, but it was very hot. The doorknob. [BROWN opens palm of right hand]

SCHOTTLAND: I see you have a bandage there. I'm sorry that happened to you. Did the doctor look at it?

BROWN: I was in the new place with Maya. She let the doctor come in. He put some medicine on my hand and the big white Band-Aid and listened to my heart with the thing that goes in his ears. And up my nose with a light.

SCHOTTLAND: Good. I'm glad the doctor checked you out. Now I need some more information about what happened. Did you open the door?

BROWN: No, it was so hot. So I went back to my bed. But I didn't get into it. I was coughing and coughing, so I went to the window.

SCHOTTLAND: Is the window right next to your bed?

BROWN: [shakes her head no] Because there is a carpet first, and then my desk. It's white with a white chair.

SCHOTTLAND: And the window? Where is that?

BROWN: On the wall. Mommy and I made the room. She said, "Wouldn't it be fun to be able to look outside when you're drawing or doing work for school?" So we moved the desk, and in the afternoon I can look out when the shade is up and see tree branches and the side of the Orloffs' house. They have two kids, but in college, so I don't play with them. They say, "Hi, April," when they're home.

SCHOTTLAND: The window is above the desk?

BROWN: [nods]

SCHOTTLAND: You said you went to the window. Was the shade up or down?

BROWN: Down.

SCHOTTLAND: All the way down?

BROWN: [nods]

SCHOTTLAND: Can you tell me what happened next?

BROWN: I climbed on the chair—the white chair, not the beanbag chair. That's pink. And then I got up onto my desk.

SCHOTTLAND: Were you standing up on the desk?

BROWN: No. On my knees. So then I touched the pull chain on the shade. It's like teeny silver beads, one after another. [demonstrates quick touch with index finger] I was scared it was hot, like the doorknob, but it wasn't. I'm not supposed to touch it, because shades are always down at night. Maybe my daddy and mommy were outside, waiting for me because my doorknob was hot and they didn't have a pot holder.

SCHOTTLAND: What did you see outside when you pulled up the shade, April?

BROWN: The big tree and the Orloffs' house. I put my face on the window to look for mommy and daddy. I didn't see them, but I thought the tree branches are big, so I was looking down on the ground for their feet.

SCHOTTLAND: And did you see them, or their shoes or their feet?

BROWN: No.

SCHOTTLAND: What happened next?

BROWN: The angel came.

SCHOTTLAND: Tell me about the angel.

BROWN: It came to my window. Its face was in the window. Then it flew back and I could see all of it. It had giant white wings. But arms and hands, too. And it told me to come out of the house.

PAGANO: Did you hear it tell you, April?

BROWN: No, but it went [gestures with both hands], *Come out, come out.*

SCHOTTLAND: Did you go out right away?

BROWN: Not right away. I'm not supposed to touch the window.

My dad set down the transcript and massaged his temples. Reliving that kind of interview, with a young child involved, would always be stressful no matter how many decades had intervened. "When she said the window was open . . ." my dad said. "We spoke with the security company. If the window was up more than, I forget—an inch or two—the contact magnets would separate and the alarm would go off. They also had superbright security lights, strobes, and a siren."

"So all this stuff was going off right then?"

He looked over at me and nodded.

"Amazing how much she was able to absorb during all that. I wouldn't have been so composed. And then along comes an angel to help her."

"I got to admit, the shrink was helpful on this. We talked after. She said fairies had replaced angels in the imagination of most girls her age. But if the girl was raised Catholic, then she would see angels as a powerful source of good. A five-year-old kid like April, no matter how bright—and she said April was highly intelligent—doesn't have a sense of what the shrink called 'relative morality.' Meaning she would still be unsure whether she should break her parents' rules during a traumatic situation. But the angel could overrule her parents' warnings about not opening the window, because it had authority and rightness, goodness, whatever."

"So she gave herself permission to break the rules to escape."

SCHOTTLAND: But you opened the window, right?

BROWN: The angel made its hands go up like *Open up the window*. So I did. But my hand hurt and I cried. I told the angel, "It hurts." It made its hands go up again, so I tried again even though it hurt my hand.

SCHOTTLAND: And the alarms were going off anyway, so you didn't have to worry about setting them off. Then what happened?

BROWN: I opened the window. The angel made me very, very strong. I jumped out.

SCHOTTLAND: Jumped out like how? Did you stand up?

BROWN: No. I sat on the flat thing and put my legs outside. I didn't have my slippers on. I fell onto the grass.

SCHOTTLAND: Where was the angel when you did this?

BROWN: It was flying away. I think it must have been my guardian angel. It had the biggest wings. White wings, like angels have, but when it moved them, I could see color sparkles. All colors. Not sprinkles, like on ice cream. Sparkles.

SCHOTTLAND: It must have been quite a sight.

BROWN: [nods]

SCHOTTLAND: I know a lot was going on, but could you tell if it was a boy angel or a girl angel?

BROWN: I couldn't tell. But it was very tall because I could see it in my window. But maybe it was flying up just a little.

SCHOTTLAND: So it wasn't one of those baby angels.

PAGANO: Cherubs.

BROWN: It was a grown-up.

SCHOTTLAND: Did you notice anything else about the angel? Its hair color or what it was wearing?

BROWN: I don't know about hair. I told you it wore a white thing.

SCHOTTLAND: I'm just making sure. I'm listening to you. And after the angel flew away?

BROWN: I didn't see my mommy and daddy. Mrs. Orloff was there in front and she kept hugging me. And then there were the outside sirens from the fire engines.

CHAPTER FOUR

I opened the window and took a deep breath of the heady green smell rising from our recently mowed lawn and the sweet scent of other people's roses wafting across the backyard. My dad sighed at this behavioral quirk I'd developed since moving to the suburbs—an affinity for fresh air. A game at Citi Field or fishing for striped bass in Jamaica Bay were okay for him, but they were planned well in advance and didn't require him to leave Queens.

I had put on one of my two businessy Zoom shirts, this one a soft yellow cotton with a traditional straight collar, with only the top button opened. Neither publishers in Cairo nor FBI counterterrorism types in DC wanted to see clavicles.

"I'm ready for my close-up," I told my dad. He was in the recliner, which he'd pulled over to the desk, but the leg rest was down and he was cradling a bunch of folders. The one on top was marked HOSEA WILLIAMS. I settled into the desk chair beside him and swiveled back and forth to find the perfect angle for getting to know the first in Seymour Brown's circle of lovelies. "This is the guy from Appalachia who taught himself Spanish and Russian?" My dad nodded. "And he was your number one suspect?" Another nod. "Do we have time before the Zoom to go through the Williams transcript?" I asked.

"Turns out it's not the transcript," he said in an anguished voice suitable for the last scene of *King Lear*. "Other stuff."

"Is there a chance you have more of the case papers in the closet?" I asked matter-of-factly. If he thought I was trying to cheer him up with false hope, he would only get more upset. I didn't want him to be a dud on the Zoom with April. He shrugged. *Possibly.* "What have you got?" I asked.

He handed the folder to me in the most blah manner possible, like *You can look but it's hardly worth bothering your vision neurons for*. But I studied the assorted reports, newspaper clippings, and sorry-ass grainy pictures. My dad had obviously photocopied them onto bumpy NYPD paper. No other law enforcement entity I knew of consistently used paper that looked as if it needed a dermatologist. I pulled out a mug shot of Williams taken in the nineties in Chicago. He was positioned against the usual backdrop of a cinder block wall.

I'd been carrying around a mental image of Hosea Williams. Actually two mental mug shots: one of a Black Hosea, the other white. It turned out the guy was white Hosea. He looked like an average blue-collar guy in his late twenties, with a reasonably well-trimmed U-shaped beard that reached the top of his breastbone. His eyes seemed naturally puffy, slightly downturned, so I couldn't read his expression. However, the latex-gloved hands in the frame holding his chin and the side of his head indicated a certain vexation he felt at being arrested.

If not for that restraint, you'd think, *Here's someone who always gets takeout from McDonald's because he likes a couple of beers with his Double Quarter Pounders and fries, so he has two cold ones in his Dodge Ram and eats in the cab*. He wasn't fat, just hefty. What you could see of his arms sticking out of his T-shirt showed that, though he may not have had the healthiest diet, he worked at being in shape. Not ripped as much as fit. You could pass him in the parking lot of a Target or sit next to him at an Islanders game and not feel threatened.

I pointed to the gloved hands in the mug shot. "What was he brought in for? Drugs?"

"At that point," my dad said, "heroin."

"He doesn't look like he was using."

"Nah, he was into merchandising. But he started out when he was still a kid as a runner for the most violent mob family in Mexican heroin that operated in Chicago. And the most successful. Hosea learned Spanish in like a couple months and ingratiated himself with some guy close to the big boss, then to *el gran jefe* himself."

Surprisingly, before he came to New York, Hosea Williams had relatively few other arrests and only one conviction—for the sale of fifteen grams of cocaine. He got six years in max security, yet somehow got out after fourteen months, which I figured meant he had done some maximum cooperating with the Chicago DA.

"Where is he now?" I asked.

"Federal prison. Not for anything violent, though. Something with money laundering." My dad spoke while giving Hosea's mug shot a menacing stare. "In Chicago, before he came here and hooked up with Seymour Brown, he figured out before almost anyone else how major crack cocaine would become. Just the fact that it could be snorted or smoked—that intensity of the high—but it didn't have to be injected. Hosea was a real strategic thinker. The local gangs couldn't see that at first. So Hosea took a hike and came to New York."

He crossed his arms loosely over his chest and relaxed, leaning back further, his *Who'd believe it?* posture. "So this was in the mid-nineties. When he got here, he fell in with some Russian mob guy who introduced him around. Within six months he pretty much gave up the drug stuff and moved over to financial crimes. That's when he taught himself Russian, which I hear is a bitch to learn."

"Who hired him?"

"Probably everybody."

I leaned over and picked out one of the grainy newspaper clippings. It showed a snappily dressed Hosea and Seymour. They appeared to have just gotten out of a car and were in the foreground. Behind them, somebody—maybe a chauffeur—was bent over the open rear door, helping someone get out of the car. Hosea was eyeing Seymour—and his livid expression was not one of a guy anticipating a pleasant evening out with the boss. The graininess of the photo and the yellowing of the paper obscured some detail, but Hosea's anger was palpable.

"Hosea would seem to have a degree of hostility," I remarked, handing the picture to my dad.

He glanced at it and handed it back. "Yeah, that's why we always kept him high on the suspect list. He really hated Seymour."

His phone alarm went off so piercingly that we both jumped. "It's time for me to call her," he said.

He forwarded the Zoom link to my email, and I clicked through on my desktop. April was already waiting. The app window opened to reveal a smiling, slender woman with long, dark-blond hair pulled into a thoughtlessly attractive high bun, trendy clear-framed glasses, and low-key makeup that still looked polished. Her camera was at the exact right height, and the room behind her was at the perfect teleconferencing angle. It looked sunny and inviting, with spring green walls, a large potted palm, and framed posters of *In a Lonely Place* and *Imitation of Life.* The shelves behind her were filled with what looked mostly like books about film. The only odd note was her earrings, which were large and looked like a pair of hunched, irritated eagles. Were they some weird display of fervent jingoism?

"April!" my dad said happily, with more vivacity than I'd heard emerge from him since maybe 1997.

"You need to unmute yourself, Detective Dan," she said in a pleasant and practiced way. I wondered if she was still teaching partly online these days.

"Oh, yeah," he said, hunting around the screen for approximately an eon before finally clicking unmute. "Hi, April!" he said, picking up his previous uncharacteristic chipper tone. "You can just call me Dan, now."

"Okay. Dan! It's so good to see you."

"It's great to see you, too. If it's all right, I have my daughter with me. Her name is Corie." I wheeled the desk chair over to make myself visible and I waved. She waved back, perhaps a touch of surprise crossing her cheerful face, but overall she seemed unfazed. "Corie used to be a special agent with the FBI and now does contract work for them. I like to bounce ideas off her. She helps me think better." He'd never said that to me in so many words, and it gave me that little parental-approval thrill that I was apparently not too old to crave.

"If you're at all uncomfortable with it—" I began.

"Not at all, not at all. Another perspective would be great! Especially from someone with your background." She beamed. "I'm sorry, I missed your name."

"It's Corie. I love your earrings, by the way." Though I liked her sense of style overall, at least what I could glean from a Zoom image, I didn't like the earrings. But I was curious to get a handle on her. She didn't seem the type to suddenly unfurl a DON'T TREAD ON ME! flag while laughing and spraying gunfire in the air, but I'd been wrong before.

She reached up and touched one of them. "Oh, these? Yeah, aren't they great? They're the falcon statue, like in *The Maltese Falcon*. I found this jeweler on Etsy who will make film earrings to order."

"Well, they did a great job!" I had seen *The Maltese Falcon* years ago with my mom during one of our TCM binges and had no recollection of what the statue looked like. But April seemed pleased with the compliment.

"Anyhow," my dad interjected.

"Anyhow!" she repeated brightly. "I'm going through this weird situation right now. Or possibly it's not weird at all, and everything's fine. But I think it's probably weird. And as a gut check, I'd love to talk to someone in law enforcement who knows a little more about my past."

My dad spread his hands out invitingly.

"Somebody might be trying to kill me?" she suggested hesitantly. "Or not!" she added, and I knew she had been staying up late alternating between whether to trust her gut or to suspect she was overreacting.

"Let's start at the beginning," my dad said. "Tell me what your everyday life is like now." He was using the same technique he'd used with five-year-old April—getting her to feel more comfortable by talking about less emotionally laden stuff.

"It's pretty boring right now," she said. "I think I told you I'm an assistant professor at Rutgers. I teach film. My specialty is American movies during the studio system, so roughly 1930 to 1960." I nodded as if I knew exactly what she meant by "the studio system," and so did my dad, though there was a chance he actually did know. "It's summer session, and I'm teaching one class online. I'm only on campus one day a week to screen the movie we're discussing, in case the students want to see it on film or the campus library doesn't have it available for streaming."

"Where are you living now?" my dad asked.

"Here. That is, New Brunswick."

"Do you live alone?" I asked.

"Yes, for the time being. My fiancée, Misaki, is doing a postdoc in Japan. I haven't seen her for four months." Her eyes moistened a little, but she blinked and her tone didn't alter. "I'm hoping she can figure out a way to move back here. It's so hard in academia for couples to find decent work near each other." She paused. "But honestly, I'm luckier than so many academics right now. I still have a tenure-track job in a place I actually want to live. That's, like, unheard of. Are you still living in Queens?"

"Can you believe I live in the suburbs now? My daughter and her family had to take me in." He patted my arm affectionately. "I think I'm going to die of fresh-air poisoning."

I added, "I know you're supposed to be miserable living with your parents when you're in your thirties, but I actually like having them around." I instantly felt bad, as it hit me that I was talking to someone who couldn't live with her parents even if she wanted to. April, though, looked entirely unbothered and smiled at us benevolently.

"So you're alone a lot of the time right now," my dad observed.

She nodded. "Which is fine, you know! I like being alone. And it doesn't really feel like I'm alone, since I talk to students so much of the day. Then there are faculty meetings, which are endless, and I get to watch movies with Misaki while video chatting, though the timing can be difficult. Sometimes I get up at five to do that."

She paused. We waited. "So here's what happened," she said. My dad nodded encouragingly.

She had been on campus heading to her office. My dad cut in to ask if her campus visit was done on a regular schedule. It was, she informed us. She screened movies every Thursday at eleven a.m. She was heading from her parking space to her building when a dark SUV suddenly gunned its engine and drove up over the curb straight at her.

"Were all four wheels up over the curb?" I asked, trying to feel out whether it really was an attack.

"Yes. It drove a good ten yards onto the grass, chasing me as I ran away." My dad and I glanced at each other. Not an accident. She seemed to understand what we were getting at, and added, "Yeah. Maybe it's not just my imagination. It was coming straight at me. Also, a couple of students walking nearby said the license plate was duct-taped over."

"So it looks like it wasn't a spontaneous thing," Dad said.

"I guess not," April replied.

"Where did you go from there?" I asked.

"First I ran away as fast as I could, but it kept coming. All of a sudden the movie *The In-Laws* popped into my head. Did you ever see it? The original, not the remake." Her brow furrowed, conveying her full disdain for the remake.

My dad exclaimed cheerfully, "Yes, hilarious movie!"

"It's now on my list," I said.

"Oh, you should definitely see it," April said. "Comedies don't usually hold up as well over time as dramas, but this one really does. Anyway, there's this one part where Peter Falk, who plays a CIA agent, yells 'Serpentine!' at poor Alan Arkin, who's running away from people shooting at him. You know, not in a straight line, but like this," and she curved her hand back and forth in front of her like a snake wriggling.

My dad laughed and said, "That scene was hilarious!" It didn't sound that hilarious to me, but I smiled encouragingly.

April saw my face and said, "Just trust me, you need to see it. I know it doesn't sound funny, but it was. Anyway, that's what I did. I ran serpentine. I don't know if it worked, but he eventually stopped and drove away."

“He? Did you see his face?” I asked.

“No. I didn’t see anything. Just the glare off the windshield. I guess I’m being sexist. It could have been a she,” April replied. “It actually seemed driverless to me, kind of like in *Christine*.” Finally, a movie I had seen and remembered clearly.

“So this sounds not only intentional, but the duct-taped license plate means it was planned,” my dad commented. “Do you think the New Brunswick police aren’t taking it seriously enough?”

“It’s not quite that,” she answered. “One of the students was the one who called 911, and she and her boyfriend were pretty upset. The police told me they’re doing forensic work on some tire marks left in the grass. I’m pretty sure they believe that someone was trying to hurt me. That’s not the issue. It’s more that they seem uninterested in my past. I tried to tell them about what happened with my parents. I certainly got sympathy, but they just kept insisting that the arson, the murders . . . they happened a long time ago. They keep wanting to know who could be angry at me now. But I really can’t think of anyone. I tend to get along with people. I mean, a few students get F’s, but just when they stop going to class. They don’t hold it against me for that.”

I nodded. It was difficult imagining someone working themselves into a murderous rage at this pretty, smiling film nerd with goofy earrings.

“And honestly, everything I know about the Mafia is from Scorsese and Coppola movies, not real life. But it seems like many of those guys hold a grudge, and I’ve read it’s the same with the Russian Mafiya. And if someone was angry enough to murder my parents in that terrible way and presumably meant to kill me too, then . . .” She looked off-screen for a minute, possibly gazing out a window, and then turned back to us.

My dad rubbed his chin, saying, “Yeah. That’s where my mind went. Your parents. Though I have to admit I’m also not sure why anyone would wait more than twenty years to come back and get you.” She nodded eagerly along with him, as if to say, *I know, that’s weird, too, right? None of it makes sense!* “Do you mind if I ask you a few more questions about the people in your current life? It’s not that I don’t believe you when you say no one wants to hurt you, I just want to get a feel for what's going on."

"Sure."

"So tell me a bit about your relationship with your students."

"I mean, it's fine," she said. "I like them, they like me. I try to be as straightforward as possible with grading so that there are no arguments. Of course, there are always a few, but nothing major."

"Are you one of those professors that socializes with your students, hosts them for parties or whatever?" he asked.

"Oh God no," she replied, so firmly that I laughed a little. "Wait, that sounds bad! It's not. It's just that I have, like, no extra time. I need to be publishing as much as possible at this point in my career. Also, during the regular semester I have about a hundred fifty students in my Intro to American Film class, so a party for them would get a bit crowded. I see the grad students at department events, but not socially one-on-one."

"Did any of your students ever seem . . . a little off?" I asked.

She grinned. "A lot of them! But they didn't seem off in a violent way. With all the school shootings, I do occasionally wonder if any one of them might be the type to shoot up a classroom. But I never had a student who made me feel threatened."

"And what are your colleagues like?" my dad asked.

"They're great. Well, mostly. Some of them are just okay. Academics can be prickly, you know. But I don't think anyone has any special quibbles with me. Besides, if any of them wanted to do me in, all they'd have to do is deny me tenure in two years. Much more devastating than death."

My dad looked up at the ceiling, resting his chin on his tented fingers. April and I waited. In a moment, he reengaged. "How's your family? The Cincinnati bunch."

"Northern Kentucky, actually. Right over the river from Cincinnati. They're okay. I don't really get to see them much," April said with just a touch of regret.

"No quarrels? Were they upset when you told them you had a girlfriend?"

"I mean, they weren't immediately like, *Tell me how I can be an ally to the community!* but I don't think it was a major shock. Now that they've met Misaki a few times, they really seem to like her. She won my grandmother over by being so much more polite than I am and always writing thank-you notes by hand."

"How often do you see the family?" I asked.

"At least once a year. I try to get back for Christmas. One of my cousins—she's twenty-two—came and stayed with me maybe a year ago because she wanted to visit New York but didn't want to pay for a hotel. She was surprised that I don't live in a mansion, because she knows I inherited some money. Oh, and I Zoom with my grandma and my aunt Patty about once a month."

I had thought my father would be getting tired or distracted by this time, but he was intensely focused. He asked April what she remembered about her past. She spoke fondly of Seymour, recalling that he had a real talent for drawing—or at least that's how it seemed to her as a child. All the pictures he drew had burned in the fire. He used to draw her funny cartoons with a character he called Mary the Canary. She didn't really have specific memories of her mother, just some strong images. She remembered catching her mother's eye in the mirror while she was at her vanity putting on makeup, and she gave April a big smile. Another memory was her mother slicing the crust from a sandwich and cutting it into dainty strips, saying, "This is how you do it when you want to be extra fancy."

Although many people knew that her parents had died in a fire when she was young, the only people who knew that her father was involved with the Mafiya—and that the fire was arson—were Misaki, the family who'd raised her, law enforcement in Brooklyn and Kentucky, and now the New Brunswick PD.

"I'm guessing you've Googled yourself. Does anything about your past show up?" my dad asked.

She shook her head. Her falcon earrings flopped around her neck, and I worried for a second that one might fly off. "Brown is such a common name. Half the time when I actually want people to be able to find me online, they can't. Besides, the murder wasn't covered in major newspapers, just local ones in Brooklyn. They weren't online at the time, I don't think. Someone might be able to find out more if they knew my parents' names, probably, but I don't remember anyone asking." She glanced at her phone. "I'm so sorry to do this, but I just want to give you a heads-up. In about ten minutes I have to go. I have a conference with a grad student."

"That's fine," I said. "Do you mind if I ask what your financial situation is like? You mentioned an inheritance."

"Yes. I've been super lucky. Assistant professors—that means I'm a professor who hasn't gotten tenure yet—generally don't have amazing salaries. But I inherited a bunch of money from my parents. Most of it was in a trust, but I also got assets from bank accounts, life insurance, and the sale of the lot the house was on. Plus there was a couple hundred thousand in cash and jewelry in a safe-deposit box. I was only allowed to open it when I turned eighteen. I reported it to the police because I was worried that it was dirty money that hadn't yet been laundered, but the Brooklyn DA's office said there was no evidence of that, so I could keep it."

"How much money do you have now?" My dad could never see the point of beating around the bush about money matters. He didn't shrink from asking people he had just met what their salary was, even though it made my mom cringe.

April turned red. "I know this sounds weird, but I really don't know. I mean. Several million." I wasn't sure whether she was embarrassed because she thought she should know how much she had or because she thought it was an unseemly amount of money. "It was handled by the trustee until I came of age, and I basically dumped it all with my financial adviser. Actually, it's a team within a big brokerage firm. It's in a couple of different accounts. I don't check often, because I don't really spend a lot. I've drawn from it to live on only when I was a grad student and to buy this house. And I have some money sent quarterly to my grandma."

My dad held up pictures of Hosea Williams and Toddy the driver. I didn't like showing her a mug shot of Hosea, but we'd decided that would be less provocative than the one of him staring daggers at her father. She didn't recognize Hosea at all, but had vague memories of Toddy from when she was a girl. She was sure she hadn't seen him recently.

She checked her phone again, so we took the hint and signed off, agreeing to meet in New Brunswick in two days so we could talk more and she could show us where the attack occurred.

"Dan. It was really so good to see you again. And great to meet you, Corie. Just talking to you folks, I already feel more secure," she said.

My dad grinned. "Really glad we had this talk. I look forward to seeing you in person."

"Bye!" With a wave, she vanished from our screens.

My dad turned to me. "So that's April Brown."

"I really like her," I said.

"I do too. She's the same person she was when she was a little girl. Smart as hell, friendly—even though both times she'd just been through a tough situation. Observant. She reminded me so much of you."

I smiled. "I should have asked her for some sci-fi recommendations. Eliza loves to watch with me, and I bet we could finally get her into black-and-white movies now."

"Well, you can ask tomorrow." Dad rubbed his temples and grimaced.

"What's up?" I asked.

"This case," he said. "Someone trying to run her down . . . It doesn't make sense. What the fuck is going on?"

Brushing my teeth that night, I had a flash of what my next day's plans needed to be: Get to the Brooklyn Public Library for one last probe of the Kim and Seymour killings. Dig deep into the weekly newspapers in and around Manhattan Beach. There had to be contemporaneous coverage on the arson-murder.

These neighborhood papers were often rich in those particulars that stupefied outsiders, gratified locals who saw their neighbors and shopkeepers in print, and occasionally offered a promising detail to investigators.

I went to the Brooklyn Library, where I found Lucy the blessèd. Lucy was the first librarian I saw when I walked in, standing behind her desk with her hands clasped as if she'd been waiting for me to arrive. She was the right librarian to find. Within minutes I was set up at a carrel with my laptop, able to access borough-wide newspapers and neighborhood weeklies. Many went back decades, at least one for more than a century.

The *Manhattan Beach Clarion* had several stories on the fire, nearly all written by one Johnny Miron Polyakov. There was a front-page headline right after the crime: FIRE KILLS COUPLE. The subhead was LITTLE GIRL ESCAPES and, beneath that, ALL IS ASHES.

Johnny seemed to pick up what any sharp journalist would see. He even elicited a quote from the neighbor who first saw April standing outside shivering, alone, in pajamas with lambs all over them: "She said, 'Where is my mommy and daddy?'" Other than the lambs, there was nothing in the account I didn't already know. Its final sentence was "Fire investigators and police are delving into the cause of the fire." The word "arson" hadn't yet appeared.

In the main photo accompanying the story, all but one of the FDNY trucks had pulled away. Fire department cars and a van, along with the usual NYPD crime scene investigation vehicles, clung to the curbs. I estimated that the time wasn't long after sunup, the sky just bright enough to illuminate the insignias on the car doors and put a sheen on a length of the crime scene tape.

In a smaller photo, three dog walkers faced the camera, mesmerized by the revolting remains that had once been the Browns' house and its owners. A couple of women pushing strollers had ventured out. One was so engrossed, she appeared about to bang little Brielle or big boy Brandon into a parked police car.

The following week, the *Clarion*'s front page had a half-page reproduction of the architect's plans for the Browns' house. On the upper part of the drawing, printed in those flawless capital letters architects use, it said, MASTER BEDROOM. An arrow pointed about three-quarters of the way into the room with the words FIRE STARTED HERE near its tip.

There was an immediacy about reading about our case in a way-back newspaper (okay, digitized way back). My eye caught the name Bobby Melvin. Later that morning, as I knew, he'd been named head of the investigation. Too bad. My dad hated him. For Bobby, the qualities my dad embraced—diligence, curiosity, a willingness to be surprised, plus inspiration—were the enemies of a fast resolution to a case.

I angled the laptop screen to try to escape the reflected glare of the fluorescent lights. That's when I saw the picture of my dad. I enlarged it to 150 percent. At first I recognized him by his boots, Wellingtons. My mom had bought them so long ago, I couldn't remember him wearing anything else. Naturally she'd gotten him those green ones, British. They could practically vocalize, *I'm off to muck out the stalls.*

He was young—older than I was now, but not by a lot. He looked so energetic and assured. There was the big block of his head, the broad shoulders pulled back, his chin lifted toward the left—probably because Bobby Melvin was standing on his right.

There was my depressed, TV-watching, cranky dad, but at his peak, when he really was one of New York's Finest. His straight back had not begun to morph into comma shape. The man in the photo was the dad of my memory.

Just to cover all bases, I looked up the crime in the traditional New York papers and found a human-interest piece, THE LITTLE SURVIVOR, in the *Daily News*. Not bad, but I missed Johnny Miron Polyakov. The article was only slightly mawkish, with one neighbor calling April "a darling child" with "big blue eyes, and so sweet and quiet, like her mother, may she rest in peace." That person spoke off the record, but a Joan Koslow was forthright enough not just to give her name, but to state that April was always clean and nicely dressed, "never overdressed. Her mother took very good care of her." Then she added that it was obvious that Seymour doted on the little girl even though "he had the reputation of being somewhat of a cold fish with everybody else. I saw him in the playground with her on weekends a few times, pushing her on the swing, actually going on the seesaw with her. April brought out the best in him. One time I heard him calling her 'April May June July,' and they both were laughing."

Joan Koslow's words, "cold fish," stuck out simply because she said that to a reporter about Seymour within a week of the awful murders. Someone might confide in a friend, *He was the worst person in the world*, understanding that it would be unseemly to say that for public consumption. Seymour truly must have been a bad guy.

CHAPTER FIVE

April, Dad, and I spent the first moment we met, standing beside her Subaru Outback, accustoming ourselves to the three-dimensional versions of each other. She was smiling broadly as she walked over to meet us.

"I am so grateful that you drove down here," she said.

"Not at all," said my dad with uncustomary gallantry. At our request, she led us to where she had parked her car six days earlier. She was shorter than I'd guessed from our virtual first meeting and so small-boned she probably needed alterations on her watchband.

"Okey doke," my dad said. "So being here will help us get a handle on what happened that day. You were heading to that building over there?"

"Right. Up to my office. It's on the fourth floor." With her chin, she pointed to a blah-looking stone-and-glass building ahead of us. "I was going to set up the projector to screen the movie for my students, then head to my office to get a little work done. And I couldn't stop obsessing about a tub of red licorice twists I left there. Five pounds, from Costco. It's like, *My name is April and I'm a red licorice addict.*"

I was amazed that April Brown could be this irrepressibly upbeat, that she could drop the thread of a narrative about how someone had tried to kill her at the mere recollection of a tub of candy. Perhaps she was simply unwilling to let her emotional guard down in front of people she didn't know very well.

April looked like a solid citizen, wearing a sleeveless white shirt with pleats in the front and pristine maroon jeans. Today her shoulder-length hair was brushed to a sheen. Her eyes behind her glasses were the winner, blue like a turquoise, with a thin, dark outline around the iris. I admit to being a little envious; I had blue eyes, but compared with hers, mine were more the color of the sky on a morning that dawned with warnings about air quality.

"You were walking toward that sidewalk, right?" Dad asked April.

"Yes. It goes to that path that leads around to the front of the building." The cement path, with stubby grass on either side, was about half the width of the sidewalk. It was a direct and charmless route to the academic building. April began walking, and we walked alongside her. "This is the route I took."

"How fast were you going?" I asked. "Strolling? Running toward the red licorice?"

"I was going about like this," April said, and sped up slightly. Still, no one would say we were going fast. It definitely wasn't a pace to attract a normal passerby's attention. We got there in under two minutes. I usually liked to take notes by hand as someone talked, but it was difficult as we were outside and walking around. Besides, I wanted her to feel as unselfconscious as possible.

"And you said there were a few other cars parked nearby?"

"Yes. Not anything like it is when regular classes are in session, but maybe a total of ten cars."

I glanced around. Three cars besides ours, and two students on the sidewalk having a conversation that required much gesticulation. A guy in his twenties was coming from the other direction. As they neared each other, he stepped down from the curb into the lot to let them pass. "Was there more action than this?"

"Definitely. More cars. A couple of cars—besides the SUV—were driving around, not just parked." She shrugged. "Not hordes, like an intro psych class during the school year. More like a linguistics seminar."

"Pedestrians?" my dad asked.

"Yes. Three or four. I don't know . . . could have been a couple more."

"Were people heading toward the building or leaving?" I asked.

"Mostly leaving," she said. "I mean, they could have had other stuff to do on campus. But most were headed toward the lot."

I stood about a foot from my dad, waiting for him to follow up on my question, but instead he started to jingle the change in his pocket. He looked like a retiree who comparison shopped for antacid. Which, actually, he was. For an uncharitable moment I was embarrassed by him. His collared shirt—a plaid so faded it had no readily identifiable colors—had wrinkles and floppy short sleeves. Also, an early-morning shaving mistake had left him with one very short sideburn that made his head look tilted. He appeared perplexed, not a quality you want to see in the veteran detective you're depending on. Finally he stopped fiddling with coins, took his hand out of his pocket, and spoke. "The first moment you were aware of the SUV . . . think back. Were you still walking in the lot or were you on the sidewalk?"

April closed her eyes. Finally, eyes still closed, she murmured, "Just trying to get a visual." Normally that would make someone in law enforcement suspect she was stalling. She was a film scholar, though, someone who sees for a living.

"No rush," he said softly.

April opened her eyes. I was half expecting some cinematic gesture, a one-two blink—*Oh my, such bright sunlight!*—but she just scratched her nose. "All right, I'm pretty sure this is how it went down." She stepped down from the curb and walked a few steps away from us diagonally. "So you two are standing in the spot I was heading toward."

Her delivery was somewhere between matter-of-fact and brisk. She wasn't showing any signs of distress: no hoarseness from a dry mouth, no arms across her chest to give herself a comforting hug. But I'd expect as much: contrary to what most people outside law enforcement think, many crime victims are not weepy or shaky—just brisk. That appeared to be April's MO. And maybe after what she'd been through as a child, she'd learned to suppress shock.

April glanced around her as if to double-check. "Right. It was just about here that I perceived that something big—the SUV—was behind me on the right. I think I saw something in my peripheral vision before I could really process it . . ." She paused. "It was something like *Big dark vehicle coming too fast*."

"Besides your peripheral vision," my dad said, "was there anything else to grab your attention? Shouting, engine noise . . . that sort of thing."

She didn't answer off the top of her head. Her eyes closed again for a few seconds. I wished all the witnesses I interviewed could be this careful and thoughtful about the information they were providing. Finally she said, "Maybe because of my job, I might be more aware of ambient sound than most people. But nothing until it was coming. Then the engine revving and tires squealing. Maybe half a second later I heard someone scream. When something comes up from behind you so fast . . . I don't know. You're aware of wrongness. Or your lizard brain kicks in and warns you to watch your ass."

"So you sensed it wasn't just a car speeding by," I said. "It was something dangerous, and it was headed for you."

"That's what was so crazy," April said. "I mean, I generally feel pretty safe walking across campus. The two of you are law enforcement, so I'm guessing a certain awareness of the possibility of peril probably figures into your thinking all the time. But with me? Totally not."

"Got it," my dad said. "Once you realized what was happening, did you notice anything more specific about the SUV?"

She shook her head.

"So can you give us a demonstration of how you got away? As close an approximation as you can of how that serpentine thing went?" He added "Please" in the instant she said "Okay."

April had been straightforward when talking about what happened. But I was also in the post-traumatic stress club, which made me think that even she might find a reenactment challenging. I asked her if she wanted me to follow her and run right behind her. "In case you feel like stopping to chat," I said lightly. I was pretty sure she'd tell us that she'd be fine, but instead, she nodded.

We went straight on the grass for a minute, and then April began to run in serpentine fashion, first to the right, a hairpin turn to the left, and a more gradual turn to the right. A moment after that she stopped and said, "I'm not sure this is exactly what I did. I was going on instinct."

"But you think this is pretty much how you went?"

"Yes. But I can't guarantee it was actually how it happened."

"I don't need a guarantee," I told her. "Now, at this point, the car had come out on the grass and was still following you, right?"

"Yes." It was only a syllable, but there was a fair amount of emotion in it. For the first time, she sounded shaky.

"Look, we don't have to perform the whole thing again. We can start up, walk the route you took. Or we can say 'Enough' and you can point out when the SUV stopped following you." I looked back toward the sidewalk, where my dad was shading his eyes, watching us closely.

With her fingertips, trying for a casual gesture, April wiped the sweat trickling down her forehead. But her strained breathing and perspiration weren't from exertion. Most likely she was reliving the terror of being someone's prey. "Listen," I told her, "you weren't only fast-thinking, you were brave. That was true when the car was after you. And it's true now—your willingness to talk about what happened and also to re-create it."

"Thank you." She rubbed her damp palms against her jeans and did what I took to be a subconscious *Chin up!* "Um, why don't we go side by side?" she asked. "I can show you at what point I realized the SUV wasn't coming at me anymore."

We walked, slower now, for not even a minute. "I was right here—" April stopped. "And the car was over there." She pointed to a spot about half the distance we had just come, near a sign with a campus map on it. "It looked like it was getting bigger and bigger. And then, all of a sudden, it lurched off, almost at a right angle, away from me."

"And then?" I asked.

"All I know is, this is the spot where I remember being all right, free of it."

We were on the grass, facing the building, a fair distance from the path. I was always terrible at judging distance, but I used Josh—slightly over six feet tall—as one of my standards. This looked like three Joshes lying head to toe to form a straight line. I checked out the terrain. Not quite flat, but all I could spot were a couple of swells—not even hillocks. I didn't understand. Nothing I saw would present a problem to a vehicle with four-wheel drive. My guess was that a huge SUV, like a Range Rover or a Chevy Suburban, should have been able to go off-road on a slightly bumpy college lawn with the ease of a lion running across the savanna. So how come it hadn't gotten its prey? Why had it suddenly driven off?

"So the car never got closer to you than from about here to there?"

"No." She took a deep breath.

"Did you get a clear sense that it was trying to run you over—seriously injure or kill you? Could it possibly have been only trying to frighten you?"

She shook her head. She didn't know. But it didn't even take ten seconds before she stopped walking. We were a few inches from the path. I stood beside her and gave my dad a time-out signal. Finally she looked at me. "My impression . . . It doesn't even qualify as an impression. But it doesn't seem as though it was someone trying to frighten me. There was a purposefulness to it. It was after me, and when I started serpentining, it got confused." Her brows rose in give-me-a-break fashion, as if she'd just heard some really stupid answer from a student. "No, not 'it.' Him. Or her. The driver seemed . . . You understand I'm just pulling this out of my ass."

"Sure. Keep pulling."

"Either the driver wasn't used to such a big car or to driving on something other than pavement."

"Gotcha," I said. "So there's that little voice inside you saying that the driver's purpose was to run you down?"

"Yes. Why they stopped? I don't have a clue." The corners of her eyes crinkled into a smile. "Oh, speaking of 'little voice.' There's a British film, *Little Voice*. Not in my Top 100, but easily Top 346."

* * *

I filled my dad in on the attack as we followed April through New Brunswick to her house. He nodded as I spoke, then checked his email and discovered that Gabriel Salazar—who had risen to second-in-command of his precinct—had emailed him some documents, including one about the Browns' finances. Considering the horror of their deaths, Seymour and Kim seemed to have lived well. They left behind what Gabriel informed us was a well-drawn will that gave April the contents of some trusts and most of their assets, minus a few small bequests. It mentioned two safe-deposit boxes, one of which had the deed to their house and ownership papers for Seymour's Mercedes. I guessed the other one had the cash and jewelry April had told us about. The boxes were in Seymour's name only.

"I looked at this stuff over the last twenty years," my dad said. "You know, like when there was a little downtime and I wanted to eat at my desk because someone's wife made blueberry muffins and they were crumbly. I'd think back to one of my cold cases. Anyway, there were a couple of things that struck me . . . not as wrong, but as odd."

"Like what?" One thing had already struck me, but I wanted to hear what he had to say.

"First of all, the will. Nearly everything went to Kim—with a trustee, which makes her sound like she was probably not a financial whiz—except for some bequests. Like to his secretary and a couple of charities. I remember thinking, *The Red Cross and the March of Dimes?* I mean, they're good causes, but what's that word you use for typical?"

"Generic?"

"Yeah. It sounds like he said to his lawyer, *Toss in a couple of charities so I don't come off like a heartless scumbag.* If something happened to him and Kim together, it all went to April. Trusts again, with a legit bank. But the weird thing was, there was no provision for guardianship for April. Like didn't they have any family? And if they didn't, wouldn't they write,

I leave my beloved daughter April in the care of my friend Joe Schmoe and his wife, Betty?"

"It does sound odd." We had left campus about ten minutes earlier and were now moving into a suburban area. April was easy to follow, as she drove well and signaled. I also had her address on my GPS, so I wasn't concerned about losing her. "It sounds like they were very isolated."

"They didn't even name a childcare agency to place her. And Kim's will was basically the same as his. No *I leave my pearls to my best friend Mary Sue.* They left the executor to decide about the kid, and who was he? Some banker with a tie clip?"

As we drove through the streets, the houses, mostly Victorian, got a little bigger, but the indication that we were getting to higher-income territory was that they were better cared for. The owners had money not just for paint jobs but for restorations and landscaping.

"You mentioned a couple of things that were odd," I said.

"Right. Actually, Connie Vaughn mentioned this. She was—I think—detective third grade back then. She thought it was funny that only Seymour had access to the safe-deposit box. She said if people have good jewelry that they keep in the bank, why would just the husband be in charge?" I nodded. That was exactly what I'd been thinking. "She said a woman would want to be the one to pick out a necklace for a big night out. But she'd also want to look at her other stuff."

"Exactly. Unless he was afraid she'd use it to run off with a boyfriend or sell it for . . . whatever. Drugs. Gambling. Money to redo the kitchen."

"Yes, but there was no evidence of anything like that."

A minute later, April slowed down, then pulled up in front of a house that made my dad and me say in unison, "Nice!"

April's house was not the grand one you might expect if you knew how much was in her brokerage accounts. But it was a lovely professor's home, clad in white-painted wood. Its Victorian trim was the green of trees in

July. As we walked up the stairs to the front porch that ran the length of the house, I noticed that nearly everything was slightly off. The stairs themselves seemed almost precisely in the center of the house, but the impressive front door, (maybe) mahogany with glass panels, was off to the right, as if some early-twentieth-century joiner hadn't liked the drawings and had slid it to where he thought it ought to be. A gable initially seemed placed directly over the front door, but as we got closer, I realized it was plunked so that its apex aligned with absolutely nothing.

But the whole effect was an off-kilter pleasure. The shrubs that needed a slight trim, the rectangle of front lawn with its couple of brown spots, and an old-fashioned porch swing with its load of mismatched pillows were imperfectly perfect. April might not have high style, but she did have an eye.

"It's such a nice day, do you want to sit outside?" April said to my dad.

"Yeah."

She led us to the main part of the porch, where there was a love seat, a wicker rocker that had a white cushion with the most modest of ruffles, and a few chairs and little tables.

My dad went through the motions of offering each of us the rocker, but before we began shaking our heads, he was already seated, giving it a back-and-forth trial run. April took a small metal chair with chipped paint, and I got the love seat.

I hesitated, as I tend to be weird about all sorts of sensory input, from smells to accidentally having someone's rough elbow touch me in a crowded elevator. I could practically sniff the mildew as I prepared to sit, feel the out-all-night dampness of the cushions, but not only was the seat dry, it had a faint just-laundered scent. Both Wynne, my BFF since first grade, and my daughter, Eliza, had, separately, murmured that I might consider whether I was slightly autistic. Josh never noticed, or at least he didn't appear to think it was odd when I told him that if he ever put his tongue in my ear, I would vomit. My mom understood totally because she had similar mishegas—she couldn't touch velvet or corduroy and had twice fainted from the smell of ammonia.

"Okay," I began. "Just to be clear. Since we Zoomed, or even since we drove here, have you had any new thoughts about the incident? If anything occurred to you about passing someone on the lawn when you were running, the shape of the SUV's headlights—the most minor detail, like 'I saw a used Kleenex on the grass'—let us know."

April pushed up her glasses so they became a headband. "Nothing. Truthfully, it's more my style to deliberately avoid overthinking about bad stuff. I do my best to put it out of my mind. Make fresh lemonade or practice my guitar. So nothing to report."

I sat back and wished I could close my eyes. Not that I was tired, but after being on campus, the shade on the porch and the slightly mossy smell of trees made me so relaxed. April's address could have been Easy Street. A woman strolled by with a mastiff and a weighty poop bag. A Prius went one way and a red contractor's pickup the other, which the residents probably considered heavy traffic. Across the street, a boy about Eliza's age wearing only shorts and giant earphones moved back and forth almost imperceptibly on a glider. I pulled a pad and pen out of the small backpack I'd been carrying.

"I know we talked about your students, that you only fail someone if they stop coming to class," I said.

"Right."

"You don't get rattled by students who don't do the work?"

"No. That happens. And there's always one or two who tell me their granny died, so they can't take the final," April said. "My exams are apparently fatal to grandparents. But as long as they make it up, I can deal."

"Ever have a student get angry with you?" my dad asked.

"I've definitely gotten some outraged emails trying to argue that an eighty-five average should be an A-minus. But I've never been stalked or anything. No threats. I mean, there may be a student who's seriously crazy, but seems normal, who could plan some kind of retribution for a C-minus. But nothing I've ever picked up." She'd had her feet tucked under her on the small metal chair, but now she put them on the floor. "Do either of you want some kind of a drink?"

I said yes to S.Pellegrino, and of course my dad suddenly sat up straight as she enumerated the three brands of beer she had on ice. She also mentioned having a bathroom on the right, down the hall past the living room. So while she went into the kitchen, we took turns taking her up on her bathroom offer. On every wall were framed stills from black-and-white movies, and I imagined how enthralled my mom would be with this.

When April brought out an unopened can of mixed nuts along with the drinks, I pondered that she seemed to be a perfect person: intelligent, down-to-earth, sane, considerate, totally pleasant. Even when talking about annoying students, there was acceptance, not hostility. She didn't appear damaged by the awful deaths of her parents and the terror of watching her home—and everything in her life—burn to the ground. She was not only a survivor, she seemed like a good soul.

So who would want to kill her? Was there someone that twisted who would come back after all those years and try to wipe out the last surviving member of Seymour Brown's family? What dangerous information could she possess? It wasn't as if, at age five, April had sat on her dad's lap, checked out his papers, and memorized all the numbers of the offshore accounts where he could have stashed his clients' money.

She shook some nuts onto separate napkins for each of us. My dad took a bunch and popped them into his mouth with a finesse that came from years at bars with cops. He smiled at April. "A blessing on your head that they're not unsalted." He followed that with a couple of swigs of beer. "Here's what I'm thinking," he said. "The plan to go after you on a campus that wasn't full of people wasn't a bad one. Maybe it was even good. A big, heavy SUV that wouldn't draw attention but could easily drive up on a sidewalk, down a path. And black or very dark blue? Excellent. Because—and here I'm going to risk upsetting you, but I want you to know what we're thinking—if you got hit by a light-colored car, it would be covered with blood, and that would complicate their chances for a clean getaway. Every other car on the road would be dialing 911. So whoever it was either chose well or had a lot of dumb luck when it came to color choice."

April gnawed on a couple of knuckles as I added, "My guess is the SUV was probably stolen and then abandoned. No one's going to risk taking it to the local car wash, where"—I hesitated, then plunged in—"the wastewater and suds would turn pink. And they wouldn't risk parking it in their own garage, where forensic techs would be sure to find enough DNA, in spite of the wash, to connect the SUV to an attack on you." She took a single almond from her napkin and examined it for a second before she popped it into her mouth—as if she had just read one of those articles on eating mindfully. "I'm not saying some psycho out to get you would plan it out in that way," I went on. "But a pro, or someone who has enough savvy to plan an attack? Definitely." I turned to my dad. "They must have CCTV coverage on campus. Right? If people were allowed on campus, presumably it would be working. If the campus cops weren't monitoring it twenty-four seven, at least they'd have it. And the same with the New Brunswick police."

"Right." He set his beer down beside his chair and rocked forward, leaning in toward April. "Now, besides the cops on the scene," he said to her, "did you speak to any detectives from the New Brunswick police?"

"Yes. Two of them interviewed me." She picked up her phone. "Should I text you their contact information?"

"Yes, and to Corie also. Do we have your permission to speak to them on your behalf?"

"Totally," April said. "I'll call and tell them I would appreciate it if they cooperated with you. The main detective looks a lot like Austin Stoker in *Assault on Precinct 13*. John Carpenter film, extremely 1970s. Anyway, I'll call him." She took a deep breath. "You've already spent a lot of time coming down here, going to campus, and you'll be speaking with the local police. I'd feel better if going forward I could pay—"

My dad cut her off. "No. The case was never closed. I thought about it on the NYPD's dime and now on my pension. So when you called . . . Consider it a package deal. I owe it to you and your parents."

April lowered her head. It was a bow of gratitude. Plus, I thought, an acknowledgment that she shouldn't push the payment business. When she lifted her chin, I noticed she wasn't teary, although she swallowed with effort, a reaction noticeable to someone with a trained eye. The upside of resilience is the ability to bottle up fragility and loss. It's also the cost. "Thank you," she said.

"You're welcome," my dad said.

"Ultimately the reason why I contacted you was that I wondered—considering that what my dad did might be not quite legal—if this could be some kind of revenge thing? A mob hit?"

"I'm definitely not an expert on Russian mobsters," I told her. "But everyone who deals with them knows they not only employ brutality, they're also creative with it. They not only want to leave the other guy dead, they want to make an impression: *Hey, fuck us over and you'll die just like this.*"

"Was my dad actually a member of the mob? Or did he just work with them? I don't remember anything Russian growing up." April frowned, as if trying to recall her dad popping out with a "*Dasvidaniya!*" one night, but clearly nothing came to her. Otherwise, she seemed very calm when asking about her father's criminality. Did coming from such a man upset her? Did she ever worry whether she had inherited not only her smarts from him but also his tendency to lie, cheat, steal?

"No," my dad said. "He wasn't in the mob. Whatever his background, he was hired help. Very high-level, though. In his field, he was considered one of the top accountants."

April chewed thoughtfully on another couple of nuts, washing them down with a swig of beer from her bottle. "So whatever crime the mobsters got their money from, they gave it to him . . . To do what? Besides doing the tax returns and telling them how to structure their financial stuff. Actual money laundering? I really know nothing about that except what I've seen in *Breaking Bad, The Wire, Ozark.*"

"Those should give you at least a sense of how it works," I said. I felt confident in my ability to explain this, as terrorists routinely laundered their drug trade profits. I'd also heard my dad explain it to Eliza the other night. "Let's say you're a criminal. You have some military-grade weapons you'd like to sell to some bad guys. It's illegal, of course, but you find your buyers, and they buy from you without a hitch. Suppose you get a couple million dollars for it. Obviously, you're going to want to spend that money. You can't just keep giant piles of cash. Or you can, but it's hard. If you use twenties—which are less traceable than hundreds—that actually takes up more room than you'd think. It's hard to hide. If the cops ever raid your house, it's a bunch of physical evidence. Also, if you get that kind of money, you're going to want to make big purchases. A new house—well, this one's so lovely and cozy, you'd just be buying a vacation home."

"Oh, thanks," April said. "I love it here, it's really my dream house."

I smiled and went on. "Or other purchases. Cars, jewelry. A boat."

"A Jet Ski!" April jumped in. "I've never tried, but doesn't it look fun?"

"I've never done it either, but it does," I agreed. I nestled down further in the love seat, which was more comfortable than outdoor furniture had any right to be. "Anyway, you can't just dump a pile of bills on the table to buy these things without raising a ton of questions. You need your dirty money—that you got from criminality—to look like clean money that you earned legitimately. So if you're an illegal arms dealer with a pile of dirty money, you need that money cleaned. Laundered. You want it to seem like legitimate money. So you'd need people to do what your dad did."

She nodded thoughtfully. "And what exactly did he do to make the money seem legit?"

I hadn't yet dug into Seymour's background enough, so I glanced at my father. He said, "Honestly, he was so good, I'm not sure if we know everything he did. We do know he used a bunch of accounting tricks—offshore accounts that aren't monitored by the Feds, dummy businesses with fake earnings. I don't know if he did this, but one common way among the Vory—that's the Russian Mafiya—in New York at that time was overpaying for real estate. You might pay too much for a property to someone who's in on the scam. They might kick some of the overpayment back. There's no single way to launder money, or we'd catch them easily. It takes a lot of creativity. Your father was like an artist when it came to hiding the origins of dirty money. He kept the money in motion, from account to account, investment to investment, until it could no longer be traced."

April smiled ruefully.

"Besides being imaginative and being a real thinker, he had the know-how. He also had contacts all over the world," my dad said.

"That seems useful, in its own way." Her forehead creases became visible as she tried to puzzle it out. "So why do you think they wanted to kill him if he was so useful to them and good at his job?"

My dad shot her a sympathetic glance, but didn't shy away from being straightforward. "It's hard to say. We're not even sure they're the ones who killed your parents. Of course, if someone has the kind of criminal connections that your dad did, it's going to be the first place we look when he's murdered. It's possible he was skimming money off the top, or that they thought he was cooperating with law enforcement. He wasn't, but they could have been wrong. But we looked at the Vory, and we just didn't see a motivation for them to do that. That doesn't mean there wasn't one person who hated him enough to do it—we just never found him. I always thought it was his partner, the Honorable Hosea, who did it because he felt he wasn't getting his fair share. I mean, your dad's business was to hide money. Wouldn't come as a shock if he hid it from his partner."

"Well, we all have our areas of expertise, I guess." April sighed, pressing her fingers to her temples. I could finally see that the discussion was upsetting her. "Where is the partner now?"

"In prison. So he definitely wasn't driving the SUV. Which is not to say he had nothing to do with it, but he himself has an alibi."

She took another swig of beer. "So, ultimately, here's why I called. The New Brunswick PD seem like competent, serious people. But I'm worried they won't dig deep enough. What happened to my parents could be totally irrelevant. I can accept that. But until we know more, it shouldn't be ignored."

My dad rubbed the top of his head and squinched his eyes. He looked hot and uncomfortable. "Yeah . . . here's the thing. I get where these cops are coming from in a way."

I added, "The detective working the case would be thinking that the Russians could have come back to find you anytime in the past two decades. You never went under a different name or anything."

"I know. Really, I do. It's just that—"

"But," my father cut in firmly. "I worry the same thing as you." She looked up at him, visibly relieved that she wasn't crazy for wondering about it. He continued, "No one seems to want to kill you now. But someone tried to kill you when you were younger. At least, they didn't care if you died. They killed your parents. Now of course, it could be a coincidence. But in my opinion, lightning doesn't usually strike twice in the same place."

"Tell you what," I said. "Let the New Brunswick police follow the leads about your present-day life. Because it really could be something like that, and they should be following up. But my dad and I can take a closer look at the people from your past as well."

She smiled at us gratefully.

CHAPTER SIX

The trip to New Brunswick (rather, the elation I felt the next day, belting out "Jump Then Fall" as I waited for my dog Lulu to sniff seventeen hundred spots along our route before choosing the most exquisite repository for her morning poop) made me realize that Long Island post-pandemic life with PTSD had become a touch numbing.

Not that I needed danger to feel energized, though there had been a brief interval in my life when I'd driven an allegedly bulletproof car the 231 miles from Baghdad to Erbil and back again for risky business. Another time I had waylaid the wife of the US liaison of al-Qaeda in Lebanon in her tiny dressing area in the long corridor in the loungewear department at Macy's. My boss gave me five minutes to turn her, saying, "Don't feel pressured, but if one or both of you got killed, the director would be beyond pissed." I convinced her to spill what she'd overheard about a plot to bomb the Brooklyn Battery Tunnel. Then I left her in her cubicle and strolled past her bodyguards, who resembled Scylla and Charybdis, waiting outside the dressing room.

Now my life was so unremittingly suburban that my whole mood had lifted after a single visit to a film professor in New Jersey. Lawns seemed a deeper green, quick waves from neighbors prophesied deep community roots.

I returned from my walk with Lulu to find my parents sitting six inches apart at the big kitchen table, holding hands and gazing at each other with unfocused eyes that signified something I didn't want to know about. "Anyone want coffee, tea?" I asked in a vigorous voice. My dad said he was coffeed out and my mom drew back her head and tilted it to the side, considering.

Finally she said, "There's a piece of ginger in the bottom drawer of the fridge. Maybe a cup of ginger tea, or are you saving it for something?"

"I forgot it was in there. It's yours, but it's probably old enough to be bat mitzvahed."

"I'm sure it's fine. I'll make it. Would you like some?" I nodded as she stood. Her long bathrobe had a wide ruffle all around, from neckline to hem, and she looked ultra-*charmant*, like she was a theater major again at Brooklyn College playing the role of Lady Whoever in a drawing-room comedy. "I heard you two had a marvelously productive day yesterday," she said.

"It was great," I said. "You'd really like her." As she chopped the ginger, I told her about April's framed black-and-white movie photos in the bathroom.

"Definitely an idea to steal!" she announced. "Now, what are the two of you planning for today?"

Before I could come out with a long *uhhh* to stall until I thought of something, my dad announced, "We're going to Manhattan Beach in Brooklyn. I want to check out the crime scene."

My mom was reaching for the teapot, but I took over reaching as she turned to him and said, "Casing the joint, Detective?"

"There's no joint to case anymore. The house burned down years ago, but yeah, you can still pick up a lot by seeing the neighborhood. Thought it would be a good idea to let Corie get a feel for it, see what insights she has." My mom beamed at both of us: at our bonding, at our newfound hustle, at the spring returning to my dad's step.

An hour later, my dad and I were driving along Jamaica Bay in Brooklyn when some hawks whooshed by our windshield, headed for a strip of shore. "Dead body washed up," he said.

"Did you ever think it might be a horseshoe crab?"

"Not for a minute."

* * *

We stood on the sidewalk outside 310 Reynolds Avenue, which had once been the Browns' address in Manhattan Beach. The sun illuminated the sea mist suspended in the air, and for our first few moments there, random pedestrians, cars—even the heinous house that now had a giant "310" welded into its wrought iron gate—appeared as sublime as one of Renoir's seascapes.

My dad opened the old canvas messenger bag he'd brought and pulled out an envelope with the pictures from the night of the arson and the days after. "This is from the pile Gabriel Salazar brought over. These were taken by the cops at the scene. The rest, with the skinny white borders . . . those came from the fire marshal's files."

The crime scene photos were helpful in grasping how the Browns' house had been situated on its lot. That corner plot of land where the house once stood was now entirely engulfed by an immense Spanish hacienda/Norman castle and the wall surrounding it. Not even a blade of grass could find space to grow.

"I've seen worse," my dad said. "But Jesus H. Christ, this place could bring home the bronze for ugly. Manhattan Beach used to be more gracious living." He pointed to the house next door—a saltbox colonial, shingles painted white, with yellow shutters and window boxes, topped by a simple gable roof. "I bet the next guy who owns that will tear it down and put up something with two towers and a moat."

"That one is as pretty as it gets," I agreed. The shingled house was timeless: if they'd been house-hunting in Brooklyn and spotted it, Abigail Adams would have turned to John and said, *That is so us!*

But whoever had rebuilt on Seymour Brown's land appeared not to be embarrassed by being nouveau riche, and probably believed the example of the colonial style next door was pathetic. If you are nouveau riche—as long as your money is clean or safely laundered—let the whole world know!

I lowered my head to put myself back in the past, examining the first photos taken the night of the fire. The first few showed a blaze that had already consumed most of the roof and part of the second floor. In subsequent photos, the fire had fanned out, so the flames appeared like a hand splayed out over the house—deliberately trying to hide everything it could from view. "You see how the flames are pale, almost white?" Dad pointed out.

"Sure. I know it has something to do with the chemistry of the accelerant they used to set the fire. Except I forget what fuel it signifies."

"Gasoline. A gasoline fire has yellow or sometimes white flames," he said. "Look, it's important to notice that, and then run all the tests. But even the next day, you could still smell the gas a half a block away. I mean, from the get-go everybody knew it wasn't that someone just fell asleep with a cigarette."

I glanced down at the photos. "And gasoline gives off this kind of black smoke, right?"

"Yeah."

When viewed from the front, the only parts of the Browns' house still visible in the photos were narrow strips at either end. They were right near the corners of the first story of the house and hadn't yet burned, though their flat surface had sooty streaks from the smoke. They were pitted and splotched where chunks of the burning upper level must have hit. The one-car garage was still standing, unscathed. Even with its smoke residue, it seemed a detached onlooker.

"What was that building material?" I asked.

"Stucco," my dad said. "The flat kind. Not with the swirlies like cake icing."

I went back to the photos, hoping something would pop out at me. I divided each one visually into segments, checking for each detail. Nothing about the house itself, although in a couple of the shots I could see that at the side of the driveway, right near the sidewalk, there were two garbage cans with lids and two smaller bins for recyclables. "Was the next day garbage collection, or did they just not put their cans away?"

"The next morning," my dad said, "we went through everything. Took fingerprints off all the bottles and cans. We got Seymour's from his office and Kim's from stuff she kept in the garage in containers on shelves. Christmas tree ornaments, summer toys for the kid, like a blow-up pool. No nonfamily fingerprints."

"Did the NYPD or the fire department check any of the neighbor's cans?" I asked. "I can't see an arsonist throwing away a lighter or a book of matches into the Browns' trash can."

My dad let out a long sigh, so even before he spoke, I knew his answer. "They were so busy guarding the crime scene that no one noticed the Sanitation Department truck coming through the neighborhood starting at eight the next morning."

Just then his phone went off, an old-fashioned telephone ring. "Hey," he said in that robust male-to-male voice. "I appreciate you getting back to me so soon." He mouthed something to me, most likely telling whom he was talking to, but for all I could tell, he could have been saying the Pledge of Allegiance. I had no clue. So I closed my eyes for a minute and let the sun shine down on my face. I listened to my dad's "yeahs" and "uh-huhs," the rumble of a truck passing us over potholed streets, Olivia Rodrigo pouring her heart out from an open-windowed car a block or two away.

Then I saw my dad's cheeks inflate with annoyance. He exhaled slowly and silently and said, "Detective, I understand. You don't need my help handling your case. I'm a lot older than you, but I was once where you were. I remember pushy private investigators." He closed his eyes as the detective had his say, a long one, interrupted only by my dad's occasional "Right" and "I get it." Finally he said, "I'm only interested in the historical aspect of this case. I recognize and respect your turf. I'm just trying to get the basics. And I'll hand over anything I get." For my dad to use diplomacy rather than his usual congenial-bulldozer style meant the other detective was super possessive of his info. A couple of minutes of silence told me my dad had managed to convince the other detective that he was okay. At the end there was a cool but courteous goodbye.

"So?" I tapped my foot as I waited for him to say something, but as I was tapping sneakers on a car mat, he wasn't galvanized. He opened a zipper on the outside of the messenger bag and took out his notepad and pen.

"Shhh! I need to write this." I kept silent. Law enforcement types understand that "Quiet" from a colleague is a command that should be taken seriously—unlike civilians who can't resist *C'mon, just give me a vague idea* or crane their necks to read upside down. Finally he spoke. "It was the New Brunswick detective working on April's case. I left word for him last night when we got home from New Jersey. Obviously he's under pressure, not just to solve it, but to keep the professor happy without letting her bring in her own team of investigators. That would be a no-confidence vote for him. That's why I pushed the historical business."

"Did he give you anything?"

"Eventually he told me that the campus cops accessed the university's CCTV footage. He agreed that it does look like the SUV was either chasing her or at least trying to scare her. He even said he'd try to get me in if I want to see it myself, but in his opinion, it does not look like a car whose brakes failed. The driver was steering and headed toward her, not trying to avoid hitting her."

"But then, whoever it was just gave up," I said. The wind must have changed just then, because I got a few sublime whiffs of Atlantic Ocean air and mused about whether Seymour's breathing in that moist and salty brew every day kept that word "offshore" always on his mind.

"'Gave up' is right. The detective, Ricardo Jones— Doesn't that sound like a TV series? Probably on CBS. Anyway, my new buddy Ricardo says the tapes show the SUV leaving campus at a north exit and making a left. The problem is, that's where visual coverage ended. On that particular street in New Brunswick, there's no CCTV. His theory is the SUV was headed to the turnpike or the Garden State Parkway."

"But didn't they consider it could also have been a local, heading home to . . . wherever? Elm Street in New Brunswick?"

"Yeah, that's a possibility, too," my dad said. "Oh, he did mention that the CCTV footage backed up what a couple of bystanders reported, that the license plates—front and back—were obscured."

"But they didn't drive on the turnpike or the Garden State with taped-over license plates." I knew from anti-terrorism work that CCTV and pole cameras on highways are programmed to alert authorities when a vehicle has no license plate, or a covered one. A computerized warning is dispatched in a nanosecond, and the warning has to be responded to.

My dad nodded twice, slowly. Then he said, "So maybe they stopped a few blocks away and pulled the tape off. By now they could be anywhere. On Elm Street in New Brunswick or the Oregon coast." I knew how pointless it was to search for a black SUV of indeterminate make in the Western Hemisphere. We had to come up with some other way to find the person who chased down April.

As if following the same cue, Dad and I snapped out of our mind trip to New Brunswick to refocus on where we actually were—in Brooklyn. I glanced at a high window in one of the turrets of the humongous hacienda/castle. Someone up there was gazing down, unsure of what to make of us. My dad, too, was watching the window, but then he shrugged his shoulders, indifferent.

Brooklyn would have to wait a minute. He wasn't totally finished with New Jersey. "Ricardo told me they've got zilch on April Brown. No record, no complaints, a solid citizen. And the city hasn't had any hate crimes targeting gays or lesbians for a while. Personally, he said, he never experienced anyone getting a bug up their ass about a lesbian professor. It's a college town."

He put his notebook and pen back into his messenger bag and pulled out what appeared to be a couple of architectural drawings. "I swore to Salazar I'd return these by Friday." He started unfolding them. "I bet you ten bucks that whoever is up there in the window will be out here in the next five minutes."

"Three minutes," I countered. "Do you have any badge-looking thing you could flash?"

"Don't borrow trouble," he said. "We'll deal with it." That's where we differed. Given the slightest hitch, I would instantly start drawing up a list of responses, and keep the bullet points coming. That was in addition to my ready stock of long-planned defenses for more likely problems. I'd been if/then ever since I was a kid, and PTSD had turned that tendency up to eleven. He, on the other hand, simply assumed that his training and experience would take over. "So look here, Corie. These are a couple of the drawings from when Seymour remodeled the place. They changed the whole upstairs into one fancy master suite." He unfolded the huge renderings and put one on top of the other. The first was the site plan, a drawing of the house shape—basically a square, though pushing to the northeast, trying hard to be a rectangle. It was located on an irregular corner plot of land.

Even though the Browns' house took up much less of the lot than the current Hacienda Hideous, I could see that it would be tough for an arsonist trying to escape to find camouflage. True, there were trees, represented by green circles, but most of them were no larger than a dime. The only large tree was the one on the side of the house, near where April's bedroom had been; that was the size of a quarter.

"Anyone trying to get away unseen would have to race from tree to tree," my dad said. "Like in that cartoon where the wolf goes *swoosh* and all of a sudden he's behind the next tree. You know the one I mean."

I said yeah, then quickly changed the subject so I wouldn't have to listen to his recollections of cartoons beloved by Boomers. "Was there any conclusion as to which way the arsonist left?" I asked. "Front or back door?"

"No actual physical evidence, but from the photos of the fire, we got a pretty good circumstantial picture of what happened. It started in their bedroom. The way the fire spread—and the way it burned through the middle of the roof here first—indicated that they were either tied up, unconscious, or dead when the arsonist poured gasoline over them. Can you imagine being tied up and smelling the gasoline, hearing the match . . . It hardly ever happens, but that case gave me nightmares." He shuddered. "Wake-up-screamers. Couldn't get the images out of my head, and I'd never been a guy given to images."

"The first time you hear something horrific . . . It's awful and vivid and you can't not think about it, see it," I told him. "At least for me. But then I learned to narrow my focus to only what was important to my case. If I kept reacting to the big-picture horribleness, I'd be too rattled to be effective." I was surprised to hear myself add, "But I think it made me a colder person."

He started to say something along the lines of my still being a sweetie, but I waved my hand dismissively and he took the hint. Finally he said, "Cops deal with it in different ways. I tried to imagine that someone had shot the Browns first, so they wouldn't have seen the fire come closer. I knew there was zero evidence for or against that, though. Anyhow, the fire burned the ceiling and the roof almost directly above the bed, and the opening gave it more oxygen. That section started collapsing inward before the rest of the master suite. Eventually, the whole second floor went up, so the fire investigators thought the perpetrator kept pouring gasoline as he went down the stairs."

I pictured someone going downstairs pouring gasoline out of one of those five-gallon containers, tried to get in their head so I could see why they were doing it in that way. "Let's hope the Browns were already dead—"

"Just say whatever you have to say. Don't worry about my feelings."

I said, "Maybe the perp didn't burn the stairs to block off an escape route, although we've got to consider that. Maybe he/she/they didn't want the firefighters getting upstairs to save Seymour and Kim."

"Could be," my dad said.

"Also, the longer it burned, the more oxygen it got because the roof was burned up and the less evidence there would be."

"Yup."

"They weren't burning the stairs to get April, right?"

"No." He pointed to the architectural drawing of the first floor. "Her room is over here, on the side, pretty far from the stairs. And it was one of the last places to burn. So it's not likely he dumped gasoline there. Either he didn't want her to die or didn't know she was there."

"But the arsonist didn't actually save her or try to get her out."

"Right. So if he did know she was there, he didn't give enough of a fuck to save her life. Would have been easy enough."

I shook my head, then closed my eyes, trying to picture the staircase that night. "The stairs, at some point, were in flames."

"Right."

"And they are closer to the front of the house than the back."

"By a lot," he agreed.

"So why would someone committing arson and homicide risk going around the burning stairs to the back door? The heat alone was so intense. And I assume the flames were spreading. It's more sensible to just go right out the front door. I mean, this is on the assumption that the neighbors weren't aware of the fire yet, or just staring at the flames on the top floor, or calling 911. It's more logical just to walk out, head down, go around the corner, keep going."

While the architectural drawings for the Browns' house showed a relatively good-size backyard for Brooklyn—there was even a teeny square with the neatly written HOT TUB inside it—the front entrance was much closer to the sidewalk. Easy to dart away quickly. However, if someone had exited through the back door, they'd have to go into someone else's yard and risk being seen, or come back around to the front anyway. The north side of the house also faced a street, so anyone climbing out a window could be seen. The south side of the house, where April had crawled out of her window, was so close to the neighbors' that whoever had originally put the tree in had clearly underestimated its growth potential.

My dad took the other drawing and put it over the site plan. It was the PROPOSED SECOND FLOOR 1616 SQUARE FEET. It had a large bedroom, a study, his and her bathrooms, as well as a combo gym and solarium—a great setup.

It had always been important to me to get a feel for people's stuff. Studying a subject's sock drawer or gun cabinet can add another dimension, and when I got to explore the places where they lived, it was as informative as a Big Five Personality Test. True, all I could see so far in this case was the neighborhood, the crime scene photos, and a couple of drawings, but already it had given me a clearer picture of the perpetrator's movements. It also got me wondering about a couple who would design a house where a little kid is left alone downstairs. Had that been something they both wanted, or had either Seymour or Kim insisted? From the little I knew, they both seemed like caring parents, or caring enough. Had one of them pushed for uber-privacy? Or did they just have great faith, in those not-so-digitized days, in their baby monitor?

"Are you sure there was no other bedroom on the first floor?" I asked. "Doesn't it seem weird that when the wife was so young, they would have cut off the possibility of having a second child?"

"Absolutely. There was a tiny bedroom and bath off the main part of the finished basement. Nothing near the kid. But it wasn't your typical house. Like, look at how big this kitchen is, but the dining room is really small. If you had Thanksgiving there, you could cook up a banquet, but then when you moved to the dining room, it would basically fit the three of them and the turkey. But this living room, it's like the lobby of the Waldorf-Astoria!"

"Did they have big parties or anything?" I asked.

My dad sucked in his upper lip, closed his eyes, and did a little head bobbing, one of his Deep Concentration signals. "Shhh!" he said, though I hadn't made a sound. Finally he said, "Right. Cocktail parties. Big cocktail parties with waiters bringing drinks and hors d'oeuvres. One of his other clients, I think a Bulgarian, told us about them. So much food, the guy said, you didn't have to eat dinner afterward. And you know how they had his and her bathrooms upstairs? Well, they had two bathrooms downstairs, too. One right off April's room, and one for the guests."

I thought, *Not a bad idea: Who'd want some hammered guest peeing on their kid's toilet seat?* Just then, the front door of Hacienda Hideous flew open. A guy in a red plaid bathrobe over a thin white undershirt clomped down the front steps and strode toward us. He was short and wide, but not fat, more like someone who compensated for being short by leaving no muscle group undeveloped.

When he got near the car, he put his hands on his hips and pulled himself up to his full five feet six inches. "What do you think you're doing here?" He wasn't quite spoiling for a fight, though he probably wouldn't have said no if one was offered. Mostly he was establishing his primacy. The sidewalk might be legally designated a public thoroughfare, but we'd better fucking watch ourselves.

"We're doing some research into a historical crime," I said. Then I added "sir," since he'd begun shifting back and forth in his leather bedroom slippers, as if he were debating which side to take: historical crime, for or against. "You may know that—"

"I know," he said, shoving his hands into the pockets of the robe. I had modeled my clear-eyed, direct gaze on my dad's—even before I went off to Quantico. No judgment, no fear, no anger. The man seemed to want to make a Powerful Homeowner impression, like a rancher in an old western. Then he relented a bit to pull his robe closer to his body. The arms akimbo business must have been allowing too much breeze from his knees northward. "You're talking about the arson on this property," he added.

"Right," my dad said. "Were you the one who purchased the land from the Browns' estate?"

"Yeah. But like, two years later. Through the bank. Never knew the guy, his wife." My dad's direct gaze was more practiced than mine, and more effective in getting the guy to move from hostility into neutral territory. He even offered, "You know there was nothing left of the house, not even a nail."

"Yeah, we heard," my dad said. "But the records show there was a detached garage that wasn't burned down."

"You want to know something else? It took that stupid bank eighteen months to figure out that the sight of that little garage standing there by itself was what my broker called 'curb unappeal.' Eerie. They couldn't get it sold for nothing."

"'Eerie' is a good word for it," my dad said.

"Really a disturbing reminder," I added.

"So I wouldn't say I got it for a song, but trust me, they were glad to get it off their hands. By the way, I didn't introduce myself. I'm Dr. Sean Moscowitz. I practice a couple miles from here, on the border of Manhattan Beach and Brighton Beach."

"Are you a doctor, dentist—" my dad asked.

"Podiatrist. Great area to practice in. The beach. People want, you can only imagine, fit feet."

"Absolutely," I said, then glanced behind him. "You really built yourself an amazing house."

"Thank you," he said with gracious humility. Then, though he hadn't asked, I introduced my dad as Dan Scho . . . letting the name get mushed in my mouth, a retired NYPD detective-authenticator, a title I made up on the spot. I was his forensic consultant, Cor . . . Gell . . .

"So you never met either of the Browns?" my dad asked casually.

Dr. Moscowitz shook his head. "They weren't patients."

I gave it one last shot. "Ever meet anyone who did know them?"

He started to shake his head and then stopped, raising a finger as in *Wait a minute!* "As a matter of fact . . . I completely forgot this because it was so many years ago. One of my patients heard I was building here. It turns out she was a friend of the wife! This is some wonderful lady, my patient. Natasha, but goes by Tasha. Takes her feet seriously. Not just in the cosmetic sense."

"Do you happen to recall her last name?" I asked.

"Of course. She comes every three months, like clockwork. Sobol. S-o-b-o-l."

When we got home, I left my dad in the kitchen making himself a snack and went upstairs to my office. I swiveled in my chair, getting a 360-degree view of the pink walls. There were lovely windows in the room, which looked out onto—or really, into—several treetops in our backyard. A peaceful room. It could be a really nice space to work in if it didn't look quite so much like what it was: that is, New Wife Took Down Mirrored Wall in First Wife's Gym to Create Home Office. I jotted down my 407th mental reminder to call my best friend Wynne at some point to help me redecorate.

I fished around in my jeans pocket and smoothed out the paper with the name I had scribbled as we left Manhattan Beach. Natasha Sobol. An initial Google search revealed several Natasha Sobols, so I started with social media sites. On Facebook there was someone who looked similar to what Kim's age would be now—though her avatar was so Facetuned and filtered and pouty-lipped, it was hard to tell—and lived in Brooklyn. The account was private, though. Same on WhatsApp. No one on Twitter seemed to fit the bill, as far as I could tell, nor on Instagram. I saved my favorite for last: LinkedIn. Obviously, LinkedIn was not my number one social media site for frittering away time on capybara videos. But I'd found that when investigating cases, it could be a surprisingly fruitful source. Even people who were generally circumspect about every other social media site left old résumés posted on LinkedIn, and they could be gold mines of personal information.

And once again, LinkedIn came through. "Natasha Sobol, Independent Promoter/Distributor at La Tubéreuse Scented Candles, Brooklyn, New York." Her headshot was professionally done and very glamorous, displaying a woman of uncertain age with sparkling eyes, a round face, and eyebrows heavily penciled into skeptical sweeps of brown. Her résumé revealed that she had graduated from Kingsborough Community College in Brooklyn in 1991 with an associate's degree in communications: this had to be the right person. At the top, directly under her name, she had listed her address, email address, and phone. There was no employment listed until about ten years ago, when she had been a part-time beauty adviser and then an assistant manager for client experience at a Sephora in Boerum Hill. Two years ago she discovered the eighth wonder of the world: scented candles. I checked out La Tubéreuse. As I'd guessed, it was a multilevel marketing company. I hoped that meant she'd be more receptive than most to being contacted by a stranger.

I considered texting or emailing, but decided a message on LinkedIn was the least weird way to contact her. My current LinkedIn bio was much more sparing in details than hers. There was a too-flattering photo, with my hair whipping around my face, that Josh had taken on a walk near the bay and that had come out fortuitously perfect. My listed profession was "Freelance Arabic Fiction Scout." I glanced at Natasha Sobol's skeptical eyebrows one more time and decided that she was the type to do at least a perfunctory check on a stranger who contacted her out of the blue, so I changed my profession to "Cofounder and Investigator, Schottland & Geller Investigations, LLC."

I'd once made a half-assed website for my work as a literary scout at cgeller.com, which never crashed from overuse. I went to it and quickly subbed in some new text about Schottland & Geller Investigations, with my dad and me as partners, added a stylized black-and-white background picture of a fingerprint, updated the SEO, and linked it to my LinkedIn bio. I added "*hablamos español*" and "نحن نتحدث العربية."

It might not have made thousands of employers want to hire us, but it was good enough. I tested a search for "Corie Geller" on an incognito browser, and the site was the first thing that popped up.

"Hey!" I wrote in a LinkedIn message to Natasha Sobol. "Sorry to contact you out of the blue, but I'm a private investigator who has been hired to look into a historical murder case. The victims were Seymour and Kimberly Brown, and I understand you knew Kimberly. I was wondering if we could talk if you have a bit of free time."

I was expecting to wait, but she replied in less than five minutes. "sure let's talk do u have facetime or skype or whatever?"

I sent her my info, and within just a few minutes my phone was vibrating on the table.

"Hello," Natasha Sobol breathed with a down-to-fuck voice, like Marilyn Monroe but lower pitched. Her dark hair with caramel highlights fell down below her boobs and was parted in the middle with soft waves, a brunette version of Fox News–host hair.

"Hi, Natasha!" I said too loudly and cheerfully. I realized I was smoothing my hair in an unconscious and futile attempt to match her glossiness, and willed myself to stop.

"You can call me Tasha." Tasha did look older than her Facebook and LinkedIn pictures, though I still wouldn't have guessed she was pushing fifty. "Tasha. Okay, it's nice to meet you. I'm Corie Geller. As I mentioned, I'm investigating the murder of Seymour and Kimberly Brown. I got your name from Sean Moscowitz, the podiatrist. He told me you and Kimberly had been friends." Tasha nodded. She certainly didn't look the type to avoid a friendship with Vory connections. Her frozen forehead, lip fillers, eyelash extensions, and full makeup on a weekday afternoon gave off the vibe of a Real Housewife ready to toss wine in her ex–best friend's face. "So you knew them?"

"Oh yeah. I got to know her when we met on the playground when our kids made friends. They were two years old or something like that, born in the same month. Oh my God, that was, like, forever ago. Now Taylor's a physician's assistant and," she added with a note of pride in her voice, "she's got one of her own on the way."

"Congratulations!" I said, wondering just how digressive this conversation was going to be. "Boy or girl?"

"Girl," she said triumphantly. "But I told her, 'Just as long as it's healthy,' am I right?"

I agreed that I, too, preferred healthy children over a specific gender and steered her back toward April's parents before I wound up hearing about the nursery color scheme. "What was Kim like?"

"She was always . . . Well, you know." She paused.

"Actually, I don't," I said. "You're the first person I've spoken to who knew her well. Other than April. She's my client."

"April! Oh my God, the little girl? Well, of course she's curious about what happened, the poor thing. How could she not be? How is she doing? I always wondered. I would say to Max—Max is my husband—can we find out how the little Brown girl is doing? And he said they found some relative who lived outside of New York and there was no way to find out."

"She's doing fine. She's a professor in New Jersey."

Her wide blue eyes got even wider. "Get. Out. No way! See, I'm not really surprised, though, because Seymour was so smart. Max always had a ton of respect for him, even though he didn't do business with him. Is she married? Does she have kids?"

"No, but I gather she's in a serious relationship." Before she could follow up with more questions about April, I asked, "Was Kim smart?"

"Kim? Oh, no. I mean, she wasn't, like, majorly dumb or anything. But she wasn't like Seymour."

"Tell me a little more about her."

"Well, she was nice. I guess. Very pretty. Good makeup, good clothes. She was probably size zero or something like that. Teeny. We would meet at the playground with our kids, and she always brought extra Goldfish and juice boxes for Taylor. When they started school, we would get manicures together. We went out to dinner sometimes as couples. It's hard to say, really. She was always a little quiet and just shut down whenever Seymour was around."

"Was he a domineering type?"

Tasha nodded earnestly. "Totally. Max always said he heard he had a nasty temper, and that's why he'd never do business with him. I never saw it. Actually, he could be borderline charming. But I totally believe it. I mean, this was a while ago, the 1990s . . ." She paused.

I got a sense it would be a good moment for a compliment, so I said, "You so don't look like someone who was married in the nineties."

She grinned and said, "And I'm almost a grandma, can you believe it?"

"I would never believe it!" I said, hand over my heart, shaking my head in wonder, though a little afraid that my compliments might be over the top. I needn't have worried.

"Oh my God, you're so sweet. I started using Retin-A and wearing sunscreen every day all the way back in, well, the nineties. That's key."

I nodded solemnly. "So you were saying? I think about Seymour's temper?"

"Right. Wait, what was I saying? Oh yeah. So Max and me, we're both the children of immigrants. His parents came from Russia, mine from Ukraine. But our marriage . . . even though we married young—probably too young, but whatever—we have a very modern marriage. We're equal, totally. But Seymour and Kim? They were, like, Old World."

"Old World how?"

She pursed her lips, at least as much as the Botox and fillers would allow. "Oh, you know. It's been a while." I nodded, and she went on. "But just like, whatever he said went. He made all the decisions. I know you're younger than me, but trust me. Even back then it was weird and old-fashioned. Kim told me they didn't even have a joint bank account. He gave her an allowance. And it wasn't a huge allowance, either, not compared to what he could have given."

"They had a lot of money?"

"He had. Tons. And here's the thing. At least this is what Max told me. I'm sure he wasn't supposed to, but we wind up telling each other everything. He told me that Seymour bought a huge apartment in Park Slope for his girl on the side. Meanwhile he was nickel-and-diming poor Kim. People still wore fur back then, and most of us had some cute and casual fur around. We called it fun fur. And a mink for going out nonlocal. There were two sables in the neighborhood, also. All Kim had was a fox jacket."

This was interesting. My dad had said that they'd had word that Seymour ran around. But an apartment in Park Slope—even back in the nineties—didn't sound like a fling. A much more serious relationship. I made a note to find out more about the girlfriend. "Given he was controlling and had a temper, were there any signs that Seymour was abusive to Kim?" I asked.

Tasha seemed a little distracted as she answered, as if she were looking at something else. "She never said he was, but I wouldn't die of shock. Like I said, Max said he could be a real asshole."

"Have you ever heard the name Hose or Hosea Williams?"

She shook her head. "Was he on the Mets?"

I started to explain, but she cut me off. "Look, I'm so sorry, I really want to help, but I have to run. But listen. Tonight I'm having a couple of friends over. We're going to have some wine, watch *The Bachelor*. We have a screen outside by the pool. At least one of them knew Kim, and the other might have too. Do you want to come over and join us? You could ask all of us. And have fun!"

I got the strong sense that I was also going to be urged to purchase some scented candles. But I figured that was a good trade for learning more about Seymour and Kim. "Yes, count me in!"

"Great!" She gave me the address, and I scribbled it down.

After we said our goodbyes, I went to the top of the stairs and bellowed in the way that I knew drove Josh batshit—but I was too lazy to go downstairs. "Eliza?!"

"What?!" she screeched back, and I knew poor Josh was having a heart attack.

"Want to watch *The Bachelor* with me? I have to catch up on this season." She didn't answer, but I heard her eagerly trotting toward the stairs.

CHAPTER SEVEN

"I only saw Tasha once, on FaceTime," I was telling Wynne Fairclough, my best friend, as the two of us talked on FaceTime.

Wynne's hair, in a plain, pulled-back ponytail, was just how it had been when we were six years old. Now, though, it was infused with some exorbitant hair gel that supposedly penetrated the cellular level, which sounded to me like an iffy proposition. Her face, whether on the phone or close up in bright sunlight, looked as poreless as it had in first grade.

She admitted to spending forty minutes a day listening to her happy playlist—mostly Vivaldi and Telemann—while doing her skin-care routine and applying makeup to achieve the apparently-no-makeup radiance that had made her a style icon. Add to that time spent test-driving new product. (It annoyed me that the fashionable had decreed, for reasons unknown, that "product," like "sheep," could not have a plural *s*.)

Even at age six she had been a commanding presence. Not by being authoritative or a bully, nor through emitting pulsars of virtue. She strolled into Mrs. Warner's classroom at the top of her game. Every single day, she didn't have even one imperfection—or at least that's how she came across. Her sneakers could be clean or dirty, but that became the look. Ditto jeans with Ts until she switched to button-down shirts. When it came to first-grade chic, Wynne ruled.

She was generous with her gift too, helping girls roll up their sleeves, realigning the shoulder seams on boys' T-shirts whether they wanted help or not. When Petra Cruz walked down the hall holding up the giant rectangle of oaktag that was her Trees project, Wynne shook her head fast: *No, no, no!* Even I, not exactly an aesthete, knew the taped-on pictures cut from magazines or newspapers wouldn't do it for Mrs. Warner. "You want me to show you how to fix it?" Wynne asked, hearing *yes* before Petra actually said it.

We followed Wynne as she grabbed the oaktag and raced around the corner into the girls' room. Within seconds she was raking through our backpacks, finding only red and green colored pencils, some glue, an already peeled stub of a violet-blue crayon, and a twelve-inch ruler. She went to work. "I'm going to take off the pictures and put them back. So they look . . . more better. Then you draw the leaf of each tree"—Wynne carefully untaped the first picture, stuck it about a millimeter from where it had been, then pointed to a spot just above the upper right-hand corner—"and make it look like it's from that tree. Bigger than the one I drew on the back. Come on, don't be scared."

When Petra handed in the much-improved poster, Mrs. Warner was transported: "Look at the detail! This is A work."

I picked up a carrot Eliza had peeled and left on the counter after taking only one bite. Munching, I asked Wynne, "You know that look when a woman has a ton of stuff put into her face? Fillers, Botox?"

"How can you even ask? Of course. They're so pumped with Juvéderm, their cheeks and jaw meld, and their skin is so smooth they look like hard-boiled eggs. Didn't you ever notice that half the upper-middle-class women over forty resemble each other, like first cousins?"

"That's Tasha! I couldn't see her body, but I'll bet she's super slim. She has this puffed-out face with overlush lips. They looked like they'd been extruded, like purple sausage meat."

"I bet the color was oxblood, not purple," Wynne corrected. "And the plumped-up lips? She probably has a dermatologist who's still paying off her Maserati. Why inject just one syringe when you can double it? And that's become what patients want."

"I think Tasha may have the biggest cheeks in the 718-area code. But there was still something pretty about her. Well, I wasn't thrilled with the purple lipstick."

"Oxblood." Since the first grade, I'd learned that there was no subject—from toenail length to the expansion of the universe—on which Wynne didn't have an opinion. "You might want to rethink the color."

"Or I might not."

After graduating with a BA in art history from Hunter College, Wynne became a fashion photo stylist and, later, an editor at *Vogue*. She wasn't even thirty when she opened her own design firm. Wynne Fairclough's taste was splendid. An article in *W* called her a "life designer," helping the superrich choose everything from salad bowls to cars to cowl-neck sweaters—art in their apartments, candlesticks in their country homes, collections of essays, novels, biographies to set on the nightstands in their guest rooms. She counseled them on charities that merited their donations and the most scrumptious brand of Sicilian orange marmalade to make breakfast *perfetto*.

My friendship with Wynne had likely diminished the discombobulation I might have experienced when I married Josh, going from a government salary and a studio apartment to inherited wealth and an insanely large home on multiple acres.

Now, after all these years being completely unbothered by her single status, Wynne was engaged. She'd met her fiancé, Gordon Parks Rafael, a year earlier, when she was visiting me in the hospital, right after I escaped my kidnapper. She rushed back to my bedside to report she'd met a TGG—totally gorgeous guy, initials we'd been using since seventh grade. As she was on her way down, he had gotten onto the elevator. "Light brown skin, huge eyes like Kalamata olives." The name on his ID had both an MD and a PhD after it. A half-Black, half-Jewish infectious disease specialist. Infectious disease was just another specialty when she met him, but somehow, like everything Wynne touched, it was now suddenly fashionable and exciting. But what wowed Wynne in that first nanosecond was the cut of his white cotton dress shirt. She asked him where he'd bought it. By the next evening, they were an item.

"All right," she said after another few minutes of talk, "I totally get Tasha. She probably wears Le Parfum de Therese."

"What does that mean?" I asked.

"It means jasmine, but in an exquisite way. Most likely she's socially confident and underplays her intelligence. Trust me on this." I did. "Now, go upstairs to your closet. We need to style you for tonight."

"Okay, but don't tell me I have nothing suitable and that I should go out and buy a chartreuse plunge bra. Work with what I have."

Phone in hand, I walked back and forth in front of my hanging row of pants a couple of times, which was not exactly a hike. "Wide-leg pants are back," Wynne informed me. "Didn't you keep any? I remember you had a dark gray—"

"No. All I have now is what's here. There's no secret closet with my good stuff in it."

We, or rather Wynne, finally decided on dark skinny jeans, a simple cami, and a cropped leather moto jacket. "Don't even think of flat sandals," she warned me. "This is the equivalent of dressing for an important meeting in her conference room, and she's CEO." Finally, Wynne approved of the highest-heeled sandals I owned, which I'd bought on sale in 2008 in De Gaulle Airport on a stopover from Doha. I had never wound up wearing them, because even trying them on hurt. "One more thing. Don't obsess about your hair. You'll be a couple of blocks from the ocean, so it's going to frizz. Big fucking deal, and anyway, you frizz in an endearing way."

When I called her back to model the results, she gave me one of her genuine smiles. "Now you're a Real Housewife of South Brooklyn!"

I headed down to the kitchen, holding the banister far too tightly to compensate for the heels I wasn't yet used to. I started making a smoothie to drink in the car along the way.

Eliza had been extremely serious when it came to her responsibility to make me at least passably conversant in Bachelorology. We'd spent a good chunk of the day watching the episodes that had aired so far this season, Eliza pausing every two minutes to explain the nuances and variations on the rose ceremony and hometown visits. While I added diced avocado to my frozen fruit and milk in the blender so I could pretend that my smoothie was healthy, she scrolled Instagram for general opinions on the current contestants. Lulu gazed up at me, tail wagging pleadingly, as if she thought I might be sneaking some liver into the blender, too. I handed her a Milk-Bone, and she scooted away to eat it in the hallway, just in case I changed my mind and decided to crunch on it myself.

"Everyone hates Arielle!" Eliza announced.

"But I like Arielle. She's bitter and funny."

"They think she's not there to get engaged. That she's just there to promote her tech start-up."

"But that's part of why I like her," I said.

Eliza huffed with feigned irritation at my inability to catch the spirit of the show. "They think Ryan is a total sweetheart and she'll break his heart if he lets her."

I considered. "That's true enough. For a not-overly-bright hottie, he seems unusually kind. Any manipulative woman could wrap him around her finger."

"They would make a terrible couple," Eliza opined. I couldn't argue, and solemnly agreed that despite my own preference for Arielle, it would be better for all involved if he chose Courtney.

I slurped up the remains of my smoothie as I pulled up to Tasha's house. Enormous, though more tasteful than Dr. Moscowitz's nearby castle. I ruefully realized that it had a pretty similar feel to my own home, which had been so lovingly and expensively overdone by Josh's first wife, Dawn.

Tasha had told me we'd be watching the show outside. Unsure of whether to come to the front door or around the back, I peeked over the fence. There was Tasha, with two other women, sitting on a sectional couch under an arbor entwined with flowering vines and twinkling lights. She waved a hello that could have been seen from two miles away on a clear enough day. "Corie!" she said, springing up to help when it became clear I was having a moment of trouble with her gate mechanism.

She was exactly as middle-aged gorgeous as she had seemed on video chat. She was taller than average, with a teeny waist. Her breasts were as overplumped as her lips. The latter had switched from the oxblood matte to a heavily lacquered pale coral. Even from six feet, I could see that her apparently strong, striking eyebrows were mere wisps that were artfully filled in. I said a quick prayer of thanks that Wynne had consulted with me on clothing, because I wasn't remotely overdressed for the occasion.

"Your hair looks amazing," she said, reaching over to scrunch it and pat it. I willed myself not to recoil, or even take a tiny step backward from this proximity to a stranger.

"Thanks so much!" I cheerfully replied. "Oh my God, I love what you've done out here." The lot was small, like that of most Brooklyn single-family homes, but the Sobols had maximized the entertainment possibilities of every last square foot. Besides the sectional, there were several cozy chairs. An outdoor TV screen mounted on the wall of the house rivaled the screen size of the art house theater I'd gone to when I lived in DC, a venue too sincere to sell popcorn. Behind the seating area was an expansive outdoor kitchen, stainless steel and gleaming stone, which—in addition to a grill large enough to accommodate a freshly killed woolly mammoth—included a sink, a refrigerator, and a six-burner stove.

There were indeed several scented candles around, with a sharp, clean smell that reminded me of something I couldn't quite place. The label, gold and black with art deco letters, said LA TUBÉREUSE—CITRONNELLE ET CÈDRE. It came to me—they smelled like a snazzier version of the citronella candles I bought at the hardware store to keep away mosquitoes. "Let me introduce you," Tasha cooed. I waved awkwardly and hoped that the two women on the couch who were standing up didn't decide they needed to shake my hand. They didn't, staying where they were. "This is Olga Kozlova, she's my cousin and my best friend, for, like, ever. And Gina Licchoveri. We've also been friends for so long. How long is it?"

Gina was five feet one and maybe a hundred pounds on her most bloated day. The only things about her that were big were her eyes, which were deep brown and so wide she looked perpetually amazed. "Oh God," she said quietly with a fond smile. "Like, twenty-five years?"

"We are so fucking old!" Tasha laughed and clapped a hand to her cheek in mock shock.

"Shut up! Don't even talk about it!" Olga laughed. Her hair was waved in the exact same style as Tasha's, but just a few shades lighter. "It's so nice to meet you, Corie. Tasha was just telling us about you."

"It's so nice of you to have me!"

"Everyone, sit down," Tasha urged. "Let me get you a drink, Corie. We have wine, beer, diet soda, water?"

"I'll have wine, thanks."

"Red or white or rosé?"

I pictured myself spilling red wine all over the pale gray couch, so I said, "Rosé."

She opened the fridge. "Grenache-style rosé, Mourvèdre . . ." She picked up another bottle and frowned at the label: "Pink moscato?" She shrugged slightly, apparently baffled as to how pink moscato wound up in her fridge.

"Mourvèdre," I decided, not that I'd ever tasted it or even heard of it. I just wanted to say the name. Within a few seconds I was holding a full glass large enough to bathe a dachshund.

"What part of Long Island are you from?" Olga asked, sitting down.

"Nassau County," I answered. "The North Shore."

"Where?" she persisted, her eyes on mine.

"Shorehaven?" I said, hesitantly.

"Oh, I know it," she said confidently.

"You do?" I was surprised. The town was small, maybe twenty thousand people, and hardly a destination for people who live in Brooklyn.

"Yes. I have a lot of friends who live on Long Island," she said.

"It's on the water, right?" asked Tasha.

"Yes," I said.

"I love it there," said Olga. "So much of Long Island is superficial, you know what I mean?" Tasha nodded, and I tried to picture the level of superficiality that it would take to leave Tasha and Olga cold. "But the people in Shorehaven seemed different. Real. You know what I mean?"

"I think I do," I said. We chatted a bit while Tasha set out trays of mozzarella balls and cherry tomatoes drizzled with balsamic vinegar, and chips and guacamole with cilantro and red onion sprinkled artfully over it. I learned that Olga was a stay-at-home mom, with her youngest child, a teenager, the only one of her kids still living at home. We shared an eye roll over the difficulties of parenting teenagers. Gina, a pharmacist, was much more subdued than Olga and Tasha, who were so brightly colored, literally and figuratively. I wondered how she'd fallen in with them.

The sun had finally set, but since it was a little more than a week past the summer solstice, the sky wasn't willing to give up all its light, staying a dark, rich blue. Olga checked her watch. "It's *Bachelor* time!" she squealed.

"My favorite is Arielle," I said. They all swung their heads to look at me, and I felt a second of panic, as if I'd somehow blown my cover. I had to remind myself that I wasn't pretending to be anyone I wasn't. I was there as Corie Geller, investigator of historical murders, and they knew that. "She's funny," I said defensively. "Though I really hope Ryan doesn't end up with her."

Everyone nodded. "Right?!" Tasha said, and clicked the TV on.

Tasha's guac was delicious, and I had to stop myself from eating the entire bowl. I was as riveted by the episode as they were and joined them in cheering on Ryan's tentative kiss of Courtney and scoffing at Becca's tearful, and clearly false, insistence that she was definitely not still in love with the boyfriend who dumped her seven months ago. Happily, though Ryan may have lacked a nuanced understanding of human motivations—or even a basic one—he seemed to recognize that Becca might not be on the level. Courtney—and Arielle—were safe for another week.

Afterward, we were all slightly fried from the emotional roller coaster we'd been on, plus our roles as love coaches. Olga, spent, sat unnaturally silent. Gina, low-key but obviously emotional, rested her hand on her chest. In a soft, constricted voice, she said, "Can you believe Madison? Doesn't she see what her life will be?"

"Okay!" Tasha sounded a little like a drill sergeant calling out *Attention!* "We need to talk about the murder."

All eyes were on Tasha, who had enough charisma to lead her troops across the Rubicon, if she were ever so inclined. "Like I told you, Corie is a detective with years of experience, even though she looks twenty-four." I smiled and shook my head. Tasha amended her estimate: "Fine. Twenty-six. So I'm going to give her the floor. If any of you get chilly, there are shawls in the bamboo chest."

I moved toward the edge of my chair, resting my wrists just above my knees so I was leaning toward them. Kind of like a storyteller about to say *Once upon a time.* "A little more than twenty years ago, there was a family living about half a mile from here, on Reynolds Street. Kim and Seymour Brown and their five-year-old, April. You've all heard what happened to them . . . that someone got into their house with gasoline. I won't go into the details, because they are horrendous, but Kim and Seymour died. April managed to climb out of her window, which was on the first floor."

"I heard they found Kim's engagement ring in the ashes," Tasha said. "Or is that one of those urban things?"

"Urban legends?" I asked. She nodded. "No. It's pretty much true. They found a diamond." I paused and looked at each of them to see if this sort of talk was too disturbing, but they seemed okay. So far, not even a shudder. "The diamond was intact. But because of evidence downstairs, they assume the fire got hotter as it consumed more . . . got more fuel."

I stopped there. Of the three women, Gina was the quietest—but the easiest to read. Her knuckles had gone right up to her mouth during a couple of heartrending conflicts on *The Bachelor*. With the TV off and stars twinkling above the potted palm trees, Gina shivered and rubbed her upper arms. Tasha strode over to the bamboo chest, pulled out a shawl, and draped it around Gina. Tasha struck me not so much as nurturing, but as someone who felt obliged to make sure that everything was all right—more nurse than mommy. Still, if she wasn't loving, she came across as benevolent.

A moment later I understood Gina's shivering. We were so close to the ocean, and the night air was salty and damp and cooling rapidly. I put on my jacket and zipped it up halfway.

"Do you happen to know what happened to the little girl?" Gina asked me. The voice was subdued, as if she were dreading to hear the answer.

"April's doing fine!" I told her. "Luckily, she was a resilient kid. The police and the Department of Social Services worked hard on her case and finally found some close relatives—Kim's—in Kentucky. April wound up living with her grandmother, and it worked out. She's an assistant professor at a great college, is in a relationship, and seems really well-liked in her community."

Gina exhaled slowly. Olga was delighted. Clearly Olga Kozlova could handle hearing about the fire that engulfed her friend and her friend's husband. She was realistic enough to acknowledge that horrible stuff happens. But her disposition led her to seek out sweetness and light. She struck me as someone who loved darling handbags with surprise compartments and movies with happy endings. At the words "in a relationship," she tilted her head and said, "Awww."

I would have loved another glass of Tasha's excellent rosé just to maintain my mood, but it was after ten, and I wanted to be alert during the questioning as well as on the drive home. I switched to Perrier—even though I'd always disliked its brash bubbles—dropped in a couple of pieces of lime, and returned to my chair, a wide rattan throne with cushions fit for a czarina.

"First, I should let you know that April is our client. As I told Tasha, in this case I'm partnering with a former NYPD detective who worked on the arson-homicide. He and April have been exchanging holiday cards every year since."

"That is so touching!" Olga said.

I nodded.

"I mean, you think of some tough cop, and there he is in the Hallmark store—"

Tasha cut her off. "She's able to pay you?" Tasha asked me. She sounded precisely on the midpoint between concerned and nosy. Her expression was hard to read; her eyebrows appeared quizzical, but they were so intensely crayoned I couldn't be sure. "I mean, college professors don't make a ton of money, and to find out all about what happened . . ."

I was pretty sure Tasha was trying to discover whether April had inherited anything significant from her parents. It seemed like a good topic to avoid, so I said, "April didn't hire us specifically to find out about her parents' deaths. After she left, she never went back to Brooklyn, and she seems to have no knowledge of any of her parents' friends, business associates, whatever. But she does have some good memories of both Kim and Seymour—"

Olga cut in. "So how come she hired you?"

"I'm getting there," I told them. "Just a bit more background. April's led a pretty quiet life. She's not worldly, but on the other hand, she's definitely not naïve. She has what it takes to be a professor. She's smart, self-disciplined, intellectually curious. She has a PhD in cinema studies—"

"She makes movies?" Olga demanded.

I shook my head. "Watches them, analyzes them, compares them with other art forms. Teaches them. A lot of it is very technical, but basically, she loves movies. Anyway, she leads a quiet life. She's engaged to a woman who lives in Japan, doing some scholarly work, and they can't be together until they can arrange their careers a little differently. She teaches, gets together with friends and colleagues, keeps in touch with her grandma in Kentucky, but that's pretty much it."

Tasha, ever the hostess, put out more plates of food. She offered wooden bowls of nuts equipped with folk art nutcrackers—little sailors, farmers with pitchforks, doctors with stethoscopes—you stuck a nut between their legs and *crack!*

I explained to them in detail what had happened to April that day with the SUV.

Almost in unison, Olga and Gina said, "Oh my God!" Olga uncrossed her legs and planted her sandals on the tile floor. They were so terrifyingly high-heeled I wouldn't even have tried standing in them. I was already looking forward to the moment I could peel off my much lower heels. She leaned forward. Her nail polish and rings captured the rays of light and shot them back in sparkles.

I went on. "Without a doubt, if April hadn't taken evasive action, the SUV would have run her down. That's according to witnesses and the video the campus surveillance cameras picked up."

"What did she do?" Tasha demanded, letting her jaw drop after the last word.

"She managed to run where the SUV couldn't get to her."

Suddenly all three were calling out further questions. The best way to handle that was not to answer any of them immediately. I stood, went to the refrigerator, and got another Perrier. I kept standing, letting them take the conversational lead. I wasn't looking for a specific piece of information—no *Where were you on the night of . . .*—but instead trying to get a feel for who Seymour and Kim were and how the people in their lives saw them. If I let the women talk, rather than asking specific questions, I hoped I'd get to see what they thought was important to understand about the Browns.

"So why would someone try to hurt her? Kill her?" Tasha seemed upset that such a decent person, who'd already lost so much, could be the target of a bad guy. Her gleaming mouth formed an upside-down U.

"We haven't come close to an explanation, and we don't want to assume it was a random psychopath until we've exhausted every other possibility. And April agrees. In fact, before we began to work on the case, she brought up her parents' deaths with the local police."

"And?" Tasha said harshly. "What did they tell her? Let me guess, they said, *No way. That was then, this is now.* I swear to God, cops give me acid reflux."

"Well, I don't think April was thrilled with that response either. And it seemed to me that, yes, twenty years is a very long time, and it is highly unlikely that April overheard some crucial conversation that she still hasn't remembered. Or, if she saw the arsonist walking down the street, she'd immediately remember what she'd forgotten all these years and would yell out, *You killed my parents!* But the Browns . . . well, Seymour, anyway, was not the typical accountant. A lot of his clients were involved in crime, mostly organized, mostly the Russian Mafiya, the Vory." I held up my hand before they could chime in, as they all seemed eager to do. "I know they also operate in Ukraine, Moldova, Belarus, et cetera, et cetera. And, of course, in the US."

"I can see that you're the careful type, Corie. I like that you did your homework," Gina said.

"Thank you. So let's talk about both the Browns. When I FaceTimed with Tasha, she said she had met Seymour, but what about you and Olga?"

Gina was on the verge of answering—her mouth started to open—but Olga was probably so used to being the designated talker that she jumped in. "No, we didn't know Seymour. Never met him. I mean, we met Kim through Tasha. We used to take salads to the beach and eat at a picnic table before we had to pick up the kids at school, and one day Tasha said to us, 'There's this sweet girl married to an accountant. He's been around, but she hasn't. Anyway, she's from out of town and has . . . some . . . What was it, Tash? That kind of shock."

"Culture shock," Tasha said. "What's with you about that word? Culture, culture shock. It's not like you're not smart."

"I know, but it's like a mental block with that word. Anyway, she was this really nice girl, nice house, nothing flashy, had a darling little girl, but she was always walking around with the kid in a stroller. Kim was what my mother used to call all dressed up with no place to go—"

"Full makeup. Looking lonely," Tasha cut in. "That was the point about culture shock. She only spoke English. Maybe by then she learned '*spasibo*,' but I'd be surprised. But also, she was from Kentucky. You know what's in Kentucky? The Kentucky Derby. There must be something else, but nobody ever said anything to me about it. So I don't know when Kim met Seymour, or where, because he wasn't a Kentucky kind of guy." Tasha's eyes lit up, and she held up her index finger into a *wait a sec* gesture. "I just thought of something else! Kentucky Fried Chicken!" She massaged the diamond ring on her left hand. "Sometimes . . . when Max is out of town, I get a bucket of extra-crispy chicken wings delivered and . . . Orgasm! Anyway, I don't know when Kim came to New York. But she was a fish out of water."

"Except . . ." Gina began. We stretched our necks toward her, watching her lips for recognizable words. Half her speech wound up sounding like the peeps of chicks in baby animal videos. "Kim never tried to get into the water," Gina continued. "Okay, we live in New York City, but how different are we? We work or we're stay-at-home moms. It's not like we go clubbing and come home at five in the morning blitzed from party drugs. And what's to fit in? I'm Italian, and this definitely isn't an Italian neighborhood. BFD. Do you think they expect me to do that Russian dance where the women walk around waving handkerchiefs and do those high kicks?"

"The Barynya," Olga said. She waited for Gina to resume, but as Gina had just finished talking more than she had the whole evening, there was a silence that Olga had no problem filling. "Another thing. She was young, okay? I mean, younger than we were. But not like four generations younger."

"I know totally what Olga is saying," Tasha said to me. "So Kim was maybe four or five years younger than us. But she acted super girlish. Always asking did I think she should wear pants or a dress to some restaurant. If it was dinner with one of Seymour's clients, should she try to start a conversation with the wife or just sit there and let the men talk? What happens if the wife is older? Like what do you say to someone who's fifty?"

"Couldn't you just put that down to normal social anxiety?" I asked.

"It was normal," Tasha said, "except it was too much. I know this sounds terrible, because Kim was really as sweet as sugar and also she died in such an awful way, but sometimes I wanted to lose her number."

"Do you think you would have eventually?"

Tasha said, "I'm not sure. I felt guilty after she died for having hoped she'd make some other friends and drop me. And I was a little upset with Max because he was, like, too glad when I took Kim under my wing, which I did of my own free will. Because Seymour . . . not that Max ever used Seymour as an accountant or had anything to do with him in business, but Max knew Seymour was a guy who 'mattered in the community.' Do you get what I'm saying?"

"That Seymour was well-connected and you'd rather please someone like that than piss him off."

"Right." Tasha paused. "But aren't there limits to how nice you have to be? It's not like Kim was the boss's wife."

Gina peeped, and all three of us turned to her. "If you happen to remember, about six months before she got killed, I told you, 'Okay, I'm a pharmacist. I never play physician. But I know a thing or two about the human condition.'" Even though her volume was still low, she was more emphatic. I hardly had to strain to hear her anymore. "Remember I told both of you that her blah-ness could be minor depression? Remember, Tasha? And Olga, you said maybe I was right, that Kim did look exhausted half the time. And then you said okay, that fatigue could be a symptom, though maybe it was because she didn't have enough help in the house."

Tasha held up both hands, a my-turn-to-talk signal that caused the two others to stop. "I was over at her house and I brought a bunch of my old *Architectural Digests*, because I wanted to show her about pendant lamps. We were sitting at her table in the kitchen, and all the lights were on and she's turning pages, looking. She had smudgy circles under her eyes, and it wasn't from non-waterproof mascara. She was exhausted." Tasha touched her eyelids, though gently enough to keep her gold and plum eye shadow pristine. "So I said to her, 'Kim, you need a break. You know it, I know it. And probably Seymour knows it too. Maybe he's afraid to suggest getting a cleaning lady because you might take it as criticism.' Well, we both knew that was bullshit, but I wanted to give her a way to save face if he said no."

"He had more money than God," Olga said. "Why would he say no?"

"Maybe he was one of those control freak guys who thinks that a wife does absolutely everything," Tasha said. "Whatever, Kim clearly needed help at home. So I figured I would push a little. Naturally, she asked me fifteen different times how to approach it with Seymour. And finally I told her just to tell him straight: 'Seymour, I need help in the house.'"

"Did she ever get anybody?" Gina asked.

"That's the thing," Tasha said, shaking her head sadly. "She made such a huge deal of it, but when she asked Seymour, he said it was okay. This was like—I'm guessing here—maybe a month before the fire."

I slid over a few inches to get a better take on Olga's dominatrix shoes, with metal spikes for heels and much ado about pointy grommets around the ankle straps. My butt and the backs of my thighs got wet, as all the humidity that had accumulated on the cushions since I sat down had soaked through my jeans. I looked toward Tasha, the only one of the three who had really known Seymour.

"So you knew them both and saw them together as a couple," I said. "Was he overbearing with her in public as well?"

"Totally," she said.

"But there is some common wisdom out there that opposites attract, or at least do well together," I suggested. "Do you think it could have been a happy marriage?"

Tasha screwed up her face to ponder my question. Though not asked, the others—maybe unconsciously—gave me quick answers. Gina performed the standard exhalation/eye-rolling duet, as in *God give me patience*, while Olga shook her head no.

"If anyone else has an opinion . . ." I added.

"Well, I never saw them together—" Gina began.

Olga cut her off. "I saw them together one time, at a cocktail party for Brighton Ballet Theater. I think one of Seymour's clients was on the board. Kim was wearing a dress with a tulle skirt and satin ballet flats. Normally I'd think, well, it's a little literal. Except she pulled it off! So adorable. He looked old enough to be almost her father, but he was wearing a white dinner jacket and came off like a short George Clooney. Without the beard. Not that I know how tall George Clooney is, but Seymour was what? Five eight? Anyway, they did make a good-looking couple. But I noticed that they didn't talk to each other the whole night. Like at all, even when they were standing next to each other."

Tasha raised her eyebrows to signal *dubious*. Then she fluffed her hair, parted her voluminous lips, and said, "Meh." Recrossing her legs, she added, "Not 'almost' happy. You want my personal opinion? If you are going to be happily married to someone, you have to be able to have some fun. Playfulness, you know? I don't think there was much play in either of them. So *not* happy"—she flashed us a too-wide emoji smile—"but they kind of loved each other in their own way."

"Except one thing, Tasha," Gina said. "You told us he had a girlfriend that he bought a place for in Park Slope. How much love could he have had for his wife when he's spending so much money on someone else?"

Tasha flipped her hand. "A lot of guys need girlfriends. For sex, and also as a guy thing. If all the men he dealt with had a gold Rolex and a Tag Heuer for sports, don't you think he'd want the Tag too?"

"Can you give me an example of how Seymour and Kim loved each other?" I asked.

She stayed silent for a moment, as if waiting for assorted neurons to fire. "Okay. Kim looked up to him because he was so smart. Like, where did all the VIPs go for financial advice? They totally looked up to Seymour, and Kim was impressed by it. This was her husband, and he had a college degree and was really upscale, and word got around that he had a waiting list for clients. And he loved . . . I think—because he was kind of a mystery and didn't really have friends to go to a Giants game with—that he loved Kim because she was so all-American. Every time we saw them, he let it out that she was from Kentucky, like that was such an asset. I'm not sure why—it wasn't like he was an immigrant. He didn't even have a New York accent. He could have been from anywhere. Probably he was also turned on by her youngness."

"Do you know what the age difference was?" I asked. My dad had been doing some background checking, much easier now that so much had been digitized since the time of the murders. Curiously, there was a six-year difference between the birth date on Seymour's driver's license and the one on his CPA license with New York State. In and of itself, its main significance was that his identity was fluid.

"This is just a guess," Tasha said. "Ten or fifteen years."

"Fifteen to twenty," Olga countered. She ran the tips of her fingers over her high Slavic cheekbones. "Let me tell you, Seymour totally had an eye job. Like no bags, and Jake Gyllenhaal eyes. Not blue, but puppy dog. That's the first thing I thought when I saw him, eye job, and then Kim showed me a picture of him and April when she was a baby and I was one hundred percent positive. Not that I would ever say anything, but even with the work he had done, he looked more young grandfather than older father."

Tasha shrugged. "Olg, I'm not going to argue with you. Whatever. But he totally adored that child. And Max noticed one night at dinner that Seymour said, 'April is a little genius. And she looks so much like Kim.' Two completely separate ideas—smarts from him, prettiness from her. Anyway, after the fire and all that horrible stuff, Max and I were talking about them. He said in his opinion, Seymour would never have left Kim, because she'd given him that wonderful child. And I said, the real love of Seymour's life was April. And Max said, 'You're absolutely right!'"

I was curious about a pretty young woman having a five-year-old as competition. "Did any of you ever have a sense that Kim was jealous of April, or that she and Seymour fought over her?"

There was a jingling of jewelry as the three women leaned forward or shook their heads. Gina said, "I mean, April was such a nice, easy kid. Who could resist her?"

"Listen, you're a little on edge with the first child," Tasha said. "But Kim would talk about how they played tea party and beauty salon and how fun it was. When Seymour finally said she could hire someone, she asked me if I knew of anyone who was good with kids also. That was important to her. And with references."

"Right," Olga said. "You asked me, and I said my sister-in-law's niece had come over about a year before."

"Except she was the one whose English wasn't so great," Tasha said, and Olga nodded. "And Kim said she had to have someone who spoke English. Someone had told her that Irish girls were good. Which I thought sounded like saying *I want someone white* without using the words, but I wasn't going to start a fight with her. She's from Kentucky, or maybe it was him who wanted that. Anyway, I told her to put an ad in the *Irish Standard*, where girls wanting jobs look. I told her to be sure to put in 'experienced' to discourage anyone eighteen with a cute Irish brogue."

"But she never found anyone," I said.

"She never had time," Tasha said, shaking her head. "So soon after . . . What a shock! I swear, it took me months not to picture the fire every day."

After some more chatter that largely repeated the themes we had already touched on—"He had a driver, and it never occurred to him to ask if she needed help with babysitting?"—I took my leave. Of course Tasha buttonholed me—with surprising subtlety—about whether I was interested in scented candles, and I was happy to oblige. We all hugged and promised we'd be in touch. Tasha met my eyes as I unlatched the gate: "I'm very, *very* interested. Please let me know if you find out anything."

I promised I would, took one final sniff of that fresh ocean scent, and headed back to my car.

CHAPTER EIGHT

After months of homebound life, my visit to Brooklyn had been bracing. Unlike nights out with the Long Island women I'd met, I didn't have to hear exhaustive discussions about the ACT scores seniors needed to get into Bowdoin. None of them tried to see whether it was worth getting to know me by asking what my husband did or where I'd gone to college. It was a girls' night the way I liked it—some raunchy remarks at the TV and a little too much wine.

My parents were still up when I got home. They had always worked late hours in their professional lives and had kept the habit in retirement. My mom wanted to hear every detail, as if I were seventeen again and just back from a date with an intellectually gifted hunk. My dad actually had his little spiral-bound pad and pen on the table beside his mug of warm milk and honey; he'd been drinking that concoction nightly before bedtime since he was five. It didn't matter if he was staggering from fatigue, booze, or (once) just back from the hospital, where they'd extracted a bullet from his shoulder. He strummed the spiral with his pen to get my attention. "I got a few items I want to go over with you," he said. I felt bad, though not bad enough to keep from asking if he could wait till morning. The instant I heard his "Sure," I realized I'd hurt his feelings. But the trouble with having a detective as a dad was if I feigned enthusiasm, he'd know in two seconds.

Upstairs, Josh was reading in bed, although I could see from the way his eyes floated from the page to me that he was drifting off. "I wanted to see that you got home all right," he said. In a life filled with enough men that there were some (Brandt and Brent, hairy Hamid) I could remember only because their names or qualities alliterated, my husband was the one guy I'd ever slept with who actually wore pajamas.

"That's so sweet," I said, wondering, *He wants to see if I got home?* Wouldn't my having been part of a successful undercover op that foiled a plot to blow up jet fuel pipelines that led to JFK—or on a team that stopped US jihadists from smuggling the explosive RDX to an offshoot of Hezbollah, or, on my own, outwitting an attempt to kill me—give him confidence enough that I could survive two and a half hours of watching *The Bachelor* in Brooklyn?

"Sweet? I don't see myself as sweet," he said. Neither did I, actually. Though I did wonder if he had his own PTSD—though not technically diagnosable—from when I had been kidnapped and he didn't know if I was dead or alive or ever coming home. "Gallant?" he suggested.

"Sure. Gallant is good. Shows machismo, but doesn't beat its chest. Like your pajamas." I took off my clothes and made them into a relatively neat pile, since we'd officially left the stage of the relationship that involved wanton tossing of panties. I could see underneath his pajamas that he was getting into the same mood I was already in. I leaned in for a kiss, then paused. "You do know, Josh, that after this is over, when we should be falling asleep in each other's arms, I'm going to have to get out of bed and take off my makeup."

"And floss and brush your teeth," he added.

"You want to wait until I do that?"

"No."

"Okay." I slid under the blanket and started unbuttoning his pajama top.

The next morning, I was still buoyed by my night out in Brooklyn, and not just from the info I garnered. I enjoyed being with Tasha in particular. She was dauntless, like a steelworker in a Soviet poster, yet also benevolent. If Dr. Zhivago had wound up with a woman like her instead of Lara, she'd have stuck with him, joined him on the streetcar, and resuscitated him, and the novel could have had a happy ending.

I brought my coffee to my office in a travel container, even though I wasn't leaving the house, a habit I'd finally acquired after sloshing coffee in a mug onto pastel T-shirts dozens of times. I settled in and took a long, slow sip, grateful that I was finally able to afford truly excellent coffee. I turned on my computer. At the beginning of the pandemic I had added an extra monitor to professionalize my home office. Even though I'd already been working from home, seeing others' Instagram home office setups had motivated me to up my game. I told myself that I needed it when doing FBI contract work from home. The extra screen would help me keep track of Arabic-English translations, although I wound up using it more for streaming my favorite Arabic-language show, *Al Hayba,* and watching slideshows of baby animals.

Knowing that my dad was reliably ten minutes late, I skimmed through my Twitter list of Arabic-speaking journalists. Since I had slowed down my work as a scout for Arabic literature, I was determined to read something in the language every day. Fiction, poetry, but news was a plus. It catapulted me out of Long Island World back to the Middle East. If my life were a pie chart, Long Island would be a hefty slice, about a third, and delicious. It included my husband and daughter and great coffee. But two-thirds of the pie comprised my career, my nearly lifelong friendship with Wynne, all my other relationships—Queens College friends, assorted spooks, including a DEA agent I still thought about every day, a fiction editor in Cairo I sometimes Skyped with, my parents. It was reading and streaming and jaunts to museums and theaters. Running. Music. Audiobooks. But in the year between my kidnapping and the day April Brown texted my dad, a lot of that bigger chunk of pie had dried up and fallen into crumbs.

I heard footsteps, along with another, more unfamiliar sound. I swiveled to face my open door, and there was my dad, unusually wide-eyed for the hour. His vacation-size four-wheel suitcase was rolling beside him. Instead of his usual "Hiya, kiddo," he stopped and gave me a loose version of an NYPD roll call salute.

He was unusually spruced up. Seeing him in a white dress shirt after months of T-shirts from his Mets collection was jarring. I had told him to be a little less casual than his usual sick day chic as I wanted him to Zoom Tasha with me. If he was anticipating an interview with a cooperating witness, he shouldn't come across as a retired cop from the Auto Theft unit in a YA GOTTA BELIEVE Mets T-shirt. My mom had probably done his hair; there was a vague scent in my office, more lilac than sandalwood. The almost well-fitting gray cotton pants he had on were also a shock to the system. Since the end of April he'd been wearing an unending supply of khaki shorts: he, the family non-shopper, had gone on a mad, hot dog–fueled rampage in Costco when accompanying my mom. The dozen pairs of shorts he'd bought looked manufactured from recycled lunch bags, sewn on a machine that only did topstitching.

His grooming was disquieting as well. His vanishing hair looked strangely thick. His face was total smoothness; I couldn't spot one dot of unshaved stubble. I glanced at his suitcase. Every summer, they used to go to North Carolina for the Flat Rock Playhouse, the Blackberry Festival, and visits to retired cop friends. But they hadn't gone since Covid. So where were they off to?

"What's with the suitcase?" I asked.

"I've got all the stuff," he said.

"'Stuff' is a little broad. What kind of stuff?" He was perfectly capable of hiding giant tubs of pretzels to avoid my mom's lectures on the evils of refined carbs, perhaps planning to hide them in my office closet.

"For the April Brown case. I figured if we're going to work together, we need to get some sort of a system going. This is one hell of a big room, so we could get a file drawer or cabinet. Something. My contribution."

"I can—"

"Shush," he said. "Listen, last night, when you were in Brooklyn, I drove your mother back to our place because she missed some sandals. I'm not sure whether she meant she missed them like she forgot them, or that her heart was breaking. And no, I didn't ask. Anyhow, I checked our downstairs storage locker. And guess what? I found another evidence box full of stuff I copied on the Brown case!" My heart surged, as if I just had a hit of some new wonder drug. "I haven't looked through it all yet. But I did see that it had my list of everybody we interviewed back then. Jogged my memory, because it was me who put the names in that particular order."

"In order of what?" I began. "Who was most likely—"

"Nah. It was in order of who of Seymour's associates would have the most information about him. I admit there was some guesswork in that. But what was the downside? If I was wrong, I'd have wasted time. Like even if I got to everyone on the list, the big fish could've gotten away." As he spoke, he picked up speed. His words tumbled over one another.

"That's true . . ." I managed before he charged on.

"Except it bugged me that half the goddamn cops and your geniuses in the FBI tended to investigate each name as it came up. In chronological order and insanely thorough. Like they'd tell me, 'Hey, Dan, there was a receipt for underwear that Seymour bought the afternoon before the fire! We gotta drive into Manhattan and spend an hour with the salesman.' You tell me. How likely is it that Seymour said to the guy wrapping up a dozen undershirts, 'Gee whiz, I'm scared my client Shmuel Kaminsky is out to get me'?"

"Not likely," I agreed, "and anyway, buying a dozen undershirts is not the act of a man who believes he's doomed."

My dad was quiet. Probably strolling down Homicide Memory Lane. So I rolled the suitcase over to a window seat, lifted it up there, suppressed a grunt. I imagined Dawn, when the room had been her gym, sitting on one of the two window seats, cooling down from whatever exercises promoted her size zeroness. Maybe she'd gazed out and meditated on the stones in the driveway. They formed a meticulous herringbone pattern, as if the paving were for the carriages of Tudor England's nobility rather than her friend Felicity Kleinberg's Volvo.

I opened the suitcase. One glance assured me that it was filled with the paperwork my dad had copied or borrowed at the precinct. Nearly all of it—except for a couple of binders and a notebook—was the paperwork he and I had brought over earlier from his apartment. I waved a manila envelope I hadn't seen before in his direction, implicitly asking if I could open it. He nodded okay, so I sat between the suitcase wheels and the wall, though the window seat was so narrow I managed to squeeze in only a hip and half a butt cheek.

Nothing in the envelope looked like a list, but there was a stack of paper stapled together in the typical way of my father, which meant that out of the five or six times he whomped down on the stapler, only a single staple held everything together. The rest remained to convey teeny puncture wounds. I checked out the pages.

Naturally it had the usual names, DOBs, ID numbers from any prison time or military service. But it was a stack, not a list. Only a single witness per page. Nearly all of them were pictured with duplicates of their mug shots or newspaper photos, plus a couple of empty squares. Along with that, my dad had circled in red summaries of felonies each had been arrested for. Occasionally there were descriptions of allegedly lawful business activity that had a vaguely fishy smell. Each page had its subject's family members circled in blue and personal friends floating inside cartoon thought bubbles.

The guy with top billing, page one, was my dad's prime suspect: Hosea Williams—the multilingual, sociopathic opportunist who left Chicago's crack cocaine world to hook up with the Russian mob. I turned to page two. In second place for knowledge about Seymour's doings was Toddy Mirante, his driver; based on what I knew, I agreed with both assessments. If Toddy was any smarter than his reputation suggested and his hearing was good, he might have gotten the gist of every cell phone conversation and back seat discussion. He might even have had ideas about how to monetize the info.

I learned that Toddy had also made the suspect list. The main reason he was considered was because of his actions the week of Seymour's murder. Up to that point, Toddy had an unblemished attendance record. Yet he had taken off from work for three days with an alleged ear infection. And the third day turned out to be the one that ended with the fire.

Intent to kill—or unpremeditated bacteria? Either way, it was a break in Toddy's pattern that the cops immediately noticed.

"Dad, with Toddy . . . When the detectives got to his place in the Bronx early the morning after the fire, he was there?"

"Yeah. He lived with his mother. We got there about five thirty in the morning and woke her up. A little lady in a big bathrobe. We asked where he was, and she just turned around and walked toward his room. She didn't say 'wait outside,' so we followed her. He was sound asleep."

"Any smell of gasoline or fire residue?" I asked.

"None. And trust me, we sniffed. And when they executed a search warrant a few hours later, nothing on him or on the clothes in the hamper. They even took a sample of the lint in the dryer filter. Anyway, when we woke him up, he was mostly befuddled but also terrified. He kept saying, 'Wha', wha', who are you?' even though we said 'Police' loud enough to wake the neighbors. My partner practically touched the tip of the man's nose with his shield. It didn't strike me that he was faking being asleep."

"What happened then?"

"We took the mother into the living room, and one of the guys questioned her while we got a statement from Toddy. He said he had put the car in the garage a couple of blocks away, returned a couple of movies to Blockbuster, and taken out a couple more. The mother backed him up. She said they had dinner and watched *Muriel's Wedding*. He started complaining about an earache, so she gave him two aspirin when he went to bed. He'd been sick for three days."

"Did he go to a doctor?"

"No. His only alibi is his mother."

"Do you think it's possible he set the fire?"

"Possible," my dad said. He rubbed his well-shaven chin. "Not probable. No one, and I mean not one single person, even hinted that Toddy would have had a motive."

"Unless he just hated his boss," I suggested.

"Lots of people hate their bosses, but they usually don't kill them."

I got up from the window seat and started to pace. "But Toddy's boss wound up dead. Like, is it possible that the murder has nothing to do with Seymour being mob-affiliated, but because he was an asshole boss? From what I've heard of him, he doesn't seem like the guy to be super understanding when his employee takes three days off for an earache."

Dad scratched his head, flattening his careful combing. "I don't think so, but who knows. Toddy seemed easygoing. You'd think, *Nice—and stupid*. He may be the type who gets very upset when his boss loses his shit at him, but he wouldn't get even by killing him." He took his time inhaling and exhaling. "Maybe we should talk to your new friend in Brooklyn now. This Tasha might have some memory of Toddy that could give us a lead."

That morning over coffee, I had given him a condensed version of my impressions of Tasha and company. "It could pay off to locate the driver," I said. "He'd be tough to interview. I gather he's less than brilliant, and the chances of him comprehending a conversation he overheard and then being able to remember it aren't . . . What's the word? Optimal. But he may remember something, even if he doesn't know how important it is."

My dad crossed his arms tightly across his chest. The FBI's body language course that I took in 2005 would have called the gesture "oppositional." For a few seconds his mouth was as tight as his arms. Finally, he said, "Let's just see if we can track him down. My impression of Toddy is that even if he wasn't too dumb to think of arson, he could never have carried out a plan well enough to survive it. And it didn't jibe with what we learned about him: the brains of a hamster—a nice hamster."

I texted Tasha, thanking her for a fabulous time, praising her buffalo mozzarella and her outdoor living room. She texted back almost instantly, "loooved meeting u/ we all think u r the best!!!" I managed to wait a full two minutes, then asked if she was okay with Zooming me and my dad about the case.

"Checking my cal," came back. I wasn't too worried as I watched the three flickering dots. She was self-assured and straightforward. No panicked *Let-me-come-up-with-an-excuse* pause because she'd gotten cold feet. "How abt in 15 min?" she wrote. "Rest of wk cray."

It took my dad and me much of that time to arrange our chairs so we each took up approximately half the screen. Also, we had to angle the computer camera so the top of his head or my jaw wasn't cut off when we both were in frame.

He was seated at a higher level. I'd given him my desk chair, and I was using a small, needlepointed armchair I'd taken from a corner of the dining room. Comfortable enough, though built on a scale for minuscule eighteenth-century people. I had no clue why Dawn had bought it. Maybe zealous hostesses earlier in the 2000s deemed it mandatory to hire a stenographer to perch on it and record guests' reactions: *After a first sip, Kiki Sykes-Rubin would have no truck with the escarole soup.*

A minute before the call, my dad stood and headed toward the door. He believed in being a minute or two late for any meeting with a witness. It was an inoffensive delay, yet it gave most people up to 120 seconds to work up some anxiety. To his mind, a rattled witness was more useful than a calm one. I believed the opposite, so when Tasha came on, I gave her my highest-wattage smile.

She looked as put-together as she had the night before. Her shirt was a thin black cotton speckled with minuscule bumps, like a chic rash. Simple. She'd ditched the complex collection of gold chains. She grinned back and asked, "How are you?" very slowly as her eyes flicked around, not so surreptitiously checking out my office.

"My dad will be here in just a minute."

Finally he made his entrance. Instead of a blink frenzy, cuticle fixation—some minor show of nerves—Tasha offered a delighted "Hi there!" It wasn't flirtatious as much as pure social confidence.

"Tasha," he said, "how are you? I'm Dan Schottland." His voice wasn't his usual, but the familiar good-cop tone I'd heard ever since I was a kid listening in as he talked on the phone. It was deep to establish authority and also crooner-smooth to show composure. Then as now, his volume was turned down somewhat, so he still sounded in command, although

Tasha would have to pay attention to what he was saying. "Thanks for agreeing to talk to me."

"No problem!"

Having been trained in interview techniques, I saw that in their initial contact, she sat up straighter and lifted her chin. It was a way of acknowledging, whether she was conscious of it or not, that his authority was greater.

Throughout my training I'd always been hyperaware of these female tells—the hair touching, the fingertip nibble that existed even in the most self-possessed of us. One of my tells, which I got to see on video in an interrogation techniques seminar, was head tilting. I acted like a devoted beagle. Fortunately, all six of us in the class were videoed, so I was able to see an excellent male tell: Mr. Uxorious Catholic rotating his wedding ring when questioned by a really hot agent.

My dad cleared his throat and began. "Did you ever see Seymour being aggressive or losing control with Kim or anyone else? Physically or verbally."

"That can include humiliating or belittling them," I added.

"Sort of," Tasha said. "I definitely heard some stories that he had a very hot temper, and it wouldn't shock me if he lost it. But I never personally saw him, like, yelling. There are people in the world who are nasty to waiters, and that was definitely Seymour. And he would talk more to Max, my husband, and kind of act like wives weren't worth his time. But nothing obvious."

"Did Kim know about the girlfriend in Park Slope? Did the two of them ever meet?" I asked.

"I'm almost sure she didn't. She really didn't have anyone to talk to besides me. Which is kind of sad, because we weren't that close. But I think she would have told me if she had known," Tasha said.

My dad nodded thoughtfully. "How much did you know about Seymour's business?"

"I heard he was an accountant to a lot of mob guys. Some who just weren't totally legit and some who were total monsters."

"Do you know how he helped them?" I asked.

"He helped with their taxes." She let out a sharp laugh at her own joke. "No. He had a reputation for being money launderer to the stars—or the stars in his world. But I don't know specifically what he did or anything."

My dad and I shot each other a glance. We each knew what the other was thinking: Tasha wouldn't be able to shed any light on the details of Seymour's criminality, but she could help us understand his social connections better.

"Do you remember the Browns' driver?" my dad asked. "His name was Toddy. Toddy Mirante."

"Kind of." Tasha was sitting in a Zoom-perfect carved wood chair, what Wynne would probably call either "the best of Sri Lankan craftsmanship" or "a piece of shit." Behind her were bookshelves with English and Russian titles, heavy on Russian nobility—not that I could read Russian, but I knew the Cyrillic alphabet well enough to figure that Екатерина was Catherine the Great, who, I also knew, did not fuck a horse but did fuck over about five million Jews by forcing them into the Pale of Settlement.

"Did you ever have a conversation with him?" Dad asked her.

"It's hard to remember. I think I saw him a couple of times. Kind of *Hello, how are you?* He would take them to a restaurant where we met them for dinner, and when we finished, they'd just stand in front and Toddy would drive up in the car and they'd get in. Well, Toddy would get out and get them into the car. But—call me old-fashioned"—she smiled and shrugged, as if my dad had said, *Oh, of course you're not old-fashioned*—"I can't get past that 'ladies first' is the way a guy should live his life. Car wise, door wise. Except every single time, Toddy opened the door for Seymour first. Then when Seymour was in, he went around for Kim."

"Ladies second," I remarked.

"In that world . . ." Tasha said. "And Seymour wasn't in the mob. He wasn't even Russian. Even my husband, Max . . . When he saw Toddy opening the door for Seymour first? Oh my God, his eyebrows went all the way up to his hairline—which, it so happens, is receding, but he refuses to get a prescription cream for it. Anyway . . ." She took a breath, preparing for her conclusion. "We were talking on the way home, and he said—Max said—that whether you're a selfish misogynist or one of these men who push into elevators before women . . . Even if you're one of those, you treat your wife with respect. At least out in public."

"At least," my dad agreed.

"Do you think this was Toddy's idea of how a driver should act—or Seymour's?"

"Oh, it had to be Seymour's. He would have corrected Toddy otherwise. If I remember right, he seemed more upscale than some of the chauffeurs for certain types around South Brooklyn. Seriously. While they're waiting for the people they drive, they get out of their cars and talk. Even back then, giant Orthodox crosses tattooed on their throats, snakes or barbed wire on their necks. Like they'd come out of a Siberian prison instead of Rikers Island. Real Vory guys stopped getting tats years ago. But their drivers? Seymour would die first rather than have someone like that working for him."

"What would he want?" my dad asked.

Tasha pursed her lips, a generous display of muted flamingo matte. "Well . . . respectable. Not, like, in a black suit with an English accent." She looked up, trying to recall. "Toddy was more the kind of guy a doctor or lawyer would have. Professional, polite. If you saw him opening the car door for Seymour, you'd think the boss was a business leader, not some accountant who cleaned up dirty money for lowlifes."

"So that was no secret. You'd heard Seymour was a money launderer," my dad remarked.

"Max—my husband—said that was his reputation at the tennis club. But he said it was okay to go out to dinner with them because no one thought Seymour was actually in the mob or did anything horrible. And he knew I liked Kim and felt sorry for her."

"Did Toddy ever drive you and Kim anywhere?" I asked.

Tasha screwed up her forehead to the extent her Botox permitted. "Maybe one time he took us shopping in the city? SoHo, back when there were cute little shops instead of Uniqlo."

"Did you get a sense of what he was like?"

"No. Not that I remember. Well, like, I'm sure he said to Kim, 'Where would you like me to pick you up, Mrs. Brown?' But that was just one day. Maybe two. He probably needed to be available almost all the time for Seymour. You know, I really like this, being questioned by two detectives. It's like being on *Mindhunter*, except not creepy."

Together, we both smiled at her. I took a sip of lukewarm coffee and a few droplets trickled onto my T-shirt. As I reached for a tissue, I asked, "Hey, Tasha, how would you like to help us with the investigation?" Out of the corner of my eye I saw my dad's head whip around to look at me. But I could also sense that he was willing to see where I was going with this.

Tasha's focus went from the big picture to just me. "You're kidding!"

"You could talk to Toddy for us. Nothing dangerous." Before she could conjure up a vision of herself in Louis Vuitton body armor, I added, "That means no in-person meeting. Phone is okay, but video chat would be better."

"Why?"

"It will up your credibility with him, because he'll recognize you. And it's important for us to get a read on his reactions," my dad explained.

"We'd go over your role until you feel secure." I had spotted some small columns on her bookshelves earlier and managed to recognize Doric and Corinthian. Now I realized they were her merchandise. "I forgot to say this before, Tasha . . . I just love your candles! That freesia scent!"

"Thank you!"

My dad nodded a quick homage to candles and then got back to Toddy. "You would be the perfect person to contact Toddy Mirante, find out what he can remember." I was relieved that he was going along with my idea. And it was clear that Tasha liked the description of herself as "the perfect person." He added, "You're a natural when it comes to making people feel comfortable."

I loved that she nodded in agreement. "Also," I added, "you have that connection with him from way back."

She gave us an uncertain look. "It's like, close to zero."

"We know, but it's more than we have. He's more likely to open up to you. And you're so good with making people feel comfortable. The way you did with Kim."

"You're not kidding? Really?"

"Really!"

I glanced over to my dad. He'd narrowed his right eye to achieve his Wise Man look: *I see the world as it is*. "Really," he repeated.

"Oh my God, it would be like . . . So exciting. But I wouldn't act excited." Her eyes, now blazing and wide, moved right back to my dad, not seeing me. *Sic transit gloria* sisterhood. "So you honestly think I can do it, Dan?" she asked.

"We wouldn't ask if we didn't think you could handle it. Let us figure out the best approach."

"Great!" she said.

I sensed that my dad had been expecting to map it out with me and me alone, but if her conversation needed to sound natural, she had to be in on the planning.

"So here's some background, Tasha," I told her. "The only reason Toddy was ever under suspicion was that for three days before the fire he didn't show up for work. By the time he felt well enough to go back, Seymour and Kim were dead. The house burned to the ground. It's a miracle that April survived. So we—and you—have to consider the possibility that he set the fire and escaped. Given all we know about him, that kind of crime is out of whack with his personality. Easy, low-key guy, according to everyone who was interviewed. No sign of aggression or grievances. No problem with taking orders."

"And that's where I come in," Tasha said. She looked ready to jump out of her fancy chair and get going. "Because he's kind of . . . Well, he's cute, but you don't see it that much. If he was a girl, you'd call him mousy. You know? So if two sharp detectives like you and Corie are questioning him, he'd be a wreck. 'Oooh, authority figures,'" she mimicked. "I admit, that's just a guess. Sure, he'd give you facts. But with me, he wouldn't be in any rush to get off the phone. It was so awful, and even now, twenty years later, he'll still need to talk about it. It was probably the biggest deal in his life."

CHAPTER NINE

Tasha and I made a good team, since her obvious delight in detail made up for my *Let's get this over with* approach. Even before I finished a current background check on Toddy, she had created a four-level outline that included every recollection she had of him, including talking too loudly, presumably so he could be heard by the passengers in back. She outlined his relationship with each of the Browns, which I took to be a combo of fuzzy memories and creativity. She devoted a couple of Roman numerals to evaluating the qualities of Seymour, Kim, and even April that might appeal to Toddy—or not.

"You did a terrific job," I told her. "Great idea, thinking about his relationship with April."

"You know what struck me? Maybe Toddy felt like a loser and resented a kindergarten kid with so many privileges."

"Maybe he did," I told her. "It's a good insight. But let me tell you why you should keep it on the back burner. Investigators tend to lead with what they've already learned. Most often, what's 'likely' will pan out, but we want to keep our minds open."

Tasha was sitting at a shiny white desk. It had one of those old-timey three-paneled mirrors, so it probably worked overtime as a makeup table. Her pearly nail polish perfectly matched the desk, though I wasn't sure if that was intentional. "So from what we have about Toddy's life," I went on, "he wasn't exactly Mr. Assertive. Compliant people can be hostile or resentful, but most of the time they don't act on those negative feelings."

"But you don't rule it out," she said.

"Absolutely not. But in this case, we have to remember that whoever tried to run April over with an SUV lacked confidence driving off-road. Toddy was a professional driver. He wouldn't have gotten scared off by a few bumps."

"Maybe he was faking being a bad driver to confuse the cops!"

I was direct with Tasha about the TV episode she seemed to have running in her head. "Faking it might have convinced the cops that the SUV was driven by an amateur," I told her. "But if Toddy really wanted to hurt April? It was a waste of time for him to go to New Brunswick, drive like he had a learner's permit, and then leave before doing any real damage. And I can't see hating someone for twenty years for being a spoiled brat. At least, that can't be the only reason why you hate them or want them dead."

Tasha smiled in comprehension. "I so get it!" Her perfect teeth gleamed in the flattering brightness of a soft, unseen light source. "Also, who the hell would chase a professor and then not follow through? Right? She'd be analyzing what happened for the next ten years and also be on the lookout twenty-four seven. But it's also weird for the Vory to do. Listen, I grew up in Brighton Beach. Some of my best friends' fathers . . . At home, some were sweeties, some were shits. But when they did business, they were strictly animals. From everything I ever heard, they hardly ever send warnings. Anyone who deals with them knows how bad they are. And when they go after someone, it's three weeks in the ICU. Minimum."

"Yeah. That's another reason this case is so tough to figure out," I said. "And what would the Vory want her to keep quiet about? Her feelings about *Notorious*?"

"I know that movie! Or maybe it was *Suspicion*. I get those one-name movies mixed up. I forgot she teaches film. I took an intro course at Kingsborough. Loved it. But I didn't think *Citizen Kane* was the best movie ever."

Part of me was tempted to go along for the ride on Tasha's tangent this time. But I knew I had to get her focused, so I said, "Oh, by the way, from what we know about Toddy, he wasn't mobbed up. The closest he came to the mob was, well, driving for Seymour." I remembered another point I'd meant to bring up. "Besides finding what he knows, if anything, it could be helpful to get a clearer picture of what he's doing now. Like whether he sees any of those guys around, the ones who dealt with Seymour. I tend to doubt it because he's living in Connecticut now, driving for some hedge fund guy who lives in Greenwich."

"Does he like it?" she asked.

"You're the detective."

I had found Toddy on Facebook. He didn't post often, but once in a while he would take a picture during the day, presumably when his boss was in a long meeting. *Revolutionary War battlefield, right here off the NJ Tpke!* A few months later, sitting at an outside table with two other grinning middle-aged men and two humongous pizzas loaded with toppings. *Marcus High '86 Michael, Anthony, Toddy together again!* Actually, the bulk of his Likes and Comments seemed to be from the same Michael and Anthony from high school.

I held my phone parallel to the monitor so Tasha could see the photos. "That's Toddy holding the napkin," she said. "It was probably tucked into his shirt. He's put on a few. But no more unibrow! Isn't it amazing, how you remember what you never knew you knew?"

"It is," I agreed. While I was showing her stuff, I held up a printout of the phones available on the prepaid plan. We were planning to get her a phone she could use for contacting Toddy. I could have set up her own phone with a special number—assuming that she connected with him and he was willing to talk on-screen—but I didn't want to give her the leeway you have with your own phone, fiddling with location services, turning off encryption, or adding nosy, permissions-grabbing apps.

After she finally settled between a Samsung and a Motorola, we had fun picking out a name and password for a new email address. I also decided to create a burner Facebook account—against their rules, but so useful. Assuming he might recall her first name but not her last, Sobol, we decided to give her a different Russian surname beginning with S: Sokolov.

"Even guys who aren't dangerous can be creepy or annoying. You don't need him knowing your life."

"This is so undercover!" she said.

"Total deep cover," I agreed. While I was at it, I asked her to edit her actual profile, stuff like changing the specific "Manhattan Beach" to a more abstract "Brooklyn."

"When will I get the new phone?" Tasha asked. "I'm a little anxious." She pulled in her lower lip as if to chew nervously, but she clearly had trained herself in lipstick preservation, so the day's opalescent orange remained intact. "I never used an Android before."

"Trust me, you don't need a PhD in telecommunications. You'll get used to it in no time. But first I'm sending it to an ex-hacker who freelances for law enforcement agencies now and then. We'll get it to you soon. He'll install an app that can record both sides of a Skype or Zoom, audio and video, and the person on the other side won't know what's happening. It varies by state, but in New York, it's legal. Anyway, the ex-hacker will also disable the GPS, put in a privacy extension and a VPN. That's virtual private network."

"Is it expensive?"

"No. This isn't high-tech. Well, to me it is. That's why my dad and I use an expert. But just to be cautious. Private investigators almost always do it."

I hadn't a clue if most PIs actually did this. When I sounded out my dad, he said it couldn't hurt; his old colleagues who'd become licensed PIs were major cheerleaders for due diligence. We didn't even think of asking Josh. We both knew he'd not only give us the legislative history of interstate wiretapping, he would wind up warning us that it was "on the cusp of legality."

"Theoretically," I said, "if someone wanted to track your new phone, they wouldn't be able to. It can make it look like you're calling from Switzerland or Swaziland. But we'll make it look like New Jersey, okay?"

"I hear Ridgewood is really nice," Tasha said. I told her I'd heard that too. Then I assigned her to pick out a few pictures for me to post on the new account. Nobody else's face but hers, nothing political, only standard pictures, like vacation scenery, a just-deceased pop star ("She was so full of life!"), or the cupcakes she makes every Fourth of July ("The one day a year I'm okay with red velvet cake"). I backdated a bunch of the posts, a suggestion from our hacker-consultant.

Then she asked, not hesitantly, if I would like her business, A Thousand Candles, on social media. When I went to her Facebook page, I saw that her candles came not only in a variety of scents but in a variety of shapes. I owed it to her to give a heart rather than a thumbs-up, though I wondered how my being a fangirl of merchandise like an eight-inch penis candle with a wick coming out of the urethra opening would go over on my next security clearance.

With her new phone, Tasha's newly created alter ego, Natasha Sokolov, joined Facebook with a photo of her holding a platter of salad: gorgeous, vivid vegetables on a bed of teeny lettuces. *Book club tonight. We're reading* Scandalous, *about Winston Churchill's mom. All I can say is—beyond OMG! (Pic taken bef I put on the feta & vinaigrette.)* In the picture, Tasha looked as good as the salad, crisp and bright and slightly excessive, in white jeans, a blue shirt, and maybe two necklaces more than were customarily worn in Ridgewood, New Jersey.

She sent Toddy a friend request the following morning. By midday, Tasha texted, disheartened that he hadn't accepted her. "T cud keep me hanging forever. Right?"

Since I hadn't specifically told her I had been in the FBI and worked with them from time to time, I texted, "This is what cops do. They wait." I was pleased I sounded so noir-ish, as if Lauren Bacall had been cast in one of Humphrey Bogart's roles. A few minutes later, just as I was wishing it wouldn't seem creepy to text April to tell her about this forties film thought that I'd come up with, Tasha wrote, "am officially his friend!!!"

I sent her back, "Set a timer 4 hrs, 15 min and then message him who you are & that you'd like to talk. NOT BEFORE." I had explained that a regular slice of time—two hours, say—is the sign of someone letting a specific amount of time pass. A giveaway. "Not bef," she texted.

"Count on me. I'll send message we planned about me at a red light seeing a big Mercedes w beige leather seats like he drove & remembering him as nice guy & looked him up on FB. Wud love to speak to him sometime."

"Don't want to seem bossy, telling you what to say. I know u got this. Just I know how to get people to talk."

"lol," she wrote, followed shortly by a GIF of Gus the chicken guy in *Breaking Bad*. Then: "Sorry. 'Get people to talk' just reminded me. I don't think you had people tortured!"

"np. Just making sure he doesn't feel pressured. You don't want him thinking he needs to be careful."

Toddy responded almost immediately after Tasha messaged him. She updated me with screenshots as they communicated. Of course he remembered her! He recalled driving Mrs. Brown over to her house and taking them shopping and out to lunch a lot. The "a lot" didn't jibe with Tasha's memory, but his recollection turned her and Kim into closer friends than they actually were.

Tasha asked if they could talk, because she had something to tell him—it was nothing weird or bad, she assured him. Toddy asked for her number and whether it was all right to call sometime around lunch tomorrow. She said totally, but he should know her phone was a Samsung, so she couldn't FaceTime, but Skype or Zoom was fine. Tasha's acting as if she assumed it would be a video call worked the way I'd hoped. Toddy messaged that he was looking forward to seeing her again.

My dad was in New Brunswick for the day, looking over the police interviews that the detective heading up the case, Ricardo Jones, was reluctantly allowing him to read. Dad was concerned that we were too focused on the connection between the attack on April and the murders of Kim and Seymour so long ago. He wanted to see for himself that none of the people the New Brunswick PD had interviewed—students, colleagues—raised any red flags.

"Technically, they're not supposed to share that info with me," he had told me early that morning. "I don't even have a PI license. And I'm based on Long Island, so *Hey you help me, I'll help you* doesn't work as well. But I called Jones. He'd sounded smart, but not easy to deal with. Right? Usual suspicion of outside talent, plus he's not the most outgoing guy in the first place. I think I told you that. Except this time he said, 'Let me check to see if it's okay.' And I said back, 'Check what? I happen to know the victim herself requested that you guys cooperate with me. I'm not some schmuck off the street who's never seen an incident report before.' So then he performs a three-act drama of throat clearing. Finally he says, 'You can come by the next time you're in New Brunswick. Just check that I'll be on duty.' So I said, 'You on today?'"

"You're a retired police detective," I said to him, "so you should understand the pressure this guy is getting from the higher-ups. Also, maybe he has a bug up his butt about the NYPD, thinks you'll be arrogant and second-guess him."

He'd waved his hand as if such picayune matters were beneath his consideration, then demanded for the third time that I save Tasha's interview with Toddy so he could watch when he got back to the house.

I hung up with my dad and focused on getting Tasha ready. The settings the hacker-consultant had set on the recording app would make it start automatically and keep going throughout the entire call. Tasha had taken the burner phone on a house tour for me, and I decided that her kitchen table was the best location. She looked pretty in there, but not seductive. Another plus was that off to the side was a window with a tree large enough to read suburbia, not city or beach. The light wasn't glaring, though it was sunny enough to communicate *Nothing hidden here.*

Nothing hidden, except me. I would be watching the call in real time. In case she needed a prompt or a lifeline, I would text her on her own phone.

When her phone did ring, so did mine. I picked up in time to see her beaming at Toddy. "Oh my God! It's so good to see you!"

He smiled back, but it was clear he was nervous, or maybe confused as to why she was getting in touch. “Good to see you too.” He was seated outside, alone, at a rusting picnic table in what would be a serious contender for the title of America’s Bleakest Roadside Park. About a hundred feet behind him, beyond the patches of dying grass dotting the hard, brown dirt, was a highway with loud trucks rumbling by. “You really haven’t changed,” he added.

“See? I remember you were a nice guy,” she said, “and I was right.”

Earlier, I’d checked through my dad’s files and found a copy of Toddy’s chauffeur’s license from the time he worked for Seymour. He’d had a unibrow then, though now a space had been cleared. His weight on the license was listed at 172 pounds, but this had edged upward, probably two hundred. He had been handsome once, I guessed, though by now his forehead had three horizontal furrows across it. The corners of his lips had contracted over time, so he looked like he was perpetually trying to figure out whether he was the only one smelling something funky.

“So tell me what you’re doing now,” Tasha said. “Are you still living in the Bronx?”

“Yes. I take care of my mom,” he said, a barely perceptible shrug indicating his embarrassment. Not a major lie, but we knew he lived in Connecticut.

“That’s so nice!” she said. “I hate when people don’t take care of their own.”

He smiled quickly—Tasha’s charm was an elemental force of nature—but a second later seemed to hope she’d get to the point. Mosquitoes kept dive-bombing his left ear, and he tried again and again to get them off by lifting his shoulder to squish them without making a fuss.

“So you may be wondering why I got in touch with you. The Mercedes reminded me, but you came to mind for another reason,” Tasha said, and his eyes widened, inviting her to continue. She launched into the story of April almost getting run down.

I shook my head, squeezed my eyes shut, and rubbed my temples in slow, small circles. All this preparation—Tasha’s outline, the burner phone, the fake email—and I had forgotten to tell her not to mention what happened to April. Toddy was more likely than Tasha to still be chummy with people in Seymour's orbit. I didn't want to alert anyone that someone was asking questions about a connection between the attack on April and the murder of her parents. But there was nothing to be done about it now, and hopefully she could still get useful information. "So you know me," she said. "I can't just let that go. I have to try to figure out what happened! I doubt it has anything to do with Seymour and Kim, but I just wanted to get another perspective. April already went through so much as a kid."

Toddy looked more uncomfortable than ever. "Oh wow. Poor kid. Well, I guess she's not a kid anymore. But . . . yeah." He seemed to be looking for some guidance on what he was supposed to say next.

I texted Tasha, "ask him what Seymour was like." I did want to hear what he had to say on that, but I also wanted Toddy to start to feel more comfortable, that he wasn't going to be raked over the coals. Yet.

Tasha barely flicked her eyes down to read my text and then asked him about Seymour. "I mean, I have my own memories, but he didn't talk much to me," she added. "But someone can definitely be one thing to his wife's friend and something else to the people who work for him."

Toddy nodded and rubbed his flat hand over his balding head. "Yeah. I mean, he was really smart. You could tell. And successful and stuff. It was a good, steady job and I miss it in some ways. But he was . . ." He trailed off, as if hoping she would finish his sentence for him.

"He was what?" Tasha asked patiently.

He pursed his lips, then answered. "Well, he was kind of a jerk sometimes. I'm not talking about how he treated me. Just generally."

"I can't say that shocks me. But in what way? What kinds of things?"

"So, this one time, he and Mrs. Brown were in the car after a dinner out. They came back to the car early but didn't tell me why. And I could tell from the conversation—not that I was listening on purpose . . ."

"Of course not!" exclaimed Tasha. "I could always tell what a really really good person you are. You're an upright guy, unlike so many of the drivers I knew."

I cringed a little at her effusiveness, but it worked. He visibly relaxed and started to speak more fluidly. "Yeah, so I overheard them kind of arguing because Seymour had punched a busboy. Mrs. Brown was upset."

"Really!" breathed Tasha. She leaned forward, lips slightly parted, boobs straining at her shirt. We had tried to downplay her ageless hotness, but it just came so naturally to her.

"Yeah. Apparently Mr. Brown punched the busboy because the guy took the bread away too soon. And the restaurant didn't even ask Mr. Brown to leave! I guess he was such a big deal, or maybe he'd done some accounting work for them or something. He decided he'd had it and just walked out. And I don't think Mrs. Brown would have felt comfortable after that."

"No, I don't think she would," Tasha murmured.

"And this other time?" Toddy continued. Tasha nodded. "We were stuck in traffic. Frustrating, right? Everyone's frustrated. This guy just leans on his horn. Mr. Brown gets out, walks back, right to the guy's open window, reaches in, and slams his head down against the steering wheel!"

"So he could really lose his shit," Tasha observed.

"Yeah," Toddy agreed.

"Ask abt gf in park slope," I texted, which autocorrected to "park sloop," but I figured she'd know what I meant.

This time I didn't even see Tasha glance down, but without missing a beat, she said, "I felt bad for Kim sometimes. We all knew Seymour had that girlfriend in Park Slope."

"Oh yeah, I remember her."

"What was her story?"

"Her name was Luisa de León. Hispanic. Gorgeous, just gorgeous. But very professional. Nice. Friendly, nice to everyone. I guess she had good self-esteem."

"Hmm, 'professional.' Do you know what her job was? Or is?"

Toddy scratched his head. "No, I don't know if I ever knew."

Tasha tented her fingers and perched her chin thoughtfully on them, as if she were listening to a great professor hold forth on *The Epic of*

Gilgamesh. "Was Seymour really into her? Or was she just, you know"—she shrugged and gave him a wry smile—"a side piece?"

"Oh, no," Toddy answered emphatically. "He was totally into her. He'd had other women, but never more than—I don't know—like a month or two. Once he started seeing Luisa, he went every chance he could. And he took her out to dinner and stuff. Broadway shows. He'd never done that with any of the others." For the first time, Tasha let a half second go unfilled. That was enough for Toddy to add, "Not that he would ever have left Mrs. Brown for her. He loved her in his own way, but one woman wouldn't cut it for him."

"Did you get the impression that Kim Brown really loved Seymour? Or was she staying for his money or for April?" Tasha asked. *Excellent!* I thought.

"She was in love with him, I think," Toddy said. "The older man, but not too old. Rich, important."

"Come to think about it, I did see Kim as a one-man woman," Tasha said thoughtfully.

"I mean, not that she'd talk to me about personal stuff, but you pick up a lot in that driver's seat."

"Totally! And you're a very perceptive guy. Oh, I forgot to ask. Do you happen to remember that Luisa's address?" Tasha asked, as if she knew she was asking too much of any human.

He shook his head, frustrated at coming up short for her. "I want to say Eighth Avenue, but who knows. At one point I could have driven there blindfolded." A truck on the highway behind him honked loudly, and he whipped his head around to see, revealing a more prominent bald spot than was visible from the front. He turned back and grinned awkwardly.

"Was anyone mad at Seymour?" I texted, and Tasha inquired. I already knew the answer he had given the police, but I wanted to see if he was still telling the same story.

Toddy had relaxed a bit since the beginning of the call, but he drew his shoulders up and together at this question. Tasha sat with a pleasant look, as if she'd asked him about the weather. "I got the impression some guys in the Mafiya weren't too crazy about him. But I don't know their names or anything about them. And don't forget Hose. Talk about angry!"

"Hose?" Tasha asked, her nose wrinkling in apparent confusion.

"Yeah, Hose. Hosea, his name was. Or is, I guess. He was Seymour's assistant, but not like a secretary. Really smart guy. He helped him with everything, running the business. But they fought sometimes, especially toward the end. I had the idea Hose thought Seymour might be cheating him somehow, but I don't know for sure. Anyway, one time I was pretty sure I heard him tell Hose that he thought the Russians were threatening him." This jibed with what Toddy had told the police. Now he hesitated, then went on. "I was driving both of them. Seymour was on the phone—remember those giant phones with antennas from the nineties? Anyway, it was an angry conversation with some clients. Then Seymour screamed into the phone, 'Why are you talking to me in Russian? I don't fucking speak Russian!' and handed the phone to Hose."

"Was Hose Russian?"

"No, he was like from the South. Said 'y'all.' But he spoke Russian. Part of how he was so helpful to Mr. Brown. Anyway, Hosea talks to these guys in Russian, in a calming kind of way. When he hung up, Seymour asked, 'Was that a threat? Were they fucking threatening me?' Hosea said no, they weren't. They were just looking for reassurance. Something like that."

Tasha widened her eyes. She was ten minutes into her career as freelance detective and she had already gotten more out of Toddy than the police had. Though Toddy's newfound openness may also have been due to the time elapsed since the murder and his diminishing fear of anyone involved. "Did Hosea seem upset by the phone call?" she pressed.

"Nah. But he wasn't the type to get upset, like, ever. Very cool guy. He spoke Spanish too, like a native."

"Cool how? Stylish? Charming? Jokey? Unemotional?" She looked at Toddy expectantly, and her lash augmentation made a graceful canopy—wide-eyed curiosity, but not the least bit girlish. *Good for you, Tasha!* I thought.

"I wouldn't really know about style or whatever. But steady, you know? Never laughing or yelling. Like a manager at the DMV or something."

I texted, "ask if he saw the house burning." This was a roundabout way of checking up on his alibi without seeming as if she suspected him in any way. If what he told the cops was true, he shouldn't have seen it.

She asked, and he closed his eyes as if trying to remember—though I would have thought that wasn't something you forget, even after twenty years. He opened them and said, "No, I'd been with my mom that night. Didn't see it until the next day. Amazing, the whole house just . . . evaporated. Who can imagine anything like that? I had nightmares after that for so long."

"I don't mean to upset you." Tasha put her hand over her heart in concern. "I lived nearby, so I remember seeing that empty space for a long time before it was rebuilt. It took a while before it stopped hitting me in that way."

"No, I'm not upset. Well, I guess you never really forget something like that. He wasn't the best boss I ever had, but believe me, there were worse. You know, okay for a boss. And she was the nicest lady. And that poor kid. It's just . . . these are bad memories."

Tasha oozed sympathy—"Of course! My God. You went through so much!"—and somehow in her capable hands it did not seem over-the-top. "Were you close to him? I mean, I know he was your boss and everything, so it's weird. Was he nice to you?" I mentally high-fived Tasha for asking the question before I could text it.

"I mean. He was okay. I definitely didn't want him dead or anything."

Tasha shook her head, eyes wide. *Of course not!*

"He said good morning, thank you, that kind of stuff. Really didn't seem to see me other than that." Toddy paused. "Mrs. Brown was the nicest, though."

"I know, right? I still miss her!"

He nodded. "She would let me come in the house and watch TV when I had a few hours to kill before picking up Mr. Brown again. So I wouldn't have to wait in the car."

I texted, "Seymour a good dad to April?"

"Was he nice to April?" Tasha asked smoothly. "I remember the kid totally. She was such a sweetheart. Quiet and so unbelievably smart."

"Yeah, she was great. Sweet is the right word. Not bratty at all, even though she was so rich. And Mr. Brown absolutely loved her. The sun rose and set on her, you know?"

"That's what I saw too. Did Kim—sorry, I mean Mrs. Brown. Don't take this the wrong way, but did Mrs. Brown ever flirt with you?" No response. "The only reason I ask is I think I remember her telling me she thought you were cute—a big guy, but so gentle and polite."

"Oh, no!" Toddy remained even-keeled, although he brought up one hand to his mouth to bite his nails. Each nail had a slender half circle of gray-brown dirt underneath, and I shuddered to think what germs he was ingesting. "I mean, I'm a guy who lives with his mom in the Bronx. Even if she wasn't such a straight shooter, she would have better taste than that."

"Do not ever sell yourself short, Toddy Mirante!" she instructed. After catching each other up on what else they'd done since that time, they said their goodbyes and promised to keep the other informed if they got any news.

Less than two seconds later, my phone rang.

"Oh my God, how'd I do?" she breathed.

I told her, with all sincerity, how amazing she'd been. That she'd gotten Toddy to let his guard down. That she'd gone over all the important points. That I felt I was getting to know some of the people involved in a more personal way, which was super important. Then I asked, "Why did you ask about whether Kim was flirting with him?"

"I don't know exactly. It just popped into my head. She seemed lonely and sad sometimes. And she probably didn't see any other men without

Seymour around. A girl like her would be happier knowing that other men notice."

"Yeah, that makes sense. Again, thanks so much. This was such a huge help."

"No problem!" she said brightly. "And you have to keep in touch with me and let me know what's going on. I'm invested now!"

I promised I would.

"And let me know if I can do any more detecting! I love this stuff!"

CHAPTER TEN

It was such a gorgeous morning that we were all in the backyard by nine thirty. My dad and I had decided to share some of the details of what we'd discovered. We wanted the whole family on our side, ideally cheering us on, if or when we decided we had to dash out in the middle of dinner or take a couple of days to do a stakeout.

Dad and I sat beside each other on an old English-style bench—the kind with an arched back and slats. I did most of the talking, my dad peppering my recitation with a few extra details I forgot to include. My mom, on a wooden deck chair, arranged her skirt around her knees as if she were expecting to be served elevenses. She'd already fluffed out her hair several times. Eliza was on the lawn in threadbare shorts and a SAVE THE TURTLES T-shirt that she'd either slept in or laundered at midnight. Josh was hunkered down on a footrest, his long legs forming an isosceles triangle with a missing base, though an intriguing apex. His judicial robe was neatly folded beside him on the grass because he had a ten o'clock argument on a motion, but he'd wanted to hear our progress report.

My dad said, "The cop heading up the case in New Brunswick, Ricardo Jones. At first he was all official, 'case in progress so therefore I can't reveal any details of our investigation to outsiders.' I gave him an argument—not nasty or anything. Got zilch from that. But I took him out to lunch, and we really talked. I got him to understand that I'm coming from a different place, from the historical angle, and I'm not trying to take over. He finally let a little hot air out of his balloon."

Eliza took this as an inadvertent fart remark and lowered her head. While that muffled any laughter, the rhythmic up and down of her shoulders gave her away. I'd noticed that today's high school kids—who had such mature social consciences, who would march against racism and for gun control—remained emotional nine-year-olds when it came to flatulence. Judge Josh narrowed his eyes and gave her a look that could mute a courtroom in a microsecond. But Eliza, head bent either to study the grass or recuperate from the giggles, missed it entirely.

My dad continued: "Jones didn't become my best buddy, but at least he gave me a rundown on what they had. He's the kind who knows that the more you talk, the more you can inadvertently give away. Listen, without a doubt he's getting pressure from the campus cops and his own command. But what the hell did he think I'd do, call the *Star-Ledger*?"

"Maybe," Josh said. "Not an unreasonable conjecture."

"I'll bet the Admissions Office was applying coercion as well," my mom remarked. She stretched out her neck, her pre-performance movement. The words that came out sounded ripe, sophisticated, like the voice-over for a luxury moisturizer. "They don't want to change their motto to 'Expect the unexpected at Rutgers.'"

"You said it." My dad winked at her.

"Was it worth the trip back to New Brunswick?" Josh asked Dad.

"Oh yeah. In person, he's looser. I got to see the footage from the campus police's CCTV that they'd copied and handed over to the New Brunswick cops. Not that I learned anything earthshaking. They really had done a thorough investigation."

"What was in the footage?" I asked.

"Nothing much except for a black SUV with tinted windows and taped-over license plates, front and back. It was clearly someone not used to driving on anything except asphalt. You might not realize it, but even the smoothest-looking incline has bumps and gouges. You could see the driver's elbows raised, turning the wheel back and forth the way a little kid does. But details like race, sex, age? *Gornisht.*"

"Height?" my mom suggested. "How close was his head to the roof of the car?"

"From the half second I saw when he wasn't bumping around, about average. But who the hell knows? He could have been slouching down. That could take away another couple of inches." He cleared his throat, then did it again. Ragweed or a pronouncement.

"So here's what I realized. Once the SUV got off the grass, the driver was okay."

Eliza raised her hand as if she were in class, and he nodded at her. "Like he was relieved," she said. "'Finally, a real road.'"

"Good point, kiddo," my dad said. "All I can tell you is that was my impression too, but there's no way to tell for sure. Once the driver hit the road, he took a pretty fast tour of that part of the campus. A pretty fast tour, but he got around. Made several turns. Got to a dead end and did a U-ie. So almost at the end of the on-campus footage, after the SUV got back on asphalt—four minutes, fifty-two seconds. When it came to getting out of Rutgers, this driver didn't know his ass from a hole in the ground."

Josh stood and, with what I could tell was sincere reluctance, announced, "I have to get on blah-blah-blah"—the program the federal judiciary used instead of Zoom. He'd said the name about fifty times, but the word or acronym had an odd ability to avoid being captured by my long-term memory. "It's interesting," he said. "In trials, probative evidence like this is admissible, though it's not objective evidence, like a fingerprint on the gun. When you're looking at a few seconds of video, even a frame, it's not necessarily reliable."

"What's probative?" Eliza asked.

"Proving or demonstrating something."

"It sounds skeevy."

"Depends on what you're proving," Josh said. They smiled at each other. Then he went on. "Film can be surprisingly misleading. They're still writing books about the Zapruder film of the Kennedy assassination." My mom leaned forward, as if she had a riveting opinion to express, but Josh skillfully avoided noticing her, stood, and picked up his robe. Then he double-timed toward the house.

I asked my dad, "Did you get anything else useful from Jones?"

"A list of people they ruled out, including the few kids April flunked because they stopped coming to class. And she told them about someone else she didn't mention to us, an alt-right guy who stood up and applauded after she showed them a clip from a silent film about the Ku Klux Klan—"

"*Birth of a Nation*," my mom said.

"Right. Anyway, she told the kid in professor-like language that she didn't put up with shit like that and he either had to control himself for the whole semester or drop the class. He dropped it. But he was alibied for the SUV day. He's been a flagger on a road repair crew since May. Has to clock in and out."

"And that's all they've gotten?" I asked.

"Well, they checked the fiancée-girlfriend who's in Japan, but no travel on her passport since she got to Kyoto. They didn't go any further because everyone they interviewed said she and April have a solid relationship."

"This isn't exactly an episode on Netflix," I said.

"Not even half a thrill," my dad replied. "According to Jones, they listened to April about the Vory. Naturally he said they didn't brush her off. But he said she had no names, no leads for them. They requested some records from the NYPD, but they hadn't gotten anything. Still, they could have pursued it more. You can't tell me people from New Jersey don't know from pushiness."

"Sounds like April's right. They've written off the arson."

"Yeah. I bought him lunch at a Pakistani restaurant and gave him an overview of the case over tandoori chicken legs. We talked about fucking budget cuts and how I was once where he's at now, not being able to do the one thing you're good at—your job. So we're Ric and Dan. At least I have someone in case I need anything else."

At my dad's request, we headed into the kitchen where it was air-conditioned. Eliza filled her bottle with ice water and said she had to get ready for her summer courses at the local community college. I guessed she wasn't as mesmerized by the details of the case as I'd thought, since

I knew her classes didn't start for three hours. She'd picked Intro to Chinese and a course about relativity and black holes. (When we asked her why, she'd shrugged and exhaled three weary syllables. We figured they were *I don't know*.)

My mom—what was left of our audience—took her hot water and sliced a lemon so thinly transparent that when she held it up over the cup, it looked indecent. I heated some ginger tea my mom had made a few days earlier, but instead of tasting like liquid wellness, it tasted more like water that had been hanging around in a faucet long enough to absorb every toxic mineral in the Long Island aquifer. I dumped it and grabbed a Coke Zero. My dad was in Manly Cop Mode, so he took a pod of the extra-bold and made a mug of black coffee that seemed to plop more than stream out of the machine. We sat around the kitchen table in a moment of comforting family silence. If that silence had possessed a voice, it might have said, *Isn't it great that it's just the three of us for a little while?*

My dad carefully cut out two pictures of Luisa de León he had just printed from her real estate company's website. I pinned them to our bulletin board, where we kept a visual track of the relationships among the people involved. Usually there was one person in the center of my boards. This time, there were two: Seymour and April.

My dad was creating a database entry for Luisa as I stared at her picture, rubbing my chin and tilting my head sideways, hoping to see her in a different light. I realized I must look like a Sotheby's art appraiser, so I straightened my head. She was professionally dressed in a pinstripe suit, her perfect manicure on display. Her only jewelry was a pair of tiny pearl earrings—no engagement or wedding rings. Her hair was long and dark and impossibly shiny, her eyes the color of darkest chocolate, and her smile open and welcoming. I was sure people had been telling her forever that she had adorable dimples. I could see how Seymour had fallen so hard. But her evident warmth ensured that women would find her engaging as well. I wasn't remotely surprised that she appeared to have been successful in sales.

Her website bio hinted that she represented high-end clients, which my dad and I immediately agreed meant that I had to call Wynne. He sat listening to my end while I dialed her and started pacing, as I often did on the phone.

Wynne first berated me for having left her last text on "read" for more than three hours now.

"I was with my family!" I protested.

"Oh, I see. Like being with your family and your kid is a priority." She laughed.

"I'm just warped that way."

"You're warped in many ways. So anyway, what's up? Or did you call to discuss the *Bridgerton* meme I sent?"

I filled her in on Luisa and asked if she knew anyone who might be able to tell me more.

"I mean, I know some guys in Hedge Fund Brooklyn, and I'll definitely get in touch with them, but you know what might be better?" she asked.

"Hmmmm?"

"She'll know who I am." Wynne said this with total assurance and not a trace of arrogance. "I'll call her, tell her you're my client and friend. Tell her you're tired of being a Long Island matron, that you want some Brooklyn in your life. That I want you to see one of the houses she's showing. That way, you can ask her some stuff, or maybe just get a feel for her. But that should be helpful, right?"

I nodded, then remembered I was on the phone. "Yes, definitely."

"Unlike most of the people you interview, I bet, she will do anything to keep the conversation going."

Most of the people? That would be unlike any interviews I'd conducted as an FBI agent, even with the loneliest of willing informants. I told Wynne to go ahead.

A couple of hours later Wynne texted me a Brooklyn address and a time when Luisa would be showing us the house. "She will already know how much your LI house is worth," said the text bubble that popped onto my screen, followed two seconds later by "and remember to dress as rich as you actually are, ffs!" with a diamond emoji.

I had done my best, even asking Josh if I could borrow Dawn's monstrously huge diamond earrings. He was saving them for Eliza when she was old enough.

"Of course!" he'd said, then cleared his throat. "You know, I could buy you serious earrings if you'd like."

"God no!" I replied, and immediately regretted my vehemence.

He seemed unfazed at my implicit insult of his first wife. "You seem to like more practical gifts," he observed, as if he were David Attenborough commenting on one of the attributes of a gazelle.

On the drive to the house, I fantasized about various possible futures in which Josh, Eliza, and I moved to Brooklyn. We would attend art gallery openings and museum exhibits, go to the opera, see offbeat theater productions. Every so often I'd remind myself how much I hated moving and that I couldn't force Eliza to leave her friends in high school. And then I'd tumble immediately back into my fantasy world and see myself jogging by the lake in Prospect Park.

I parked around the corner from the house we were going to see. Though the day was hot, the large, elegant old trees that lined the streets seemed determined to keep me cool as I walked. I sent them a message of thanks, since I'd been afraid I'd show up to meet Luisa with two giant sweat circles under my pits.

I turned onto what I was bizarrely imagining as "my block," as if I already lived in the house. I could see Wynne and Luisa chatting. Luisa turned toward me, and I waved my hand over my head like I was trying to direct an airplane or something. I reminded myself once again that I didn't have to be so eager to ingratiate myself—that I already had something Luisa wanted. Her cheeks crinkled into her charming dimples, and I felt as if we already knew each other. Her picture on the website had not been airbrushed. She was, like Tasha, beautiful and ageless. Unlike Tasha,

I could see no evidence of fillers or Botox or lifts. Wynne introduced us with a formality I wasn't used to from her.

"I know why you chose to look at this property," Luisa said knowingly in a throaty voice with a little laugh. Wynne smiled inscrutably, and I guessed she'd just chosen a random expensive house from Luisa's listed properties. Luisa glanced back at me and explained. "There are so many 1860s Italianate brownstones in New York, and many of them look like this on the outside. The acanthus brackets," she said, gesturing above the door, which was framed with leaf carvings.

I nodded knowingly, as if I already knew what acanthus brackets were and as if I hadn't already thought the house was unusually beautiful and stately.

"But people just gutted these brownstones. The eighties!" she said with dismay, and Wynne shook her head empathetically and clucked. "This house, though. It's different. One of the purest examples of the Italianate era I've seen. So many period details are preserved. I can't wait to show you!" She glanced at Wynne. I realized that she might be very interested in getting my commission, but she was far more interested in winning over Wynne, who could presumably bring her not only me but endless supplies of rich people who fretted about the period details of the Italianate era. But it struck me, too, that she really had passion for what she was doing.

She sailed up the staircase, and we followed. "Forty-two hundred square feet. And wait till you see the closet space! Usually you can't get that with preserved historical detail." Wynne murmured in sad agreement over the brutal trade-off between historical detail and closet space. "I just have to show you this," Luisa said excitedly to Wynne, her patter continuing as we stepped through the entranceway to what I guessed was the living room. The room was attractive in a *Downton Abbey* way, except it was overstuffed with quirky furniture. Tchotchkes concealed too many table surfaces and obscured the books on the shelves. Wynne started taking pictures of the fireplace for her records. I wandered over to a stuffed peacock. Its glassy eyes stared out of its blue speckled head as if it were anguished, realizing that it was taxidermied and would never again get to walk in a garden.

I sensed that Luisa was hoping for some sort of reaction from me, so I made a polite comment about the woodwork, which was indeed mind-boggling. Wynne smiled but murmured something about how there can be too obsequious an attention to period detail. Luisa quickly dialed back her Ode to Eras Past and began chirping cheerfully that going with a lighter, more modern color could bring some light in.

Although I knew perfectly well that sweet dimples didn't render someone incapable of murder, I just couldn't imagine that this bubbly Realtor leading us up the stairs into the second-floor bedrooms, gesturing excitedly at the sunlight coming through the stained glass transom and making pretty color patterns on the floor, could burn someone to death. On the other hand, I had trouble imagining her having a long-term affair with a married criminal, and I knew she had done that.

Though the house—minus the glut of contents—was beautiful, I found my fantasy life in Brooklyn fading. I had complained about our Long Island McMansion enough, both out loud and to myself, but I found myself thinking, *This isn't home to me.* I even missed Dawn's decorating style, which at least left space to move around in. I took a ton of pictures that I said I'd show Josh, and I asked all the potential homeowner questions I could think of, like how the heat worked and what the pipes were made of. I hoped I sounded serious enough about buying the house—about buying any house—that Luisa would want to continue talking to me.

Finally, Luisa regretfully noted that the homeowners would be back with their dog any minute, and we had to leave. As we stepped into the warm humidity of the day, I was racking my brain to think of a way to continue talking to Luisa. As it turned out, I needn't have bothered.

"Would you like to see any other places? I'm currently showing several properties of this caliber," she said, crinkling her eyes in the sunlight. I told her, truthfully, that I would like to, but my leg was hurting due to an old injury. I didn't mention that the injury was the one I'd gotten during my kidnapping the year before.

Luisa suddenly gasped in excitement. "I have a great idea!" Her level of excitement seemed on a par with what Ben Franklin's must have been when he felt the electricity through his key. "Let's go back to my place. You can get off your feet." She turned to Wynne. "And maybe you could give me some ideas on how you coordinate historical details with updated decor. Not that I'd ever think of asking you to do your work for free," she added hurriedly. "But I'd be glad to pay for just some broad outlines. I am such a fan of your lifestyles. My building is beaux arts, with a little art nouveau thrown in for good measure." Wynne would certainly have agreed to go to Luisa's house for my sake, but her eyes lit up at Luisa's description.

"I'd be happy to, but I hope you don't mind if I take pictures. Just for my idea books, nothing public." Luisa brightly agreed, giving us her nearby address.

I had less luck parking this time and wound up several blocks away from Luisa's. I paused in the car, fingering my LED flashlight amulet. This would be the first time I'd been so close to a possible suspect since my kidnapping. I mentally monitored my body for the physical expressions of my PTSD: no ringing in my ears, no flush of cold adrenaline in my legs. Normal breathing and heart rate. I did a minute of slow breaths just in case and headed over.

Once again, Luisa and Wynne had arrived before me. I started to jog a little, a precarious proposition with my sore leg and heels. Luisa waved her arms and shook her head, telling me not to rush. I slowed a little and came up beside them as Luisa was describing in elaborate detail the history of the house that was her home and office.

She invited us in and took us to her office on the first floor. It was entirely uncluttered in a way I couldn't manage even if I had a week's advance warning that the Queen of England was dropping by. And Luisa hadn't been expecting any company. The only thing on the desk was a sleek Mac laptop. "Would you like some hibiscus iced tea?" she asked us graciously.

We would. As Luisa left to get the tea, Wynne whispered to me. "See this thing here?" She tapped a credenza with an inlaid wood design of stylized parrots with snooty beaks. I nodded. "It's actually a filing cabinet. Nice piece. No lock. I'll get her upstairs. You stay down because of your leg. I'll try to talk really loud or something while we're coming back."

"Don't be too loud," I warned. Wynne gave me an *as if!* look.

Luisa brought back three tall glasses of red liquid over ice, each with a tiny mint leaf on top and a silicone straw, like we were in a restaurant. She placed a coaster on her desk, set one of the iced teas on it, and motioned me over while flipping open her laptop. "Corie, let me set you up here. You see these folders on the desktop? These are my current properties. Let me show you a couple. Not Manhattan, right?" No, no, I assured her. Only Brooklyn. Wynne, an inveterate Manhattanite since her first moment of adulthood, gave me a wry smile.

Luisa looked at my face closely, as if she were searching my skin for blackheads, and moved three of the folders in the center of the screen. "Flip through these and tell me what you think. Honest opinion!"

"Of course!" I said.

"Would you mind giving me a tour while she looks?" Wynne asked.

"Sometimes when you say 'the pleasure is all mine,' you don't mean a word of it. But this time, really, the pleasure is all mine."

I breathed a secret sigh of relief at how easy that had been. As they moved into the living room, embarking on an intense discussion of crown moldings, I immediately started looking through her computer files.

First I checked the websites of major banks, but she didn't have a saved password login to any of them that I could think of. She seemed to save her files onto Dropbox and not iCloud. I scanned through the files as quickly as I could. Mostly properties, it seemed, though I took a gander at a folder called EFILE and nearly choked on my hibiscus tea when I saw her declared income for 2019. I made a mental note to ask Wynne if it aligned with what a high-end Realtor could make. Another folder called INS had insurance information: car, home, two pieces of jewelry. A life insurance policy had a beneficiary named Valeria de León. I wondered if this was maybe a mom or a sister.

Her PHOTOS folder was split into "prop" and "pers." The personal photos went back to 2006, though I supposed I couldn't expect her to have digital photos of Seymour. There were thousands, so I started clicking on random pictures from each month. She seemed to travel to resorts with the same group of friends surprisingly often. In 2014 a guy started appearing in her pictures. He was about her age—five or ten years older than me—and superhot: brooding, with chiseled chin, luxuriant dark brows, and golden-skinned forearms that looked as if they were created by God to complement perfectly a white button-down shirt with rolled-up sleeves. Far too hot to be another sugar daddy like Seymour. In April 2017 a grinning Luisa was showing off a diamond engagement ring to admiring friends. And after November 2017, the guy wasn't in any more pictures and Luisa wasn't wearing a ring.

I heard them heading upstairs as Wynne said, "This oak!" I rushed over to the filing cabinet. It was indeed filled with file drawers, though they weren't the boxy file drawers I'd expected. They lay flat, as if they contained artworks rather than regular papers. The drawers were labeled with neat, tiny labels that made little immediate sense. One was 08BL, another was 98FLG. I guessed the first numbers were years and started flipping through ones that started with 9's. I gasped, suddenly remembering that I couldn't let the computer go to sleep, as it was surely password protected. I wouldn't have a good explanation for that. I ran back, moved the cursor around, and ran back to the files.

I was right—the first numbers were years, though I still had no idea what the letters meant. A lot of what was in there was memorabilia, not documents. A college transcript (she'd had a 3.6 GPA); a sheet of wallet-size class photos from high school, her chin resting unnaturally on her fist, one of the pictures cut out; about three hundred Christmas cards from 1993. I heard footsteps above my head and wasn't sure if they were on their way up or back down. I'd become so absorbed in looking that I lost track of time. I ran to the computer to touch the trackpad again and raced back, banging my hip against the table.

The drawer marked 95LJ3 was where I found them. A blank manila folder contained several official-looking documents. I saw Seymour's and Luisa's name on both of them. I whipped my phone out and started photographing them all without examining them, flipping through the pages as quickly as I could.

I heard Luisa ask in a louder voice than she had been using, "Do you take smaller jobs? I mean, not like whole lifestyles? Like personal image, clothes, hair, makeup?"

Though I hadn't yet snapped all the pictures, I hurried the papers back into the folder as I heard Wynne answer, "I used to, but these days I prefer a more holistic approach," as their shoes clicked near the top of the stairs.

And then, the familiar symptoms: the ringing in my ears, the shortness of breath. What a moment for my PTSD to come racing back. My heart pounded like it was trying to break through my rib cage. Back at the desk, I did what Dr. Greenblatt had taught me, attempting to force air through my nose while pinching it shut and bearing down like I had to poop. It worked. I could feel the symptoms receding, though my large intestine hadn't fully comprehended that the bearing-down thing was only a psychological maneuver.

When they walked back into the room, my head was still bowed while I exhaled through the O my mouth was making. And I was slightly bent at the waist.

"Oh my God, are you okay?" Luisa rushed to my side. Wynne looked at me, concerned and quizzical. I could tell she wasn't quite sure if I really felt bad or if I was playing Luisa in some way.

I looked up, my cheeks hot, and laughed. "I am so ridiculously sorry," I said.

"Don't be," said Wynne. "What's going on?"

"It's this new diet I'm doing. Intermittent fasting. I get light-headed sometimes."

A calm washed over Luisa's face as she nodded knowingly. "Oh, I've been there," she said, rubbing my arm as if we were close friends. "Remember that crazy lemonade diet? I fainted! In the subway! It was so embarrassing. I woke up while this huge guy was helping me onto a seat. And then I gained all the weight back in, like, two weeks." We chuckled together at the rigors of dieting. "Did you see any properties you like?" she asked hopefully.

CHAPTER ELEVEN

I stood in my home office, throwing out one page after another, while my dad admonished me to be careful and not throw away anything important.

"Okay, thanks," I told him. "My plan was to throw the important stuff away, but now that you reminded me, I'll only get rid of the irrelevant stuff." He huffed, picked a crumpled paper out of the recycling bin, and smoothed it out to see what I'd so thoughtlessly discarded. Then he crumpled it back up, tossed it, and sat heavily in my office chair.

The minute I'd gotten home, I'd printed out all my photos of the papers from Luisa's filing cabinet that I'd taken with my phone. Most of them were unrelated to anything we were looking for. An exam for an interior design course at Pratt Institute (she'd gotten an 87), car insurance papers for a 1992 Saturn, an expired warranty for a KitchenAid mixer. For someone so neat, Luisa didn't seem to get rid of very much.

I separated all the banking and legal documents and spread them on the desk so my dad could look at them at the same time. My heart thumped as I realized what was laid out right in front of me. "Check these out," I said, grinning and tapping two of them.

"What the hell . . . 'See More Brown'?" Dad read. "Oh God, like Seymour Brown." He shook his head. "And they called this guy a genius. Anyway, you had more cases with money laundering than I did. I need you to explain this to me like I'm five."

I was by no means a money laundering expert, but you couldn't do terrorism law enforcement without knowing some basics. One of the papers I showed him was titled "Articles of Organization" for a business called See More Brown, LLC. No names on that one, but the other page was a contract listing Seymour Brown and Luisa de León as owners. "LLC just stands for limited liability company," I said. "That's it. From what I remember, any business that's not a corporation can be an LLC. A dog-grooming operation, a check-cashing service."

My dad jiggled his leg impatiently while I found an ancient scrunchie in my pocket and took the opportunity to pull my hair off my face. "Anyway, an LLC can be a perfectly legitimate way to organize your business. You set up separate banking and stuff. That way you can keep track of your income and expenses. You pay taxes as a partnership, not corporate taxes. Most important, I guess, you're not personally liable if the business goes under. You wouldn't have to pay the business's debts with your own money."

My dad gestured toward the papers. "But this isn't a legitimate business."

"Presumably not, because Seymour wasn't a 'pillar of the legit business community' kind of guy. But we don't know that for sure yet."

"I hope it's not a legitimate business. Who would buy something from a company called See More Brown?" My dad's chin suddenly struck a thoughtful angle. "Unless it's a plumbing company . . ."

"I remember when you were the adult in the room."

"I decided to regress. So tell me, how would a guy like Seymour use this arrangement for an illegitimate business?"

"So, here's how it might work. See More Brown would not be intended to make money in the usual way. Like, it wouldn't make a product or provide a service."

"Okay."

"It would be what's called a shell company. Like, it's not a real company, with secretaries and an office suite in an industrial park or whatever. And it's not a nail salon on Main Street. It doesn't make profits. But even a shell company can be legit in many cases," I added. I saw I was losing my dad and decided to cut short my Josh-like digression enumerating the legitimate uses of LLCs. "A guy like Seymour, though, might open a business bank account for See More Brown and stash money there that he doesn't want anyone to know he has."

"Like the IRS."

"Yeah, or the FBI, or maybe even the Vory. His wife, for all I know. Also, the business can buy and sell stuff he doesn't want anyone to know he's buying and selling. Like if he wants to buy a car and doesn't want anyone to know he's buying it, he can do it with the business bank account."

"Makes sense. Diet Coke?" he asked, opening the mini fridge I'd recently stowed next to my desk.

"LaCroix," I said. "Not the coconut, it tastes like suntan lotion. Blech. Eliza loves it."

"I need caffeine." He handed me a grapefruit flavor, popped his Coke Zero, and settled back in the chair, waiting for more.

I had a few sips of my drink and continued. "Okay, so if you're Seymour and you're a proud co-owner of the new business See More Brown, you're not going to open the business's bank account at the local bank on the corner of Main Street. Or at Citibank or whatever. Because they are going to require information about the business, and it will be easy for anyone to see that it's your money. You'll do it . . ."

"Offshore!" my dad interjected, as if he'd gotten the Final Jeopardy answer.

"Right, offshore." Although I knew better, I always pictured an "offshore bank" as a booth set up on a white sand beach and staffed by an impossibly hot, shirtless, sun-bronzed stoner, offering piña coladas, puka necklaces, and checking accounts. "A lot of these offshore places—the Caymans and Bermuda and Switzerland—their banks have different rules than US banks. They don't require you to attach your name to the bank account, or they make your name hard to find. They don't make it as easy for the Feds—or anyone else—to discover that the million dollars that belongs to See More Brown, LLC, is really controlled by the guy named Seymour Brown."

"Got it."

"Though we—that is, the FBI, the SEC, FINRA—have gotten much better at tracing money than we were in Seymour's day. It's a lot more sophisticated now."

"Feds fuck up everyone's good time," my dad said with a lopsided smile.

"Always," I agreed.

"So if Luisa's name is on here, does that mean she's in on it? This matches her signature on other papers."

"Right, and she has copies of the paperwork, so it doesn't seem like he stole her identity or anything. She could be in on it, or he could have lied to her about what he was doing."

"So what did they use the company to hide?" he asked.

"That's what we need to figure out," I said, poking at him to oust him from my chair. He sighed with a drama that rivaled my mom's and settled on the couch while I sat in the chair so I could use the laptop for quick internet searches.

We were both startled five seconds later when Candy Crush music blared from his phone. "Sorry," he murmured, muting it.

It was about forty-five minutes later that I cleared my throat. He tore his eyes away from Candy Crush with some initial difficulty but then gave me his full attention. "So here's what I've got. It seems like See More Brown—the company, not the person—bought at least two properties. One of them is the Park Slope place where Luisa lived."

My dad got up and went over to the Luisa time line we'd created on our giant whiteboard. "This place?" he asked, pointing to a spot on the time line.

"Yeah," I said. "That one seems like a legitimate purchase. It was bought by the LLC in 1993 for one point seven million from a Mrs. Judith Steiner. I can't see much about Mrs. Steiner online, but that price seems similar to other stuff sold nearby at the time. Here's the thing, though." I paused.

"What?" he asked impatiently.

"It was a four-bedroom. With a dining room and a maid's room and a washer/dryer."

"So?"

"Is that the kind of place you buy your mistress?" I asked. "No matter what she does in bed?" He shook his head slowly as I continued. "That's an apartment for a family, not a mistress. I'm not really sure what to make of it. Maybe there's some scam I'm not seeing, but we know she really did live there."

"Maybe he told her he was leaving Kim and he was going to marry her and start a family," my dad speculated. "That's a lot of money to string along a mistress, though. He could have bought a luxury one-bedroom in Manhattan for less than that back then."

I tipped my chair back too far, spilling grapefruit LaCroix on the front of my pink T-shirt. "Crap!" I said, blotting the spill with a tissue. The tissue disintegrated into teeny strings, making everything look worse. I forced myself to let it go and focus on what Luisa and Seymour, adulterous nineties couple, were thinking. "Maybe he told Luisa he was leaving Kim, and he meant it."

My dad raised his eyebrows at that. "What's the other property?" he asked.

"That's the fishier one," I answered happily. "1434 Bell Street."

"Less fancy neighborhood," he observed.

"Much," I replied, handing him some documents. "But look. The company bought it for two point eight million in July 1994. The building includes two apartments and a ground-floor store, but still. They're small, and it's not a great neighborhood. That was way too much money. They sold it a few months before Seymour died. Nine hundred and seventy-five thousand dollars."

My dad smacked the papers with the back of his hand. "This is always confusing to me," he complained. "How does he make money when he spent way too much on the place and sold it for less?" He glanced around, as if hoping his Global Econ professor from college was hiding behind my desk and would pop up and make it totally understandable.

"The short answer is that he and the building's seller were both in on the scam. Both of them knew the building wasn't worth that much. This is why they did it: Let's say Seymour has a client who suddenly has big-time cash on his hands. Drugs or whatever. The client can't just deposit it in his personal bank account without raising a ton of questions."

My dad waved his hand in irritable beckoning circles, as if to say, *Yeah, yeah, I understand this, get to the point.*

"So Seymour puts that money into the Caymans account. The Caymans bankers don't ask annoying questions about where the money came from." Dad inclined his head, and I continued. "But the client wants to start spending that money. He can't drive over to Costco with a Caymans debit card, right? So here's how Seymour solves that problem. One of his LLCs, like See More Brown, uses that Caymans account to pay too much for something. Like a building. Now that two point eight million is in the seller's bank account and they can use it. And if anyone asks where all that money came from, they can just say, 'I sold this real estate. A totally legit transaction.'"

"So the seller they bought the place from would have to be in on it," my dad hazarded.

"Absolutely," I said. "That's the person who is going to get to use the money. So that's probably the client, or a close associate."

He looked at the papers in his hands, and his eyes brightened. "The seller is Clifford Shapiro!"

"You know who he is?"

"Vaguely. He's a Vory hanger-on. Or was. Don't know what he's doing these days. I'm sure I could find out."

"We'll have to," I commented.

"Anyway, what happened to the nine hundred seventy-five thou they got when they sold the building?"

"I'm not sure. It might have still been in the offshore bank account."

"So when Seymour was killed, his and Luisa's LLC had a family apartment worth almost two mil and maybe another mil in the bank. What happens to LLC money when one of the owners dies?"

"It depends," I said, grabbing the LLC operating agreement and scanning it. "So, yeah. Look! There's a clause here saying that if either of the LLC members dies, the other has the right to buy the shares from their estate. I mean, the clause is a page and a half, but that's the essence."

"So Luisa got the money."

"As far as I can tell. Yes."

Our eyes met.

"So Seymour died, and then she started her dream business," he murmured.

Toyota, Chevy, Polaris blue, Arctic silver. It never mattered what the colors were called. My dad's cars were always such a dull gray they looked like his grandfather's first act on coming to America had been to buy gallons of the dullest-color paint from the Sears Roebuck catalog. It turned out to be perfect for a stakeout vehicle; this gray was so dreary your eyes immediately sought something brighter. Sure, there was a voice that tinkled in your ear *unmarked police car*, but your senses were so dulled you couldn't hear it. And the worst of it was, he bought it because he liked it, not because he wanted to fly under the radar.

So there I was, across the street and one house back from Luisa de León's town house, grayed out. I'd driven to Brooklyn in my beloved red Outback—admittedly not a car for a stakeout. But it gave my dad a chance to take my car back to Long Island, have a shower, a meal, and his mug of milk and honey before a long sleep. Then he'd be raring to go. He had a much higher tolerance for surveillance than I. And Luisa would recognize me if she caught a full view of my face.

It wasn't an urgent stakeout in response to a crisis. We just wanted to get a sense of how she lived. *Anything oddinary*, as Eliza would say. Five buff guys ringing her bell at midnight? Others having a key to her front door or basement entrance? Flat pizza boxes so heavy the delivery guy's knees buckled, and you wondered, *Pepperoni and meatballs? Uranium-238?*

My dad and I both knew that a stakeout in such a quiet neighborhood was unlikely to pay off big-time. In the sixteen hours he'd watched her, Luisa had gone out twice. The first time, a town car pulled up to her house and took her to a high-rise in Dumbo overlooking the East River. Even if she was checking out an immense duplex, how long could that take? Though my dad didn't know real estate, he knew how his city worked. He estimated an hour and a half: look, haggle, pretend to walk out, haggle some more, then finally list. He came in ten minutes under.

The car then took her to a fancy Italian deli, where she spent fewer than ten minutes, emerging with a shopping bag and a bouquet of flowers. After that, back home. The other time she'd gone for what he called a run in Prospect Park an hour before sunset; since he had been able to keep her in sight, it was more likely a brisk walk.

Meanwhile, I tried a couple of Bureau databases I'd used a year earlier and found one that still accepted my username and password. The Bureau had a reputation for being digitally challenged, even when cyberlover Mueller had been director. And the last administration's Justice Department had put politically appointed Lapel Pin People in charge. The mementos of their tenure were chaos and forty-nine-inch LED-lit monitors on too many desks.

But I didn't have to challenge the system too hard . . . or call my DEA ex-boyfriend to come to my rescue. Researching Luisa's background did not seem to require anyone with a top secret clearance. Other than her initial ventures with Seymour, Luisa seemed to have remained untainted in what was usually considered an exceptionally grubby business.

Her life was all out there, easy to track: after Seymour was killed, she became sole owner of the properties. And with Brooklyn becoming an object of universal desire, she sold her Park Slope family four-bedroom, paid all taxes due, and began buying and rehabbing other apartments in the neighborhood. According to a four-year-old piece on her in *Breukelen* magazine, after a couple of years, the thrill she got from her own ingenuity—a six-bottle refrigerator above a built-in wine rack below the shelves of the book nook she had magically created in a two-bedroom apartment!—turned into a yawn. She stopped investing in fixer-uppers and focused solely on being a real estate agent.

Word of her indefatigable efforts on behalf of her clients spread from wealthy Latinos, her first clients, to all of moneyed Brooklyn. Luisa's turf was the whole borough now. She showed her clients grand new condos in Williamsburg, brownstones in Park Slope, Victorians in Flatbush, brick town houses in Brooklyn Heights, Dutch Colonials in Bay Ridge. Nearly everyone called her a pleasure to deal with.

In the entire twelve hours I spent on her relatively quiet street, she remained inside. There were no visitors, no ring-and-bring drug couriers, no meals delivered. A couple of times I climbed over the seat to the back, hunkered down under an old rain poncho, and peed into a female urinal. (I hadn't done that often enough in my law enforcement life to be truly pristine at it. However, my sneakers and my dad's floor mats remained dry, so I called it a win.) Followed by much Purell. Several bites of turkey wrap, sips of iced tea. I read part of *Embrace on Brooklyn Bridge*, an Arabic-language novel.

It seemed ridiculous to be spending time trying to get a handle on someone whose life seemed so open. But with one scratch of a match, Luisa had gotten enough capital to finance her life's work. Horrible serendipity? Or had she lit the flame? Seymour must have thought himself so clever, inserting a clause that would guarantee him full ownership should anything happen to Luisa. Instead, vice versa.

It was possible that Luisa was still involved with the Vory. High-end real estate was still an effective way to launder money. But she sought publicity for her career, which she'd avoid if she were a criminal. And it was significant that she sold properties to named individuals, not shell companies; the prices seemed commensurate with similar properties. For her, offshore money would mean buying a condo in Isla Verde for her parents' winter delight.

About an hour and a half before my dad was due to take over, I called him. "We could spend weeks here," I said, "and watch her do the same thing. If she's into anything criminal, she's going to be doing it virtually."

"Funny," he said. "When I didn't hear from you, I said to myself, 'Either Corie is onto something big or she's bored but forgot how to talk on a phone.'"

"I just remembered how to talk on a phone now." I paused long enough to clear my throat from whatever allergen was having a night out in Prospect Park. "Do you want to meet me here and take over the surveillance, or should we pack it in?"

"Come on home," he said reluctantly. "If there's something to get, you're right. It would be online, and we can't—Fourth Amendment and all that crap. Fine—it's not crap."

After a two a.m. drive home on an almost-deserted Grand Central Parkway, I showered, gave Lulu a belly rub since she was lying on her back on the bath mat and blocking my exit. Then I climbed into bed with Josh. He smelled of lime, musk, and clean pajamas. I did hear a murmur of "I love . . ." but if the next word was "you," I was already asleep.

The following evening, while I was wiping down the counters and Josh was loading the dishwasher, I asked whether juries had trouble understanding money laundering. He said that the lawyers actually took such pains to explain the alleged dodge that except for the one or two jurors who'd been nodding off throughout most of a trial, the majority seemed to get it—until they left the courtroom to deliberate. After a few hours, his bailiffs reported fists banging on the table, yelling, crying, which sometimes led to a hung jury.

Josh said they usually understood the big idea: any disguised monetary transaction was money laundering. But precisely how that was done was often too much for them. No matter how many explanations he sent back to them, they couldn't get their heads around the complexity of the maneuvers—an onshore money market account to an offshore bank to shares listed on the Tokyo Stock Exchange to real estate in Geneva.

"You know," Josh said, "Seymour's murder—and his wife's—is somewhat analogous to money laundering." He placed his beloved yellow scraping spatula in the top rack and closed the dishwasher with his hip. His "somewhat analogous" augured a conversational mood. Actually, a pontificating mood, which meant me listening while he used snore-inducing words like "pretextual." I began to regret asking and disguised a yawn by compressing my lips, even though I knew it would bring forth even more yawns. Handsome men—whether judges, geologists, or porn stars—had grown up with appreciative audiences. He simply assumed I was ready for him to continue. "All right . . . Think about a felony-murder charge, an intentional killing while committing some other crime."

"Okay," I said.

"Arson is a similar kind of crime. It can be deliberately confusing, meant to conceal evidence of the crime—the victim, the perpetrator, and the motive. That's why it's so much harder to make a case or get a conviction."

"Josh," I said, taking his hand, large and warm and still a little damp.

He held my hand against his chest, and I could feel the crinkle of hair under his cotton shirt. But he would not be dissuaded from explaining. "I wonder if there's something about the SUV attack that's similar. Maybe it's not a straightforward attack, but something meant to sow confusion."

I started to lead him upstairs. "Yeah. I need to know what the SUV driver was trying to accomplish. Death? Terror? Money? If they wanted April to part with information she's been holding back since she was five years old—which doesn't exactly cause me to be in awe of their intelligence—they could have held her at gunpoint in her own house. Or kidnapped her." I took a deep breath and let it out slowly through puckered lips. "On the other hand, maybe it was an egregious error and they were actually trying to run over someone in the Anthropology Department."

CHAPTER TWELVE

Now that we had a much better—if still incomplete—understanding of the older crimes, it was probably time for my dad and me to focus our efforts more directly on identifying the driver who had gone after April.

Lulu came to my side of the bed a little before six a.m. and made a pathetic sound somewhere between a whimper and a harsh bark of outrage. I peered over the edge of the mattress to see what was going on. She had a wild expression that looked less like her dog parents and more like her distant wolf forebears: *Fuck you and your housebreaking*. Rather than risk a mess on the rug, I pulled on yesterday's jeans and a cami so boxy and shapeless I could get away without a bra.

Outside, Lulu did her business and bounced along for three steps at a time, then sniffed whatever delight was nearest her nose. I gently urged her with the leash, but with a quick turn of her head, she planted her paws in place and stared past me, head raised, muzzle open. An amazed look, as if God had appeared in the distance—but I could see nothing that was out of place. She stretched out her short front legs and did a full-on downward dog, just in case. Then she seemed to forget whatever it was that she'd found so compelling, and we continued on our way.

Even though the plastic surgeon who'd fixed my leg as best she could assured me that it was okay to run, I was still apprehensive that the fourteen-inch skin graft would drop off like some skanky, long-forgotten Band-Aid. I decided a brief jog would hit the spot and held the knotted plastic poop bag in my left hand. After a WTF moment, Lulu not only kept up with me, she pulled me along, her tiny legs blurry with motion. I hadn't run braless since sixth grade, and my boobs felt like a pair of maracas in a salsa number.

I couldn't get the case off my mind. I was hesitant to suggest to my dad the plan that had been forming in my mind: that we revisit Jersey. He had done more than due diligence there so recently, cultivating relationships with the local police and shelling out for Pakistani chicken legs. But it seemed like our most promising next step.

Inside the house, I unhooked Lulu's leash, scooped some kibble into her bowl in her nook near the back door, and walked into the kitchen to wash my hands. "I'm thinking we should go back to New Brunswick," I announced.

"For what?" my dad asked. He was the only one awake so far. I headed to the coffee carafe and held it up questioningly. He nodded wordlessly: yes, the coffee was freshly made. As I poured my cup, I could hear Lulu snarfing down her food, her registration tag clanking against the bowl. Grabbing my usual no-brainer breakfast, a banana and the jar of peanut butter, I sat next to him at the table.

"First and most importantly," I said, "we need to update April about Luisa. It's a significant lead in her case. It's also a sensitive topic, her dad cheating on her mom; I think it would be better if we broke it to her—and showed her Luisa's picture—in person." Dad nodded, and I continued. "Also, I dug up an old FBI checklist we used to use when we interviewed witnesses to assess whether a crime was committed by a stalker or a random maniac. I don't expect it to be especially illuminating, but it's possible it could stir up some of her memories that might be useful for us."

My dad agreed to go, more readily than I had expected. "I can show her my Russians!" he exclaimed.

"I thought one of them was Moldovan."

He waved his hand, as if he could not concern himself with picayune details. Several days earlier, while going through the case files, he'd discovered a handwritten note on a random piece of torn-off yellow lined paper. It wasn't his handwriting, and he wasn't quite sure whose it was. The note said that while all of Seymour's clients must have been upset that the money he was laundering was now beyond their grasp, it was rumored that two Vory members, Alexei Buga and Vovka Kravtsov, had been beyond upset, enraged to discover that with Seymour's death, they weren't able to access anything. Probably millions.

We both thought it unlikely that they would hurt April now, even if they knew about the money she'd inherited and believed it was "rightfully" theirs. It's not as if killing her would let them get their hands on it. But they were known to be way more vicious than the average Vory psychopath, and we didn't exactly have a plethora of leads. So we'd agreed to follow up. Dad hit up Gabriel Salazar again and wound up with a couple of recent mug shots: Alexei and Vovka were popular with the cops, go-to suspects for particularly barbarous crimes.

A couple of hours later my dad called April and asked if we could get together. No answer to whodunit yet, but we'd found some bits and pieces we wanted to run by her. He said he would stop at the Italian deli and bring sandwiches or salads down to New Brunswick so she didn't have to fuss. We could sit out on her porch and go over the case. She must have offered to provide us lunch, because he said, "People from New Jersey never realize that we have just as good Italian food on Long Island. Maybe better. We're bringing it just to show you." It was the first time I'd heard him talking up Long Island rather than Queens. He hung up, looking satisfied. "She wants a classic Italian sub, no oil and vinegar, because it will make the bread soggy. She said she can add it there."

"I love seeing the two of you together," April told us as she ushered us into her cheery, welcoming house. "Your whole father-daughter thing."

"We are really lucky," I said, still mindful that she didn't have the same.

My dad patted my shoulder affectionately. He turned to me and said, "Maybe we could start with your checklist thingy."

"Sure!" April said. "But is it the kind of thing you can ask me while I get us ready to eat? I'm starving."

I said that was fine and followed her through her living room, with its tall fireplace and nappable couch. I noticed on my right a slightly open door that had an old-fashioned faceted glass knob, and I glanced in to see a room whose windows were covered by heavy black curtains. "What's in here?" I asked, trying not to sound like I was thinking, *Weird, to say nothing of suspicious.*

"Oooo," she said, clearly excited to show us. "This is my baby. Come look." She flipped on a light and ushered me into a small room with forest green walls. It was dominated by a screen at one end, which faced six welcoming chairs, in two rows of three. "It's my screening room. As you can probably tell, if I had to choose between this and my kitchen, I'd order in three meals a day. I had this room built from a chunk of the living room, which was huge for the house anyway. And I stuck in a guest bathroom by taking a slice out of the kitchen, so I wouldn't have to go too far when I was watching Branagh's *Hamlet.* Four hours!"

"This is awesome!" I said, plunking myself into one of the chairs and staring at the screen, as if I expected a movie to start flickering across it. My dad stood in the doorway, leaning against the jamb.

"Right?" she said. "So I can watch TV or anything in here. But I also have a film projector. There's just a quality that real film has that you can't capture with digital." She gestured toward the back of the room, and I swiveled around to see a wall with a glass square cutout and a small door that I initially thought was a cabinet door. On second glance, I saw that it had a keypad lock. "Some of the reels are worth a mint now, so the insurance woman said I needed a serious lock."

April opened it as I popped out of my seat to peer over her shoulder. The projection space was surprisingly tight, dominated by a large gray metal projector next to a stool. Film reels were packed from floor to ceiling, though they looked organized and had labels in tiny, neat handwriting. An awesome collection: I was jealous and told her so, my dad nodding his agreement.

In the kitchen, she poured us iced tea, unwrapped the sandwiches we'd brought, and put them on plates. I began the checklist. She gamely answered my questions: Anything vandalized—from a knocked-down mailbox to the standard vicious message sprayed on a garage door? Dents in her car? Hang-ups or threatening calls? Neighborhood dogs barking in the night? Odd smells? "I wish I could be of more help," she said. "But no. Nothing."

I loved that even though the plates she had set at the table in her dining room didn't match, they each had an olive-y green as part of their pattern and they somehow all worked together. Even though we were in New Jersey, the Mezzogiorno seemed very close. She offered us a drizzle of oil and balsamic vinegar, which my dad accepted and I declined, and she decorated her own sandwich with them.

I commented that the paintings on the wall—a series of portraits of women, all with striking, bold, flat colors—looked like they were all painted by the same artist. April, delighted that I'd noticed, explained that her fiancée, Misaki, had a background in visual arts and still liked to paint as a hobby. The portraits were of some of April's favorite female movie characters, including Cher in *Moonstruck* and Pam Grier in *Foxy Brown*. I said truthfully how good the paintings were.

As we ate, my dad attempted to extract an admission from April that Long Island Italian was indeed as good as New Jersey Italian. She pretended to demur. On my father's howl of faux outrage, she laughingly said that it was as delicious as any she'd had.

We sat for a few minutes, eating more than talking. Eventually my dad paused and took a long slurp of iced tea. Then he leaned in to speak to her quietly, almost as if I weren't there. "You and your father . . ." He swallowed hard, which meant he was about to say something corny. He could do it as a father or husband, or sometimes a friend. As a cop, he did it reluctantly, only when the need for bonding outweighed his aversion to the mockery of his peers. "You didn't have him for long, but the two of you had a great beginning." April's eyes grew shiny, and she blinked hard. "I remember, right off the bat," he went on, "when I was first assigned to the case, how everyone I interviewed said how devoted he was to you. It wasn't in answer to a question, either. It's what people remembered about him."

"Maybe people remembered that because it was the only good thing about him they could think of." She looked him straight in the eye as she spoke, almost like a challenge: *I dare you to get mushy.*

"Maybe," my dad said. "I wouldn't call him"—he searched for a word—"beloved. But the good news is, you were."

"I thought he was the best man in the whole world," April said. "After he was killed, those first few years, I started picking up bits of conversation. So by the time I was eight or nine, in Kentucky, I knew that 'best' wasn't such an accurate adjective. I tried to figure it out."

"Not so easy at that age," I commented.

"It wasn't. What I decided in the end was that I was a one-off to him. Special. It wasn't only that he was good to me, he wanted to be with me. I don't ever remember him being aggressive or argumentative with anyone else when he and I were together. I gather he wasn't like that in other situations."

"Was it just you and your dad who were close?" I asked. "Did he bring your mom in at all?"

April closed her eyes for a few seconds. "I guess . . . I know we did things as a family. Recently, since the whole thing with the SUV, some memories have come back. I assume they're memories, not mini-scenarios I've concocted to comfort myself."

"You don't have to curate them," I assured her. "Memories, imaginings. It doesn't matter. We're not looking for testimony as much as something that'll give us a clearer slant on things."

"Okay. Well, I remember being at the beach and him angling the umbrella so my mom had shade. And another time, being in a rose garden with them, which must have been the Brooklyn Botanic Garden. He was taking a video of me and my mom running around and smelling different rosebushes, inhaling as deep as we could. We were laughing a lot. I have a feeling he must have had a VHS camcorder, but who knows. I did one of my grad student papers for a Film and Finance seminar on how VHS beat out Betamax, so maybe I'm paying homage to my own research."

My dad gave her an encouraging smile, but as she'd just taken a bite of her sandwich, she shook her head, chewed some more, and said through the provolone and Genoa salami, "That's it."

I guessed she would give anything to watch that scene in the rose garden play and replay. If only that one cassette hadn't burned, she could have caught a glimpse of her early childhood.

"Mmmm, this sandwich," she said, resting it on the plate but not letting go of it. "You know, for the first few years after the fire, between going to a psychologist and being with my grandma—cooking and watching game shows and going to church—I learned how to distract myself from thinking about it. It really helped, along with what I suppose is natural resilience. The downside is that willful amnesia cut me off from the first act of my life."

"I'm glad you kept up with my dad," I said. "He always cherished your Christmas cards." "Cherish" wasn't a Dad verb. But April struck me as someone open to emotion and occasional schmaltz; you couldn't specialize in American movies during the mid-twentieth century without a willingness to tolerate sappiness.

"I loved his cards too," she said. "Until I was a teenager, he sent me the Peanuts ones. He signed his name in cursive and, next to the picture of Charlie Brown, he drew a stick figure of a girl in a skirt, with my braids, and printed underneath them in tiny letters, 'Charlie Brown and April Brown.'"

"Besides my dad, was there anyone else from your first act who contacted you?"

"My grandma told me much later that a year after I came to Kentucky, someone from Social Services in New York sent a form to her and one to my psychologist, to check that I was okay and still in treatment. Some formality before closing the case."

I saw my dad take out his notepad, scribble something, and immediately return to his lunch. He was a no-pork guy, so he'd opted for mozzarella and tomato with basil after deciding that his usual eggplant parm wouldn't survive the trip well.

"Anyone else?" I asked. "Maybe a neighbor from Brooklyn . . . or the parents of one of your friends from school helped them write to you?" I paused, then apologized. "No. This is terrible, interrogating you when we should be stuffing our mouths."

"So let's keep eating," my father decided. April, who had never totally stopped, gave him a thumbs-up. She ate in enthusiastic bites, stretched out her legs and crossed her ankles before tucking them underneath her. Her no-show white socks had a bright stripe of chartreuse just below the ankle. She looked more undergraduate than tenure-track, and I was sure she was carded every time she went to a bar where she wasn't known. Nevertheless, there was also something commanding about her; whoever stood by the bar door grumbling "ID" over and over would add "please" when April came in.

We cleaned up lunch in about five minutes. "I was asking if anyone from New York—besides my dad and whoever from Social Services sent the form—got in touch with you. Your friends from school, friends of your parents?" She gave it some thought, then shook her head. "I know how young you were when you got to Kentucky, met your family for the first time. But did any of them ever mention mail being forwarded to you by the post office? Even an invitation to a kid's birthday party?"

"No. Growing up, I half expected a miracle card from heaven on a couple of my birthdays, but I never got one. That sounds pathetic. But it probably came from the fact that even though my grandma was born in Kentucky, she was still very Irish Catholic and a believer in miracles. Like telling me Saint Brigid was personally watching out for me. Later, when I started thinking about coming out to her, I decided it would make it easier for her if I told her I thought it was God's plan for me. At some level, I felt she must have sensed I was a lesbian right from the get-go. Brigid is such a feminist saint. Anyway, to answer your question, no, I never got anything from New York."

"Would your grandma have told you about someone connected with the mob or an associate of your father's trying to contact you? Not when you were five, but as you got older?"

"She was very protective of me. Part of it was what I'd been through. But the other—I'm guessing at this—was who my parents were. Right before I went off to college, she told me about what my mother had been like as a kid, how she kept running off to be with older men who could show her a good time. She admitted that she was sorry she'd been too strict, partly because my mom was so gullible. And when she ran away and didn't come back, my grandma said she was devastated. She felt if she hadn't been so harsh, my mom might have stayed. Of course, she never found out about their marriage and my father till after their deaths. But she once commented that for my mom, he must have been the ultimate Mr. Good Time."

"Between the time your mother left for good and the date of your parents' marriage license was four months," my dad told her. "So it didn't take her long to find her type of man." He reached into Josh's old litigation bag, which he'd borrowed for the day, a squared-off leather case large enough to hold handfuls of files. He drew out a folder and showed her a copy of Kimberly and Seymour Brown's marriage license. Legit, signed, and sealed. Well, not so legit: right on the certificate it said age 18. She'd been sixteen.

April looked at it for a moment and then said, "Oh my God! She was just a girl. I never completely processed that. And my dad was thirty-four!" She was wearing a Henley T-shirt, and she clapped her hand over the three buttons. Then she shook her head as if to clear it. It was a move made by someone who must have seen the thousand films in which actors responded to shocking news, but it seemed sincere. "And you still haven't found any family for him?" she asked.

"No," my dad told her. "Even though a lot of backup information for professional licensees has been digitized, what we found in our search for Seymour Brown is basically what we found during the first weeks after his death. His certified public accountant's license is registered with the New York State Department of Education. That's required. It says he's a graduate of Pace University. The state has a lot of requirements, including an official college transcript. But there was no record of him at Pace back then, no record now."

"Lots of people lie about their histories," I said. "They give themselves college degrees, brilliant internships, awards for public service. But if you dig a little, you usually can find some record of where they were during the four years they claimed to be at Yale—or Pace. But there's no trace of your dad anywhere; it's as if a person with the name Seymour Brown sprang into existence the day he applied for his CPA license."

April nodded, but she hugged herself and rubbed her arms as if the temperature had dropped twenty degrees. "I'm really okay talking about this," she assured us.

My dad grinned at her. "Even as a kid, you were pretty unflappable—that's one of those words you read but never use, and here I am using it." His face fell into seriousness. "What we don't know about your father could fill a library. I could see the cold-case writing on the wall a week after the fire, because the man—husband, father, homeowner, CPA—was missing in most of the places you normally look. I sent a cop on desk duty over to the Municipal Building to check for all first-name Seymours born on the day he usually used as his DOB. I thought maybe he changed his last name from something ethnic to Brown. Just one other Seymour born on that date. Last name was Davis, and he co-owned a fish store in Washington Heights."

"It's not like he was the invisible man, but in a way he was—" I said.

I knew I'd inadvertently made a film allusion, because April managed a half smile. "If you haven't seen the 1933 original, you should," she said. "Anyway, sorry to interrupt."

My dad had obviously seen the movie, and the sudden brightness in his eyes signaled that he was about to follow her digression. I spoke before he could open his mouth. "He really was a CPA," I told her. "A Seymour Brown took the exam that's required, a big one that's in four parts. You needed a seventy-five, and all his scores were in the nineties."

"So not a complete fraud," April said.

"Not at all, in terms of his having the qualifications to do what he did. People taking that test had to sign in when they went into the exam room, and his signature was comparable to the one he used in his practice. And back then, you needed to work under the supervision of a licensed CPA before you even took the exam, and he had: a solo practitioner whose clients were in the plumbing supply business. That guy died of cancer about three years after your dad went out on his own."

"So he sort of busted out of Zeus's head like Athena, except as a full-fledged accountant," April said.

I nodded in agreement. "It's still possible that Seymour Brown was his actual name and somehow the birth wasn't recorded in the city and we didn't find any possibles in all the databases. But if his name was something else, he still was born somewhere. He had parents, but we don't know anything about them. We know he married your mom and had you." April looked downcast, so I continued. "And you know he adored you. He also respected your mind, took you to the library, to the movies every week. You had a father who not only loved you but enjoyed your company."

I was congratulating myself on how well I had lifted her mood when the breeze shifted and floated through the open window and I got a whiff of some lovely flower scent. If I closed my eyes, I could picture myself reclining under a palm in Marrakesh. April asked, "Anybody feel like coffee? Tea?" and soon I was sipping a giant glass of iced coffee with enough sugar and half-and-half to qualify as dessert. My dad opted for hot coffee. April sat back down with a can of Diet Coke.

"You know," she mused, "the only time I feel sadness about my parents is when I realize that all I have are memories—and maybe some of those are faux memories. When you showed me the copy of their marriage license, I saw my mom's signature for the first time. The *y* in Kimberly had an extra little loop at the end. Feminine, playful. It was great to see, but I wish I had something of hers. I'm not a jewelry person, but maybe a locket or a silver cross on a thin chain. I picture that as her style, though for all I know she could have gone for a giant gold necklace, like the ones Elizabeth Taylor wore in *Cleopatra*. Or if I could have the framed picture of her and my dad that I think she kept on her nightstand. And I wish I had something of his, too. I pictured him as having a serious watch—expensive, but not gaudy. Or some favorite book that he wrote his name in."

"So you've never seen a picture of your mom as an adult?" I asked.

"No. Oh, I'm so glad you mentioned it! I almost forgot. When all this started, I asked my grandmother if she still had photos of my mom when she was a teenager. She sent me copies. Hang on while I get them." She ducked into the living room and reemerged less than thirty seconds later, carrying an orange tote bag that said DAMN THESE HEELS LGBTQ FILM FESTIVAL, which I had to admit was cooler than my FBI ACADEMY QUANTICO VA duffel. She pulled out a couple of photos, five-by-eights, and handed one to me and one to my dad.

I studied teenage Kim's school picture, then looked up at April. They both had exquisite eyes, blue with a touch of green so they looked made of turquoise. Except Kim's had every kind of makeup you can put on eyes and lashes; her hair sparkled from the spray she used. April wore only a touch of mascara or was just blessed with thick brown lashes. Dad and I exchanged photos. The other was of Kim and two other girls, their arms around each other's waists, posed like every other picture of girlfriends since the invention of the camera. Again, lots of makeup and much blond hair—though on all three of them. Kim's mouth turned up, but her lips didn't part, as if she were trying to hide bad teeth. However, since her teeth had looked fine at the time of her school shot, I assumed she had now reached her rebel stage.

"I know," April said. "Marked resemblance, right?"

"Pretty much," my dad said.

"I wonder how it made my grandma feel when I arrived in Kentucky looking so much like a younger version of my mom."

I hadn't thought of that, but it must have been rough. "Did you see these pictures right off the bat when you got to Kentucky?" I asked.

April shook her head. "No. My grandma and my aunt Patty both put them away right before I met them. I'm sure if they'd had pictures of my mom when she was an adult, they would have been all over the house. My aunt probably would have made a collage. But they talked it over with the priest and decided to show me after I was confirmed, which was in seventh grade." She pulled out another folder. "When I was eighteen, I came into my inheritance. I flew to New York to meet the executor of my dad's will. He took me to a bank in Manhattan and said, 'You'll be seeing everything in your father's vault.' Vault. I was already into film, and I was picturing . . . There's a great scene in *Marathon Man* with an open bank vault that gives the frame such depth."

"Terrific movie!" my dad said.

"Beautifully made," she said, but I couldn't tell if she agreed that it was terrific. "But this wasn't a vault at all, just a big drawer lined with felt. It wasn't even the actual safety-deposit box my dad had, because soon after they were killed, the police had to open it to go through it. But Mr. Toomey—he was the executor, a lawyer—had someone take a chronological series of pictures as the police opened the drawer and took out each item. My grandma said, 'There's a canny Irishman for you.' She was so happy my dad's estate had been in good hands." April cleared her throat. "Obviously, my grandma can be a little parochial."

She opened the folder and showed us the photographs of the vault contents. She asked my dad if he'd been there that day, but he said that his senior on the case, Bobby Melvin, had gone. "Bobby loved working the homicides of the rich. Or at least the upper middle class," Dad groused. "Some kid got shot in Brownsville, he never gave a crap. Assigned it out the minute it came to his desk." April shook her head, commiserating with my dad about some people's terrible values. My dad went on, saying that he had seen these bank photos a few days after they were taken, and as he looked at each one now, he remembered it. There was a picture of a wad of bonds and stock certificates, then pictures of each individually. Titles to Seymour's car, two houses—the one in Manhattan Beach and another, which sounded to me like a mansion, on the South Carolina shore. One of those velvet bags I'd only seen in movies, with thirty-seven uncut jewels. The bag looked deflated, as if bereft from the loss of its contents, and a rainbow of gemstones were arranged around it.

"The only thing I kept was the light blue one," April said. She pointed to a pale blue round stone in the shot. "It's a Montana sapphire. I just had the feeling he got that one for my mom. For her eyes. Maybe he was going to make it into a ring." I nodded. April was a bright-sider, which I assumed was how she'd survived.

The next picture was a dark red shaving kit, and the following one was the $100,000 inside it. I knew that was getting-away money, not walking-around money. Enough to get Seymour to wherever his real wealth was kept, but not so much to automatically trigger an IRS investigation. The Browns' wills were there as well, though the safe-deposit box was only in Seymour's name. Kim would have had no access. Also, there was a notebook—in the backup photo, a close-up of a blank page like all the rest. I noted the raggedy remains of pages torn out.

The notebook reminded me of how the launderers for Hezbollah in South America operated. The minute a transaction was complete, every dollar or euro amount, every secret account number written on a single sheet of paper got destroyed. Now they have digital backup, but in the late nineties they had two guys, one in the Western Hemisphere, one in the Eastern, memorize every digit along with an alphanumeric code for the recipient.

"So the executor you met when you were eighteen, Mr. Toomey, was the same guy who'd supervised the pictures?" my dad asked.

"Yes, same man, but the police or New York State had them put it in another branch of the bank. But he came along. He was fine," April said. "I brought a lawyer, Larry Roth. His father was in my aunt Patty's high school metal band." My dad grinned, and she added, "How else do you find a trusts and estates lawyer in New York City? So I wound up with Larry Roth, who turned out to be an awesome guy. He came with me to meet Mr. Toomey, who reminded me of the Broderick Crawford character in *Born Yesterday*. Overbearing, arrogant, and that was when he was trying to be nice. I could tell he was super pissed when I walked into his office with my own attorney. He went from white to deep red in three seconds. Oh, and he was wearing a monster ring and he kept banging his hand on his desk to make a point."

"And he had a lot of points," I surmised.

"Oh yeah," April agreed. "And even though I had an idea of what my dad was involved in, I couldn't believe he had picked this guy. Anyway, Larry wasn't fazed by the bluster and made sure the other lawyer didn't pull any sneaky stuff. A few months later, when everything was done and the jewels and the beach house in South Carolina were sold, I was worth over seven million dollars."

We knew she had inherited a healthy sum. But seven mil caused an eyebrow raise. I said, "Holy shit! I assume the South Carolina house must have gone up in value from the time you were five to when you were eighteen."

"Not as much as you'd think," she said. "It's, like, ridiculously large and has direct access to the beach. My dad and his partner—some company—paid almost three million for it. Maybe that wouldn't be shocking in the Hamptons even then, but no one was paying those prices down there, even for mansions. They overpaid."

"That's money laundering," my dad said. "I think we tried to trace it at the time, but the shell company was a dead end."

"But why did I wind up with the house?" April asked.

"I can give you lots of possibles," I told her, "but no definites. Maybe it was just some investment he made, and the shell company was Seymour Brown himself. Maybe he wanted some insurance in case the Vory turned on him. Maybe he skimmed something off the top of a larger deal. Or this could have been step two or three of a much longer process. The reason we're interested is because your ownership and the sale benefited you but might have damaged someone else's interests."

"But that was when I was almost nineteen. Who nurses a grudge for that long?"

"That's one of our questions," Dad said. "Anyway, we'd like to talk to this Mr. Toomey, if he's still around. And also your lawyer, Mr. Roth. Just to see if we can jog their memories, get some lead, though truthfully, it's a long shot. We'll need you to call them and give your permission for us to do it. They'll probably want something in writing, too."

"No problem."

"And while Mr. Roth is at it, a copy of your will, assuming you have one."

"Sure."

I excused myself to pee. When I came back, April was giving my dad a synopsis of *Born Yesterday*. When he followed my example and went to the bathroom, I asked April whether she had made a will and who would benefit from it. She said she had. There was a trust for taking care of her grandmother along with bequests to her grandma and Aunt Patty and her daughters. She also left a sizable amount to an LGBTQ charity and the Children's Defense Fund. The rest, including her house, went to Misaki, her fiancée.

"Not that I think your aunt Patty is going to order a hit," I told her.

"What about Pride New Jersey?" she joked.

"I've heard they're ruthless."

When my dad came back, he reached into the litigation bag he'd brought. For a minute I thought he was going to offer April the bag of sourdough pretzels he was saving for the ride home, but he took out the recent photos of his Russian and Moldovan, the mobbed-up clients who'd been so agitated by Seymour's murder. "Our turn for picture time. See if you can recognize any of these." He gave the first to her, saying she should take her time. "They're relatively recent pictures, so if you saw them within the past year, say, maybe you'll remember. Imagine them in a suit, a T-shirt, whatever."

She looked closely, really studied it, and I realized it was a good thing to have a film scholar making an ID. She shook her head after the first. "Who is he?"

"We don't like to say anything before a potential witness looks at photos. If I say this guy is an actor with the New York Shakespeare Festival, you're going to have a certain reaction to that." He showed her the second photo, another man, about twenty years younger than the first. Again April spent time looking and then shook her head. Once Dad was certain that she didn't recognize the two men, he told her who they were. "They aren't really connected to each other, other than being part of the Vory. The first one's a Moldovan, Alexei Buga. The second picture is a Russian guy named Vovka Kravtsov. They both had business dealings with your father during the year he was killed. We heard rumors about them being very, very upset by his death. Not out of grief. More like they were crazed because he supposedly had their money somewhere offshore, but they had no idea where. No idea how to track it down."

I took out some pictures of Luisa de León from ads and articles about her. Eliza had cropped and printed them for me, so they were all the same size. "Do you recognize her?" I asked.

"No. I would have remembered her. She is so attractive. How old is she?"

"Forties," I said.

"Are you going to tell me she's in the Vory?" she joked.

"No, she's not in the Vory." I paused. April looked up. "When you do an investigation, all sorts of people turn up. Like her. She was your dad's girlfriend."

"From when he and my mom were married?"

"Yes."

She slowly handed the pictures back to my dad. I did a once-over to see how she was. Not shaken by the revelation. Well, a tightness in her jaw, a change for someone whose demeanor seemed naturally upbeat—chin held high, an open-eyed way of looking at the world, an easy-come smile. As we got up to leave, I made small talk, asking her what her favorite science fiction movie was, hoping she wouldn't say *2001*, which I thought was pretentious. The question relaxed her, and she seemed to revert to her positive self, rubbing her temples with her index fingers as if to speed cogitation. Finally she said, "I think I'm contractually obligated to say *2001: A Space Odyssey*. *Solaris* by Tarkovsky, and some even might count *Man with a Movie Camera* as science fiction." I hadn't seen it, so I obviously wasn't going to argue whether it was canonically science fiction. She continued. "I would say *Ghost in the Shell,* and . . . I think *Her.* I'm not counting films like *ET* and *Terminator 2* that are buddy movies, father-son movies. Oh, and if you're including dystopic films, then—"

My dad leaned over to zip up the bag.

As we were headed to the car, I spoke as softly as I could to April. "Your dad's girlfriend. She's lovely, smart. Successful. Of course, we're not mentioning her name. That's standard practice. She was in a couple of business deals with him. Nothing major, and she seems on the up-and-up now. But she did benefit from his death. And though she came into our sights recently, as we've been reinvestigating, she's got to be considered a possible—"

"Subject?" April more mouthed the word than said it.

"Yes."

"A killer?"

"Possibly. She does have a great smile though."

April agreed.

CHAPTER THIRTEEN

When we got into the car, my dad transferred a pretzel to his mouth as he belted himself into the passenger seat. "How come you didn't mention Luisa's name?" he asked. "Are you worried about April chasing her down so she could learn more?"

"Yeah. Luisa's photos make her look totally good-hearted. It's natural to want to approach her."

"Smooth move, kiddo." He held out his bag of pretzels. "Want one?" I shook my head, he looked relieved, and I steered the car north.

My dad didn't snore on the inhale when he slept, but growled deep and loud in his throat as he exhaled, drowning out a couple of punch lines on a *Wait Wait . . . Don't Tell Me* podcast. As we drove over the Verrazzano-Narrows Bridge, his growl became a snort. I glanced over, realizing he was up. No yawn, no stretch. He was wide-awake in an instant. Though I turned my eyes back to the road, I could see him brushing salt crystals and pretzel crumbs from his shirt.

"I like this," he said. "You chauffeuring me around. It's a good thing I taught you to drive, so I can just close my eyes and relax."

"Works for me," I said. "Are we really going to interview Buga and the other one who gave money to Seymour and never got it back?"

"The other one is Vovka Kravtsov. Vovka is a nickname for Vladimir."

"Live and learn. If I call him Vov, will he be offended?"

"If he doesn't break your nose, you'll know he's okay with it," he said.

"Why is it worth questioning them now?"

"I just want to hear what they say about April, specifically. Not that I think they'll say much, but there's always a chance something will dribble out. I also want to see if they have any insight into Luisa or any of Seymour's sidekicks. Insight into his dealings. Seymour never got too buddy-buddy with his clients. An occasional dinner. No golf game. But these two came to him particularly late in the game and were a cut above the rest. They were vicious, but they understood that napkins belong on laps."

There was blessedly little traffic. I gave the Outback a touch more gas and whizzed along Shore Parkway in Brooklyn feeling kickass, like I was driving a convertible along the Basse Corniche. "Napkins can't be used for garroting?" I asked my dad.

"Only if you're out of wire. But listen, I was thinking we should each get a private investigator license. The real McCoy, not some shit like a business card with the FBI seal that says Retired Special Agents Bowling League or whatever the hell you've been flashing."

"The federal equivalent to what you've been flashing," I said. "But why do we need it? We've been doing fine."

"You get taken more seriously, both by civilians and law enforcement. Not that it makes everyone spill their guts immediately, but it might make someone who is reluctant open up a bit more," he replied. "And you're already a pro at getting people to spill. This can only help."

"Don't you have to take an exam? I don't want to deal with all that."

He waved that away. "Lulu could pass this exam. Seriously. It's nothing."

"All right," I said slowly. I wasn't quite sure why I felt hesitant. It seemed like a commitment to something big, though it wasn't as if a PI license came with the obligation of doing it full-time.

"It would also show that somebody hired us, that someone put some money into taking this case seriously. I can fast-track the licenses."

Among the things not to say to your dad is *I can fast-track them faster*. So I told him, "Okay. I'm in."

A few months after Josh and I got married, we'd decided we needed a regular date night. Not in the sense of waiting for the kid to go to sleep so

I could put on my crotchless panties and play. An actual grown-up date at some chic spot in Manhattan or a foodie place in Brooklyn, have drinks, dinner, flirt, and converse. We did it every Thursday.

That Thursday we did a casual version, winding up at the public beach about a mile from our house. It was a wide stretch of sand strewn with mussel shells and the exoskeletons of horseshoe crabs. Long strands of seaweed, so dark they looked more black than green, were scattered gracefully about, as if by a set designer. At that time of evening we had the beach to ourselves except for one guy a good distance from us who was throwing a tennis ball into the water for an ecstatic Labrador.

Josh and I walked here so often we knew every crag and boulder by heart. Looking at Long Island Sound, if you lowered your eyes to half-mast, you'd believe you were on the edge of America, that there was nothing but salt water until Europe. Actually, you were seven or eight nautical miles across from your fellow suburbanites at a similar public beach in Westchester who probably understood that they were facing Long Island but were feeling *Ah, la belle France!*

"I know we agreed not to talk about work on a date night," I said, "but I need to talk about work."

"Okay," Josh said. He set up our low-to-the-ground beach chairs next to some dramatically tall grasses waving in the breeze.

I brought him up to speed on our trip back to April's, with the details about executors, lawyers, stocks and bonds, jewels, plus Buga and Vovka and how they'd felt violated by Seymour's death. "So you dealt with people in the Russian mob—Vory—when you were an assistant in the Southern District, right?"

"Yes," he said. "Wire fraud, insider trading. Almost any white-collar crime that comes to mind. Oh, I remember a case of a Bulgarian selling mustard gas to Iraq. Part of his defense was that he didn't know it was toxic. Russians, Ukrainians, Kazakhs . . . They all have communities in Brooklyn, so you're going to find mobsters who commit federal crimes. No different from Colombians, Italians, Eastern European Jews, the old Irish gangs."

"Well, the Russians aren't structured in pyramid fashion, like a family with one guy at the top," I said. I was thinking "pyramidic" might be the correct adjective, but didn't want Josh to say, *Oh, you must mean pyramidesque—or pyramidified.*

He opened our backpack and took out the grapes and cheese we'd brought. I pulled a couple of rubber bands off the blue ice, freeing the vodka we'd poured into a water bottle. "You know what's funny?" he said. "As a judge in the Eastern District, I get more trials with defendants from all those former Soviet Union countries than I ever did as an assistant in the SDNY." He opened the bottle, saying, "*Na zdorovie,*" as he took a drink. I said something like that back to him. "So you think it was a Russian or a Kazakh who chased your client around Rutgers in an SUV?" he asked.

"I'm semi-considering it, mostly because my other option is Luisa de León, and that's not sitting right with me." I relieved him of the bottle and handed him grapes and cheese in a single glass container. My mother had done her *I'm appalled* double blink as she watched me combine them, although she remained silent—probably because Josh was in the kitchen. "Truthfully, we have doubts about either Buga or the other guy going after April, but we still have to check them out. Their doing it would be like saying, 'I'm going to burn down that guy's house, along with the guy in it and—Hey, this is the fun part!—I'd be burning down the hundreds of thousands or millions I handed over to him, because I'll never learn where it is.'"

"I'm with you," Josh said. "And it's not as if they have anything to gain by going after April now. It would be pointless revenge. Actually, I agree with you ninety-eight percent."

"The two percent?"

"And you tell me you suck at math. The two percent is if one of them is psychotic. Then, if he's upset that Seymour Brown wouldn't disclose how he'd layered the funds . . . well, Seymour and his family can burn in hell. Crazy and self-sabotaging? Of course. But it's not a line of work that requires a cost-benefit analysis before each hit."

I sighed and popped a few grapes. Josh took off his boating shoes and rubbed his soles along the sand. He was a man who would not consider flip-flops. "It's true that the Mafiya, the Vory, has been around for centuries. Not in the United States, though. But in Russia, whether it was under the czars or the Soviets, they were known to do anything. They did it for vengeance, to preserve their reputation for being savage, and they did it to live."

"Sometimes for pleasure," I suggested.

"That too," Josh said. "They had absolutely no hope of justice, from the czar down to the guards in the gulags, so they killed and tortured to survive. But in the US, it's a new Vory. They've adapted their behavior. They see their own compatriots making enormous successes of themselves in what we think of as American terms. Legally. They still have a rough reputation, even compared with other criminal groups. But they feel the pressure not to be perceived as animals. They know respect counts here at least as much as fear." Josh mindlessly poked at an inert shell of a dead horseshoe crab with a small branch he'd been fiddling with. "Funny. Seymour's job was to make his clients look clean. Not just to stay out of prison, but to be accepted. Actually he wanted that for himself, too. Maybe he got it, in his own eyes, by making the Russians look up to him as a financial wizard but also as someone tough enough not to suck up to them. Well, for a while, anyway."

I thought of three-a.m. wake-ups as good for bladders and bad for psyches. We lie in the dark recalling the past, which means that the willful ignorance we use to get through the day collapses and we peer into a hellhole: our failures, missed chances to show kindness or honor. As for the future, those dark-of-the-night forecasts always call for a moonless sky and cold rain. Any chance of seeing a road to redemption is virtually nil.

Double that if you've had a career in law enforcement.

That night after the beach, we'd brought home several pints of ice cream for the family and had a kitchen celebration of nothing but Jeni's

Darkest Chocolate and Graeter's Black Raspberry Chocolate Chip. It was still working its magic when I poked my phone and saw it was 3:18 a.m., so I didn't cringe from past or impending disasters. Instead, I went to the bathroom, then padded down the hall to my office entrance. Lulu followed, looking put-upon.

About a year earlier, when my leg was still healing, my dad had dropped by and put up a chinning bar for me—for recovering my upper-body strength after too much time off waiting for an infection to heal and a skin graft to take. But really he wanted to remind me that being able to kick ass and endure pain had saved my life, and I needed to regain that skill to feel safe again. I hadn't had a fitness routine in so long, but when the cold metal hit my hands, I was surprised to find myself still able to observe noticeable biceps when I tried the first set of pull-ups.

I had moved on to lats when Josh appeared, saying, "I was wondering where you were." Even though his voice was hushed, I let out a shriek and dropped to the floor. It didn't say much about my Krav Maga martial arts mindset, which supposedly included a heightened awareness of my surroundings. I was clear enough, though, to realize that his casual hello was an attempt at sangfroid—imperturbable guys like him don't fall apart if there's a pillow, blanket, and no wife at three in the morning.

"I'm fine," I told him.

"I figured you were, but I was just curious where you'd gone." He pulled at his pajama cuffs as if aligning the sleeves of a starched formal shirt for a black-tie evening.

Just as several snide replies were vying with each other in my head, I decided to lay off. He'd lost one wife to sudden death, and he'd almost lost me to a killer-kidnapper, so snide was unfair. I said instead, "Wasn't it fun being down at the beach tonight, just the two of us?" By that time I had my arms around him, and I sensed he was nodding. After a sweet moment, we gave mutual pat-pat dismissals on each other's backs and gently let go. "Want to come in?" I asked. He hesitated, being a man of regular habits, then apparently decided that by now sleep was a lost cause, and he followed me in.

Josh wasn't a frequent visitor to my office, so he seemed surprised (pleasantly) at the Zoom nook I'd created by the bookshelves as well as surprised (unpleasantly) by a pile of papers on the floor, part of a wrapper from an apricot nut bar, and a printout for Wynne of "8 Secrets to Long Hair Just Like Sherihan" from *Vogue Arabia* strewn on the rug around my recliner. "It's weird to have clients instead of witnesses," I told him. "I mean, I don't feel the need to coddle April, but I do want her to feel she's getting her money's worth. Not that she's paying. But it's right that she feels she trusted us and that we're giving her our best."

We sat on the couch, and I put my feet up in case he felt the urge to give a foot massage. "When I left the US Attorney's to go to Shannon Little," Josh said, "it felt something like that—I owed something to the clients. In a different way than I did when I worked for the government." Shannon Little was the private law firm he'd worked at—and made a fortune—after he'd been a prosecutor and before he became a judge. He rested my left foot on his leg and wrapped it in his hands. The warmth felt wonderful in the air-conditioned night. "Look, I enjoyed the firm, becoming a partner, a rainmaker."

"I know." He was stretching out my toes. It felt great, and what felt even greater was that he had never once expected me to rub his feet. I wasn't fond of other people's feet.

"My partners, the associates, the staff . . . I liked nearly all of them. But nothing I've done before or after being an assistant on a government salary can compare. The camaraderie in knowing we were all using all our smarts and knowledge of the law to go after the bad guys. We had such a sense of purpose." He hesitated. "That FBI retirement party where we met? Even after all those years in the firm and on the bench, I couldn't wait to go. I always loved being part of that life."

"You could have gone back. Or found a job opening for a good guy somewhere else."

His lower lip turned into something close to a pout, if he were the sort who pouted. "I left at the time because I felt I should have a grown-up job, not cops and robbers."

"Cops and robbers is exactly what I've been missing," I told him. "I felt that sense of purpose, too. Being a literary scout didn't cut it. Once in a while I felt gratified about bringing a good book to English readers, but having to slog through five mediocre historical novels about intrigue in King Farouk's court?" He pressed his thumb deep into the ball of my foot, and I exhaled one of those spa sighs of total relaxation. "Of course it was my choice. New husband, new daughter. I needed time to find my way. Plus I was tired of being the one who got called to convince the women in terrorists' lives to open up to me. Corie Geller, women specialist, gold medaling at getting terrified wives and sisters and daughters and girlfriends to turn against the awful men in their lives.

"And I was just as good at interrogating men, for God's sake. Fundamentalist pricks almost always underestimated me. But my bosses, not even once, made me their first choice to break down the actual bad guys. So *wadaeaan*, FBI." Josh's brows went up, which suggested he was startled not to know something. "It's a more informal way of saying goodbye in Arabic," I explained. "And *'ahlaan*, publishing. But now I'm thinking *wadaeaan* again, this time to publishing."

"I know," Josh said. I gestured, *Come on, tell me more.* "I've thought for a long time that you should find something better-suited to you. Just because you love reading and are intrigued by other cultures doesn't mean sitting alone in a room all day reading and writing book reports is great for you. You like being out there." Josh had found his place in the world—he was perfectly suited to being part of the legal system's elite. He wasn't even aware of how much he needed—in his case literally—to be looked up to. "On the other hand," he continued, "while I'm not suggesting that you be overcautious—"

I cut him off. "Undercaution is part of my charm." I felt a doggy lick on my free ankle and I patted the couch. Lulu leapt up, but instead of climbing into my lap to canoodle, she started to burrow her nose between the cushions. "Speaking of undercaution, my dad and I are going to get private investigator's licenses." His jaw didn't drop, but his mouth loosened.

"He says he'll fast-track them. And everyone says the exam is ridiculously easy."

Josh had a slew of questions. Where would I start out—with a major corporate-serving spook agency? And my dad? Hook up with another Homicide retiree? Or some established PI who did background and matrimonial investigations? Maybe with—

"I'm thinking my dad and me. Together. Schottland & Geller. Oh, with 'Private Investigations' after it. Or Private Investigators? I'm going to talk to him tomorrow, but after his coffee."

CHAPTER FOURTEEN

I carefully slid the pad of my thumb under the Coke Zero tab, gently working it open as quietly as possible. It snapped and hissed for what seemed like an hour while I pointlessly shushed it. Finally it subsided enough so I could take a teeny slurp, hoping to infuse my meandering mind with some caffeine.

I was holed up in Wynne's guest room watching Wynne and Luisa chatting, sipping their third glasses of wine. The night before, I'd installed a tiny but effective camera I'd rented from a spy-on-your-spouse store on the Lower East Side, a place that had the dimensions and ambiance of a toilet booth in a bus station.

The camera had a built-in mic, and I'd stuck it high in the corner of Wynne's living room. It would record in places she and Luisa would most likely sit. For reassurance, I stuck another mic just outside the French doors leading to Wynne's terrace.

The two of them were still talking—as they had been for the past two hours. Now they were dissecting what they were calling "the Gestalt style effects" of various architectural and decor details. I had been intrigued for the first twenty minutes or so, but by this point they'd returned to the topic of color temperature for the third time. At one point I almost dozed off on the guest room's enormous bed where I was lying. The mattress was too soft, though, and as my muscles relaxed, I ended up almost rolling on top of the laptop I was using to watch them.

Two days before, Wynne had called me without texting first, which always meant Something Big had happened.

"What's up?" I asked.

"Oh my God, Corie. Luisa called me!" Wynne was as breathless as she'd been as a teenager telling me she'd been assigned to the same group project as her crush Jared Finsey, who earnestly carried a sketch pad wherever he went and whose light brown skater-boy hair kept flopping into his eyes. "Luisa wants to pick my brain, she says, on how she can incorporate whole lifestyles into her real estate business. Of course, I think she's just cultivating me for referrals, but whatever. Isn't that great?"

"Yes?" I was hesitant, not quite sure what her enthusiasm was about. It's not as if she needed Luisa's business.

"So I have an idea how I can get her talking about Seymour." Wynne was near her peak of ebullience, talking like a podcast playing at 1.5x. I was touched. Not only was she apparently as excited about my investigation as I was, but she wanted to be a part of it. "I'll invite her here," she said. "I'll pretend it's my usual first step with a new client, except you can set up a camera that you can watch." She paused. "I'll tell her I'll have to charge her my initial style consult fee."

I wasn't sure how much that was, but I guessed it was probably an amount even Dawn might gulp at. "It's awesome that you're doing this, but are you sure it's a good idea?"

"She'll pay," Wynne said with unmitigated confidence. "It will make her feel like she's the one trying to get something from me."

"I mean, what if she realizes—not now, but eventually—that you had a part in our investigating her? What if she bad-mouths you? She seems to know a lot of rich people."

"Luisa can't possibly hurt my business," Wynne answered flatly.

I tried and failed to imagine what it was like to move through the world knowing I was that good at something, and also that everyone else believed just as deeply that I was gifted beyond all other mortals.

Being careful of her insanely expensive bed linens, I took another swig of my Coke Zero and leaned back into the pile of approximately thirty-seven minimalist shams and *don't call us decorative* decorative pillows on the bed. Then I raised my feet and examined them against the white of the ceiling, considering whether I should get a darker blue pedicure next time.

Wynne was now gesturing at her own surroundings to make a design point. She had stood up and glided over near the open French doors that led to her modest-size terrace, which she jokingly called Fairclough Acres. Her left half was now past the edge of the screen, but I could still see most of her as she spoke.

"So . . ." she was saying to Luisa. "My style here."

"Unembellished," Luisa replied.

"Stark," Wynne corrected her, smiling. "Partly because I want to provide a proper showspace for the art. But also, look out here." She gestured to the terrace.

I'd always loved Fairclough Acres. She had managed to make the space a haven from city life. She would change it up for each season, but in summertime it was dripping with palms and tropical-looking plants with giant red and yellow flowers. I would lie in her hammock after an edible to watch the clouds puff by and the jets slowly streak across the sky. The perfume of her jasmine plants would drift over me while downtown Manhattan melted away. I always half expected to hear a cawing parrot and a monkey clutching a vine while screeching *oo-oo-oo-AH-AH-AH*.

Before I married Josh, when I was still living in a studio whose focal piece of furniture was a queen-size Ikea platform bed with a Target duvet, I was never very jealous of Wynne's money. Two luxuries of hers, though, gave me a pang. One was that she had a washer and dryer in her apartment, whereas I had to go down to the cobwebbed basement with the hissing, clanging steam heat and pick my way warily past the mad-scientist-looking fellow tenant who seemed always to do his laundry at the same time as I did. The other luxury was her terrace. Now Wynne glanced over her shoulder through her French doors. "And meanwhile, these plantings are lush. Very much embellished. You walk through these doors, and you're walking into a very different place. When it's done on purpose, not just haphazardly, big style contrasts can be really effective. They aren't discombobulating at all. They make up a whole that is greater than the sum of the parts. Occasionally you need a dividing line that promises a new mood."

Luisa nodded eagerly. *I get it!*

Wynne appeared to be slightly unsteady as she headed back to the seat across from Luisa while clutching an ugly ormolu vase in her right hand. I'd seen her drink much more than three glasses of wine with no change in her gait whatsoever, so I guessed she was faking drunk to encourage Luisa to also feel more uninhibited.

Wynne waved the vase around. "See this? Not stark." She gestured at the whole room to show how the ornate green and gold didn't belong. "I keep this around to remind me what not to do," she said, gazing down at it. Her usually upright yogafied shoulders were rounded. Her words were not slurred, just slightly thicker than usual.

"What do you mean?" Luisa asked.

Wynne didn't answer but sucked in a deep breath and tilted her head back, blinking hard.

"I'm so sorry, I didn't mean to . . ." Luisa said, abashed.

"No, no, no. Don't apologize. I brought it up." Wynne drew in an unsteady breath. "There was this guy. I was young. So young. Twenty-three. And he was . . ." Luisa shifted closer and patted Wynne's arm, dark eyes open wide with rapt sympathy. "He was married, of course. I was stupid, and I believed his bullshit." Luisa nodded vigorously. "I'd dated guys before, even ones a bit older than me. But they were boys. He was the first adult I dated, you know what I mean?"

"Absolutely," Luisa said. "When you're young . . ."

Wynne nodded. "Right. He seemed to me to be so competent. And confident. At every aspect of life. At his work, at knowing which wine to pick, at socializing with any group of people. And of course"—she shrugged slightly—"in bed."

"Believe me," Luisa said. "We've all been there."

"His name was Gerard," Wynne continued, which confirmed my suspicions that she was in fact describing her real relationship with an arrogant, manipulative fuck with froggy eyes; even with a kiss, he would never be a prince. I had disliked him on sight and, as I got to know him, came to detest him. "He never admitted any insecurity he felt," she added. "That's what I thought it meant to be strong. Oh God, I was so pathetic." She shook her head and took a long, slow sip of wine. Luisa and I waited.

Wynne went on. "Everything was about him. Anytime I mentioned something that was going on with me—I was an assistant stylist at *Vogue* then—we would somehow wind up talking about how it reminded him of something that had happened to him. I never asked myself, *Isn't this weird behavior*? And every time he was in a shitty mood or pissed about something work-related, he'd turn on me. And I believed he was justified, you know? If I just did everything better, better, better, he wouldn't have to descend into a mood. Since he wasn't happy, it was my fault."

"Textbook narcissist," Luisa murmured, shaking her head.

"And I was the textbook pushover. Eventually," Wynne said, "we went on this ski trip. Vermont. It was supposed to be a three-day weekend where we could de-stress. So we were walking down the hallway of our hotel and I took his hand and smiled up at him. All of a sudden he yanked his hand away and started walking fast. I tried to catch up, and we passed this guy and he and Gerard said hi to each other. Turns out, the other guy was his kids' pediatrician. Gerard's face was flushed almost purple, and he wouldn't speak to me. I don't think he was worried the guy would tell his wife, he was just embarrassed to be seen, you know? So we went to dinner and Gerard started telling me how needy I was and how he had no patience for this sort of thing. I mean, what the fuck? What had I said that was needy? I hadn't even asked for the emotional bare minimum from this guy. When we got back to the room, he started packing. It was ten thirty, and we left that night."

"Do *not* blame yourself. We can never let those assholes get away with defining who we are." I noted Luisa had switched to "we," sisterhood mode. "You, me . . . We know who we are."

Wynne shot her a grateful look. "That's why I keep this vase. Because he got it for me, and I was shocked at how little taste he had. And that he could be so clueless about what I would want. But I tried to tell myself it was just a different sensibility, the Louis XV period." She smiled ruefully. "Anyway. I'm so lucky I got out when I did. She got up and refilled her own wineglass and then looked inquiringly at Luisa, who willingly extended hers. "I'm so grateful that something inside me made me realize before my twenty-fourth birthday that I'd love to get married, but I'd rather be single than stuck with an egomaniacal fuck."

Luisa laughed and held up her ringless left hand. "Oh my God, girl, same." They clinked glasses, and each took a deep sip. I could see even over the video feed that Luisa's eyes were shining both from emotion and too much wine. "I have the exact same. Well, not exactly. But that guy who made me realize what I needed. Or what I don't need."

Wynne nodded and leaned back expectantly. Luisa put her wineglass down and placed her hands on her knees. For a second I was afraid she was getting up to go. Instead, she took a shaky inhale, then let it out and began. "There was this guy. I was young, he was married." She rolled her eyes at the triteness of her own story. "The thing is—like what you had, he was different from anyone else I had dated. At that point I was used to guys who wanted to be with me because they liked the way I looked, that I was the upbeat type. Not for who I was, a complete person. Well, there was one professor I hooked up with in college who wanted to teach me more about Proust. I kind of hinted that I didn't like Proust, but nothing I could say would have stopped him."

"Ugh," commented Wynne, "though I do like Proust."

"Definitely ugh. And Proust is great, he's just not my thing. In any case, the professor didn't last more than a couple of weeks. This other guy, he cared about me. Or made me feel like he did."

Wynne nodded encouragingly.

"Like I told him all about my plans to start in the real estate business, and he was really interested. Not just giving advice, but hearing the details of what I wanted and encouraging me. I still wonder if I would have chosen some other career if it weren't for him."

Luisa put her face in her hands. I pulled the laptop screen close to my nose to see if she was crying. Her shoulders were still, though. In a few seconds she lifted her head. There were no tears, but she was clearly moved recalling Seymour. "Of course, he told me he'd leave his wife." Even though I would have a recording, I made a quick note on the pad that had been sitting on the ruffled pillow next to me. "And of course, I believed him. I was so, so young, but I still knew not to completely trust everything he said. Also, he had a young kid he talked about all the time. He would have had a really rough time saying goodbye to her. But I had pretty good reason to think he was telling the truth about wanting to be with me."

I guessed that reason was the apartment they'd purchased together. To Luisa, who probably knew he wasn't on the up-and-up, but might not realize how money laundering worked, it would look like Seymour had put his money where his mouth was. He had invested large sums in their future together. I still had no way of knowing if he ever considered moving into that apartment with her or if he was using it to kill two birds with one stone: mollifying Luisa and laundering Vory money.

"But did he wind up leaving her?" Wynne asked gently, ingenuously.

"No, but . . . well, to this day, I don't know whether he would have or not, but the thing is, he died."

"Oh my God!" Wynne exclaimed. "What happened? How old was he?"

"You know, I don't remember exactly. Late thirties? Younger than me now, which is completely insane. He seemed so ancient to me back then. I had to explain to him who the Smashing Pumpkins were." She emitted a brief, bitter laugh. "He was killed."

"Wait, what?!" Even though I was trained to spot lies, Wynne's apparent shock might well have fooled me.

Luisa nodded. She seemed shaken by the reminiscence. "Someone set his house on fire. His wife and little girl were in there, too." Wynne looked stricken, and maybe she was, hearing the story from someone so close to Seymour. "Beyond horrible," Luisa said with a gulp. "The little girl escaped and lived, but he and his wife died."

"And they didn't think it was just a regular house fire?"

"No. I forget the details, but the CSI or whoever they were could tell it was arson. My guy had been involved in some iffy business deals, so I guess it wasn't too surprising. To the cops, I mean. I just about died of shock. I only found out he had died when the investigators showed up to interview me." Luisa shook her head. "I hadn't heard from him for a few days. I worried that he was ghosting me, but I kept telling myself not to be so clingy."

Wynne's eyes looked like they were about to pop out of her head, though maybe the wine had loosened them up. "Did they think you did it?"

"No. Or, I don't know. Maybe they weren't sure, but I didn't get that impression. They asked me where I was that night and stuff, and whether we'd fought, but their questions were a lot more about what I knew about his sketchy business stuff. And I knew next to nothing about that. I mean, I'd gathered the broad outlines, but he wasn't the kind of guy to let those details slip."

"Was it drugs?" Wynne asked.

"I don't think so. I never really found out the details. But I think it was more, like, financial stuff."

Wynne chuckled grimly. "Sounds like our young selves had similar taste in men."

"I know, right?" Luisa said, agreeing. She paused. "Terrible taste. This is going to sound horrible, but . . ."

Wynne waved her hand as if to say, *No judgments here.*

"I'm kind of glad he died sometimes? I mean, not in that horrible way. Jesus, burning to death is, like, the worst. And his poor wife. Who the fuck would be willing to kill a whole family like that? It's insane, right? But. I could have been miserable if I'd stayed with him."

Wynne leaned in and gave her a hug, rubbing the back of her head as if she were comforting a small child. She glanced up at the camera over Luisa's shoulder and gave me a wink.

The door to the guest room cracked open, and Wynne's head popped through. "How'd I do?" she asked.

I pulled her into the room and held her hands in pure joy. "That was so awesome. I can't thank you enough."

"Did it help with your case?"

"You were wonderful. The better I understand where she's coming from—and more important, where Seymour was coming from—the clearer judgments we can make."

Wynne sat on the edge of the bed and flopped backward, as if she were exhausted. "That was, like, my big undercover spy moment."

"And I like how long you talked about decorating. The boyfriend stuff really seemed to come up naturally. Not everyone can do that. You were great." I started to put on my shoes. "Though I have to admit, I was zoning out while you were talking about the demise of dark wood furniture."

"So was I," admitted Wynne. "She's such a decent, sweet person for a possible murderer, but not very original." I started to get up to grab my purse, and she said, "Hang on a sec."

"What's up?" I asked. I sat back down to listen.

"You seem to be serious about getting into investigating as a career."

"I think I'm pretty serious," I said.

"Good, we're on the same page," Wynne said. "I want to help you. Not just with this kind of thing, talking with people, but with what I'm good at. Let me help make you an office." When she got excited about a project, she seemed to be surrounded by an electric field. During fourth grade she'd almost lit up the Queens night sky when she conceived of a matzo collage for PS 101's Festival of Spring.

Wynne had frequently offered her design services to me since I moved in with Josh. She would claim that Dawn's foolishly expensive, excessively inoffensive dreary pink suburban taste pained her ("actual, physical pain," she'd say) more than genuine, authentically bad taste would. And I had always said no. When Josh's and my engagement was a done deal, I changed the bedroom. That's in the Second Wives' Rulebook. But otherwise I'd let the house be.

Part of it was that despite his reassurances otherwise, I never felt quite like Josh's money was also mine. I could spend it on clothes and books and lunches with friends without a thought, but I was hesitant about something that would wind up costing thousands of dollars. Becoming a wife and mother and starting out as a literary scout was major; I'd had no energy to give to decorating, and as much as I loved Wynne and could deal with her, I wasn't sure I wanted to battle over the price of some mid-century switch plate.

Another, deeper part of me worried that I had usurped Dawn's role. I'd married her husband, adopted her daughter. Erasing her from her home felt like erasing her from having existed. As if she'd start to disappear even from photographs, like in *Back to the Future*. And so I lived with more shell pink than anyone other than a six-year-old girl should be able to stand. And if I didn't feel at home there, I convinced myself that it didn't seem such a high price to pay. I'd moved from rental to rental since I left my parents' home at age eighteen. I'd never felt at home. Or truly tried to make one.

Wynne looked at me, her eyes round and surprisingly serious. "I know you think this is no big deal. Or 'it's just the way that a house looks' or whatever. But your environment helps facilitate what you do. I could help you work better."

"It's not that I don't think it's a big deal," I said, automatically getting ready to turn her down again. But this time I paused. It was one thing to have Dawn's stuff in the rooms I shared with Josh and Eliza. This was going to be my room. I'd be in it every day. I'd be thinking in it, planning in it, talking in it, wasting time in it. When my dad/partner came to work, we'd have conference calls with law enforcement, Zoom with clients. Maybe it could be a place where I could slurp my lunchtime ramen while scrolling through Insta and not cringe because I'd caught a glimpse of Dawn's suedelike wallpaper that, to me, resembled human skin.

Wynne saw my hesitation. "This is about what you want. I'm not going to do it to my taste. It's about empowering you, and this is the best way I know how to do it."

"Well, you also do it by being, you know, my friend who listens to me. But I hear you." I thought for a moment. "My dad, though."

"Oh please, I can handle your dad. He thinks it's not a real place to work if it doesn't have cinder block walls and gunmetal gray filing cabinets."

"I'd add a dying ficus plant in one corner for maximum authenticity."

Wynne grinned. "By the time I'm through with him, he'll adore eggshell paint and think the whole redesign was his idea. And laugh at how he actually fought having matte paints. He'll say, *I must've been nuts.*"

CHAPTER FIFTEEN

There's no more delicious way to be a detective than to drive to the town dock, climb down to the water's edge, sit on a rock, and call your old boyfriend about your current case.

That old boyfriend with whom you will forever, sort of, remain in love. Not that either of you ever owned up to the "forever" part. But even after all these years, you suspect he feels the same about you.

Not that it mattered. Sami and I were far too temperamentally unsuited to sustain permanent coupling. If he went two weeks without slipping into a developing country to infiltrate a terrorist organization, he would start to get antsy. And I wanted to put down roots.

Sami Bashir and I. Muslim and Jew. While that barrier was not insurmountable, it was problematic. Neither of us was a Holy Roller, but we believed enough so we could never disavow.

We both worked for the Department of Justice. Not exactly a meet cute: he was an agent with the DEA, I with the FBI, and we were thrown together as members of New York's Joint Terrorism Task Force. That gave us lots of chances to exchange snide remarks about each other's agencies and also to spend a great deal of time together.

Sami went undercover throughout the Western Hemisphere. He played a drug dealer, drug buyer, terrorist, arms dealer, corrupt banker. He could play anything, except maybe a DEA agent, because no matter whether he was clean-shaven or bearded, buzz cut, in a kufi skullcap, ponytailed, or shiny-headed, no one could look at him and think *Drug Enforcement Agency*. An adjective like "disreputable" would flash through their mind, and that would be the most positive view. When Sami was in his role, he came across as more reprehensible than some of the thugs and fanatics he worked to vanquish.

For once, the early-morning wind was blowing my hair off my face, not into my mouth. But I could tell by the length of the wait until we were connected that there would be no video. It wasn't crappy internet service; the call passed through a series of security checks. Sami was out of the country in a place that even a person with my level of security clearance shouldn't know about. So my pale beige foundation and dark brown mascara and peach lip balm to produce a natural self who glowed (as if from sunbeams shooting up from the bay) was wasted effort.

"Been a long time," he said in Spanish, so I knew he was probably in Paraguay or Argentina. If he were in his native country, Brazil, he'd greet me in Portuguese and then, when I said *Bom dia,* he'd switch to Spanish and tell me, *That's right, you only have those two words of Portuguese.*

If he'd answered my call in Arabic, I'd have assumed he was undercover and not visiting his Uncle Lateef. The tri-border region in South America had some Muslim communities, and among them were Muslim radicals who sold drugs to finance their ops in the Americas.

Sami asked, "How are you doing? You? Your family?"

"We're fine. Thanks for asking. I talked my parents into moving in with us."

"And your husband and daughter are good with that?"

"Yeah."

"And are you good with that?"

"*Más o menos,*" I said. So-so. "No. Seriously, it's going well. My mom loves having an audience and she's a huge help. And my dad and I talk shop a lot." The big rock I'd thought was level was actually sloped. I moved my sneakers into a crevice and shifted my butt until it sensed (as butts are wont to do) a more level space. "And you and your folks?" His parents lived in New Jersey.

"They're fine." He paused. "I got Covid at the end of March. Bad."

"Oh, my God!" The Spanish, *¡Ay Dios mío!* sounded much more intense than the English would have. "How bad was it? I was thinking of you because I heard things got really rough in Brazil."

He responded with a few bars of some old Spanish song—"'*A veces espero/tal vez . . .*'"—and substituted *la mierda*—shit—for whatever the real lyrics were. But Sami the Lighthearted was his one cover that didn't work.

"So it was awful?"

"Stomach and fever mostly. My lungs weren't too bad, but I was so weak that every time I coughed there was nothing that didn't hurt."

"I'm so sorry, Sami."

"I didn't want to die that way. Bullets, okay. Cancer, it happens. In a pile of my own excrement—and then have my corpse stuck in a refrigerated truck with a Freon leak and not get buried for a month? Didn't like that."

"Could you get to a hospital?"

"Too dangerous—in lots of ways."

I realized I had reached into my shirt and was gripping the little flashlight I wore on a chain. "Was there anyone to bring you food and water?"

"No. Nothing in the fridge because I had just moved into the place. I was thinking how I needed to get out and buy some stuff, but then I thought, *I'll just close my eyes for a few minutes*. Then I woke up in the middle of the night the sickest I've ever been."

I didn't have time to repeat "I'm so sorry," because he was on a roll and I didn't want to interrupt him. He generally wasn't a long-form dude.

"People say the second week is the worst. Try the second day."

His bout with the virus was so brutal that my coughing for ten days in the guest room and losing my sense of smell—worried that I'd never taste pizza again—was trivial by comparison, so I didn't mention it.

"Was the drinking water okay?" I asked.

"It's usually okay, if it's boiled. The times I could get up, I boiled it. At least whoever lived there before me, or the one before him, left some big bottles of a Paraguayan knockoff of Gatorade. He must have been a runner. That was it. The blue stuff and water, unless you count a can of mackerel I never ate. Just looking at the picture of the fish made me sicker, but the TV wasn't working, so it was all I had. Hey, Corie, are you going to ask if I thought about you when I thought I was going to die?"

I laughed and wanted to say something sardonic like *Do you think I'd own up to such narcissism?* Except nothing came to mind, so I used it as a chance to clear my throat, because I was choked up. "You did think about me," I told him.

"Oh yeah."

Silence, not too awkward. "Sami."

"What?"

"Sometimes I think about you, too." I was midway between talking and croaking. "You know 'sometimes' means 'a lot.'"

"Of course," he said. "So you and your father are talking shop. Going over old glories?" It took a second more for it to click for him. "Or new glories? Working on something again?"

Get to the point, I ordered myself.

When I came to New York to join the Task Force, I had to report to a supervisory special agent who was a misogynist shit and an anti-Semite. After the second time he stared at my boobs and called me Miss Shapiro, I said "Schottland" and crossed my arms over my chest. The third time, I brought along a few Post-its, wrote "Coral Schottland" on the first one—just in case. It was only another two days before he said, "Just state your business, Miss Shulman," so I peeled off the top Post-it and smacked it onto his old-time paper calendar.

After that, to make sure he got the information he needed before I found myself throwing a pamphlet about anti-Semitism at him, I began spouting information the instant I walked through his door. He was a known nonreader of reports, so I delivered multisyllabic observations, breakthroughs, suggestions, and conclusions. I blasted them out like a fusillade and never took more than three minutes. I went so fast the term "briefing" became inadequate.

So it was easy to give Sami a succinct summary of the homicides, arson, Seymour's links to the Russian mob, and the attempt to kill or frighten April Brown.

"And you need me to do something, right?" Sami asked. "What?" One thing I liked about him, in addition to everything else, was that he didn't get pissy if I needed a favor. Usually.

I asked him if he could look into Seymour's . . . Who knew what Hose was, exactly? His partner or assistant or enforcer? Supposedly Hosea Williams had given up dealing drugs when he left Chicago. I wanted to know if Sami had any access to information about Hose's Chicago connections through the DEA—info that might not have been available to the NYPD in the 1990s.

"I don't know how long it will take," Sami said. "I have to get out, get a few things, but I've been really busy." We didn't have any secret code, but I knew him and his work well enough to guess he meant he needed his Task Force phone, the one he used to exchange photos and files and access official databases. Clearly, on this assignment, his phone had to be left off campus.

"No problem," I said with what must have been barfogenic sincerity, because he mimicked me, and we both laughed.

He called me back five days later while Josh and I were in the den enthralled by a documentary on bird cognition. Seriously. New Caledonian crows could make hooked tools! I leaned over Lulu—who would never tempt a documentarian to make a film about her cognition—who lay between us, and pressed pause. Then I went out into the hallway and stuck in an earbud.

"Sorry," Sami said. "I had important stuff to do." He was in a noisy area. It sounded as if someone was fixing a truck, revving its engine again and again. "Okay, listen up, dude," he said. "Here's what I can tell you. Your friend Hose hadn't been involved with drugs since he left Chicago. You know he got six years at Pontiac, max-security?"

"Right," I said. "But he only served fourteen months. Was that for very, very good behavior?"

"If by good behavior you mean selectively disclosing knowledge of the methods used by the CJNG—that's the Cártel Jalisco Nueva Generación—"

"You think I don't know what CJNG stands for?"

"—to take over Sinaloa markets in Chicago."

"Sorry I jumped down your throat," I said.

"The only thing new about that is the apology," Sami said. "Accepted. So because Hose gave the government the CJNG's methods, he got out of Chicago without even having to testify against anyone. That's how golden his info was. When he got to New York, he started hanging out in Brighton Beach, got himself a couple of Russian girlfriends. Within a year he was doing business with a few Russian mob guys who were into prostitution and pornography." He paused. "Corie, this is where you say, 'A class act.'"

"Missed my shot," I said. "And he actually learned Russian by this time?"

"Initially, well enough to get along, but not enough to finish off a liter of vodka and still remember how to conjugate his verbs. But by year two, he was fluent, working for a whole bunch of guys. Gambling, fencing, extortion. Their usual shit."

"Any trouble with the law? State or federal?"

"From what I could tell, in addition to languages, he has a gift for ratting his way out of rough situations."

"So why is he enjoying the comforts of Otisville?" I asked. "And how come he was sent to a medium security prison, with his record?" I'd forgotten for a moment about the crows and parrots and Josh. However, Lulu must have had a touch of border collie in her DNA because she came up behind me and nosed my Achilles tendon to herd me back into the den. I leaned in the door, holding up a finger indicating *Just one second* to Josh, but he was focused on the *New York Times* Spelling Bee puzzle on his phone and waved his hand to say *No rush*.

"It wasn't drugs this time," Sami said. "He started going around calling himself a crypto financial adviser. Money laundering. Amazing, the asshole cannot stay out of trouble, but he's a brilliant asshole. He always makes the most of any situation." I picked up the dog so she wouldn't keep nudging me. She started trying to lick something irresistible around that separation between my nostrils, and I twisted my head out of her reach and tried to mute my *Blech!* while Sami said, "Seymour hired him to work with a few Russian-speaking clients, took a liking to him, and started teaching him to do more sophisticated work. Does that match with what you have?"

"Yes, it does. What's your impression of what Seymour saw in Hose? He never trusted anyone before. But he seemed to really take to him. He wasn't a mentor to anyone else, as far as we know. Well, except by all accounts he was a very devoted and involved father to April."

"Who knows? If life were a movie, it would be because he saw Hose as the son he never had. But it could be just that his business was expanding, and he needed help that very few people had the knowledge and the learning capacity to give," Sami said. "And the lack of morals. Also, Hose was born in the US, so unlike other Russian speakers that he could hire, Seymour trusted that his ultimate loyalty wouldn't be to other Russians. Although 'trust' may not be the best word. Can you ever really trust a guy who was best friends with the Mexican drug cartels? And then flipped?"

"There aren't many accounting majors who took seminars in the concealment of tainted money. You make do with the best you can get," I said.

"So if they had a good mentor-mentee thing going on, why do you suspect him?"

"Because Hose started bringing in some clients to invest with them, but Seymour didn't trust him enough to tell him where he put all their money. It turned out that when Seymour died, Hose couldn't get his clients' money back."

Sami was quiet for a moment. Then he asked, "What else do you need?"

"You've already given me so much time," I told him. "Except I'm not done. I have another favor to ask."

"So what do you want, *cariño*?"

"I want to know how to get into Otisville and speak with Hosea. Getting people to talk is what I do best."

"The visitation rooms there are not open consistently. The only ones who consistently gain in-person access are the prisoners' lawyers, and from what little I've heard, the Bureau of Prisons isn't even giving any guarantees on that. Things keep changing. I guess I'd try to do it through his lawyer."

And then, Sami being Sami—aware of how awful I felt because I didn't have anything more to ask and didn't know what else I could say, and he also didn't know what he could say, and neither of us knew when or if we'd speak again—did what I hoped he would do, because I wasn't brave enough: he hung up.

Laurette Simmons, Hose's attorney, refused to speak to me. After I called six times and left messages, both terse and rococo, someone finally answered. I managed to get out "Hi, this is Corie Gell—" but he'd heard enough.

"Ms. Simmons does not wish to speak with you." He enunciated each word with precision and chopped it off at the end; a sensitive soul would find his *t* in "not" almost too harsh to bear. "She does not permit her clients to interact with—" Suddenly his voice seized up, as though his breakfast protein shake was making a comeback. "They do not communicate with private investigators."

I would have pitied him, except he used "does not wish to speak with you" instead of "does not want to speak with you." I had an urge to say something so scathing it would haunt him for the rest of his life—but nothing hurtful enough came to mind. Calling a felon's lawyer was easier back in the day when I could say, *This is Special Agent Corie Schottland with the Federal Bureau of Investigation*. After I married Josh and left the Bureau, my name morphed into Corie Geller. My new intro—*I'm Corie Geller, private investigator*—clearly made lawyers and their assistants wary. Or disdainful. There was a wonderful world of rejection awaiting me, who had always prided myself on my ability to connect and persuade.

"Ms. Simmons's client is currently residing in Otisville Correctional Facility. While my client is willing—"

"No."

"You cannot be successfully supercilious by cutting off the person you want to demean in mid-sentence," I said, a lot faster than he would have. "Speaking of 'sentence,' my client is willing to foot the bill for a year of Hiroshi Yamauchi's services for Hosea Williams in exchange for my getting to speak with him. Hiroshi Yamauchi is considered—"

"I happen to know who Hiroshi Yamauchi is," the assistant said. "The prison consultant."

Regrettably, I recalled my belief that decency is effective. So I responded with an upbeat, "That's right," and didn't add *you ass*. However, decency did not mean taking shit. So I said, "I need to speak with Ms. Simmons now."

"One moment, please." The phone played *The Four Seasons*, which I liked, though not in one ear. I yawned, then spaced out. "Autumn" went on long enough to move into puffer vest weather.

Prison consultants were either former employees of the Bureau of Prisons or smart ex-convicts who had served their sentences and turned their grasp of surviving the system into a business. White-collar criminal lawyers sometimes referred to the consultants as "concierges."

Services like those provided by the Yamauchi Group didn't come cheap. Yamauchi, whose first job had been as a correctional officer at thirty-five thou a year, had risen through the BOP's ranks to become regional director of its mid-Atlantic division. He'd retired twelve years earlier. "The week after I retired, I got business cards and new stationery," he told me and my dad when we'd met with him two days earlier. "My whole career at the Bureau of Prisons, I watched, I listened. I got to understand how this system operates. It operates badly, but that's what I have to work with, understanding 'badly,' understanding it in all its different forms."

Currently he was charging four hundred bucks per hour. Dad and I pitched him that we were a start-up whose principals were so highly regarded in law enforcement circles, professional courtesy was simply smart business. Yamauchi said, "I don't know about that, but I'll give you a break."

Inevitably, the marginalized folks—who got caught on CCTV waving a Smith & Wesson .38 at a gas station or sold ten grams of PCP to a guy who came off like a cool dude but was actually an ice sculpture posing as a DEA agent—got screwed: not only literally in the holding pen just outside the courtroom at their arraignment, but figuratively and painfully by every aspect of the system. They didn't get a Yamauchi to see them through.

My dad said it reminded him of one of his sister Ruthie's favorite Borscht Belt jokes: An old guy was sitting on a park bench. A bird came flying by and took a dump right on his head. As it flew off, the man yelled after the bird, "For the rich, you sing!"

I yawned again. I'd been so far away from mindfulness that *The Four Seasons* seemed to have made it to Hanukkah/Christmas/Kwanzaa by the time Hosea Williams's lawyer finally answered.

"What is this?" Laurette Simmons sounded amused. "A private investigator offering Hiroshi's services to my client? Do you have any concept of what that man charges per hour, my dear?"

"Yes." I saw no need to mention his discount or her "my dear." What I did need was to get actionable info from Hose.

Initially, I'd insisted to my dad that I wanted to pony up for Yamauchi's fee. We'd already told April that the case was going to be pro bono, but if we were going to make a go of an investigations business, this would be an investment in our future. Dad flatly refused. April was already getting our considerable skills for free, he said. Besides, we already knew it wouldn't be a financial hardship for her. So I agreed we'd ask April.

Together, we'd called her. Dad tapped my arm when she answered—to show he wanted to be the one doing the talking. There is one man alive who knew Seymour's business interests, he told her. And that's Hose, and of course Hose wasn't going to talk to us out of the goodness of his heart. We needed to make sure it was to his advantage. But we could offer him something he wanted—the leverage that would make him open up.

My dad spoke clearly but with intensity. He explained to April who Yamauchi was and the services he provided. It would cost a lot of money, sure. But the information Hose gave us could be the key to unlocking April's family history, and maybe the threats that faced her now. When he finished, he paused, ready to parry any objections April might raise. But she simply said, "Okay, sure. How should I get the money to you?"

"Yamauchi charges four hundred an hour," I informed Simmons. "His fee is not an issue." Before she could come up with yet another way to condescend, I told her that my client was the sole survivor of the arson-murder that had killed Hose's onetime partner twenty years earlier. She still seemed suspicious that I was scamming her, and she was just trying to figure out what kind of scam it was.

"And no doubt you are about to assure me that you aren't planning to pin something on Mr. Williams," she said, her sarcasm less than effective as she'd been snide to begin with.

"I'm planning on helping you save his ass by having my client pay for a year—up to seventy-five hour-long sessions—with Hiroshi Yamauchi and his group," I replied. "By that time your client should be residing in a minimum or low-security facility and looking forward to his freedom."

"And the reason for this munificence?" Laurette Simmons asked. Her question was followed by an odd, liquidy sound: maybe she was taking teeny sips of scalding tea. It occurred to me that perhaps I viewed her harshly because I couldn't shake the notion that women naturally tend toward courtesy, or at least civility. Would I really take notice of a disagreeable male lawyer and wonder, *Why is he acting like this?*

"The munificence comes from my client's need to know," I said. "Someone tried to murder her."

"This is the child of that Seymour person," she said, to make things clear.

"Except she's not a child anymore. And she didn't go into the family business. She's got a PhD and teaches at Rutgers."

"So why would someone go after her if she is leading such a blameless existence?" Somehow her stress on the word "blameless," along with an adenoid quality to her voice, made it sound as if she thought April was beyond contempt. I could understand that a lawyer needs to protect her client. Though maybe Hose was such a pain in the butt she didn't want to have to talk to him.

"Whoever went after her may have wanted revenge that has to do with her father. Hosea Williams wasn't the only one who lost hundreds of thousands or millions when Seymour died. It's possible they may have gone after his daughter for retribution."

"But Hosea was in Otisville when your client was attacked," Simmons said. A major glug of whatever she was drinking, so it must have cooled. I mentally switched her drink from tea to Irish coffee. "Locked up nice and tight, and they do head counts five times a day. We call that an alibi."

"So do we," I said, "and that's how you know I'm not looking to implicate your client in any way, Ms. Simmons." This wasn't quite true. I certainly wouldn't mind if Hose somehow implicated himself. But I wanted to set her mind at ease. "Hose can give me background on the case that no one else can. That's all I'm looking for. And what you're looking for is a way to improve his situation. Let's help each other."

Yamauchi was already proving he was worth with every penny. Within twenty-four hours he had arranged a Zoom conference with Laurette Simmons, his own chief corporate counsel, the deputy assistant somebody from the BOP who wore a scarf decorated with teddy bears, and the warden at Otisville. He'd coached me on what points I needed to get across.

Having heard Laurette Simmons on the phone, I had pictured her as about fifty, figuring the database had her age input incorrectly. Nope, eighty-three. On Zoom she looked like a desiccated cream puff in a white suit jacket and pearls, a froth of dyed platinum hair or a wig, and super-pale skin. Her lipstick sank into the crevasses that radiated around her lips. I'd never realized how good the resolution was on my monitor.

The consultations on whether I could interview Hosea Williams didn't take as long as the Paris Peace Accords, and they weren't as complex, but I could sense that each participant wanted to be heard. Needed to be heard. At length.

Eventually I muted everyone but myself and said, "This isn't a hostage negotiation, so I don't have to show seemingly endless patience while I let you all vent. But a life is at risk. You all know about my client and how her parents were murdered in an arson-homicide when she was five years old. Recently—you all have a copy of the report from Detective Ricardo Jones of the New Brunswick, New Jersey, PD—an attempt was made on her life. I believe there is a possibility that the two crimes are linked, and there is only one individual with the memory and inside information who can shed light on this. Hosea Williams. I've spoken with each of you about my background both at FBI Headquarters in DC and the Joint Terrorism Task Force in New York. I've invited you to check me out further. I've answered your questions and listened to your suggestions.

"Warden DeKalb, I appreciate your concern about your inmates' and officers' health and welfare, and I would follow your rules to the letter." I stopped there; he looked as if anyone trying to boost his ego would irritate him.

"Ms. Harrison," I went on to the Bureau of Prisons rep. "If you and your colleagues had managed only to keep your sanity during the worst of Covid, I'd salute you for it, but you've done so much more. The way you've kept friends and families of the inmates informed . . ." Blah, blah—I troweled it on. Yamauchi told me that getting her to represent the BOP for the conference was a stroke of luck because she was susceptible to flattery. Though I was tempted to offer a final blah and tell her how cute her scarf was, it would probably nauseate Warden DeKalb. And as Yamauchi had told me, ultimately the warden would be the Decider.

My computer always shut down with a sigh, that exhalation of release that comes to us humans as well when the day is at last over and we unhook the tormenting bra. I still stayed bent over, peering at the screen, until finally I ordered my shoulders to unhunch. Slowly, I extended my legs and sidestepped in my chair until I was facing the couch.

My dad smiled an understated cop smile, not his seal-of-approval daddy grin. This was, after all, business. But he did give the accolade that worked for either role: "Kiddo, you did good."

CHAPTER SIXTEEN

Hosea Williams wasn't long on charm, but when he was brought into a lawyer's consultation room, his handcuffed wrists attached to a belly chain, he gave a polite "Hey, Miss Laurette." His lips hardly moved. "How're you?" He did smile fleetingly, like someone who regrets his teeth, although one of the presentencing reports I'd read noted that he'd gotten a new and fancier set when he'd been the Mexican cartels' *número tres o cuatro* in Chicago. More likely he'd developed some jailhouse wariness. Hose nodded to me and murmured, "Ms. Geller."

I could hear his Appalachian accent even in those few words. Since I'd gone back over all the documentation on Hosea Williams the day before, I knew he'd spent his first fifteen years in Grimms Landing, West Virginia, a town that lacked an apostrophe, though it seemed he turned his back on it for other reasons.

The corrections officer who helped him into in a padded, armless chair took a short chain welded to the table and, earning a C-minus for manual dexterity, padlocked the chain to Hose's cuffs, so that his hands would be visible at all times. The officer made a sound like "Eh?" and Hose said "Uh." I translated it as *Is this okay for you?* And *Yeah, it's okay.*

Laurette Simmons snapped, "Guard, is this really necessary?" The corrections officer eyed her for as long as he could without risking a reprimand for disrespect and nodded, *Yes, it is necessary*. I understood why he'd eye her. On Zoom, I had found her compelling; she'd been dressed entirely in white, from pearls to frilly shirt and jacket to nail polish. This time she had a pale pink scarf with darker pink ribbons swirling across it and a pink wrap dress, a pink band on her watch. Her shoes, nails, and lipstick were an intense strawberry.

Since that first all-white day, I'd asked a couple of my friends in the Bureau about her. She did white-collar cases, not terrorism, but they'd heard of her and her outfits. Several shades of green, ditto with blue, and so on through the rest of the rainbow, as well as black. Her theory was that jurors would look forward to what the defense counsel's color of the day would be. Their marveling (or, infrequently, aversion) would keep them aware of her, as in *What a character!*

And yet I gave her credit for taking the time to meet us out here. What lawyer wanted to see her client in prison and be reminded of *guilty* ringing through the courtroom? What lawyer, knowing this client had spent everything on the trial and had zip left to pay for an appeal, would shell out for an Uber and make a four-hour round trip from Manhattan just to let that client get a shot at better treatment in prison or an earlier release?

Once the corrections officer had left, I turned to Hose. Maybe it was the light, but he looked paler than when he'd first walked in. His hands on the table had contracted into fists. Not white-knuckled fists, but clenched.

He didn't look much like the pictures of him that I'd seen. In the mug shot for money laundering crimes, he'd been a clean-shaven middle-aged man—tired-looking, his face flabby all around the bottom, looking like a molded lemon mousse I recently made that needed a touch more gelatin. I'd expected him to deteriorate even further in prison, but now Hose had a full, well-groomed beard and looked beyond fit. His neck was so full of muscles that it seemed to emerge from the middle of his shoulders. Even his face looked exercised; what first looked like high cheekbones, on second glance appeared to be more muscles, as if cheek workouts were part of his routine.

I began with a few questions about his parents, siblings, and his leaving for Chicago. He said he didn't run away from home as much as walked off without an argument or a final goodbye. Hose's delivery was easy, not rushed. He had probably told his story often enough to lawyers, parole boards, and prison shrinks. He sounded close to sincere.

As Hose told it, his father was an alcoholic, given mostly to silence but also to rare and terrorizing bouts of violence. His mother was probably also an alcoholic, but at least she loved him and his four siblings. He fondly described her uncanny ability to hear a song just once and play it on her guitar. He had a knack for school, he said, but he was turned off by his indifferent and burned-out teachers. He did most of his real learning on his own.

Hose's first crime, just before his fifteenth birthday, was stealing a pickup from the neighbor. He drove to Charleston, West Virginia, less than an hour away. He was alone and had never driven before. He broke into a drugstore through a bathroom window, stole all the 'ludes and Sopor in the store, and amazed Grimms Landing's sole significant drug dealer, who handed over three hundred dollars. He returned the truck to its owner's house before daybreak.

The first thing he bought was a new microwave to replace the one that had broken two years earlier. A couple of months later, so his mother would think he was working his butt off after school at a lumberyard, he spent the rest of the money on her dream, a sewing machine. But she sensed that something wasn't right and told him to take it back. He was so ashamed that he took off.

I'd taken the CIA course on how to spot liars and MIT's Cues to Deception seminars to bolster my interviewing technique. But I still wasn't sure how much truth there was in that first chapter of Hose's memoir. It had too many signs of an oft-told tale, too many pauses at the perfect places for dramatic effect. I couldn't see what he would gain by lying, except perhaps my sympathy for the bright kid with the hard luck.

"Okay. I'm going to jump around with my questions," I told him, "so if you're looking for any logical sequence, it might not be apparent. Also, something you say may lead me to go off on what might seem like a tangent."

"But I can rest assured it's not a tangent?" Hose asked. Despite the cuffs, chains, and uniform, he had the low-key smile of a hotshot. One side of his mouth was raised in acknowledgment of being mildly diverted.

"If you like," I said, "you can also rest assured that this interview isn't a gotcha. As I told your lawyer, I'm not trying to get you blamed for anything or trying to extract information that would extend your sentence or put you in danger."

"She told me that." Hose didn't even glance at Laurette Simmons as he said that. His eyes were glued to mine, which might have been a fifth-grade power play or simply intense concentration. "Nice to hear it in your own words. But I can't say for sure I believe it's God's honest truth."

I nodded. I was grateful they had made me surrender my jacket when we came through the lawyers' entrance. There was a small vent in the room, but whatever fresh air came through it had to vie with the dankness and residual body odors that clung to the cinder block walls. Though I didn't want to turn around, I guessed that Simmons was getting as pink as her ensemble.

"All right," Hose said. Not only had his fists unclenched, he was doing some finger wiggling. "You need me because you want to know if whoever tried to run over Seymour's girl had anything to do with the fire that killed him and his wife. And I need you because I can't pay for Yamauchi."

"In a nutshell," I said.

Suddenly Hose's eyes lit up, and he started shaking his index finger at me. "Okay, now I know where the name of your firm comes from. Schottland & Geller. I couldn't remember, and it was bugging me. Schottland. That wouldn't happen to be the cop who questioned me about Seymour and his wife? Over and over and over."

"Yes, he worked the case. Seymour's daughter initially contacted us because of his familiarity with the murders. He's my business partner."

"You didn't tell me about this!" Simmons snapped. I was grateful that I couldn't catch her eye, as she was seated behind me.

I paused, and so did Hose. He scrutinized the bracket welded into the table that held the chain padlocked to a doubled link in his belly chain.

"Detective Schottland questioned you twice, and you were never arrested," I said. "No charges were ever brought. He is now retired from the NYPD. That's all the relevant information. Are the two of you good to go?"

Laurette may have been about to object, when Hose said, "Good to go, Ms. Geller." She hesitated and then gave a quick nod, deciding not to press further.

"Great." I switched to Spanish. "I'm impressed with your language skills. I hear that Russian is really hard to learn. Did you take any lessons or use an app? I guess it would have been DVDs or a CD-ROM back then."

"No. Mostly I listened and did what they call that total immersion thing, except I didn't know in those days that it had a name." Hose was completely fluent. He never paused for even a second to come up with a word. "Same thing when I learned Spanish, back in Chicago. Get yourself a girlfriend or two so you can't cheat and speak English."

I laughed, and before Laurette Simmons could throw a fit, I turned to her. Her face and forearms were glowing from the heat and had a glaze of sweat. She'd taken off her scarf. "I was just checking on Mr. Williams's fluency in Spanish. Don't worry, I don't know any Russian, and we'll continue in English."

I turned back to Hose. "I'm impressed how you learned two languages, along with learning from Seymour how to do the complex financial manipulations necessary for money laundering."

"I call it accounting," he said.

"Okay. But you clearly are a smart guy." He tilted his head, granting the point modestly. "Let's agree for the moment that you had good reasons to keep Seymour alive."

"For the moment?" Hose repeated. He cocked his head almost imperceptibly and raised his right brow, alert for signs of danger from me.

"To be clear." I sat up straighter—not because I was about to lay my cards on the table, though I was. But the molded plastic seat had a way of pressing itself directly into my tailbone. "Right now, I don't think you have a motive, and I don't think you killed Seymour. Is it possible there's something I don't know? Well, as I said, you're smart. And you're in here, so I know you're capable of committing crimes. So of course I think there's a possibility that you're hiding something."

He shrugged. "Or you think there's a possibility I'm hiding a lot of things." He seemed on the brink of enjoying himself. "You're smart too. If I'm hiding something important, you've got a better shot at figuring it out than most." I heard Laurette snort at his banter, but she didn't say anything.

"But you know my main purpose here is not to investigate Seymour's and Kim's deaths," I went on. "I'm not trying to see someone charged for a double murder from the 1990s. Sure, I am interested in who killed them, but only because it might give me more information about who tried to hurt or kill my client—their daughter." Hose gave a quick nod of acknowledgment. Some—but not all—of the heightened alertness in his face and neck muscles melted away. "So here's why I want to talk to you. When a guy like you is being questioned by the police for a murder and he knows he's on the list of suspects, he's going to think long and hard about who really did it. I want to know what you came up with. I don't need hard evidence, because, again, I'm not trying to lock someone up for that murder. I want your theories."

Hose emitted a brief, loud chuckle. "During the murder investigation I wanted to ask, 'How fucking dumb are you guys?' I mean the cops."

I bristled for my dad's sake but stayed impassive. "Why were the cops dumb?"

"Well, for one thing, they're supposed to find out whodunit. Right? And they didn't. But that's their job. They have the time and the resources to figure that shit out."

"That's true," I said, resisting my desire for a snarky comeback. I had to admit there was truth in that. There were reasons for it, like near-total incineration of evidence, including DNA, a superior officer—Bobby Melvin—who was a fan of superficiality because it was fast. But I was sure that while my dad didn't blame himself, he didn't consider the case one of his finest moments.

We both paused again. Hose broke first and filled the silence. "I could give you names of guys who hated him the most, even more than the rest hated him. But were they fixing to burn down his house with him and his wife in it? No, and no again. Because ninety percent of them would lose millions if he got killed. And the other ten percent were the ninety percent's kin." I liked the way his Appalachian accent made "kin" two syllables. "So whether they hated Seymour or just thought he was badder than bad didn't matter. Because none of them would do it."

"And definitely no one would stew for twenty years and then attempt to kill April, his daughter?" I asked.

"There could be someone who'd kill a kid, but no way after all this time. After Seymour died, we had to change all our policies on accounting. Create layers of redundancy, like in any business. So if anyone got hit by a bus—or burned alive or whatever—the clients could still access their money."

Laurette leaned forward. "Hosea," she said warningly. "Self-incrimination." He offered his half-grin and jauntily pointed a finger at her, as if to say, *Oops, my bad—you've got a great point.*

I waved my hand in a way that I hoped indicated my utter lack of interest in incriminating Hose for money laundering.

He went on without my prompting him. "They would have given anything to have Seymour alive and kicking. Number one reason was he always got the job done—clean, no sloppy mistakes. Number two, if they pressured him too hard to know the whereabouts of their money, he'd drop them like a hot potato, and even when they begged him to take them back in, he'd say, 'You're dead to me.'"

"He'd talk to them like that?" I asked, and even before I was finished, he started nodding. "I've heard the Vory could make the Norte del Valle Cartel look like a gentlemen's club," I said.

"I don't think he had any fear of them. He was the genius at what he did, and they wanted him to keep doing it. He knew that, but his real power was not being afraid of anyone, anywhere. He must've been born that way."

"So a dead Seymour was worthless on a financial level."

"Right. Well, worse than worthless. He cost them," he said. "Though, you know . . ."

"I know what?"

"There could be somebody in that group—his clients—who had reasons I don't know about. Who took their money out first or forced him to give away the info on where their money was. Maybe before he died, he was held at gunpoint and asked for account numbers and passwords. You asked for my theories, that's one of them." I nodded and was about to speak when he cut me off. "And you know I didn't do that, right? Because some of those guys, the ones who had been my clients, might have killed me too when they lost their money. It took me fucking forever to get myself back in good graces."

I agreed that that made sense and suggested we take a break. After using the bathroom and Purell-ing it up as if I were prepping for surgery, I sat in a corner of the attorneys' room, put on noise-canceling headphones, and listened to rain in the forest, which my mom would call *most pleasant*. I ate the sandwich I'd ordered from the prison commissary, which she would definitely not call *most pleasant*. But at least it turned out to be what I'd asked for, an American cheese sandwich with nothing on it except a label that said it was made according to CDC standards. Laurette ate only an apple she'd brought with her.

When Hose was brought back in, the corrections officer was more hurried as he locked the cuffs onto the chain, and the long sleeve of Hose's green uniform rose enough so a tattoo was displayed on his wrist. It was a full-color woman's hand with a red, clawlike manicure. Her nails were gouging his skin. Bubbles of blood had formed around them in a different shade of red. I wondered if the rest of her was slithering around him and if it got tedious with her forever humping on his back. Or was the point that her other hand was lower down, raking his balls? But I couldn't imagine balls getting tattooed. I asked, "What was it like with the clients when the news got around that Seymour and Kim Brown had been killed?"

"Total chaos," Hose said. "Shock at first, I guess. I was the one who had to tell them that I couldn't get their money. Or at least some of it. For the ones I could get, I tried to persuade them to leave it with me. Some did, some didn't." He frowned, looking down. "They wanted me for regular accounting work, of course, not money laundering." I waved my hand, indicating my lack of interest in such picayune details. "After that," he went on, "everyone was running off to meetings, or for secret appointments with criminal lawyers."

"And what about you?" I asked. "Did you have meetings or go to a lawyer?"

Hose, with an admirable sense of drama, smacked his head against the table, barely avoiding hitting the chain. "Meetings?" he roared. He had been calm until this point, and the abrupt mood shift was startling. "Every client of mine—small stuff Seymour wouldn't have given the time of day to. They wanted me to meet them. They screamed into the phone, 'Now!' They came to my condo. One waved a gun in my doorman's face to get my apartment number. They grabbed my shirt, shook me. 'Where is my money?' 'How the fuck could you not know what he was doing?' I couldn't walk down the street because people recognized me as Seymour's man. So Seymour's big clients wanted me too. One had his goons grab me, hold me down till he could send a couple of his top guys to bring me to him.

"And it wasn't just about money. They were scared that maybe someone in Washington like the IRS or Treasury—who knew about Seymour but didn't have anything to use against him—maybe the Feds saw that fire. What if they came nosing around? I'm guessing the only reason I'm still alive is that the Russians were worried I had a way to alert the Feds in case anything happened to me. And of course, they realized how good I was."

"No attempts on your life?" I asked.

"No." He was calm again. "Back then, I was scared. I admit it. But finally it hit me that I was the closest thing they had to him, their last hope. They played on the side of honey, not vinegar. Well, their version of honey, anyway. Not that they wanted to play it that way, but I was too valuable." His confidence reminded me, weirdly, of Wynne's. Not bragging and not brash, just an assurance that he had a unique set of skills. He stopped to drink water from a water bottle a corrections officer had brought in. As we waited for the guy to leave, I watched Hose's puffy eyes, deep in thought, looking at a place that was nowhere.

"Ready to continue?" I asked.

Instead of saying yes or no, he cleared his throat and said, "I was the only one Seymour ever chose to work with. Like, as a colleague, not a secretary."

"Why you, do you think?" I asked with the most pleasant expression I could muster, so the question was more *Of all your superior qualities, which impressed Seymour the most?*

His stare into space must have been productive because his answer was instantaneous. "My Russian. Some of them, they were so dug in with their own kind that they couldn't learn English. Some of them just got off the boat. They come and go, these people. Or they'd speak it when they didn't want Seymour to understand and then say 'Oh, sorry,' like they forgot they were talking Russian."

"And he trusted you —"

"He trusted me because I'm smart. I learned the language like"—even cuffed, he snapped the fingers of both hands and made a sharp sound—"like it was a snap. I picked up accounting faster than he did, he told me. But probably mostly he trusted me because we were two Americans. You can't trust them the same way. They're loyal to each other first. Even when their English is okay, you don't know what's in their heads. They're just plain foreign. I'm not saying it's a bad thing. They're not like us, and we're not like them."

I nodded as an acknowledgment of what he had said, though I worried for a second that I was acquiescing to a statement about the otherness of Slavs. "Let's forget about Russians now," I said. "Before, you mentioned that Russians with motives you don't know about was one of your theories. What were your other theories?"

"Seymour could be an asshole," Hose said.

"I've heard of some of the things he did. He could be a bully, vicious."

"That's true, but 'bully' sounds like he was a shithead during third-grade recess. Seymour was a complete asshole—even in that world. I'm sure a hundred people thought at some point, *I wish that guy was dead*."

"But who would have acted on it?" I asked.

Hose widened his eyes and shook his head in perplexity, exhaling slowly. But he gamely went on. "One of his old girlfriends, maybe. I mean, he had a pretty enough wife, but by maybe a month after they got married, he always had something on the side. At least one. He said he needed more than any one woman could give him. And he could be real nice to them at first, give them expensive stuff, jewelry. One he bought an apartment." He waited and then added, "One time he said it wasn't just sex that made him have girlfriends."

"Then what was it?"

"I didn't want to ask him. You learned with Seymour to just to take what he said and leave it at that."

"Did he physically abuse any of his girlfriends?"

"Not that I ever heard, but you know. People do stuff when they're in private." I was about to follow up, but he cut me off. "If you asked any questions at all, he'd get so mad. Sometimes insane. You never knew what he'd do. Throw over the watercooler and walk out. Scream at me and his secretary, Carly, 'I want that all dry when I get back.'"

"Any physical violence toward either of you?" I asked.

"No. He wouldn't lay a hand on Carly. He needed her. He dropped all his papers and forms on her desk, and she always had a system so he could find them."

I didn't repeat the question or ask anything else for a moment. Keeping quiet like that was always hard for me, as I grew up in a house where there was never an awkward silence. But I'd learned that silence could be very valuable in an interview, to see where the subject's thoughts went.

I was counting *twenty-two banana, twenty-three,* when Hose said, "One time I told him someone from the Nicosia Bank of Exchange called, wanted Seymour to call him back. But Seymour forgot. And then he wouldn't believe that I had told him to call the guy. He grabbed my ear and started twisting it around till I thought he would tear it off. He kept screaming, 'You better start remembering.'" Hose tried to cover his face, forgetting that his hands were palms down and he was chained to the table. He lowered his head. "Just a week before, he told me that the next year he was going to give me a piece of the business, that we'd be partners."

I let him settle himself. I didn't think he was crying, but the memory was obviously still painful—which was in its own way impressive, given that Hose had consorted with the scum of the earth for his entire adult life. This time I broke the silence by asking him if he'd ever seen or heard about Seymour hurting his wife or daughter. "No," he said. "The little girl? Never! The wife? Again, I don't know. It's not like he was a knight in shining armor. But I didn't see anything. Like she didn't have bruises or wear long sleeves in the summer or sunglasses indoors or whatever."

"So maybe he could be a jerk to her, but no signs of abuse."

"No. I mean, I never really talked to her much, one on one. But I didn't notice anything."

"Did you ever meet any of his girlfriends?" I asked.

Hose shook his head. "But I did know that part of his fun was being cruel. When he got tired of a girl, he'd just drop her. No goodbye, no explanation. He'd stop showing up or calling and then in a couple of days, they'd call the office. He'd tell Carly to say he didn't want to speak to her. Or didn't have time for her. And she always said it."

"So Carly would do the breakups."

"Sometimes the girls wouldn't believe her and kept calling again and again. In time, like a week or two, he'd come out from his private office and say in a loud voice, 'Why can't that stupid bitch get the message?' Or 'ugly bitch,' or 'old.' But I think in a fucked-up way he got off on that."

"You said a loud voice. Was he yelling? Did he lose it?" As unnoticeably as possible, I lifted my right butt cheek and then my left off the molded plastic, hoping to relieve some of the tailbone pressure.

"No. Just loud enough for the girl to hear every word. I remember, after he was killed, someone said he made regular bad look good. I never heard that way of putting it, but it was right. He was cruel for no reason. He'd be fine one minute and the next minute so terrible, and there was no explaining it. Or he'd find a stupid reason and go batshit. A dumb thing where most guys would say, *Waste of time*."

"Do you think any of the women he humiliated knew where he lived?"

"I doubt it. The house was in the name of a shell corporation. Couldn't be traced. Like everything else."

Feeling a trickle of sweat rolling down the corner of my right eye, like a tear, I asked, "Are you familiar with the name Luisa de León?"

"Yeah. She was a girlfriend. The most serious. I'm not saying she was serious like she never smiled, I'm saying she was the one he was most serious about. She was the one I was talking about before, with the apartment."

"Do you have any thoughts about her?"

He shrugged. "I mean, she wound up with an apartment, right? So there's that." I appreciated that he could so readily see everyone's motives. He'd have made a good detective had life given him just a few more advantages at the start. "But he wasn't a dick to her, at least that I heard. I think she might have been different to him. Not just another girlfriend. Jewelry is one thing, but fucking real estate is a whole other ball of wax. He once told me that she was a smart cookie. I don't remember him saying anything nice about the other ones. Except, like . . ." I gestured for him to continue. He seemed embarrassed but went on. "That they were hot or good in bed or something."

I wasn't quite sure why a guy with Hose's tattoos would get squeamish alluding to sex, but I went on. "Did he ever do anything hurtful to clients he dropped? Or didn't drop."

"No. That's another thing. He had self-control. Never once hurt a client or acted like an animal. But if you were in a car with him and his driver got stuck in traffic, he'd yell the same thing over and over, like 'dickhead' or 'you asshole' to the driver." I pictured Toddy, sitting up front, taking the invective. "Over and over, so many times. I could sometimes feel vomit in my throat. You know?"

"It sounds horrible."

"And his wife. She had beautiful blue eyes, cute body. I heard from people who went out with them, one time he went after her for wearing too much makeup, told her she looked like a slut with all the stuff on her eyes and why did she want to look like a whore instead of a wife? That time he didn't yell. He said it in a low voice. But someone's wife was sitting next to him. She heard it and told her husband. The husband told me about it, said his wife thought he did it because he was embarrassed by her."

"Embarrassed by Kim?" I said.

"Yeah. I guess she was less upscale or something, even though she always looked good to me. The other wives there that night were older, knew how to handle themselves."

"Any other points of friction?" I asked.

"Oh yeah! She went through his briefcase and found out about the apartment he'd bought Luisa and made her co-owner. Fireworks like the Fourth of July! But he was a genius liar and convinced Kim that Luisa was a legit real estate investor. They were partners in this deal. Give the guy credit. He told Kim, 'I'll take you to her office, introduce you. You'll see.' And Kim bought it. Or at least Seymour told me she bought it. But Kim was not what you'd call brilliant."

"This has been really helpful so far. Anyone else he treated badly?" I asked.

Hose shrugged. "He'd go after anybody he thought was beneath him. Like the janitor in the office building. Or waiters. It makes everyone at the table feel terrible. This one time? The waiter's wearing a pin that says GEORGE. He's a Spanish guy. And what do you know, Seymour kept calling him 'Jorge' in this terrible accent. Like, 'Jorge, my steak better be medium-rare. You write that down, Jorge.' Later, when we were leaving, he says to this George guy, 'I'll leave the tip in cash.' Like being nice to make up for being a shit. He's holding this wad of money. George leaves, and Seymour peels off three bills real slow, like they were hundreds. But they're a ten and two singles. You know what the check for dinner was?

A hundred and ninety-six dollars! I mean, even back then guys like him would leave eighteen to twenty percent."

I shook my head. "Did anyone say anything? Or were they all afraid of confronting him?"

"Afraid of confronting him," he confirmed. "Also, he had their money."

I smoothed the space between my brows, which, if I ever decided to get Botox, would be the first place. It soothed me for a moment, at least enough to ask yet another question about Seymour's bullying. "Did he ever put down people who weren't beneath him, the ones with more power? Like some of the heavy hitters in the Russian mob. Were they safe from him?"

"He was careful about that. With all clients, really, but especially the big ones. Once in a while he'd say something that was true, but shouldn't have been said. Like this one real giant Kazakh, who had contracts all around the world for some oily shit to clean rifles. He was wearing a new pair of those wire glasses, and Seymour says, 'Nice, Omar. Real gold frames, I bet. They look good on you, nice to see you're finally making an effort.' But he didn't do that too much. I'm still not sure if it was a power trip or he was clueless."

"But little April never got any of his malice," I observed.

"I like that word," Hose said. "Malice. No, little April was the light of his life. She was the only one in the world he had nothing but good feelings for. He told me he worried about her because she was so pretty and smart. Maybe even a genius, and what kind of normal guy would want a girl like that?"

"But he was okay to you most of the time? Forgetting the ear for a minute, which is hard to do, he mentored you, right? Taught you accounting, let you bring in the clients he ordinarily wouldn't bother with."

Hose shook his head. "I mean, I'm glad I learned that stuff. But no, he wasn't okay. One of my other theories is that whoever killed him used to work for him. Not anyone specific, just someone who worked with him at some point." I widened my eyes, inviting him to continue. "I swear I'm not thinking of anyone specific. I don't know anyone who used to work for him and got fired or whatever." Hose drew in a breath. "He did teach me, let me work with him. All around Brooklyn, folks were telling me I was the first one he ever trusted."

"Do you think they were right? Did he have faith in you, respect?"

"No. I think he liked my smartness. But he had trouble having faith in me. Maybe it was me being intelligent. Could he have sensed that maybe one day I'd outgrow him." I didn't hear a question mark: better to take it as a statement and not react. "Seymour didn't believe in anyone. Maybe Luisa a bit. But he was too cynical, probably, to really trust anyone. Just his little girl. She was four or five, but he thought no one else in the world could outshine her. She was the only one worth his while. And me? After all I done, after all the shit I took, he still didn't tell me the stuff I needed to know to save the business—and my own ass—if anything ever happened to him."

"And what about your trust in him?" I asked, touching the tips of my fingers and thumbs together, church steeple–style: another of the tells I'd learned at Quantico. About to ask a gotcha question, I instantly pulled my hands apart, which showed how out of practice I was. If you catch yourself sending out a signal, consider it sent. Trying to cut it short was itself an attention grabber.

"Depends what you mean by 'trust.' I never doubted that he could lie to me or drop me. But I knew he needed me—and I knew he had no one else. Carly could sort stuff, organize everything. But I could think. He needed someone to help him because the business kept growing. It got to be too much work for any man, even one with a great mind. A couple of times he said stuff like 'Hey, partner-to-be.' I trusted that because I knew he couldn't do what he wanted to do without me. There wasn't a backlog of Russian-talking, supersmart finance dudes around he could choose from who weren't scared to deal with guys from the Vory . . ."

"But was it about a month before he was killed . . . You went into a restaurant where he was having dinner with a couple of mob guys. You walked up to his table and began shouting that you weren't getting your fair cut, that he was hiding money from you."

"I thought this interview wasn't about me," he said wryly.

I shook my head. "I'm trying to understand the guy."

Another of his half-grins. "Yeah, your partner, that Detective Schottland, went on and on about that dinner when he interviewed me. I remember." He bent his head over so he could scratch an itch with his shackled hands. "So, yeah. I was pissed. I was giving him his cut of my clients. Ten percent. And he didn't even do any work on the accounts. But he was hiding clients from me. I wasn't getting my cut. Which was only one percent! Even with the clients I was working on."

"What did Seymour do?" I asked.

"He had the headwaiter throw me out. But no big deal. We made up."

"So you essentially gave him permission to hide his clients from you?" I asked, using my amped-up eyebrow raise, developed when I first began having to distance myself from a manacled prisoner.

"No," Hose said, extending the syllable. Probably taking time to think of a passable answer. "He said he was sorry about the misunderstanding. He was going to cut me in more gradually. He explained and then got out of his chair and reached out across the desk to shake hands. No hard feelings."

"Do you really think there were no hard feelings?"

He shrugged. "Do I think it was really a misunderstanding? No. Do I think he saw how pissed I was and decided to find a way to fix the situation and keep me on? Yes. When it comes down to it, he was an asshole, and, okay, I can be an asshole, but to this day I still think he needed me."

I pushed back the chair and stretched out. Then I said, "Okay, Hose, you've got your prison consultant."

He seemed surprised that our meeting was over. His thanks weren't profuse, but they were touching because some of the unexpressed emotion behind them came through. Laurette Simmons gave me nothing but silence, and when I turned, her head was lowered. Pink chin and jowls draped over her scarf and filled in the V of her pink dress. But it was a good pink, I thought. Blood flowing. And she breathed evenly and easily.

Hose asked, "Did I give you anything you can use?"

"I think so," I told him, and smiled. Whether the smile was genuine was a question even I couldn't answer.

CHAPTER SEVENTEEN

"Momby," Eliza said. "Why do they call it an invited talk? No one was checking off names."

"Right. And no red velvet rope." April Brown had finally made it to Long Island, though it was for a film talk, not our case. "I think 'invited' means that Hofstra's film department asked April Brown to come and speak," I explained. "She's an expert on this subject. She's given this lecture at different colleges and thought we might want to hear it."

"A band tour," Eliza said, "minus the merch." My kid liked dipping into future selves, and I guessed this was her vision of second-semester-college cynical mode. "Maybe non-invited people just push their way in because they're obsessed with hearing about"—she glanced at what had just been projected on the screen—"Outside Looking In: Class and Womanhood in *Stella Dallas*."

The title of the talk was accompanied by a couple of shots from the 1937 movie projected above it. In one, the actress Barbara Stanwyck, dressed in Depression anti-chic—an oversize coat and sad hat—was standing in the rain outside a stately iron fence. The other shot showed what she was staring at inside—a society wedding, the mandatory beautiful bride and guests so elegantly decked out that it was like a deliberate middle finger to the masses.

Beneath that was APRIL BROWN, ASSISTANT PROFESSOR OF CINEMA STUDIES, RUTGERS UNIVERSITY.

"She told me it was a way of getting feedback on her work," I said. "She talks about her ideas, and based on the questions and comments she gets, she makes changes to her writing before her article gets published."

We waited, seated in a lecture hall that had curved, tiered seats looking down at a lectern and screen. Eliza rested her head on my shoulder, which wasn't easy because she was so much taller. But she scrunched down, and it felt good. The pandemic, first the lockdown and then a hybrid schedule, had been rough on her, as it had on almost every kid. She'd spent most of her time on devices. Whether due to the sudden changes in the world, or her age—I'd always suspected it was both—she'd been at her most distant from us. She'd occasionally sit through entire meals with only a shrug and an eye roll. But since then, some of her good nature felt it safe to return. The compressed horizontal line under her nose went back to being a mouth. She'd actually asked to come with me to hear April.

"So did you learn anything from the guy in jail?" Eliza asked.

"Yes. I don't know if it's a help or not. None of the awful people Seymour did business with—to call them scum would be overpraising them—had a motive to commit a double murder. At least not one we know about yet. And to do it in such a sickening way. In fact, the opposite is true. From what Hosea Williams said, they had every reason to wish Seymour would live and be well, which makes sense."

"And his wife," Eliza added.

"Of course." I hesitated and then went for it. "But there was one girlfriend—"

"From before he was married?"

"During," I said. Eliza's eyes flickered only for an instant. "She had something in the way of a financial motive because of a real estate deal she and Seymour were in."

"So is she the main suspect?"

"No, but mostly because she doesn't seem to be a murderer. She's so likable and non-crazy. Also, she just doesn't seem like she would risk throwing her life away for money. I'm trying to find a balance between trusting my gut on this and recognizing that any of us, even experts in interrogation, sometimes get tricked."

I'd been checking out the not-quite crowd: a handful of faculty sitting far enough from one another that there was zero possibility of conversation or even lipreading, maybe thirty grad students, and perhaps a dozen undergrads. My daughter surveyed all, especially the ones nearer her age. She seemed particularly captivated by an ensemble of sweatpants, a KEEP YOUR THEOCRACY OUT OF MY DEMOCRACY T-shirt, and what she whispered were Ugg flip-flop slippers, which I assumed was a hint.

Eliza and I were the only ones whispering to each other. April wasn't due to speak for a couple more minutes, yet the academic audience seemed to be there less for the shared experience of a lecture and more for some solitary purpose, like an intro to Taoist meditation techniques.

April entered from a door on the right that was so sleek I hadn't noticed it earlier. She was accompanied by a short, trim man wearing a pressed white shirt with an incongruous leather vest and a bolo tie. They were both still laughing at something one of them had said.

The man headed straight for the lectern while April hung back by the entrance and waited. He seemed to assume that everyone there knew who he was, and he didn't introduce himself. "We are so pleased to have April Brown with us today. She has made the long trek all the way from New Jersey"—he paused for laughter at his witticism, and a few in the audience were kind enough or obsequious enough to oblige—"where she is an assistant professor at Rutgers. Her work on the depictions of class in the films of the Hollywood studio system—often engaging with gender or queer studies—has been truly groundbreaking. We had a wonderful time at the faculty lunch with her today, and I heard from the grad students that their meet-and-greet with her went very well." Several grad students around the room nodded, and April looked pleased.

"Today," he went on, "she's here to talk with us about one of King Vidor's most interesting films, *Stella Dallas*. We'll follow the talk with a brief—brief!—Q and A. If you don't get a chance to ask your question, she has let me know that she's happy to have any of you reach out to her by email. So without further ado . . ." He gestured to offer her the lectern, then hurried away as she stepped in to take his place. There weren't enough people to give her a welcoming ovation, but for scattered applause, it did seem enthusiastic.

She was wearing cotton pants in a dark blue, another crisp white shirt, and a pair of dangling earrings I would have bet had something to do with *Stella Dallas*. Her light, shiny hair was in a braid down her back, and she had just enough makeup on to look like a vibrant, no-makeup person under the light that shone on her.

April carried a MacBook. She lifted her other arm in greeting. For a moment I was afraid she'd do some regrettable parody of a just-resigned Richard Nixon waving goodbye, but instead she gave some kind of Euro Hi, rotating her wrist this way, then that.

"Is that wave a thing?" I asked Eliza.

"It could be."

As April set up her MacBook to exhibit her lecture slides, I glanced back. A few more people had come in and sat randomly in the last two rows. A woman in her seventies plopped into a chair and began to peel a banana while an overdressed brunette in a business suit and cat-eye glasses primly settled herself an extra seat away from her.

Even though April was only about ten years younger, I felt a surge of maternal happiness that she had a good turnout—at least it seemed better attended than college events I'd gone to two decades earlier. Another older man was leaning against the back wall near the door, arms crossed, seeming ready to take a hike if the lecture was boring.

That was my dad. He scanned the room as if he were providing security for the event.

"*Stella Dallas,* produced well into the ascent of the Hollywood studio system, is a polished movie. It's an emotional movie—arguably an emotionally manipulative movie—in which women's lives and loves drive the events of the story. But it's different from the sort of emotional women's movie Douglas Sirk would make several years later. The attitudes *Stella* has toward both class and motherhood fall flat to today's audiences." I saw several of the film students nod their agreement as she continued.

Her talk was lively and engaging, and I was relieved to discover it was blessedly jargon-free. Or at least mostly. She peppered her points with clips of other movies, and though I'd watched a lot of the ones she was talking about with my mom, I had never taken a film class in my life. I was worried that I'd be lost, but I had no problem following her talk. Eliza was so attentive, she left her phone in her purse for the duration of the lecture. Even my dad seemed absorbed.

April showed us the end of the film, pausing on a shot of Barbara Stanwyck looking up, watching the wedding of her daughter through a window. "Here's the moment," April went on, offering a wry smile. "Stella has given up everything, including that apparently deeply selfish desire a mother has to be with her kid." The audience chuckled a bit. "And, to be clear, Stella didn't give her daughter a choice, right? Her daughter didn't consent to this. Stella deprived her daughter of the chance to choose to admit to her new social circle that her mother is lower class. I'll return to that point later; it's important.

"Stella sees her daughter through the window. The window serves as another frame, a frame within the movie frame, as if Stella were watching the movie of her daughter's escape from the sin of being lower class. The crossbars on the window emphasize the boundaries that now exist between them."

A ponytailed guy two seats down from me began scribbling furiously, and I got the strong sense that he was one of those people the bolo tie professor was warning to keep the Q and A brief. "Now just look at Stella in this shot," April said, leaving the lectern and walking over to the screen to gesture as she spoke. "We are literally looking down on her. She is behind yet another barrier—this iron fence, which casts shadows on her face. We've just seen a cop try to urge her to move along, and now we see her, framed, behind bars. The audience sees her as a criminal, rightly locked away from polite society."

April tilted her head to one side, contemplating the screen. She had been glancing occasionally at her notes as she spoke, but it had been clear all along that her talk was well-planned. Now her tone changed—she sounded reflective, as if she were pausing in her lecture to make an observation. "Barbara Stanwyck is just an extraordinary actress. Look at her face here. It's positively angelic. She radiates such kindness that even a hard, embittered film scholar like me gets taken in." Another gentle chuckle from the crowd. "It's a black-and-white movie, but with the backlighting and that aggressive Hollywood shine in her eyes, she somehow looks like she's radiating color sparkles." She turned away from the screen and continued her lecture.

When April's talk ended, she received gentle but heartfelt applause. I could imagine that her students absolutely adored her. And when the Q and A started, the ponytailed guy shot up his hand. "Please tell me why you think—to be clear, tell me exactly what your evidence is—that King Vidor meant us to see Stella as an example rather than a warning." I started to glare at his rudeness, but April was unruffled. After her explanation, when he said "And just a quick follow-up," she cut him off cleanly and sweetly, turning instead to one of the professors who was holding up a polite finger.

Earlier in the day April had gone to lunch with some members of Hofstra's media faculty and then met with grad students for a discussion. After the lecture she declared she was now off the clock, so we decided to head out for a drink. A visiting scholar had told her the name of a restaurant/bar, King Sean's, where the prices were not exorbitant but enough to discourage the undergraduate margarita-slamming crowd. Eliza protested when I told my dad to take her home, but she was mollified when he told her they'd pick up a milkshake on the way.

Outside King Sean's, there was one of those stands that usually display a menu, but this held a sign—WE HAVE RIBS OF ALL KINDS—a statement just short of gag-inducing.

The front of the restaurant was dominated by a long, shiny bar that, from the entrance looking in, appeared to be a straight line. But just before the unstaffed maître d's stand, the bar hooked slightly; it was less of an I and more of a J. Around the curve, I spotted one of the professors who had been at the lecture. He was leaning forward, talking fervently to a couple in their late forties. They appeared interested in what he was saying and taken with his passion.

Across from the bar, where we sat, there were low tables and chairs from the Age of Acrylic. Maybe King Sean said, *I want a regal look*, because all the cushions were upholstered in royal blue.

April said she should probably go say hello to Professor McDonough, and I stayed in my seat and watched her greet him. She said something that made him throw his head back and laugh, reminding me of a seal demanding fish. She said one thing more, which he apparently agreed with completely, given his bouncing head. She then headed back toward me.

April and I ordered drinks and said no thanks to baby back rib hors d'oeuvres. We were quiet as we watched the bartender, and as he set the glasses in front of us, I checked out the professor again. He was still expounding, though he turned occasionally to look at a dark-haired woman two seats down from him. She was occupied with the olives on her toothpick. I recognized her: she was one of the people who had come late to the lecture. She wore the same cat-eye glasses, and now I could see that they had red frames, the kind of specs that announced, *See, I'm my own person, not a tortoiseshell-rimmed bore.* She glanced toward us, then quickly returned to examining the olives, probably embarrassed at being caught.

I turned back to April and asked about the reviews *Stella Dallas* had gotten when it first came out. She laughed out loud. "Funny you should mention that! The notice in the *New York Times* actually says something like, 'the story is really good now, but in the future people are not going to buy it—the tragedy won't wear well.'"

"Really?" I asked. "It's so weird how they picked up on that!"

"I know, right?" she said eagerly. "Most of the other reviews were good, especially of the acting. Stanwyck and Shirley—she plays the daughter—were nominated for Oscars. A few criticized the costumes and makeup and stuff as over-the-top."

"Funny," I commented. "I assumed that was just normal for the time."

"You know, studying film, I can't tell you how many times I've thought to myself, *Oh, I guess everyone back then was just like that,* only to find people at the time commenting on a movie, saying, like, 'lol why are they so weird in this movie?'" She launched into a lengthy story about the production of *The Awful Truth*. When I admitted I hadn't seen it, her eyes widened. "Oh, seriously? But you have to! As soon as possible! It's my favorite of the Cary Grant remarriage comedies. And that's saying a lot."

I appreciated that April never made me feel like a fool for not having seen a movie she was talking about. She was simply excited that I had a wonderful new experience open to me. She took a long sip of her drink. "You don't like Long Island iced tea?" she asked.

"Long Island iced tea is never my favorite. And it should have only lemon, not one of these cherry mummies," I responded, gesturing at her incongruous maraschino.

"I'm shocked that a Long Island bar got this wrong. They should be the authorities on Long Island iced tea!" she exclaimed in mock disappointment.

I added, "Tequila, gin, vodka . . . and I think rum, plus every trendy drink ingredient the bartender has stashed under the soda gun since 1985. Too much."

"But so tasty," April said, "and so strong. It takes two or three, and you find yourself facedown on the floor, still laughing at one of your own jokes."

"Now that I have my PI license, I'll have to learn to be a morose drunk who only ever orders one brand of cheap whiskey."

A thought struck me, and I made a quick note in the little pad I'd started carrying with me, copying my dad. I tucked it away and sipped my drink, which was by now ninety percent melted ice cube.

"Hey, I just translated your earrings," I said. "That's the Cowboys' team logo, isn't it? So you get Dallas. And it's a star, and 'Stella' is Latin for 'star.' Stella Dallas! How cool is that?"

"Stella is so central to the plot I couldn't think of any other way to represent the film. His bow tie? Her handkerchief? A miniature of Stanwyck in a frowsy dress pouring coffee?"

"They are great earrings," I told her.

"Sometimes they bring a little too much delight from Texans in airports."

We paused again. Seeing the two of us in suspended animation, the bartender strolled over and inquired, "Another round?" though he dropped the "ladies" after making a brief *l* sound. April told him, "Sure," and I said, "San Pellegrino with lime, please."

April's phone vibrated a couple of times, and I assured her I would not think her rude if she took a moment to check it. Down the bar, the middle-aged couple who'd been enchanted by the professor were gone. He was sipping from a champagne glass. I wondered if Hofstra paid him enough to afford champagne midweek, or was it Espumante? I figured he was trying to appear au courant, in a striped buttoned shirt, sleeves rolled—unfortunately—to different lengths. His jeans were so pouchy in the crotch that he could tote around a baby wombat and no one would notice.

He was still eyeing the woman in the red cat-eye glasses who had been at the lecture. Mostly her back, because she'd turned away from him. From a distance, she seemed attractive, if overdressed: her black hair done in what I guessed would be called a 1920s flapper style. The bangs and the glasses were a lot for one forehead, though the look worked. After a couple of minutes of looking at her back, he must have sensed that his future held no *Shall we slip away and watch Antonioni tonight, mia amata?*

"It's Misaki," April said. "Nothing's wrong, but I just want to send a quick reply."

"Seriously, it's fine," I said. "Take your time. I'm enjoying the King Sean ambience."

I glanced back down the bar. Cat-eye shifted again, facing us even more directly. What kind of woman wore business suits with silk blouses to on-campus lectures and local bars?

I studied the bow on her blouse as it rose and fell with her deep breaths. I noticed her legs were crossed now and she was wearing almost-stiletto heels. I deeply doubted she was a grad student. The shoes and the nipped-in-waist business suit were more appropriate for the CFO of Kansas City's top insurance underwriter than for a film buff at a talk on Long Island.

Whatever brought her there, she hadn't asked a question or walked up after April's presentation just to say "Good talk." But she had followed us to the bar—though I had to admit that the last could be a coincidence.

I realized I was fiddling with the chain that held my flashlight at about the same moment I saw the professor leaving alone. April tucked her phone back into her purse, and we made small talk about the differences between Long Island and New Jersey. A couple of minutes later, Cat-eye, the professor's never-to-be-inamorata, was taking some bills from a small crossbody handbag I'd either just spotted or she'd just put on. She set them on the bar and stole a fast glance back at us. She saw that I'd caught the look and played it cool by turning her head slowly toward the door, as if she were imagining the lives of each person at the bar.

My favorite instructor at Quantico told us that if something feels weird, it very often is. Following it up might lead to zilch. But never ignore it. Okay, so was Cat-eye a fucked-up fan of Barbara Stanwyck, stalking scholars whose ideas she didn't approve of? Maybe the girlfriend or wife of whoever drove the SUV, scoping us out in four-inch heels? Maybe she was the driver herself?

"April," I said softly, "there are a couple of people who came here tonight who were also at your lecture. One was the guy you said hi to."

"Doesn't he look like Albert Einstein's twin who shaved his head but left the mustache?"

"He does! Now, there is also a woman who came into the lecture hall a few seconds before you began to speak. Sat way in the back. She's here now, down at the far end near the maître d'. She's waiting for change. Take a quick look."

April turned briefly. "The one with the Louise Brooks haircut?"

"Yes. I couldn't remember that name, otherwise I'd have thrown it in for extra cred. Ever see her before?"

She shook her head. A definite no.

When you've caught a stranger checking you out—their eyes on you, yours on them—there's a kind of electromagnetic field that affects you both, sapping your willpower to keep from double-checking whether they are eyeing you again. I purposely kept my head facing forward and listened for the sound of her heels.

I ran through a quick threat assessment in my head. Her crossbody bag was so small it couldn't hold more than a little wallet and car keys. No room for even the daintiest girly gun, though a lipstick-size canister of pepper spray was not impossible. If she'd had training in one of the martial arts, she probably would have gone for a more sportif look. The nipped-in suit jacket would restrict her arm movements. The killer heels could only kill her, since they'd trash her balance and ability to land if she dared to jump.

April, a little too boozy to realize I'd meant to alert her, was saying that Brooks was a writer as well as an . . . I didn't get the rest of the sentence because I heard a *pat-tap, pat-tap*. A new sound. Cat-eye was heading our way. She would have to pass April first, so I stood in a damn-my-butt's-going-numb way and stepped back so she'd have to move farther away from the bar or bump into me the instant she passed April's barstool.

Studying her now was easy, as she was no longer looking at us, but toward the door. Her gaze felt authentic enough for me to worry that she was actually a black-and-white cinematography geek who gets dressed up for every lecture on the subject and was timid about going up to April Brown at Hofstra, so she followed us to the bar, and then I (this thirty-something woman in white jeans, lime tank, and denim jacket) stared at her every time she happened to look April's way, so her plans to approach Professor Brown dissolved in shyness.

I noticed her skirt, though business-tight, had a slit from the hem to about a third of the way up her thigh, so she could walk at a good clip. Even in the way-high heels, she got to April sooner than I'd imagined. I was ready for something, but not for what she did.

Just as I was making sure that both her hands were empty and not reaching for a weapon, she did a quick, practiced knee bend, grabbed

April's small leather backpack from under her stool, and ran for the door. Too late to stick out my foot and trip her.

Zero need to think. My job was protecting April, not her backpack, but I knocked over the empty stool on the other side of me with enough force that Cat-eye stumbled over the royal blue vinyl cushion, put her hands out to break her fall, and dropped the backpack. I grabbed it as she somehow righted herself, took several staggering steps, and then ran out the door.

April said, "Oh my God!" then crossed herself, which seemed to surprise her. After a few seconds she said, "For God and Grandma."

"Are you okay?" I asked.

She pressed her backpack against her chest as if it were her favorite teddy bear and nodded. "Are you?"

"I'm fine. And I am not going to try to follow her. She didn't try to hurt you, and I want to hang with you just in case she has an accomplice grilling ribs in the kitchen." I turned to the bartender, who seemed frozen, waiting for the next scene to play out. "Do you have CCTV here and outside?"

"Both."

"Good. Tell your boss not to delete it." He nodded, and I turned back to April. "Listen, April," I said at my lowest, "the cops aren't likely to make a fuss over an attempted purse snatching, so I'm not pushing him to call 911. If he does, fine. But I think our time is better spent getting out of here than spending an hour at a precinct filing a report."

Even if the bartender was cool with *no harm, no foul, and no 911,* one of the other patrons might have realized what was happening and called. April insisted on paying the tab. I figured it was quicker not to argue. I opened her backpack, fished out her wallet, and in less than two minutes we were out of there.

CHAPTER EIGHTEEN

"Is your response time always so fast," April asked, "or are you always looking out for trouble?"

"Probably both," I said. "When she got up close, did any bells go off?"

"Just that she did look like Louise Brooks. That bob haircut is iconic. It's not just the hair. As she came toward us, it struck me that she was also small-boned with a heart-shaped face. I couldn't judge her height because of the heels. And it was all over so fast. But her glasses?" April tilted her head to the left, then the right, the standard *Could be this, could be that.*

"They were weird and attention-getting," I said. "Weren't they?"

"Yes," April said, "but I think they may have been a disguise. They had those tinted lenses. Amber. I only got a good look at her for a couple of seconds, but—I know this sounds weird—my reaction was *Well, this is a letdown.* And it was because she wasn't the reincarnation of Louise Brooks. I guess I had Brooks on the brain. What do they call that, priming or something? Anyway, Brooks had beautiful dark brown eyes. And I got the sense that this woman has light eyes. I mean, she wasn't trying to hide the fact that she really wasn't Louise Brooks, which would be insane. But just by having all that stuff on the upper part of her face—the shaded glasses, the bangs down to her eyebrows—she was hiding herself. It would be hard for anyone to give a good description of her."

"Excellent detective work!" I said to April.

My car was just down the street from King Sean's. It took April four tries to fit the metal catch into the seat belt buckle. She twisted around to see what was going wrong, guffawing at her failures. The Long Island iced teas she'd had were still dulling the worst of her anxiety, though she was just at the point when her bursts of laughter could turn into sobs. It had been a tough night. Despite her cheerful manner, I was pretty sure that April had not fully recovered from the SUV incident, and the attempted swipe of her backpack could unsettle her even more.

As we drove to her hotel, she stared out the window, her head tilted up like a child watching the moon following the car. As we pulled up in the hotel's semicircular driveway, the stocky doorman sat perched atop a stool way too tall for him. He seemed to sense that we didn't need help with suitcases—or else he never climbed down unless circumstances were dire.

April said, "I didn't even have time to unpack when I got here this morning. Traffic almost the whole trip." She massaged her temples as if easing the start or end of a headache. "I just had time to freshen up, then rush down."

"You must be exhausted," I said. "Shaken up, too?"

"Both, I think." She squeezed her eyes shut. Maybe that was comforting for a film expert, like sitting in darkness before light from the first few frames shines through to begin the film.

"April, would you like me to go up with you, check out the room to make sure everything's okay?"

She leaned forward to look at me. "That would be . . ." I waited for "kind" or "unnecessary," but whatever the next word was, she couldn't access it. I sensed her isolation. Her fiancée was thirteen time zones away. Misaki could only be there for April on FaceTime, so she had to deal with this alone. Though it was possible it was just a random purse snatching, the SUV pursuit paired with the attempted theft had the feel of sustained malice. The comforting possibility that the SUV attack was an accident, or that either incident was the impulse of a disturbed stranger, became even harder to believe.

I realized that she might be dreading a night in a hotel room. She had surely registered under her own name, and a hotel provided opportunities for the malevolent—as any authority on American films surely knew.

Since her normally keen mind was currently befogged, I was concerned that she could think up some dicey plan that I'd be obliged to say no to, like *I'm really okay to drive back to New Jersey tonight.* I said, "You know, I would feel a lot better if you came back to my house. We have plenty of room. We have two empty bedrooms, so it's not like you'd have to sleep on a blow-up mattress in the same room with Eliza and her guinea pig."

April considered this. "I don't want to put you out. It's not like you planned to have anyone over."

I shook my head. "I can't emphasize enough how not a bother it is. I don't even have to make up a bed—they're already made. There are towels in the bathrooms. And you've even already eaten." April still hesitated, though I wasn't sure whether she was leery of imposing or she thought she should tough it out alone for the night. "It would actually be a favor to me if you came over," I added. "I don't want to worry about how you're doing."

She smiled slightly. "I'd like that," she said. "I mean, to stay at your place. Thanks so much."

"I'm glad. Look. I don't think whoever it was would be dumb enough to come after you again tonight, but I'd feel better if you were where someone couldn't find you." She nodded. "Let's get your stuff. I'll come up with you." Another nod.

Her hotel room had a keycard entry, but I examined the door for signs of intrusion just to be sure. The strike plate, lock buttons, and bolt looked untampered with. I glanced up and saw that April had been watching me anxiously. "We're good," I told her, and saw her shoulders drop with relief. She scooped up her duffel bag from the bed and swung it over her shoulder with a swoop.

When we got back to the lobby, April took out her phone and asked for my address so she could navigate to my house. From my own experience with PTSD, I worried that she hadn't yet fully grasped what she'd been through. She could still be in fight-or-flight mode. Also, the adrenaline might be keeping her from realizing how much she'd had to drink. I told her that I would drive her back to my house in her car. My dad could drive over with me in the morning to pick up my Outback.

She led the way out the door as I texted home to let them know to expect us. By the time I finished reading Josh's reply, that he and my dad would leave now and drive over together to get my car tonight, April was in the passenger seat of her car.

As we walked into the house from the garage, Lulu woofed to show what a brute she could be, then trotted to the cookie jar, where we kept nuggets of freeze-dried liver, the reward for exemplary character. I could tell by their not being around that my mom and Eliza had virtuously chosen to subdue their curiosity. No matter how their souls cried out for information on what had happened, they would not hang in the kitchen. Naturally, they hoped, they yearned, that when April came in, she'd ask to see them and then be so revived by their vibes of sisterhood that, instinctively, she'd tell all.

I'd never had a client before, so I wasn't sure if she differed from a regular guest. I figured that either way, she could use a snack. I arranged a plate of grapes, crackers, and a small circle of sour sheep cheese Josh had picked up at the farmers market from an earnest ponytailed woman who guessed correctly that he would be riveted by a detailed description of her sheep-raising and cheese-making methods. Josh loved the cheese, telling me that I was mistaken, that it was "far from sour. That taste is a 'tang.'" I figured it could be a cheese of choice for subtle postgraduate degree types, and sure enough, April perked up when she saw it.

I took the plate plus a glass of water, and April carried her backpack. We went upstairs to what Dawn had called the Green Room, even though the only thing green was the duvet cover, which was the color of bread mold.

April looked drained. I heard Josh's and Dad's footsteps downstairs, moments apart. I told April that I'd be happy to talk more now, but I thought she might want to hit the sack. She agreed. "Morning would be better," she said. "There's a shot I'll be coherent then."

"Good. If you think of anything during the night, no matter how peripheral you tell yourself it may be, text me, I'll check it in the morning. If you want some company, feel free to call me twice to ring my phone. Don't worry about waking me or my husband. I worked in antiterrorism for years. Sleep, wake, sleep, ad infinitum. And he's a log when he sleeps. If you need to get your mind someplace else at three in the morning, you and I can go downstairs and watch a movie. You can explain the plot of *The Big Sleep* to me. Or maybe a comedy is better. Whatever you want. And there's always ice cream."

"Can't thank you enough," April said.

"You don't have to. And listen. I'm out to get the fucker who's after you. I won't stop until you're safe."

Lying in bed, I relived the night over and over: the film clips of *Stella Dallas*, a cold sip of a watered-down mojito, Cat-eye's practiced knee bend. When I replayed the lecture, I felt an idea banging around my brain, wanting to leave me and get out into the open, but there was nothing I could do to move it along. I couldn't even tell what had set it off.

April texted me only once, at about three thirty. "I'm fine. 1 ques. SUV attack and backpack attempt both failed. Does it mean anything?"

Moments after I woke up, I texted her back: "Can't be certain, but if they're linked, it could be a sign perpetrator(s) may be more hesitant or incompetent than they realize about following through."

As soon as April walked into the kitchen that morning, I could see the difference in how she held herself. Though her text to me meant that she had not had an uninterrupted night's sleep, she had a renewed energy in her step. Josh was already at work, but the rest of the family was there. I introduced April to my mom, who used all her theatrical abilities to convey in one smile her genuine pleasure that April was there and offered warm concern for her recent trouble. I was grateful my dad was not wearing shorts and a Mets T-shirt in front of our client, which meant that my mom had probably thrown herself in front of their bedroom door, barring him until he put on long pants and a grown-up shirt. He looked at my mom, his eyebrows lifted, and Mom realized through marital ESP that he meant she should grab Eliza and vamoose, leaving him to talk to April and me alone.

While Dad asked April to recount what happened the night before, I served her some steel-cut oatmeal with peaches my mom had diced into careful cubes. April complied calmly, with an attention to detail I knew my dad would appreciate.

"It's funny," she said as she concluded. "I only realized now, when wondering if this woman was the same person who drove the SUV, that I assumed the driver was a man all along. Did you ever see *The Sting*?" My dad nodded with something close to euphoria. "There's this waitress who sleeps with Robert Redford's character."

"Right!" he said. "You're surprised he goes home with her because she's"—he paused with a sudden uncharacteristic delicacy—"a homelier woman than you might think. For Robert Redford."

April nodded. "And you're also surprised when she turns out to be a hit woman because, as you come to see, you don't expect that from a woman." I hadn't seen the movie, but I knew what she meant. Even though I'd always been aware of the possibility that the SUV driver was a woman, I had been implicitly assuming the same thing all along.

April must have noted a questioning look or a head tilt because she assured me that she felt fine to drive back to New Jersey. As I walked her to her car, I said that I knew a little something about PTSD, though I didn't explain that it was as much from personal experience as from a background in law enforcement. I told her it was possible that her body might still be primed for danger. If she overreacted to a situation on the road or realized her heart was racing, she should pull over safely and take very slow breaths, imagining herself breathing in a color she liked (aqua, aqua, aqua) and breathing out a color she didn't (mustard yellow, mustard yellow, mustard yellow).

"I like mustard yellow," she said. "But yes, I hear you. Will do." She thanked us again, said how comfortable the mattress was in her room, and headed out.

"You can call them hypotheses," my dad said, gesturing to the whiteboard on which I'd inked a list in blue dry-erase, "but I'm calling them possibly useful shit to keep in the back of your head. Because it's not like one, two, three—they all have equal weight."

"I didn't say they had equal weight. They are the possibilities of who might have done this, not the probabilities," I said. "So Luisa's on the whiteboard not because I think she definitely had something to do with any of the crimes—the arson, the SUV attack, or the purse snatching—but because she had an affair with Seymour and came out ahead financially. That's a red flag until we definitively rule her out." My dad seemed to grant this, so I continued. "And one thing to add to what April said about last night. I didn't want to interrupt her, and she described it very accurately for a civilian, but it seemed to me that Cat-eye wasn't after April. At least, not this time. Only after her backpack."

"What was in the backpack? Gold doubloons?"

"She double-checked her stuff on the ride home. Nothing was missing. She had sixty-two dollars and change in her wallet, along with IDs and credit cards. Car keys, house and office keys, with a card to swipe around campus. A couple of face masks in a plastic bag. Hand sanitizer and lip gloss."

My dad settled further into his new recliner in my office. Now, more accurately, *our* office. When we first discussed starting a PI business, I'd pictured a place like Jessica Jones had—with a film noir door, our names painted on the fluted, frosted glass of the upper half. Now here we were.

Our office wasn't a disaster, but it was more cluttered than I liked. The week before, my dad and I had spoken with Wynne about what we wanted in an office. Who expected that three days later a couple of Arabic-speaking guys (I guessed from their dialects that one was Moroccan, one Somalian) would come to deliver a bunch of rolled-up Moroccan rugs to choose from.

Paint color strips leaned against the spines of books on my shelves. Wynne had set up what she assumed was a must for PIs, an enormous crazy board—cork on one side, whiteboard on the other, surrounded by an inch of black frame—on a sleek, black-lacquered easel, where it was easy to use either side. It was so soigné that Dad and I could be starring in *Law & Order, Design District.*

On the cork side, I'd already placed our photographs, using Wynne's black-only pushpins. They were pictures of everyone involved in the case, then and now, to help me remember them and perhaps see new possibilities. (Wynne had also sent along three skeins of undyed black wool from Hebridean sheep so we could run lines from pin to pin and at the same time be snaz, esoteric, and eco-friendly, which of course were the qualities clients demand in detectives.) As I pinned one that I'd seen a hundred times, I suddenly saw something I hadn't seen before. I whipped out my phone for its magnifying app and peered. Smiling to myself, I said a quick mental *thank you* to Wynne for the crazy board—it had proved its worth.

Multi-panel crazy boards are more common in movies and TV than in real life. They serve as a boon to set designers, and writers use them to help audiences remember what happened in episode four. Most investigators, though—public and private—keep track of their cases on a computer. Still, my dad and I liked to see everything at once to help us think. If we took a moment to sip our coffee or stretch our legs, we were still faced with the case, like the Ghost noodging Hamlet "to whet thy almost blunted purpose."

Props to my dad for insisting we get our licenses. Now we no longer had to bother old law enforcement buddies for database favors. At least far fewer favors. Schottland & Geller had access to some of the same public and private databases law enforcement used—from vehicle registrations to court records to asset searches.

My dad strolled over to a closet near the door to the office. Dawn used to keep her resistance bands and floor-work mat there. I'd never used it for anything; it still smelled of sweat and something spicy, like carnations—not a horrible combo, but I had a fluttery sense that the space was still somehow in her possession. I had a pages-long list of evocative smells, most of which I tried to avoid: overdone sautéed onions equaled Grandma Eva, and sawdust brought back the attic where I was held when I was kidnapped. My dad, maybe from birth or more likely from his time in Homicide, was able to ignore what was better left unsniffed. But I'd agreed to keep our office supplies there.

I turned on the surge-protector strip for our new computer with the toe of my sneaker. A bunch of random rectangles rushed toward a Big Bang in the center of the leftmost monitor of three, and Kaboom!—they formed the word TRACKER. I stared at the TRACKER logo on its shadowy background until my dad strolled over to the closet and came back. When I turned to him, a faint afterimage of TRACKER hovered over his midsection, a stainless steel water bottle in each hand and a pretzel dangling from his pinky. His bottle, naturally, had the Mets logo. Mine had LOS METS DE NUEVA YORK.

"So what do you want to track?" he asked. "Can the program access the CCTVs from the street that night?"

I was doubtful. "It would be really useful to have a picture of Cateye, though, because this thing does have facial recognition technology. I think our best bet is to check with the bar owner to see his private security footage."

I had turned on the computer to look at the transcript of the interview with five-year-old April from the night of the fire, and I displayed it on my right monitor and began reading. My dad cleared his throat, and I made a loud *Shhh!* because my grasp of what I was searching for was tenuous. He was enough like me to understand that budding thoughts are fragile. He sat down at his own computer—his desk was perpendicular to mine—and got busy two-finger typing. The speedy clicks of the plastic keys faded along with my awareness of his being near me.

I read the transcript again, twice: once to familiarize myself with the details and the second time to get a sense of April's psychology. She hadn't changed much. Even as a child, even under the most terrible circumstances, she was consistent with the person she'd become: intelligent, brave, and observant. Not wildly emotional, but capable of feeling. The idea that had been banging around my brain since the night before finally burst into the open.

"Hey," I said when his mad typing slowed. "Do you have a minute?"

"Sure."

"Remember in the transcript, when April was talking about the angel? She said, 'I could see color sparkles. All colors. Not sprinkles, like on ice cream. Sparkles.'"

"Right."

"Remember in her lecture, she showed us the film clip of Stella Dallas standing, watching her daughter's wedding through the window, and when it's over, the main character Stella walks away?"

"I remember standing in the back of the lecture room and my feet hurting."

"April was talking about how the window that the audience sees Stella through is a frame within the movie frame. The movie frame is the big rectangle, the whole screen. The window is another frame. She said something about Stella being framed for us to see, and then she herself looks through the window. Like she's watching another film through the window—her daughter's marriage and escape from a lower social class."

"Gotcha," my dad said. He did his bobblehead nod. The furrow between his brows deepened, the creases in his forehead extending until the top of his head resembled the Tesla logo.

"I'm about to make my point," I told him.

"Good, because dinner's in about seven hours."

"It's about language." My dad rolled his eyes, but I went on. "Right after all that frame stuff, April got off the stool and stood near the screen. She said something like 'Even though the film is in black-and-white, the sparkles around her, in her eyes and from the lighting, look like they're in color.'"

My dad's jaw didn't drop, but his mouth opened into an O. "I missed 'sparkles.' Holy shit, the angel! I actually remember her saying that when she was a little kid. April talking about the angel's wings having sparkles in all colors. 'Not sprinkles.' It was her making sure . . ." He paused. Over the years, although he would never acknowledge it, he'd picked up some performance skills from my mom, like waiting a beat to draw in his audience. "Even way back then, April was teaching," he went on. "She wanted to make sure we realized the sparkles weren't something man-made, like sprinkles. They were shimmery and gave off colors when the angel moved its wings. Part of the magic. Didn't she call the woman in the movie 'angelic,' too?"

I responded slowly as I thought it through. "She may have. I can't remember specifically. But this sparkling angel outside April's window seems linked to Stella. Or at least she used the same word to describe both. In the movie, Stella is standing outside a window radiating grief and also fulfillment, because her sacrifice paid off. Okay, it's a great cinematic effect, but in the lecture April doesn't call it luminosity or splendor—scholarly words. She uses 'sparkles,' her five-year-old word."

"Yeah, it's weird," he said.

"All along I kept asking myself why this is happening now. What changed? What shifts the gears from twenty-plus years of normal life for April to being the victim of attempted murder? And now attempted theft?"

"A big question," he acknowledged.

"Right. And I don't know what the answer is yet, or if this even means anything. But it seems like that movie has a connection in April's mind to the night of her parents' murder. Whether she's aware of it or not."

He disappeared into thought, though not for long. "Maybe that's true, but how could that be the new thing that got the murderer going again? After all this time, she publishes an article about *Stella Dallas* and stuff with a frame that no one reads but a bunch of film professors?"

"Actually, I think she didn't even publish it yet. She told me sometimes people give comments on the talk and you revise the paper before it gets published."

"Okay," my dad said.

"It might be someone who doesn't give a rat's ass about cinema studies. But it might be someone keeping close tabs on April Brown. Googled her name every so often, and just recently found something new."

"Did you check yet?" he asked.

I shook my head. "This just occurred to me."

He typed in April Brown and Stella Dallas. A link to her faculty web page popped up, as well as YouTube videos of April at conferences. One was a recorded Crowdcast lecture given at the invitation of UC Irvine—the same lecture she'd just presented at Hofstra. He clicked on her faculty web page. One of the headings was "Upcoming Invited Talks," and it listed her visit to Hofstra's Department of Radio, Television, Film.

"Bingo!" he announced. My monitors could mirror his, but I got up and stood behind him to look. "Do you get what this means?" he asked.

"Yes," I told him, annoyed by the condescension in his tone. If this was going to be a partnership, I wasn't going to be his Dr. Watson, madly taking notes as Sherlock expounded. "It means that Cat-eye, or whoever is masterminding this, knew when and where April would be at a certain time." He nodded, not looking deflated, though I thought he was. "And look at the date of that first talk she gave that was posted on YouTube. Nine days before the SUV tried to run her down at Rutgers."

"So tell me what you think this has to do with sparkles," he said. Okay, maybe he hadn't been condescending.

"Ultimately, what's going on at the moments when she mentions color sparkles? In both cases, the angel and the movie, you have faces, windows, a major emotional turning point for the character. For Stella, it's watching her daughter's wedding through a window. For April, it's the angel showing her how to escape the burning house by opening a window."

He sat motionless. I could see that he realized someone had seen April lecturing about intense moments on both sides of a window—and had seen it days before the SUV came at her.

In a fluid move I'd have thought was now beyond him, he went over to the crazy board. Grabbing the blue marker I kept in a Queens College coffee mug, he turned his back to me while saying "Shh!" yet again, louder this time, and wrote:

1. YouTube vid shows April speaking about woman framed by window
2. What did 5 yr old April actually see framed in the window that night?

Still holding the marker, he turned to me. "Okay, you can talk now."

"It's coming together for you, right?" I said. Maybe it was my turn to be a little condescending.

"I'm getting closer. What about you? You got a thought or two?"

I tapped on his second line on the whiteboard. "This. What did April actually see in the window?" He looked so eager, I quickly added, "Dad, please, it's not like the case is solved. But this may be important. Let's think about what she might have seen. Probably not an actual angel, though if you believe angels exist, then why not in Brooklyn?"

"I took the angel to be a useful hallucination," my dad remarked. "That's what the shrink we consulted said, and it seemed right. Her mind created the information she needed to save her own life. If little April just thought of opening the window and getting the hell out, she might be too intimidated. An angel commanding her has the authority."

"Maybe. But what if she saw something real? An actual person? The 'angel' not only gave her the correct information of how to save her life—when even the unconscious mind of a five-year-old might not know what to do. When April hesitated, the angel was impatient and had to repeat the pantomime showing her to open the window."

"But we come back to that same question," he insisted. "Why would someone leave her alone to grow up, go off to college, and become a professor, then all of a sudden threaten her life? Over an angel? Over a hallucination or whatever? Over a feminist movie theory?" He knocked the whiteboard easel with his hip, making it slightly askew. When I realized he was just going to leave it that way, I got up to straighten it. "You're a little nuts, you know that, right?" he said.

"Irrelevant and immaterial," I said. "Okay, so it wasn't the feminist movie theory. That's an intellectual construct. What did we see in that lecture—and didn't think anything of it—that another person saw and made them want to hurt April? Or steal from her?"

He thought for a second. "That's the point, really. There doesn't seem to be anything there to threaten anyone. Except—"

"Exactly!" I cut him off. I was so excited, I had to get a word in edgewise.

"Except for one person who knew what April might have seen through a window," my dad went on. "That whatever she saw was real, that it was a person . . . who now sees a YouTube video of April talking at length about people seeing other people through windows."

I saw that he got it. "And this person realized that April might remember—or be very close to remembering—who was on the other side of her window on the night of the fire."

CHAPTER NINETEEN

As someone who'd lived in apartments almost all her life, I was more sanguine than most about being inside. But now I felt the need to clear my head. And to forget my leg. My skin graft was starting with its familiar ache-itch, as if drying up and pulling loose. I couldn't help but feel that soon it would become like an ancient parchment, disintegrating into flakes, my injury exposed and undefended again. My heart started to beat faster. PTSD.

"I have to get something in my bathroom. Why don't we meet out back in a few minutes?" I suggested to my dad.

He looked suspicious, as if it were a ploy to get him to exercise, but when I told him he could sit, he seemed willing enough. I sat in my bedroom for about ten minutes looking at a book with pictures of Islamic mosaic tile floors. I felt better and went downstairs. I had some ideas about the case and was excited to talk about them. Right or wrong, it would be good to articulate them.

I didn't have to go far to find him. He was sitting on the back steps. "I've got a theory, he said, glancing at me. "I'm not saying it's formed and ready to go."

I strolled over to some nearby pots, pinching basil flowers, something I hadn't known was a thing when I asked my landscaper friend Iris for tons of herbs. I started clipping some for a caprese salad I planned for dinner. "Funny, because I've been mulling over something also. You may be ahead of me, so why don't you go first."

"Don't expect actual evidence," he said. "I've just been thinking about the case in a different way." He shrugged, as if he didn't care whether I'd agree.

"Tell me," I said. "I'd like to hear it."

"Luisa."

"That's a name, not a theory."

"No shit, Ajax. Anyhow, you ready for it?"

"Incredibly ready."

"The whole theory is . . ." he began. "Luisa de León did it."

"No kidding! Wow, I'm a little taken aback. I keep wanting to write her off." I used this kind of statement when I interviewed witnesses—but also with my law enforcement colleagues—when I wanted them to provide more details but didn't want them to feel inhibited by my skepticism.

"Okay, so like I said," he went on, "this is a theory. But I made assumptions that seemed logical and felt right. I think you're onto something: the angel wasn't on God's payroll. It was a real person who came to the window to help April escape. I worked Robbery, Sex Crimes, Homicide. Career criminals do their job and get the hell out. There are some who skip the conscience routine: 'Oh, I must hang around to save an innocent child even though the house is up in flames and somebody's sure to have called 911 already.'"

"But you think Luisa wouldn't," I said.

"You got it. She seems like a great person. Friendly, smiley. And kind. Possibly with the exception of burning alive her boyfriend and his wife, but maybe she had a rough day."

"Maybe they were already dead. Assuming your theory is correct."

"Corie, I know she didn't say it, but in the interview—and I can't explain why—I got the impression that April felt the angel was a woman. Nurturing, patient. Yeah, I know men can be nurturing, too, but hear me out. Like the angel is thinking, *Well, the kid didn't open the window, so I'll just stand here and do that open-the-window gesture again. And I'll hang around some more—even if it's dangerous for me because the cops are probably already on their way. I'll hold off until she gets the courage to jump*. Does that sound more like Luisa? Or some psycho extortionist Seymour client named Igor?"

I finished with the basil. Instead of winding up with a handful, I had an armful. Whenever I had an excess of basil, I could usually rely on my mom to bring it to her face and inhale so hard her nostrils stuck to the mid-part of her nose. Then she'd say, "I adore fresh-picked herbs!" adding a British *h* that brought me near to matricide, though, on the other hand, she'd offer to make her "pesto alla genovese."

But she was doing a tech rehearsal for a new gig, a podcast, *Actors on a Hot Mic*. She'd beaten out six others for the grand dame or old-sport-with-dentures slot. She sensed it was because she complimented the producer-director-moderator's blink-and-you-miss-it performance as one of Falstaff's hangers-on in *Henry IV* at the Queens Theatre in the Park from the mid-aughts. She hadn't Googled it; she actually remembered it.

I gestured for my dad to follow me into the kitchen, where I stuck the basil in a pitcher of water. He clamped his lips together to demonstrate how patient he was during the forty seconds it took me to run the water and arrange the stems. Lulu accompanied us back up to the office and took what was becoming her usual place beneath my desk, beside the surge protector.

My dad chose his desk chair rather than the recliner, so I knew he meant business even before he turned on his computer. "So, my theory," he said. "Episode two. Your boyfriend in medium security told you what sounds like the truth—a new and exciting experience for him, I'm sure." I may have tilted my head so I'd look willing to hear what he had to offer, but I didn't react in any other way. "Hosea was right when he said that none of Seymour's clients and none of their mobbed-up friends had any reason to want Seymour dead. They wanted him alive. Agreed?"

"Totally," I said. "Unless I find a reason to believe otherwise."

"Believe otherwise? If you weren't my daughter, I'd say you sound like the standard cover-your-ass Fed. Anyhow, they all wanted Seymour to live and be well. Now, I don't think the only reason Luisa killed the two of them was for financial gain from that apartment she co-owned with him. Nope, you convinced me she was too self-confident, too young, too moral back then to carry out such a god-awful double murder for a million or so."

I could feel Lulu against my foot, starting to twitch and whimper. She was having a doggie nightmare. Rescue dogs are mysteries; it's rare to know what really happened to them before you adopted them. In Lu's case, she and a pregnant Chihuahua were found walking along Shorehaven Boulevard with no collars or tags. Filthy and malnourished, so more likely abandoned than lost. I lifted her onto my lap like a baby and tucked her under my chin, though having her head pressing against my larynx made speaking awkward. She settled down and breathed more regularly.

"So if you bought my reasoning that Luisa isn't the murdering type . . ." I said.

"There are plenty of people who aren't murdering types—who under normal circumstances wouldn't hurt anyone—but when push comes to shove, they can kill," he explained. "That kind of person wouldn't let a child be collateral damage. Luisa wasn't shy. My guess is she confronted him about leaving Kim and he put off answering once too often. Or maybe he was more direct. He got off being cruel to women when he broke up with them, so maybe he just told her that he wasn't leaving Kim. She was a good mother to his kid, after all. He might've said to Luisa's face, 'Hey, I don't want interesting and challenging at home. The only dumb thing about you is that you believed me when I said I would leave my wife.' Or, you know. Maybe he just beat the crap out of her, and she wouldn't take that."

He paused and checked to see if I was still with him. I was, so he kept going. "So for one of those reasons, or something else, Luisa feels betrayed. And she's still very young, maybe more impulsive than she seems now. And it just so happens that by getting rid of Seymour, she stands to gain enough money to fund her dream, her own business. Maybe that's not why she did it, but it is an added inducement. She probably knows that Seymour was private and cautious enough not to tell many people about her, so it's unlikely the police will look into her as a suspect. The one thing

I'm not sure about is that driver, Toddy. Luisa might not have known that Hosea knew about her, but she knew Toddy knew about her. He'd driven them. How did she know he wouldn't tell us?"

"Maybe she didn't know or think of him. He's just another luxury accessory that comes with a Mercedes," I said.

Dad continued. "Anyway, let's set that aside. She goes to the house, maybe kills them first—I think she would shoot them or cut their throats, she's nice—and then torches the place. Either she remembers just then that there's a kid inside, or she always knew it. So she goes over to April's window and motions her out. Once she sees April is getting out, she's on her way. She's avenged and she's rich. She starts a business, and the rest is history. No one else we know of had any motive, other than that he was generally a jerk. She had two good reasons to want him dead."

"Definitely. I can see that happening," I told him. I wasn't ready to totally toss his idea yet. Besides, it was consistent with what Hose had told me about Seymour's sadistic behavior toward women. "He was a shit par excellence. It's a solid theory. Most likely, Luisa knew there was a kid in the house, because chances are Seymour talked about April. Probably too much. Blabbing about the joys of parenthood to the single woman you've been stringing along? So not cool. But anyway. I'm willing to assume Luisa knew about April and maybe even knew that her bedroom was on the first floor."

"Good," Dad said.

"And she's definitely smart enough to have kept track of April over the years."

My dad bowed his head gracefully, though not quite like a living legend acknowledging an ovation. As he'd said about himself more than once, "Often wrong, never in doubt." It was gentle self-mockery to him, the truth to nearly everyone else.

"We still need to find evidence to back it up, of course, but that's my theory," he said.

"A really good theory," I said. "But I have something different."

"Why am I not surprised?" He did try to put a smile on it but failed—this from the man who told me almost daily throughout my childhood to think for myself.

When my dad and I started talking about forming a partnership, I asked Josh about managing his ego. Dad had been retired and depressed for so many years. If he got back into the game with me and I told him an idea sucked, what would it do to him? Not the first time when it happened, but what about the fifth or sixth?

"Then what are you going to tell him?" Josh had demanded. "'Oh, Dad, what a spectacular insight!' He'll know in a half second it's complete bullshit, that you're saying it because you think his ego is too fragile for the truth. Remember that old Harry Truman quote? It applies to both of you. 'If you can't take the heat, get out of the kitchen.'"

So now I said, "Listen, Dad, I'm not saying you're wrong. But our minds went their own separate ways and came back with different theories."

"That's what minds do," he said. I was relieved to find that Josh was right and my dad could take the heat. "It's okay by me."

"Me too. But when I told you I had a theory starting to form, the emphasis was on 'starting.' Still kind of nebulous. So right now, instead of me forcing out an idea that's more marshmallow fluff than solid reality, let's see if we can find evidence to say Luisa was the mastermind or at least that Luisa was an accessory. Or not."

"Works for me," he said, and swiveled his desk chair so he was looking at his monitor. You had to make eye contact with the retina reader on the screen every five minutes, so he glared at it, then typed in his passcode. Not even I knew what it was. But we weren't going to make the same mistake Seymour made. As a safeguard against disaster or dementia, we put our individual alphanumeric keys in signed and sealed envelopes in a safe-deposit box in the bank on Main Street.

We had already looked up Luisa de León in law enforcement databases when we first got our software. No arrests, no outstanding warrants. Now we decided to expand the search for any other interactions she might have had with local or state authorities. We focused on the precincts closest to her office and apartment in the three months before and after Seymour's murder, thinking we might find that she'd reported domestic violence. We didn't find that. We did, however, discover another encounter she'd had with police. Two weeks before the fire, Officers Francis Driscoll and James Newberger of the Seventy-Eighth Precinct in Park Slope were dispatched to the vicinity of Eighth Avenue near Carroll Street. Their report said:

> The victim, Luisa deLeon, age 23, an assistant in a real estate office, stated that at about 8:15 AM she took her usual pedestrian route from her apartment on 8th Avenue to her office[1]. She was on Carroll Street when she thought she heard a vehicle behind her on the sidewalk. She turned and saw a large black car speeding toward her.
>
> Several other witnesses fled, but two separate individuals Cherie di Napoli[2] and Kenneth Bloom[3] stayed to help Ms. DeLeon. Both reported that the said vehicle was a dark SUV[4] moving slowly until it crossed onto the sidewalk in a space between a fire hydrant and a parked car. Both witnesses said it then sped up, bunked into the tree guards around trees near the curb and then sideswiped the iron fence and gate in front of a brownstone. Lack of control/depth perception similar to DWI behavior.
>
> The victim fled the said oncoming vehicle by jumping from the sidewalk to between two parked cars and squatting low to hide herself.
>
> Neither of the witnesses or victim could give a description of the driver of the vehicle except he or she wore sunglasses[5] and a dark sweater or sweatshirt with a hood that was up. Witnesses not sure if the perpetrator saw where Ms. deLeon was hiding but did not stop or exit vehicle in question and kept driving.
>
> Ms. DeLeon, even though upset refused medical attention stating that she wasn't hurt just "really shaken up." She claimed to officers on the scene she knew of no one who would want to hurt or kill her. She said she was not dating anyone at the moment, and that

any previous relationships had ended "without bad feelings." She did agree to file a complaint and cooperate in any investigation.

[1] Knight Realty, 7th Avenue near Garfield Place

[2] Tenant in basement apt at 384 Carroll Street with above ground windows

[3] Owner/installer for Blooming Shades and Blinds, 846 Flatbush Ave, returning from sales call

[4] Mr. Bloom said the vehicle "looked like" a Toyota Land Cruiser but the model name and emblem covered with strips of black duct tape, like what covered the license plate.

[5] Ms. DiNapoli said her impression was that the sunglasses were very dark, almost black "like blind people wear."

"Can you believe it?" Dad demanded. "Schmendricks. Putting something as important as the duct-taping in a fucking footnote?"

"Yeah, I know. At least there were witnesses, so we don't have to waste time trying to find out if she was making it up."

He pushed up out of the chair and did some low-yardage pacing. "Right. But unless she made a huge deal of it, they were going to look into the drunk driver crap they had in the report, not bother with the footnote. Do drunk drivers keep a roll of duct tape in the glove compartment so they can methodically use strip after strip to obscure all the car's identifying features?"

"And how do they come up with a DWI theory for a vehicular assault that took place a little after eight fifteen in the morning?" I added. "Possible, but unlikely."

He nodded. "So bottom line, these two weren't the Seventy-Eighth's brightest bulbs. And although another detective eventually did interview Luisa"—he pointed to his screen at a different document we'd found relating to the case—"she claimed she didn't know anyone who might be out to get her, and didn't have any friends who had criminal associations. So the detective didn't get anywhere." My dad stopped pacing long enough to grab his water bottle and take a few slugs.

"But this gives us something," I said. "Two taped license plates, two decades apart. Two SUVs with drivers whose identity is obscured trying to run down two different female victims—both of whom have a connection to Seymour. Possibly a coincidence, possibly a copycat crime, but it looks to me more like one individual with no imagination and shitty driving skills."

"No imagination," my dad agreed, "but they managed to escape apprehension two times."

"True. But at least we know, for the first SUV attack, that Luisa wasn't the perpetrator," I said, "because she was the victim." He didn't argue. I went on. "We also know she probably wasn't the driver who went after April. I say 'probably' because maybe her being the victim of an SUV attack gave her the idea. But chasing down someone with an SUV feels more like one person's MO to me. That someone did the same thing twice."

"And failed twice," he said.

"Right. So here's the thing," I said. "I think that makes your Luisa theory less likely."

He didn't look thrilled. On the other hand, he didn't look angry. "Go on."

"We've been assuming all along that whoever set the fire also had something to do with the SUV attacks. Now it's possible we shouldn't assume that. It could be that Luisa set the fire, and an entirely different person is going around trying to run down people connected to Seymour Brown. I might take that seriously if someone had tried to run down Luisa after the fire. In that case, it could have been revenge for killing Seymour. But the attack was before the fire. That's crucial."

"Makes sense," he said.

"Saying that Luisa set the fire and that someone else—a person who wasn't Luisa's accomplice—drove the SUVs seems like a reach to me. Homicides happen, especially in Seymour's world. But even there, they aren't what you could call regular occurrences. So what are the chances of two different people who aren't working together, both bent on homicide, trying to kill Seymour and his nearest and dearest?"

"You're asking me what are the chances?" my dad asked. "You know. Minimal to nil."

"So unless we come across more evidence, I still think it's safe to say the person responsible for setting the fire is probably the same person—or working closely with the person—who drove the SUVs in both cases. Occam's razor."

"What's Occam's razor again?" he asked.

"That the simplest explanation—in this case, the one that involves the fewest homicidal maniacs—is probably right."

He set down his water bottle so he could chew the upper knuckle of his thumb. Then he said, "I hear that. I would still want definitive proof Luisa didn't set that fire." Just as I was about to nod to show my generous collaborative nature, he continued. "I love that database. But I don't know how to tell it to find out, finally and forever, whether Luisa has a solid alibi for the day the SUV went after April."

"Hmm," I said, which was the best I could come up with at first. He knew and I knew that it was more difficult to prove something didn't happen than that it did. "Maybe the best way is to contact your detective friend, the guy you mentored, Gabriel Salazar," I said slowly. "Ask him for Luisa's credit card purchases in the week before and the week after the SUV attack on April. Because we can't get access to that in any legit way. You can tell him you might have a big tip in a cold case soon. It'll be good to establish a relationship with him, where he can access information we need. He'll know that we're in his debt and we'll deliver whatever we can back to him."

"You told me Luisa has a driver's license?" he asked.

"Yes. I checked. But no car registered in her name. She uses one of two company limos, and the driver is her employee. She could have borrowed or rented an SUV in New Brunswick. Or maybe had a driver drop her off at a Hertz in town. But would she have whipped out her Luisa de León license?"

"Maybe she had a good fake in another name, or a just-stolen license. Can the database find rentals of dark-colored SUVs?"

"Ask it," I said. "But I was under the impression that you agreed that the two SUV attacks, even with two decades between them, were the work of the same individual."

"I don't want to be doubly sure," he said. "I want triple assurance."

I was annoyed. Wasn't he at least a little curious about my theory? At least a little more curious than getting "triple assurance" on his. And following up on the whereabouts of a seemingly upright person like Luisa could often be tougher than tracing a criminal who, in trying to hide the truth, would take steps and missteps that screamed *Deceit!*

"As of today, you have no more evidence against Luisa than you had twenty-plus years ago," I said. "Go ahead, ask the database about her whereabouts before and after April almost got run down. And then check if it can explain how Ms. Northern European or Polish Very White Person who grabbed April's backpack at King Sean's turned back into Ms. Light Brown Latina named Luisa who admittedly has a great body but weighs maybe twenty pounds more. I'll give you that eye color can be changed by contact lenses."

His response needed no words: emissions of hot air blown out of the sides of his mouth.

Most of the windows in the office faced the backyard, but he walked over to the one window on the side of the house. When we decided to make my office our office, I told him that if you looked down a little, there was an empty bird's nest tucked between the branch and trunk of a big old tree. "Move-in ready," I told him. Yet as long as I'd been living there, the nest had never been occupied. Still, it clung on, unshaken by hurricanes, nor'easters, and blizzards. This was the first time he bothered to look.

"I don't get why no birds ever came to take over this thing," my dad said. "Nice location, built to last. Good school district."

"Dad . . ." I began, offering him all the empathy I could muster, which was a lot. Except he didn't want it.

He turned back to me. "Okay. That was my two cents. Let's hear what you have."

* * *

My dad seemed weary—though part of that was the orange of the day's T-shirt, a flamboyant hue that gave his face a yellow cast. Still, he looked merely upset, not wounded.

I walked over to the crazy board and tapped on one of the photos from a news clipping that had been in his old case files. I waited and then asked, "Can you come over here for a second?"

He'd switched to the recliner and wasn't going vertical without a fight. "I've seen that a hundred times," he said. "The one with Seymour and Hosea Williams by the car, with Hosea looking enraged."

"That's the one," I said, "but that's not all I'm seeing here." He pushed the chair back into its upright position and came over. "Okay, it's a little grainy because I enlarged it, and it's from a newspaper, so the quality wasn't great to begin with. But check this out."

Hose looked so different from the man I had met with the jumpsuit and prison buzz cut. Back then, his light, straight hair was unusually thick, combed back, and styled in such a way that it appeared to form a crescent moon around his head. His suit was fitted to display powerful shoulders and show that his torso tapered (slightly) at the waist. The suit was probably gray, because it photographed very pale. Given that he was wearing what looked like a black, silky dress shirt and a black tie, his style was a late nineties version of Putative Slimeball up to No Good.

Standing beside him by the front fender of the car, Seymour Brown came off so elegantly you'd think he'd have "Sir" before his name. Dark suit, white shirt, and a tie that I guessed was a Hermès or some brand most of its wearers avoided pronouncing. If he'd been an emoticon, he'd have eyes that were two blank circles; his mouth, a dash. On the other hand, tough gangster Hose could have modeled for a weak one—mouth a woebegone arc.

"Looks like his ass just came out of the wringer," my dad said, indicating Hose.

"It's not him and it's not his ass I want you to look at." I pointed to the right side of the photo. Whoever took the picture must have been standing to the left of the two men, so that they, in the front half of Seymour's Mercedes, were most prominent. I was pointing at Toddy, the driver, who didn't look as tall as he actually was because of perspective. He was slightly bent over, holding open the foreshortened back door and reaching out to assist the passenger who'd been sitting in back. "I know what you're seeing is mostly his back, but if you look closely . . . His right wrist has that thin copper bracelet people use for—I think—arthritis, though maybe it has some other purpose. Anyway, he's still wearing the thing. When I saw him on my screen, when he was talking to Tasha? He had it on."

"That's not exactly what the DA would call a positive identification," my dad said. "What are you going to do? Put five copper bracelets in a lineup?"

"Lucky that I'm not trying to get evidence for the DA, then. I'm just talking to you, brainstorming. Take a closer look at who's in the car."

My dad prided himself on not having to wear reading glasses, mostly because when he did read, he turned on so many lights that it looked like high noon in the Sahara. He squinted, then pulled his head back, but within two seconds he returned to his desk and got the magnifying glass he used for examining photos. "That's Kim," he said. "I mean, I can't say for sure, but it's got to be. Blond, smallish. Can't tell her relative height because she's not completely standing up."

I opened the magnifying app on my phone and focused on the person who might be Kim. Luckily, she was looking up at Toddy, so most of her face was visible, if not clear. Heart-shaped face. Blond, shoulder-length hair parted on the side so there was a slight dip across her forehead. I couldn't tell whether her eyes were that magic light blue, but they definitely weren't dark. Even though I'd all but memorized that tiny part of the picture, I couldn't see if there was a resemblance to April.

Kim was dressed, possibly overdressed, for dinner. I'd have to consult Wynne about that. Her dress appeared strapless, though she had a short jacket over it. It was too grainy to see if she had any jewelry on. Any jewelry she had in her house that night of the arson was gone, I thought. Not counting the diamond in her ring that survived the fire. Whatever else had been there was melted, then vaporized.

"Dad, look how Toddy's holding her hand to help her out of the car."

"Yeah, that's a chauffeur's job."

"I know it's a chauffeur's job. But when a professional driver helps somebody, they offer their"—I tapped my forearm—"or a flat palm."

He moved the magnifying glass back and forth. "So it's sort of flat-tish, I think. What are you seeing?"

"I'm seeing his thumb over the back of her hand. He's not gently supporting her fingers. He's got her small hand completely in his big one, and his thumb extends all the way across the back of her hand up to her wrist. I'm telling you, and I know it's not evidence we could bring to the DA, but that's how a lover would hold a hand. A fast touch of flesh before she takes Seymour's arm and goes inside."

My dad did his magical forehead rub to bring forth an idea from some obscure region of his brain. "You could be onto something. Remember . . . Toddy used to watch cartoons in the Browns' basement. Kim was so 'nice' or something. We should get back to him."

"And now that we have a fuzzy photo of Kim's face, we just need another picture to try facial recognition. And April has one."

"From?"

"From her grandma. Remember? Her mom in high school with two of her friends." My dad nodded vigorously. "If we can get a baseline, we can start looking at CCTV footage of the bar."

"What for?" he asked. "I mean, we should look at that anyway, but what does that have to do with a picture of Kim and her girlfriends from the eighties?"

"Well," I said. "The woman who tried to steal April's backpack was a middle-aged white woman with light eyes. Maybe it's far-fetched, but who do we know who is connected to this case who would be a middle-aged white woman with those kind of eyes?"

"Kim's dead."

I shrugged. *Maybe, maybe not.*

CHAPTER TWENTY

"Kim—alive!" my dad exclaimed. I'd expected a whisper of shock, but he blared it so loud I jumped and made a startled sound: *Mnyaaah!* Then he bellowed, "I can't believe it!" as if I were in another room.

This was the first unexpected development—well, first unexpected theory anyway—in the Brown case in more than twenty years. Beyond unexpected for him, the cop who had stuck with the case so long.

The morning after the arson-murder, at sunrise, my dad had put on crime scene shoe covers and walked the perimeter. I pictured him slowly going around the soot and ashes, wet with firefighters' water and foam, understanding by instinct and experience that some minor crunch underfoot could have contained scattered atoms of Kim or Seymour that the horrific fire hadn't incinerated. But nothing of them could be found save for those few untestable bone fragments and that diamond.

"This is beyond great!" he said. "Terrific, Corie! Unbelievable! Kim could still be alive!"

I opened up my hands, raised them above my head, and brought them down very slowly. "Easy. It's a theory, Dad. I could be so wrong."

"But you could be so right. Okay, first things first." I was engaged in an internal debate about what he would count as a "first thing" when he announced, "We need to use this thing's"—he patted the computer—"photo recognition capabilities. Match it to the footage they have at that bar you went to."

"King Sean's."

"Yeah," he said. "April will be home by now. I'll have her scan that picture she has of her mother and email it to us ASAP. Then ask her to try and get the names of the high school friends in that photo with Kim. Also ASAP. Maybe those girls have pictures of her nobody ever bothered asking for. I won't tell her what it's for yet."

While he texted April, I called Tasha and asked her to go through whatever pictures she had. "I have every year in a box, for scrapbooking," she told me, showing me by swinging her phone around a walk-in closet that was the size of my entire first apartment in Adams Morgan in DC. I saw fabric-covered boxes tied with satin ribbon. I also asked her to check with her friends Gina and Olga to see if they had any casual shots or possibly a picture taken at an event where Kim had been.

"Tasha, I don't need great quality or full-face. They can get a lot out of a picture that has only thirty-five percent of the face showing."

"I'm on it! Gina is not really a party photo person. But if she has pictures, she will find them. Very organized, which is what you want in a pharmacist. And Olga? A slob, even though she's my cousin and my best friend, though she does put herself together beautifully. But the good news is she never throws anything out. Like she'll stuff five hundred pictures in a drawer—of her cat sleeping—or she'll have one of her boyfriends' dick from 1992—but she won't remember whose it was."

When Tasha took a breath, I told her, sincerely, that I missed her and would love to get together again. She said the same and promised she would spend the entire evening going through her stuff. And she'd get Gina to look, though she'd have to go over to Olga's the next day or it wouldn't get done.

My dad and I spent the rest of the day going over, then over again, the Kim theory. In the late afternoon we went downstairs, where we all decided to go out to dinner, though separately. He and my mom went to a fish place right on the harbor, and Josh, Eliza, and I—after debating between Chinese, Japanese, and Thai—drove into Queens for the best Mexican food in the borough, which also provided Eliza with new content to post on whatever social media app she was using these days. While she posed her food for her phone, I described to Josh the shot of Toddy's hand enclosing Kim's, along with all the time spent in the Browns' basement, supposedly watching cartoons.

The hand-holding chauffeur didn't wow him, but his eyes widened at the cartoon marathons, and he began smiling when I said, "I understand this is just a theory, and she may be looking down from heaven, shocked that I could even think of anything like this, much less bring her daughter into it by asking her to aid and abet me in facial recognition."

"A theory definitely worth pursuing," Josh told me. He was grinning now. He liked this. He always seemed to enjoy it when I was investigating, especially when I made some headway. "In this whole case, there was only one woman who was middle-aged and light-eyed, so it makes sense. Why not try to track her down? If you find her, it will show that she didn't die the night of the fire. It would prove who she is. Get a sample of her DNA and compare it with April's. And also with the grandmother's—Kim's mother." He took a two-second thought break. "Did you happen to get the glass she was drinking from at the bar?"

"No. I'm so pissed at myself. I was thinking that we weren't contacting the police anyway, and I was so preoccupied with keeping April safe and getting her out of there that—"

"Don't bite yourself in the ass," Josh said. That surprised me because—especially when talking about feelings—he was more likely to sound like an audiobook of a Henry James novel: *Don't remonstrate yourself, Corie*. "Although this could all turn out to be simply conjecture."

I took his left hand, since it was close and his right was holding a bottle of microbrew I'd never heard of. "Where would that leave me?" I asked.

"Probably disconsolate," Josh said.

Although Toddy Mirante had been a person of interest for several days after the arson and murder of both Browns, my dad's superior officer at that time, Bobby Melvin, had concluded that the driver was too stupid to have committed the act. If Toddy had tried to set a fire, Bobby was positive, he would have wound up as an ember, not a living being.

"If he was in on this with Kim, you'd think he would at least have had the brains to change his name or occupation," my dad said.

"Well, he moved out of the Bronx," I said. "Lock, stock, and mother." I looked over the steering wheel. We were driving in Connecticut on a Sunday. Not a lot of frolicking New Englanders. Hilly terrain, lots of late-summer dark green, and mile after mile of stone walls left from colonial times.

Toddy had come up in the world. His house in Norwalk, a pleasant middle- and working-class town, was an almost straight line fifteen miles up the coast from Greenwich, on Long Island Sound.

"Where he lived in the Bronx," my dad reminisced as the GPS told us we would reach our destination in point-five miles, "the houses were so close together. Not attached, but two people couldn't take out the garbage cans at the same time. The rooms were really small. Right away we separated Toddy and his mother, and if I hadn't been questioning Toddy, I could have heard every word of the other interrogation."

"But they got their stories straight back then. I read your reports from that night."

"Too straight. Like both of them talked about his earache and how she gave him aspirin, and when they said they'd been watching a video they rented, they both said it was *Muriel's Wedding*—without being asked."

"When two separate witnesses offer you the same information you haven't asked for," I said, "you have to wonder if they've worked on their story together."

The houses on Toddy's block weren't large, but there was sufficient room between them that two people could carry out their trash cans with space to spare. A couple of the houses were New England quaint, with weathered shingles and shutters. One had window boxes with pink and red flowers.

Toddy's house—in the property records he was listed as sole owner—looked as if it had been built in the sixties. It was a small Cape

Cod with beige siding, which wasn't as boring as it sounds. It all appeared well-maintained, except for the landscaping. A couple of big hydrangea bushes took care of the right side of the house. But on the left of the front steps was a long, wide rectangle of dirt with a teeny tuft of ornamental grass, like a vain bald man desperate to show he could still grow hair.

I walked around toward the back, where a wood staircase with a handrail descended from the kitchen to a small cement patio, and I guessed it would be the most likely route Toddy would take if he decided he should leave without talking to us. The view was to the south, over a low, unmanicured hedge, and it was spectacular. A strip of land sloped down to Long Island Sound, and a panoramic water view was obscured only by a couple of trees.

A familiar signal pierced the air. My dad could still do that ball game whistle with two fingers in his mouth—a gift I'd always envied. He was signaling that it was okay to come back to the front because at least one of the Mirantes was letting us in. I did a quick jog back, and it wasn't until I was on the top step, face-to-face with Toddy, that I realized that since my kidnapping, this was my first time jogging when my leg didn't hurt at all. I was so happy that I said, "Toddy, good to meet you!" with too much enthusiasm. A very small woman came up behind him and pushed him aside so she could get a better view of us. She didn't seem to think it was good to meet us.

Toddy's mother planted herself on the metal threshold of the open door. "Who are you two?" Her voice was hoarse, like a kazoo, cute and irritating at the same time. "You got business here? What?" We did the private detective intro, then handed her our IDs as she demanded. We waited while she put on glasses that had been dangling from a chain around her neck, and she appeared to read every word. "I'm Claudia Mirante," she said, handing back our credentials. She was wearing rust-colored pants and an untucked shirt with rust, teal, and white stripes, along with immaculate white sneakers. Her hair was sparse, but she wore what there was of it twisted it into a doughnut on top of her head. "What do you want with Toddy?"

"We've been hired by the daughter of your son's former employer, Seymour Brown. We just have a few questions about the case."

"April? April hired you?" Toddy asked. "What for? I guess she's all grown up by now and wants to know about her parents."

"I'm sure she'd like to hear anything you have to tell us," I said. "But actually, she retained us to investigate an attempt on her life." I was aware from listening in to Toddy's conversation with Tasha that he already knew the details of what had happened. Not surprisingly, he didn't acknowledge that. So I filled them in on her very close call with the SUV at Rutgers.

"The police down there haven't been able to come up with a suspect," my dad added, "and April is naturally concerned that whoever it was is still out there and might try again. Part of our job is to find out whether the attack had any possible connection to the arson and murders of her parents years ago."

The four of us were crowded into a tiny entrance area, just big enough for what I assumed was the coat closet. We shuffled in place until Claudia told Toddy to bring us into the sunroom. "I got a bowl of grapes," she said. "I'll bring it in." As she turned, I saw that she wore hearing aids that looked like plugs of pale pink Play-Doh.

"Mom," Toddy began, but she was off, and we followed him.

"Give me a minute," Claudia croaked from the kitchen. "I forgot if I washed the grapes, so I'm washing them again."

The sunroom must have been the biggest room in the house, probably an add-on, with a smoothed-over cement floor and a beamed ceiling that couldn't decide whether to be vaulted or flat, so it did some of each. All the furniture was covered in camel-colored leather (a fairly dark camel) and appeared to have been bought as a suite. A massive flat-screen TV took up the far wall. Aside from the sunlight, the best part of the room was a black iron woodstove. There were still some logs shoved into deep shelves built to hold them.

Toddy motioned us to the couch and sat down in a club chair near us. As Dad and I shifted to face him, his mother came in with a bowl of grapes, a bunch of cocktail napkins, and a plate of plain cookies. She placed them in front of us and settled into a love seat.

"Toddy," she said, "you going to talk to them?" But he was sitting with his hands flat, right above his knees, looking ready to spring up and get away from all of us. "He's not himself," she announced. "He almost got run over by a car. He's worried it might have been on purpose."

"I didn't say it was on purpose," he snapped at her. "I just said I can't understand how the driver didn't see me." He lifted his chin to look at me and my dad. "I was wearing a white shirt and crossing the street, in the crosswalk. It wasn't dark yet. The light just turned green for me, but the car kept going. Their traffic light had already turned red."

"When did this happen, Toddy?" my dad asked.

"Last weekend."

"Saturday night," his mother said, "around seven. He got a yen for his frozen chocolate drink—Dunkin' Donuts. So I said, 'While you're at it, pick me up a box of those little ones. You know, the doughnut holes. What you don't finish, you can stick in the freezer.'"

"Ma'am," my dad said, "it's better if Toddy tells me what happened. And that's only because I might hear something in his words that tells me, 'Hey, follow up on this.'" Claudia thought it over, then nodded, took a grape, and sat back.

"What kind of car was it?" Dad asked.

"A Corolla. That's a Toyota."

"A sedan?"

Toddy seemed to lack the nerve to tell us to leave him alone. "This was a hatchback."

"What color?"

"Blue."

"Help me out here. Anything distinctive you noticed? The front of the car came at you, right? If you think back, do you remember anything on the windshield? A decal. Something hanging from the rearview mirror?"

"I don't want you recording this. Both of you, give me your phones," Toddy demanded.

Maybe because his mother was there, he added, “Please.” She showed no signs of being embarrassed by his request.

Toddy stood and watched as we shut down our phones. He looked at me and said, “If you want, you can come with me to see where I put them.” I followed him back to the vestibule by the front door. He lifted an edge of the small rug and pushed the phones toward the middle. As he bent over, the light coming through the transom over the door shone on his hair, which emitted that orange glow men seem to get when they use hair dye. Beneath the glow was dark brown. “Okay?” he said. “We can go back now. I just want to make sure I’m not being recorded.”

“I understand.”

“Don’t think I don’t remember that guy—the other detective you’re with. He was a plainclothes cop that questioned me about the fire. The other cop woke me up and started yelling questions. But he—the guy you’re with—was nice.”

“He still is. He’s not a cop. Just a private investigator now.”

“And you?”

“Retired FBI special agent, now a PI.”

We walked back through the house, past the rooms I hadn’t gotten a chance to look at earlier. There were no paintings, no photos on the walls, no crucifixes. Almost like a witness protection house, except they had really lived there for the last fourteen years.

In the sunroom, my dad was mid-cookie and Claudia had taken possession of the bowl of grapes; she held it on her lap.

Under my shirt, a recorder was taped to my chest, up near my left shoulder, so lightweight I couldn’t feel it. It was voice-activated. On the other hand, the one my dad was wearing had been running continuously since we parked in front of the house.

“I forget what we were talking about,” Toddy said as he went right back to the club chair.

I told him, “You were about to tell us whether you saw anything on the front window of the Corolla or through the windshield.”

"Anything hanging from the rearview mirror?" my dad asked again.

"No. I don't think so, but I can't say for sure."

"And on the windshield. Any kind of decal? You don't have to know what it is, just the shape or color would help." My dad and I knew that Connecticut didn't have inspection or registration stickers, so it was no surprise when Toddy shook his head. "License plate?" Dad asked.

"Connecticut." So the plates were not taped over, like the SUVs that had gone after Luisa and April.

"How about the driver? Male, female, age, race?"

"White, I'm pretty sure," Toddy said. "It all happened so fast."

"These things do," my dad said. "What happened? How did it play out?"

"I was crossing the street, like I told you. I waited till the light changed. And then the car came barreling through, like there wasn't any traffic signal, like they had the right-of-way."

"It was a two-way street you were on, right?" Toddy nodded. "And who was nearer the center line, you or the car?"

"The car. It's a four-lane thoroughfare, two lanes on each side. So I was in the middle of the first lane and the car was coming in the second lane. But then, for whatever insane reason, he started heading over the line into my lane—"

I cut in. "Were there any other cars around? Either behind him—I assume they had stopped when the light changed—or facing the other direction?" He nodded again. "Did any of them honk their horns as a warning? Do you think anyone noticed him coming toward you?"

"Yes. Maybe two, three cars honked. And somebody was flashing their lights on and off like crazy."

"Did the driver seem to be aware of them?" my dad asked.

"I don't know," Toddy said. "They were like three feet away from me. I thought I was going to die. But then they got back into their lane."

"The one he'd been in originally?"

"Yeah."

"So did you think the blue car swerved deliberately, trying to run you down? Or was it just someone who ran a red light, wasn't paying attention to driving, maybe preoccupied with something else?"

"How could I tell? Because if the other guys hadn't honked or flashed their lights? I'd be dead. So it could have been some addict or somebody trying to get me but he got put off by . . . What do you call them? Witnesses. Jesus, I can't even think straight."

"Hey, what's wrong with you, Toddy?" his mother demanded loudly. She lifted the bowl off her lap and slammed it onto the glass tabletop. The sound was enough to make me shudder, but the glass remained intact. Toddy looked like a kid who'd been smacked in front of company. "What did you tell me about the car? Come on, spit it out."

"What?" He was practically whispering, but it wasn't as if he were trying to tell her to shut up. To me, at least, it seemed as if he couldn't figure out what she was saying.

"You told me it was a Domino's car. With that sign on top. *Stunod.* You said it was lit up. Making a pizza delivery. So tell the man. It was a bigger deal than a Connecticut license plate."

"I forgot, for Christ's sake!" he yelled. "Yes, it's the most obvious thing in the world, but I've been scared shitless and I forgot, okay?"

"What happened?" Claudia demanded. "Nothing. A dumb kid driving a car in a big rush. Fine, you were shook up. Trust me, I get it. But enough. You're still scared. It's over. You think Mr. Domino put out a contract on you?"

He repositioned himself so he was facing me and Dad, his back toward his mother. But his head turned once or twice—just a couple of degrees—although he resisted actually turning to look at her. It struck me that this was out-of-the-ordinary behavior for him, that though he might have resentments that come from being dependent, slightly dopey, meek, and maybe even aware that he was a disappointment to his mom, he loved her.

"That kind of close call," my dad said, "it shakes people up." I got up and sat beside Claudia on the love seat, just on the edge of the cushion.

I turned my head in the general direction of the side of her head, close enough to her hearing aids so she could hear me when I spoke quietly. "Mrs. Mirante, I understand you being protective of your son, wanting to be in the room while we're questioning him."

She was still playing guardian of the grapes, gripping the bowl. "I absolutely understand," I went on, keeping my voice down. "The reason I'm asking you to give us a few minutes alone with him is that some of our questions might concern his former employer, Seymour Brown, or people Seymour was close with. Please know that this isn't about you. This is standard procedure: we've found that people are more open when people who are close to them aren't in the room. We'll be asking about details of relationships, including sex, and it might embarrass him to speak with you there. It's your call, though. As you said, this is your house. All we're trying to do is get Toddy's help. And protect April Brown."

"Maybe someone is trying to get her because she went into her father's business," she said.

Claudia was tough, but I sensed that she wasn't as cold as she was trying to appear. "She barely escaped that burning house," I replied. "Both her parents were murdered. She had to go and live with relatives in Kentucky, people she never even heard of, much less met. But she did well. Went to college, then got her PhD. Now she's teaching at a university."

"Well, three cheers for her." She slowly set the grapes back on the table. Her legs had been crossed at her slightly swollen ankles, but now she put them flat on the floor.

I turned to Toddy. "You are the only one who can choose, Toddy. Talk to us. Or wait till a detective from New Jersey drives up here and liaises with a couple of your Norwalk cops and drops in for a visit. Cops gossip a lot. You wouldn't want it getting back to the Greenwich PD. I mean, some of them might know your boss."

A spring in the love seat creaked under my cushion, and out of the corner of my eye, I noted that my dad had leaned forward. Claudia made a hissing sound to get Toddy's attention. "Listen, Toddy," she said. "You don't have to talk to them or any cop from New Jersey. Toddy, you don't have to say nothing. Not to them, not to the police. Okay? You understand what I'm saying?"

"Mom, can you take your walk or something? I really want to talk to them. Maybe I could help April. You don't have to worry. Oh, listen, if you go out the front, their phones are under the little rug, so don't trip."

The front door opened and crashed shut. Toddy's heavy eyebrows lowered when his mom left, like a couple of flags descending to half-mast. Though he'd stood up to his mom, he now looked sad and confused. Deflated, too, as if some of his substance had followed her out of the room.

"You know," my dad began, "we've talked about Seymour until we're blue in the face. So let's talk about the other victim, Kim."

The mention of her name took Toddy by surprise; his brows flew back up while his jaw dropped. All he could manage was, "There is nothing much to talk about. She wasn't important. Seymour was the one they were after." I had to strain to hear him, as he hadn't put enough breath behind his words to push them out into the room.

"But important or not, she died too, right?" my dad said. "And horribly." Toddy shrugged, and if I had been new to the case, I wouldn't know whether it was out of indifference or a gesture of ineffectuality—*Can't do anything about that now*.

Finally, he thought to say, "Yeah. Actually, I felt terrible. You know how they say, sick at heart? That was me. Poor lady, going like that."

"Toddy, just to save us both some time, let me tell you what we know," I said. "We know you and Kim were having fun in the Browns' basement, and it wasn't watching cartoons, was it?"

"Who the fuck told you that?" Outrage complete with flared nostrils, but not a denial.

"Sources." We waited, but he waited, too, feeling us out. "That pizza car ran the light, heading for you, and you were way beyond frightened. Because you already knew about one attempted vehicular homicide. And as you were running and praying, or whatever you did in those few seconds, you were telling yourself, *This has got to be the same driver who went after April. She missed then, but now she's coming at me.*"

My using the pronoun "she" did not raise either of Toddy's busy eyebrows.

My dad claimed that he tended to play it down the middle when he was on the job. Not heartless, not compassionate. Direct. But when he felt it was needed, he could be threatening or, like now, Good Cop. He sensed that this would work with Toddy. "From what you've told us about the night you almost got hit, there's a good chance the driver who went after April wasn't the same one you saw coming. Different MO completely." His words were comforting. Toddy blinked, breathed deeply, relief relaxing the lines in his face. "But seeing that car coming at you, I guess it must make you sympathize with what April went through, what she must be worrying about."

"Definitely."

"And you understand that if we don't find the SUV driver, she could try it again. Or something worse."

"Terrible," Toddy said, his eagerness to be on my dad's side on full display. "A fucking nightmare." His tone shifted to mild irritation. "You keep saying 'she.'"

"Good you brought that up." Dad stood, stretched his legs, and, before sitting down again, took a cookie and tore off a handful of grapes in a way my mom would frown at. "So here's the thing," he went on. "Maybe, in your heart of hearts, you wish April Brown all the best. And maybe you don't give a shit. That doesn't matter to me. My guess is, as a detective, that Kim didn't take a job with Domino's just to get the sign. But she'll go for April again. Then it's only a matter of time. She'll be back for you. For whatever reason, April is her first priority. But, Toddy, my man, even if the Domino's car was a coincidence, you've got to realize that you are next in line."

"Kim? I swear to God, I don't know what you're talking about."

"We are talking about how Kim wants you dead. Because you know how Seymour was killed," I told him.

"You guys . . . You're so crazy. Kim is dead. D-E-A—"

"Your mom will be back soon," Dad said. "When I said it's us or the cops, I didn't want to mention Kim in front of her. Well, here we are, the first to show up, the first to confirm what you know in your gut. Okay, you don't have to speak to us. But what if Kim happens to get here before the police do? Could be tonight. Could be next week. Is there a doubt you and your mother will get what Seymour got, a terrible death?" Toddy's chin was on his chest, and he was shaking his head—*No, no*—in an attempt at denial that wasn't working. My dad kept at him. "I'm telling you, Toddy, we both know it's safer to talk to us than wait for the cops to show. This is a woman who is trying to run over her own daughter. Do you imagine Kim would think twice about coming after you and your mom?"

For an instant Toddy looked as if he hadn't heard. But then he gagged. Slapping his hands over his mouth, he got up and ran. Of course we followed, and since I got to the bathroom at the same time Toddy did, I had the pleasure of watching him vomit into the sink. His upchuck subsided but came back seconds later. He didn't even try to take a step to the toilet. My latent sexism surfaced; at least Kim would have raised the toilet seat right from the get-go.

Meanwhile, my dad rushed outside in case our guy decided a dive through the bathroom window was the way to make a run for it. I stayed where I was until Toddy was finished and had cleaned the sink. I wondered how anyone listening to my voice-activated recorder would interpret him saying "I never did that before. Hard to clean up." And then me saying "Rinse out your mouth," and then "Wash your hands and face, Toddy."

The sunroom wasn't so sunny when we came back. A couple of gray clouds was all it took to highlight the starkness of the place. The shadowy light made the concrete floor seem even darker than it was, the circles of trowel marks visible in the shadows.

CHAPTER TWENTY-ONE

"Let's get a move on," Dad ordered as he came back in. Rather than sitting beside me, he took the love seat Claudia had vacated. Looking at his rigid back, it was hard to believe that his natural habitat was a recliner, but he knew, as I did, there was no time to relax. "How long were you having a thing with Kim?"

"Jesus, that's a tough one," Toddy said. "Let me think. So long ago."

"Bullshit," I said. When a witness starts saying *Wait a minute* or even *Uhhh*, it often means they're stalling to come up with a credible response. "You think you can use up time and then your mom will come in and we'll stop. No, no. We will keep asking you in front of her. If she tries to throw us out, threatens to call the police, we'll say, 'Great, let them come, let them be enlightened.' So how long were you and Kim an item?"

Toddy hesitated. My dad went with a more sympathetic approach. "You really loved each other, huh."

Toddy hung his head. "Yeah. Well. I don't know. I thought we both felt the same way . . . but then after the fire, I waited and waited. She just fucking disappeared. I had no way to reach her. She knew exactly where to find me, though. If she wanted to. I can't believe I fell for her shit."

My dad shook his head sadly. "So how long were you two together before it happened?"

"Almost two years."

"How did it start?" my dad asked.

"She— I'd just brought her home from the city. She said, 'It's so cold. If you want to wait in the basement, I'm sure it would be okay with Seymour. There's a TV down there, and a little bathroom if you need it.' I said maybe I shouldn't till she checked with him, and she said, 'He won't care. Honest to God.'" So I watched some TV and it was warm down there. She'd left me by myself but showed me how to get out by the back door in case she was giving April a bath or something." His shoulders, which had been drawn up defensively, loosened as he spoke.

"And?"

"And after a couple of times, with her wearing tight sweaters and stuff, she said I was always welcome. The only reason I kept going there was because I didn't think she'd look twice at someone like me."

"And the sweaters," my dad added. Toddy nodded. "So, keep going."

"Around three weeks into it, I was thinking it was nice not to have to use gas station bathrooms. I'm watching TV, and Kim comes down. Asks me if everything is okay and did I want some water or something. And then she told me the girl, April, had a playdate over at a friend's and she was so bored without her little girl being there. And then the next thing I knew, she was sitting on the arm of my chair and unzipping me and kissing me. Saying that she had such a crush on me for so long. I couldn't believe it. Well, I could, because she was looking at me and I swear to God, I thought I saw love in her eyes."

"So that was the start of your affair?"

"Yeah. After it was over, I mean that first afternoon's stuff, I asked her how could she feel the way she did about somebody like me when she had Seymour. Rich. Custom suits, an all-gold Rolex. People called him a financial genius. I didn't mention the financial genius part to Kim. I don't know why. Maybe because it'd make him sound too good and she'd think, *Maybe I should rethink this*. But 'financial genius' is what everybody called him. Anyway, she put her fingers over my lips—" He demonstrated with his index and middle fingers. Even from where I was, I could see that his nails were overgrown, which was high on my list of Revolting Male Habits.

"Did Kim explain why she fell for you?"

"Oh yeah. She said, 'How can you ask how I can want you? You're so masculine and have the most beautiful smile. You have no idea how awful he is . . .' Oh wait. I think she said 'cruel.' And then she said she couldn't stand it when he snuck up from behind and started feeling her up. And then she cried about how unhappy she was, but it was five thirty and I had to go pick him up."

"Did you ask her what she meant by cruel?" I asked.

"No. But I saw him be terrible to other people. I knew. Oh my God, one time we were jammed up in traffic and a guy was blowing his horn and Seymour . . . he got out of the car and went over to the horn blower's car and smashed the guy's head against the steering wheel. He was always screaming at me, like I personally made rush hours happen. And you should've heard him on the phone. He made threats, but he never said exactly what he would do. Maybe because he didn't want to be recorded. Or he knew it was scarier to say 'You'll never see the light of day again.' What did he mean, like blind or dead? Locked up somewhere?"

"Did Kim ever say whether he was abusive to her in any way?" Dad asked.

"She told me after a while."

"How long is 'a while'?" I asked.

"I don't really remember. A couple of months, maybe. When she met me in the basement, her hand and part of her arm were bandaged with this splint thing. At first she said she tripped over the vacuum and when she put out her hands to stop falling, one got bent back. But I could see it in her eyes. She had the most beautiful eyes in the world. I remember thinking her eyes were a reflection of her beautiful soul. Can you believe how stupid I was?" I took that as a rhetorical question and let him go on. "Well, love does that to people." He sighed. "Anyway, I was staring at the Ace bandage with, like, the most aching heart. And I said, 'Tell me the truth.' And she said Seymour bent her hand all the way back until he almost broke her wrist. He had his other hand over her mouth so she wouldn't scream and wake up April."

"What were the circumstances?"

"She said Seymour wanted her to do something she just couldn't do. She said she wouldn't tell me what he wanted, but he kept bending her wrist more and more and it hurt so much that she ended up doing it. I started crying, and she kissed me and said she hadn't wanted to tell me because it was so awful I might want to kill him."

"Did you want to kill him?" I asked.

Toddy wrung his hands and then bit the knuckle of his thumb. "I don't remember. Maybe I just thought about smashing his face in. But I knew if I did that, he'd fire me. I wouldn't be able to see Kim. And then, it's not like that was the only time. She had horrible bruises once. Wouldn't even tell me." He stopped, and my dad signaled him to continue. "Another time she called me from the top of the basement stairs, asked me to come and walk her down because she was dizzy. It turned out she had a concussion. Oh, Jesus! Seymour banged her head against a shelf when she was in her closet."

"How often did you see her?"

"Two, three, four days a week."

"Was it usually when April was in school? Or after school? How did that work?"

"Usually before the kid came home or when she was at a friend's. Kim put a lock on the basement door, like from the inside, our side, so if April was home and watching TV, she couldn't get downstairs. But we didn't do that too often, and we did it quick, so the kid wouldn't even notice. And Kim said, 'Don't worry about Seymour. In his whole life, he's never come down here. I'm not sure he even knows we have a basement."

As an interrogator, I always paid attention to how folks responded not only to my questions but to their own answers. Every time Toddy cited the wit or wisdom of Kim Brown, his features softened. It amazed me how besotted he still was. He lowered his chin and raised shining eyes toward some memory. Never mind that he believed the love of his life might be trying to kill him (though I considered it far more likely that it was someone rushing a meat lover's pizza with extra cheese to Central Norwalk). However angry he might be at her, Toddy was also still crazy about those times with Kim. He seemed to have total recall of it all.

My dad took over. "At what point did one of you bring up getting Seymour out of your way?"

"Oh no. You're not going to pin this on me," Toddy said. "It was totally Kim who brought it up. Listen, you can't blame her."

"Did she tell you what he said when he abused her like that?" Dad asked.

"He said she was taking too long to get undressed, and he didn't like to be kept waiting."

Beside Homicide, my dad had been in Sex Crimes, so I could see that these claims didn't surprise him, especially considering Seymour's bent for savagery. I guessed Dad was probably thinking that the abuse did happen. As I did. Possibly she made it up to get Toddy to be willing to help her, but I didn't think so. Sociopaths can be brutalized, too.

"And you're saying Seymour was very conscious of keeping Kim quiet during these assaults?" I asked.

"Oh yeah, definitely. He was totally protective with April," Toddy said. "He wanted her to look up to him. It was a little weird."

I kept myself from leaning forward. "Weird in what sense?"

"It was like he looked up to her. You've got to admit that's weird. The kid was—I'm pretty sure—five years old. You know, some parents think their kid is the best thing in the world. But a kid is a kid. Kim said April was like God to him, and everything about her was perfect. I mean, if she was bratty, Kim couldn't complain; he wouldn't believe her. He'd say she was lying. One time he smacked her because she told him the teacher said April peed in her chair two times. Seymour said she was jealous of April because April was so smart and she was a moron from Kentucky."

Out of nowhere, my dad said to me in Spanish, "You think this guy's mad that his boss was fucking his wife?" I was startled for a second until I realized what he was doing. Once he saw that Toddy didn't react, he went on. "Needed to make sure he didn't speak Spanish. Anyway, I'm nervous about his mother coming home and changing the mood. Do you think we should go somewhere? Maybe in the backyard, on the other side of that little stone wall, by the water?"

"No. I think going outside would change the mood more than the mom. And we don't know what's on the other side. He could run for it, and we have no authority to stop him."

Toddy shifted uncomfortably. My dad gave him an apologetic smile. "Sorry. I didn't have time to look up whether you had a criminal record up here. I knew you were clean in New York in terms of arrests or convictions. I was asking about Connecticut, and my partner here says you checked out clean and gainfully employed. That takes the pressure off both of us while I'm asking you questions."

"But I'm tired," Toddy said. With two fingers, he pinched the skin just over the bridge of his nose.

"Believe me, I understand. Just a few more items I need to get to. So Seymour had all this love and respect for the little kid. But you tell me he treated his wife like garbage." Toddy nodded like a weary old man, and Dad continued. "Was there any point when you said to yourself, 'I need to get out of here'? 'Out of this job, out of this relationship. It's all toxic.'"

"Listen, man, I loved her. Keeping my job meant having Kim in my life."

"Except by staying around, you had to know that at any time, once you dropped him off, he could do whatever he wanted to her . . . Well, once the kid was asleep. It must have been so hard on you."

"Harder on her." Toddy spoke in the righteous, selfless way of a brave soldier. "She once told me that if I'd pushed her away that first afternoon and not let her into my life, she would have killed herself." He, then my dad, lowered their heads at the thought.

When they looked up, Dad peered straight across the coffee table at Toddy, kind of up and down, as if to take his measure. "Toddy," he said evenly, "at what point did Kim ask for your help?"

"What do you mean? Help? What kind of help?"

Since we'd already mentioned that we thought Kim was the killer, I'm not sure exactly who his wide-eyed-innocent routine was for.

"The kind of help that other women in her situation have asked for. Help to get rid of Seymour on a permanent basis." Toddy may have been trying out comebacks in his head: *Are you crazy? Absolutely no way! Get the fuck out of here!* But nothing came. "Let me ask you another way," Dad went on. "Don't get stuck on remembering the exact words she used. In general, how did she express her plea for your help?"

There was silence at first. His skin paled beneath his tan and then looked waxy. "She didn't ask me for anything," Toddy said. That denial, along with the effort to keep his voice from trembling, took all his energy. His breathing was close to a pant. I could see how scared he was. Of us, surely—but I guessed his fear of Kim was at the front of his mind.

"Tell me basically what she said." The request was insistent, though my dad's voice was subdued. "We've been hired to protect April, but you don't want Kim on the loose, free to do"—he lowered his voice to an ominous whisper—"something to you."

It took a while for Toddy to get calm enough to speak again. "She wanted me to help her get rid of him." He threw the sentence out, as if heaving something putrid far away from him.

"Kim wanted you to help her get rid of Seymour, right?" I asked, mindful of our recording devices.

"Yeah. Kim said there was no way she could stay in the marriage. If she asked for a divorce, she knew she'd be dead in a couple of days. It would look like a genuine accident, and everybody would feel sorry for Seymour and April."

I made a mental note that she didn't mention to Toddy the more likely possibility that Seymour would simply say good riddance but insist on total custody of April.

"So, bottom line," my dad said, "given that she thought a divorce could cost her her life, what was her idea?"

Toddy did some deep thinking. In the silence, I heard the faintest sound of the Geico gecko and realized his mom had returned and was watching TV, probably in her room.

"Kim said the only way out was to get rid of Seymour. That way, she would inherit, and then . . ." More deep breathing. "Then we could get married."

"And how did you react?"

"You've got to be kidding. I was shocked."

"So what did you do? I mean, you did love her, right? If she hadn't already been married to Seymour, you would have popped the question in a minute."

"Yeah. Of course. Seymour wasn't the only game in town, job-wise. Good drivers who know the ropes, who know how to keep their mouth shut. They can get really good money and benefits with at least a hundred private situations. I wouldn't do corporate. Though Manhattan would have been easier for me than Brooklyn in terms of the commute."

The next time my dad glanced my way, I mouthed *Mom*. I jerked my head toward the main part of the house to indicate she'd come back.

My dad didn't acknowledge me, but I knew he'd caught what I was signaling. "So what did you do when she asked for your help in getting rid of Seymour, Toddy?" he asked. "I really want to know. How did you react?"

"I told you. I was shocked. I walked out. I couldn't think of anything to say to something like that."

"You didn't say no?"

"Not in so many words. How many times do I have to say it?" An answer like this demanded an unwavering, affronted stare, but Toddy couldn't even look my dad straight in the eye.

"So she didn't tell you at that point how she planned to pull it off."

"She hadn't figured that out yet. It couldn't look like what it was. It had to look like an accident."

"The way Seymour would have done it to her," my dad suggested. "Easy for him. He had no conscience."

Toddy was relieved that my dad seemed to be seeing things his way. "Piece of cake," Toddy agreed. "And he knew all those people in the mob, so he could get help if he needed it." He shrugged. "What can you do? But yeah, she wanted it to look like Seymour had an accident, but it would be on purpose."

Suspects can get bored after too much time with one interrogator. If they don't get a fresh audience, they may start wondering how their act is playing; if they decide it's not great, they could shut it down. But my dad was on a roll, so I decided to keep quiet.

"Then what did you do when she asked you to do that?"

Toddy stared at the floor, his face flushed, his ears such a dark crimson they looked gigantic. Finally he did answer. "Well, I came back. But we just kept fighting about it—"

I interrupted. "When you were thinking of the two of you being together, what were her plans for April? Take her with you? Could you see adopting her?"

Toddy exhaled and then, lowering his chin to his chest, sadly shook his head. "No. Truth of the matter was that April worshipped her father. Kind of a mutual admiration thing. Not that she didn't love Kim, and vice versa. Seymour had a younger brother in the city, Richie."

Neither the NYPD nor FDNY investigators could trace anyone related to Seymour; for all they knew, he could have sprung full-grown from the Brooklyn Salt Marsh. Either Toddy was lying now—and he'd incriminated himself so much I didn't think that was possible— or Kim had lied to him then.

"Richie was a very successful Park Avenue doctor," Toddy went on. "He and his wife couldn't have kids of their own. Kim said the best thing would be to let April be with them. April was crazy about them."

I waited for him to say "vice versa" again. Hearing nothing, I asked, "Did you ever overhear Seymour mention a brother, or someone named Richie?"

"No."

"Did you ever drive him to a Richie's house on Park Avenue? Or pick up Dr. and Mrs. Richie?"

"No."

"Did his mobile phone ever ring and after he answered, he said, 'Hi, Richie'?"

"I don't know. No."

"But with Richie and his wife loving April so much, you two could start out fresh?"

"Yeah. Just an idea she floated."

"Before you were shocked and told her no," I said.

"Right . . ." Toddy paused. "Or it could have been after, when I came back to try and see if we could work something out without her getting rid of Seymour."

"Without her getting rid of Seymour," I repeated. "But since she started telling you about April going to his brother the doctor, how would that happen without her husband getting killed?" The look he gave me was less than fond.

He turned to my dad. "She's making it sound worse than it is. Was," he complained. "Kim wanted what was best for her little girl. That's all."

"That's not all she wanted," my dad said in the kindly voice he was using. "She wanted you."

Toddy swallowed. Even he was smart enough not to trust that gentle baritone completely, because all he did was look down at his color-blocked Nikes and mutter, "I guess so."

"I'm sure Kim wanted you for a lot of reasons." My dad's voice grew louder. "For instance, she needed somebody to carry those five-gallon cans full of gasoline. It must have been many five-gallon cans. Because the reason Seymour and his house turned to ashes was that everything was saturated with it. Did you know that each of those cans weighs about thirty pounds when it's filled? Kim was a pretty small woman. But you're a big, strong guy. You did a lot of heavy lifting for her, Toddy. You needed three days off not just to do the job, but to recuperate. You were a strong guy, but you weren't into weight training. You had to buy gas at different stations. Carrying the filled cans to the Browns' house from wherever you were hiding them. How did you manage without the neighbors seeing you?"

"It was at night. I borrowed one of those flatbed things from a construction site, what they use for bricks. But I had to hide the cans again until she got Seymour upstairs and in bed."

"When did you lug them all upstairs? Well, not all, because you needed a few to take care of the downstairs too."

What often happens when a suspect suddenly realizes it's all over is that a curtain of tears descends on their cheeks. Sometimes heaving sobs. Instead, Toddy stayed dry-eyed and silent. But his entire body began to shake. His arms and legs twitched as if he were having a seizure, and I was scared that's what it was. His head jerked around so that every second it seemed as if his face was directed at some new spot. Then, finally, it subsided. His head turned in one direction—toward the doorway. Most likely he was desperate to see if his mom had gotten home. Could she have been standing there, witnessing it all?

"Had Kim already decided on a fire, or did you come up with it together?" Dad's manner was even. He seemed mildly curious, as if inquiring on plans for a picnic. He was careful not to make Toddy feel judged.

"No. Once I said I'd help, she said she'd think about how to get it done. But she was quick that way and had it all settled in her mind two days later, or maybe three. The day after, we talked about where to get a new start. I couldn't understand why she wanted to leave New York so bad. I wanted to stay close so I could visit my mom. Like have dinner with her once a week. Kim said we would have her visit us, which would be like a vacation, because we'd move to some really nice place. She'd have a beautiful guest bedroom with its own bath. Kim said she heard Tampa was nice, but also some towns near San Diego."

"But that didn't happen," my dad said.

"No. But the next day or the day after, she had the whole plan worked out. She said the house had to burn down so that no one could find Seymour's papers, if he kept any there. She thought they would show a lot of illegal transactions, and that would mean she couldn't get her hands on the money."

"Would he keep those kinds of documents at home?" I asked. "He had an office, a secretary, safe-deposit boxes. Wouldn't he take care to hide all the information on his offshore accounts and investments?"

"Kim said she didn't really know for sure, but he'd brought stuff home in a briefcase. I saw that too."

"Where did you store the cans of gasoline?"

"There were two houses kind of next door but through the backyard. One of them had been demolished and the other was going to be. Like to make the biggest house in Manhattan Beach. But the owner was behind in payments with the contractor. The two places were fenced off, the one they'd demoed and the other one. So I had to rent a bolt cutter to cut the padlock on one of the gates to get in and out. I stuck the cans under the porch of the place that hadn't been demoed."

"How long did it take you to get all the cans together?" Dad spoke rhythmically and fast, as if backed up by a drummer. Upping the pace can be contagious and prevent the suspect from thinking too long about his answers.

"I had to go to gas stations all over Brooklyn. It was—"

"Just answer. How long?"

"It took all three days."

"Did you use Seymour's car?"

"Just for buying the gas. It went faster at the gas stations. Come in with a Mercedes, you get respect. Good service. 'Thank you, sir.'"

"The night of the fire?" my dad asked.

"I took the car back to the garage. You know, where I kept it up in the Bronx. Pretended to leave to walk home." My dad looked borderline livid. He had wanted to check Toddy's alibi by questioning the people at the garage, but his corner-cutting superior, Bobby Melvin, had told him it was a waste—too far afield. "Kim wanted to rent an Infiniti for the trip, but I said if you do that, they'll have a copy of your license and the plate number. And if I rent it—"

My dad cut him off. "Got it. Keep going."

"So instead of leaving the garage and going home, I doubled back. Half the time they left the keys in the cars. I took a Toyota Camry. That year's model, metallic gray, with a V-8. I kind of hunched down and—"

My dad's patience was wearing thin. And by now Toddy was in so deep there was no need to coddle him by listening to his embellishments. That could come later, and it wouldn't be our job. We had a single aim: to get as much info as we could in order to find Kim before she struck again.

"You drove back to Brooklyn. Where did you park the car?"

"Down the street from Manny's Superette. Busy street. It's about four blocks, but we knew fire trucks would be coming and we didn't want anyone noticing the car near Seymour's because it was our getaway."

"What happened then?"

"I'd started bringing the rest of the cans upstairs. But I had to wait until seven o'clock when the kid was asleep."

"Where was Seymour?"

"Upstairs, in their bed."

"Had she given him something or what?"

"She put something in his hamburger that made him feel dizzy and sick. She helped him upstairs and put him in bed. When he was out of it, she gave him a shot."

"An injection?"

"Yeah. Some stuff she got from a guy in Brighton Beach. He put it in the needle for her because she'd never done an injection before. He told her, 'Just stick it in and push the thing down slowly.'"

"Did you see her do it?"

"No." Toddy's answer came out in a pip-squeak voice. I could see he wanted a do-over.

But my dad's follow-up was too quick. "Was it meant to kill him or make him unconscious?"

"I don't know. By the time I got there . . . He didn't look alive, but I couldn't tell. His eyes were open, but they didn't move."

My dad was silent, as if he were reordering some mental outline. Then he said, "Part of the plan was having people think Kim died too. Why?"

"That's because the wife is always the prime suspect," Toddy said, "unless it's the woman who dies, and then they suspect the husband. So she thought it was better to make a fresh start."

"So that's why she sacrificed her diamond ring?"

"That's because diamonds are the hardest thing in the world. They wouldn't burn. And she knew she couldn't use a fake one, because they'd test it."

"So she put it on the bed?"

"I'm trying to remember," Toddy told him, looking to his sneakers for inspiration. "I think she must have done it before I got in the room."

"Tossed it on top of the bed?"

"Under the covers, I think. We talked about that because she said that's how she slept."

My dad and I were clearly on the same wavelength. He asked the question I would have asked: "How was she so sure everything would burn so there would be no identifiable remains?"

"I don't get what you mean."

"Sure you do. She needed something left of Seymour so that the medical examiner could identify his DNA. Right? She kept talking about inheriting. It would be helpful if the authorities had proof of his death. Otherwise they might think he just skipped town and burned down his house."

Toddy pressed the heel of his hand against his forehead, as if trying to squeeze out an idea. But ideas didn't come so easily for him, and he didn't have anything to say.

"Tell me," my dad persisted, "how was there supposed to be enough left of Seymour to identify, but all they could find of Kim would be her diamond engagement ring?" His tone had shifted, from Good Cop to Curious Cop, though he wasn't at all adversarial. "What I don't get is that the two of them were both sleeping in the same bed and died, right? Kim didn't take off her ring and tuck it in every night before she actually got into bed, did she?"

"Look, I have been very open with you," Toddy said, "but she was the one who planned this and maybe didn't tell me everything. I mean, there were so many details."

"I can only imagine," my dad said. "But let's start with this . . . How did Kim expect to inherit when—at least as far as the police knew—she was as dead as he was?"

"I'm not sure, but she did say that the wife inherits. But she also said she could get her hands on a lot of money. Really, tons of it—in legit banks. And also cash. She had everything covered."

"Why do I think you're not telling me the whole story?" my dad asked. His tone dropped down, as if he were a parent telling a child that he wasn't mad, just disappointed. Toddy's mouth opened wide, a mediocre imitation of shock. "Let's go back to her saying good night to her ring and putting it under the covers." Dad kept at him. "Don't you think the fire inspectors and homicide cops would ask themselves where Kim Brown was, or some residue of Kim Brown? If it had all gone according to whatever plan she had, shouldn't there at least have been a toe? A charred thighbone? Or did you use so much gasoline on the bed that there was nothing left except the diamond?"

"I didn't want to overdo it, so there would be a little of him left. But the can was heavy and some extra spilled out."

My dad's voice grew harsh and hoarse. "With all her smart planning, did Kim ever believe that the biggest, hottest flames would stay on her side of the bed and the less intense flames stay on Seymour's? That fire behaves the way you want it to? Cut the crap, Toddy. What are you leaving out? Because I have a very good idea about what it was."

Maybe he did have a good idea, but I wasn't going to bet on that. My dad had gut knowledge that something was wrong with the picture, but he couldn't see what it was. I couldn't either. I couldn't figure how Kim could imagine a new start in life without some suggestion that she had perished along with her husband. Otherwise, both the authorities and Seymour's angry, relentless mob clients who'd lost so much would be searching for her.

I set my hands on my knees and leaned forward, as if I were about to spring up. Where would Kim find a body? Grab a neighbor off the street? Break into a funeral home? Then something Tasha had told me about hit me, about urging Kim to get some help in the house: *You need to get someone.*

"Whose body was in bed with Seymour that night?" I asked.

Toddy drew back. It took him too long to say "I don't know."

"But there was a woman's body with him." At last he nodded, which didn't do much good with a recording. "Don't jerk us around," I said.

"The reason you're talking to us is that we are easier than the cops, more understanding. It gives you a chance to rehearse for opening night. Don't look so insulted, Toddy. Help us to understand now. It can help you if the Norwalk PD and the Connecticut State Police come swarming into your house." There was really no "if" involved, but I felt no obligation to share that with Toddy. "Who was she?"

"I don't know who she was," he whispered.

"Stop whispering. Talk so my partner can hear you clearly. You have no idea where a woman came from? Or is it that you don't know her name?"

"I wasn't there. She was interviewing—"

"She, meaning Kim?"

"Yes. She told Seymour she had to get someone to babysit. Help in the house, too. She couldn't go shopping with the wives of important men, or go out to dinner when the men took their wives along. They all had help. She was the only one who didn't. He finally said okay."

"So how did she go about it?" Dad asked. "And don't tell me you don't know."

Toddy's mouth must have been dry; his tongue kept popping out to lick his lips. Finally he seemed to realize it was his turn to speak. "Kim wanted somebody who spoke English. She wanted someone white. It wasn't prejudice, but for the body, in case they could tell. So she had a few girls over, from the Jobs Wanted in an Irish newspaper. She said it was funny, because her family came from Ireland, but none of these were enough like her. Either they were too tall or skinny or old. She had to have someone closer to her. Not the face, because that would go. She meant size and I guess age."

Toddy must have spotted something in one of our faces, since even seasoned interrogators can come right to the edge of losing it. He quickly added, "I swear on the Holy Bible, I didn't know about this until the night we did it. It turned out that Kim had one girl come back, and she gave her something in her tea, then brought her upstairs to lie down for a few minutes after she puked. She fell before she got on the bed, the girl, but that worked out perfect because all Kim had to do was roll her under the bed. So Seymour wouldn't see her when she brought him up!"

"What was the woman's name?" I asked.

"I don't know. I know nothing about her, I swear."

"What was your role with dealing with the woman?"

"I pulled her out from underneath."

"Was she dressed or undressed?"

"Undressed. Only because Kim said she didn't want a last-minute rush to undress her and get rid of her stuff, so she did it when the girl was almost gone. We put her in one of Kim's nightgowns. I got her up on the bed and . . . Talk about dead weight, and after three days of carrying gasoline." My dad amazingly managed to look like he was commiserating with Toddy's difficulties. It was apparently enough to keep Toddy willing to talk.

"So she was dead? How did you know Kim didn't give her some shots that made her unconscious or paralyzed her?"

"Not breathing. Cold, but not like ice or anything. Dead white in front, but red or purple on her back. Kim said gravity does that after you die."

"She read up on it?"

"She went to the library. She wanted to know so she wouldn't get scared by anything. Kim gave me the diamond ring and her wedding ring, and I put them on the girl's left hand. Not that we laughed. I swear."

"Then what?" my dad asked.

"Then Kim had to leave. To get April out of her room, and out of the house. We both had watches, and we'd decided I should give her a fifteen-minute head start. So I gave her the keys so she could drop April off someplace."

"Where?" I asked, knowing this hadn't happened.

"Maybe at one of her friends or something. A sleepover. I don't think we talked about that part. But then she could drive to pick me up a few blocks away, take me to a motel room I'd rented. That way I could wash up and put fresh clothes on. I put my stuff there in the motel room that morning."

"Okay. She left to take care of April. You waited fifteen minutes. By the bed?"

"No, I used the bathroom. Just peed, but I didn't want to look at them. I went in when it was time and started pouring. All over them. Then the whole room. Under the bed and the drapes, too."

"Keep going," my dad said.

"All over the upstairs floor. It was called the master suite. Then two cans on the stairs, but it took three, because Kim said, 'Soak the stairs.' Then a little more downstairs because Kim was afraid I'd get hurt getting out. Just enough to lead up to the stairs and ignite them. Holy crap, it went so fast. Huge. It sucked up the air. I didn't know that would happen. I was coughing and choking and everything. My eyes were killing me. Anyway, for a couple of minutes the fire stayed all inside, so I was able to get away from the house with no one seeing me."

"Where did she pick you up?" I asked.

Toddy didn't want to answer, but my dad suddenly screamed the question again. The roar of his voice was ferocious, unlike anything I'd ever heard from him in my life. It so shocked me that an instant later I pictured Mrs. Mirante hurtling through the doorway, screeching, her arthritic fingers now flame-spewing claws—like a Sila from Arabic myth. Later on I remembered the image had come from an illustration in one of my college texts.

But that petrifying instant passed. All was quiet, as if nothing had been disturbed. Finally Toddy said, "Kim never came. I was crazy with worry. Maybe she got into an accident taking April wherever she was dropping her off. After a half hour I walked back to where I parked the car. It was gone. I guess Kim just got in it and drove and drove."

CHAPTER TWENTY-TWO

"I'll get our phones," I told my dad, who was standing beside the love seat.

Toddy stood as if to accompany me. Maybe he was worried that I forgot he'd stuck them under the rug. I put my hand on his shoulder and guided him back down. "I can find them myself. You should sit."

Toddy Mirante, master of alternate routes and backstreets and collision avoidance, looked lost: the inept host with ungovernable guests and no clue how to manage or maneuver around them. I increased the pressure on his shoulder, and he plopped back into his chair.

By that time my dad had his gun out. Though he wasn't exactly pointing it at Toddy, he was facing in his direction.

"Hey," Toddy yelped. "Are you insane? Put that thing away! This is my house. I want you O-U-T. Now!"

"Easy." My dad used his placating voice. "We'll be out of here in fifteen, maybe twenty minutes. You have my word. Just have a few phone calls to make." He even offered Toddy a hint of a smile, tilting his head and lifting one side of his mouth. Interesting how so many people, when terrified, will respond to congeniality even when it comes packaged with a Glock 26. I was a bit surprised—I would have waited until a more desperate situation to draw my weapon, but I respected my dad's judgment. "I noticed you have good cell service here."

Toddy nodded almost eagerly. *Nothing like Norwalk for good communications.*

As I headed for the small entrance area, I heard the blasting TV coming from Claudia Mirante's room. It sounded like some reality cooking show competition where someone was shrieking, *Where's the chèvre?*

I was pleased to see that the little rug down the hall still had a lump in it. I lifted a corner with the tips of my nails, said "Blech!" and took our phones with my other hand.

When I came back to the sunroom, it seemed as if they hadn't moved. Toddy was leaning forward, though not about to leap up. More like a posture of hip youth counselor rapport. My dad was on his feet, gun still pointing in Toddy's general direction, though seemingly without hostile intent—easy stance, expression nearly affable. He ruined the tableau vivant by raising his left hand. Since I wasn't about to lob the phone over, I handed it to him and he asked me to keep an eye on Toddy while he made calls.

I said yes, and once I took out my gun, he holstered his.

"You've got to be kidding!" Toddy acted genuinely surprised, as though he'd expected me to be wielding a rolling pin.

"You need to be quiet," I told him. "My partner is on the phone."

Actually, catching most of my dad's mumbled talk, I realized he was playing it like an old pol. He didn't immediately call the Norwalk Police Department, as I would have done—creature of FBI's regs that I'd become.

His first call was to his former colleague Gabriel Salazar in Brooklyn South, who had helped us so much already with the case. He said Salazar should move fast, not only before the townies could grab it, but also before the more media-savvy Connecticut State Police arrived. They'd display Toddy—driver for a hedge fund tycoon and now an admitted participant in a lurid double murder—on every outlet in the tristate area.

My dad also suggested that Salazar call Connecticut to tell them he was on his way. My dad's cold case was hot again, and I knew it must be hard for him to stomach someone else taking command. But he understood that if Salazar was there, he'd be most effective in keeping the locals and staties from blowing it for a Saturday-night press release. Toddy was a dipshit accomplice, not the mastermind of an arson-murder who was on the loose. Especially not while Kim's intended victim in New Jersey needed silence and protection.

Dad also knew it would be good for future cases if Salazar realized that if he scratched our backs, we'd scratch his.

Toddy strained to catch my dad's murmurs, his scrunched expression like someone trying to hear the tones on a hearing test.

My dad's next call was to New Jersey, to Ricardo Jones of the New Brunswick PD, to give him a sixty-second summary, letting him know that April Brown's mother—*Yeah, turns out she was fucking alive the whole time!*—was the likely perpetrator of the attempted Rutgers assault and probably planning something even more heinous. April needed protection.

This postponed a call to locals for too long, and it didn't sit right with me. I didn't care what had gone down years earlier between my dad and Connecticut; for all I knew he'd gotten an unjust ticket on the Merritt Parkway. I could understand that he figured Salazar would need a few minutes to track down Norwalk's chief of police and get across the point: *This arrest gets done quietly*. But it was a tense seven-minute wait before Salazar texted him back. I was still covering Toddy, so Dad decided to give the text a public reading. "Okay to call Norwalk PD hq. Sgt. Eve Stanley."

"What?" Toddy screamed. "What do you think you're doing?"

A good question. Mine was similar: Who announces their next move in front of the suspect? Maybe a guy who's been out of the loop too long. "Toddy," I yelled, "I need you to shut the fuck up!" But now I was also concerned that—with the evidence in the recorder taped so close to my dad's heart—his judgment and training were off somewhere celebrating. Toddy was still squawking every couple of seconds in lieu of the sentences he couldn't form. Great squawks, like a starving seagull. He stopped to get more breath, and I told him, "We're trying to deal with this as best we can. You've got to get yourself under control. Your mom is going to wind up with a broken heart, but you don't have to give her a brain aneurysm."

Almost immediately he shut his mouth tight, only a couple of whimpers coming through. I stepped away from him, closer to my dad. In the most collegial tone I could muster, I spoke quietly: "We need to keep everything calm. We're so close, but we're not there yet. We still don't know where Kimberly Brown is. Let me make the other calls to the locals. Can you cover our friend here?"

Sergeant Eve Stanley sounded as fully briefed as someone could be in a few minutes. Since my dad had his gun on Toddy, I turned away enough so lip-reading was impossible, and in a hushed voice I asked, "Can you make this happen without sirens? His mom lives here with him. She's in her upper eighties. Not the fragile type, but I wouldn't want to test it. Also we're still looking for his accomplice, the one who planned the whole thing. We don't want this going public." The sergeant said something between *yah* and *ayuh* that came across as more Maine woods than Connecticut. She told me she'd also alert Social Services.

Dad said, "Can you take it from here for a few seconds? I want to get my messenger bag before the blue ice thing melts and the sandwiches go bad." He had brought neither ice nor sandwiches, but naturally I told him *No problem*. I guessed he had to pee with such urgency—a thing with men of a certain age—that he couldn't wait for Norwalk's finest to show or . . . Who knew? Clearly some important business. Having a partner means backing them up.

So while I kept my eye on Toddy, I prayed that Claudia wouldn't white-sneaker it into the sunroom as my dad was on his way out. It was too late, even for her; by telling his story, Toddy had implicated her as an accessory; she'd backed up his alibi. But I worried that her long absence was due not to being mesmerized by the Food Network, but to searching for the Mirante family shotgun, which by now she might have locked and loaded. I started to sweat, even though I was wearing a sleeveless shirt and the lightest-weight cotton jacket to hide my holster.

Probably two or three minutes passed. My dad came back with his messenger bag, mumbling, "Went out, used the laptop in the car. Downloaded the whole thing onto my laptop." He realigned his shirt collar and, in doing so, momentarily pulled aside the V made by the open top button, indicating the recorder that he had retaped to his chest.

It was good thinking. If the cops or staties got there before Salazar and asked the two of us if we'd recorded the confession, we couldn't lie. And if they demanded that we hand the recorders over, technically both recordings would be theirs. But we needed the evidence, time- and date-stamped. Well, we needed it in the hands of the NYPD and the Brooklyn DA. Also, I felt obliged to give a copy of the recording to April, not just because she was our client, but because she was also the victim's daughter.

Whether she listened to it was not our call.

CHAPTER TWENTY-THREE

The rookie-est of the six Norwalk cops who arrived five minutes later had the honor of guarding Toddy, whose right wrist had been handcuffed to a chair. A couple of minutes earlier Toddy had stood and announced, "Just going inside to grab a cold one. Does anyone want anything? I'll be back in a minute." Another cop inquired why his right hand was balled into a fist. When it was pried open, they discovered his car keys.

I briefed the remaining five on the Brown arson-murder. My dad brought them up to speed on the attempted vehicular homicide at Rutgers. By then they were hooked, even when he went on, then on some more. But he kept his performance going until Gabriel Salazar (as well as another NYPD detective and two uniformed cops) showed up.

Though the sunroom was almost as large as the rest of the house, it was starting to feel tight. My dad got us out of there by simply peeling the tape off the back of his shoulder. He held up the recorder—a thin square that reminded me of the petrified after-dinner mints my aunt Ruthie served and re-served every Hanukkah. He handed it over to Salazar, no longer the kid cop he'd kidded around with, but a rising star in the department. Salazar had risen above mere sport jackets, and looked trés VIP in a dark gray suit, white shirt, and aubergine tie. His black hair was streaked not with gray, but with silver, as if someone had gotten the memo, *Age him elegantly*. He also wore an air of authority.

He offered his card to the head of the Norwalk contingent. "It's important we keep in touch." Then he politely stepped back so Norwalk could get over to Toddy and read him his Miranda rights. I heard "You have the right to talk to a lawyer for advice before we ask you any questions . . ." and noticed Salazar stroking his perfectly trimmed mustache with thumb and middle finger. I wondered if, when he'd helped out my dad by leaking some details about the Brown case, he sensed that it was a smart move. My guess was yes, but more in the *Why not?* category, as in *The old guy was good back in the day. Maybe he'll find something.* But while he was driving up to Connecticut, Salazar probably learned how smart he had been when he got a call from headquarters reporting that the recording of Toddy's confession was loud and clear.

Otherwise, his mustache smoothing wouldn't have been that sensuous, two-fingered stroke.

Just before we hit Greenwich, Dad and I spotted a food truck still open and got their last sandwich, roast meat—though the sticker on the wrapper didn't specify from what animal—two bags of potato chips, and bottled iced tea for the ride home.

We were both worn out. At one point I pulled off onto the shoulder and told him I couldn't simultaneously drive and be subjected to his Harry Bosch-ish/Clint Eastwood-esque jazz playlist. He actually looked sorry for me but turned it off.

Smooth sailing, I thought, so I was almost as surprised as my dad when I found myself off I-95 somewhere around the Westchester-Bronx border. After a couple of minutes I found a parking space in front of a nail salon. "What are we doing here?" he asked. I didn't answer. "Corie, you okay?"

"I'm fine. Just give me a minute. I just need a second to think." But all I could come up with was that my lemon-flavored iced tea was starting to taste the way dish soap smells. At last I turned to my dad and said, "She hasn't spent the last twenty years being Kim Brown."

"I know. So we need to know who she is now. We'll get there."

"You're sure of that?" I asked him.

"No. But listen, if you've got a goal, it's better to believe you have a shot at getting there than to be pessimistic and think you're going to fall on your face and break your teeth."

"I was hoping Tasha could produce a minor miracle, but all she came up with were a couple of shots down at the beach when their kids were little. Kim digging in the sand with April. That was in the days before cell phones became common, and no one would take a Rolleiflex to the beach. It's a sweet snapshot, but April's the one looking up and smiling. Kim's head is down, like she's interested in sand."

"So we need to get that picture of her mom and her two high school friends from April," my dad said. "The one her grandmother had. I can call her—now if you want. Put on a little pressure. April isn't as efficient on this as she is on everything else. We also have that one from the newspaper, where Toddy is letting Kim out of the car."

"Yeah." I looked past my dad at the nail place and wished I could be in there getting my hands massaged. "Two old pictures, the newspaper one not even full-face." I took my phone from its niche behind the cupholder and held it against my chest as if it were a talisman with magic powers, like my flashlight.

"Who are you going to call?" Dad asked.

My answer was a shrug. Since no one came to mind, I checked the mirror on the sun visor to see if my matte lipstick had disappeared annoyingly on one lip or held up. It had held up! Maybe the sense that I made good choices like Revlon Perennial Peach made me follow my instinct in the moment and call the bartender at King Sean's.

"Been done," the bartender told me. "Said to King you needed to see the CCTV footage. But Sean wasn't sure, like was it legal to show it to PIs?" I asked to speak with Sean himself, but the bartender said he couldn't risk pissing off the boss. I should try emailing King.Sean@ . . .

"I'm not emailing anyone. The woman who tried to grab my client's backpack—attempted robbery, by the way—is a suspect in a homicide investigation. Would Sean want you to tell him something like that?"

"People call him King." Clearly he had his priorities straight, responding to the word "homicide" with a point of nomenclature.

"Fine," I told him. "I'll call him King, and I won't even hint at taking this to the Nassau County DA or the state liquor authority."

It took a minute or two for King Sean to get back to me. He had a gurgly voice, as if he'd ingested so many beverages that his voice box was permanently flooded. "Sweetheart, my footage is not your business," he began. I suggested that it actually was my business and that my name was Corie Geller. After some explaining, along with my compliments on his royal blue upholstery, he agreed to go over his footage straight off. "I'll let you know if I find a usable picture," he said liquidly. "I'm good at that." Okay, fine, he'd text me a couple of frames. I told him more than a couple and also to check any cameras that monitored the parking lot. He gave a noblesse oblige sigh and said he would give it a go.

We pulled back onto the highway and were barely into Queens when I got a text notification.

I pulled onto a relatively quiet residential street in Astoria—mostly small apartment buildings—and parked at a fire hydrant. My dad turned to the back and pulled out the Schottland & Geller laptop from under the rubber floor mat. Clearer picture than on our mobile devices. The first frames King Sean had sent were from inside the bar. The photos taken as she ran out weren't of much value because of the subdued lighting. There were a few frames of Kim stumbling, then looking back at either April or the backpack. I instantly recognized her, but I had doubts if that would be good enough for the recognition program or for a jury.

At first the frames from the CCTV in the parking lot didn't look much more promising. Kim's head was down, and there was no way of knowing if that was out of caution—not to trip over a crack in the asphalt in her heels—or to hide her face. The camera wasn't conveniently placed to capture her features as she backed up to leave. I was able to see that the car was a Ford Edge, a stubby SUV that to me always looked pained and squished, as if designed by someone fond of bondage gear. Unfortunately, the license plate wasn't in the shot.

I wondered if King had gotten bored with his assignment and just wanted to be done with it. But the last two pictures were winners. "I shouldn't have doubted him," I said to my dad. You could make out the license plate in both shots. Just as Kim was driving out of the lot, she had one-handed the wheel and grabbed a handful of hair. The photo caught her in the process of lifting off the black Louise Brooks wig. It was a couple of inches off her head, and she looked bizarre—like she was Elastigirl pulling up her scalp. I squinted, trying to suss it out, when my dad said, "So she gave up being a blonde." He wasn't even wearing his reading glasses, but he'd immediately seen that the hair under her wig was also dark. "So why is she wearing that thing?"

"Maybe for the style of it," I said. "It's a specific hairdo that people will remember. Like those red glasses are what you think of when you try to remember her eyes, right? You remember her Dutch-boy cut when you're thinking *hair*. And the bangs cover up part of her face."

"For someone who's a dope, that was a pretty smart move."

"Then why didn't she wait and pull it off after she got a couple of blocks away from the parking lot at the bar?" I switched to the King's final picture and was delighted by what I saw. "And why didn't she bother putting tape all over the license plate?" I sent the photos up to the cloud and went back to our investigative software, typing in the alphanumerics of the car's New Jersey plate. "Dumb as shit," I muttered in the second we waited for a response.

The car was rented, as my dad and I had guessed from its barcode stickers and whistle-clean plate. Not a great idea to rent a car in a state in which you attempted vehicular homicide.

"You think New Jersey's her home base?" Dad asked.

"For now. Until she gets what she came for."

While my dad called Ricardo Jones in New Brunswick to give him another update, I got out of the car to stretch my legs and have a heart-to-heart with April Brown.

"Corie!" she answered. "This is so amazing. I just got back from Trader Joe's this second and said to myself, 'Before I even put the salmon burgers in the fridge, I have to call Corie.' Can you believe I left my phone at home, on the counter in the kitchen? Otherwise I would have called you right from there. The weirdest thing happened. I was looking at the salsas, which might not be your idea of a good time and—oh sorry! Please, go ahead."

April sounded so keyed up that even though my news was essential for her to know, I decided it could hold for a few minutes. The weirdest thing had apparently happened, and she needed to natter. What I was going to tell her wasn't just an ordinary update. For April, it would be shattering as well as threatening. So I urged her to go on. Her salmon burgers could wait while she told me her big news.

Then it would be my turn to tell her that her mother—still alive, still vicious—had conspired with Toddy, the driver April said she vaguely remembered: Kim had gotten Toddy to set fire to her father along with some working-class woman, probably Irish, whom her mother had lured to the house, ostensibly for a job interview. I glanced back at my dad, still in the car, still holding the phone. I mouthed *What's going on?* and he gave me a thumbs-up, that our client had protection. Maybe I appeared dubious because he followed that gesture by lifting his arm out the open window and banging the car's roof. So I knew a New Brunswick patrol car was either on its way to April's or was already there.

"My stuff can wait," I said to April. "Tell me what happened with your thing first."

"Right. I was checking the ingredients to see if I could find one without cilantro because I'm not a fan, and someone was kind of hovering near me. I looked up and it was a student who'd been in my RKO and the Tycoons seminar two semesters ago. Easygoing, smart kid. Incredible memory for the people and the positions they held. I needed the functional org charts we were using more than he did. Anyway, he seemed to be thinking twice about saying hi to me, and he pretended he was checking out spaghetti sauces across the aisle. Awkward—and he's not an awkward guy. So I said, 'What a nice coincidence, Andre. We could have an impromptu tutorial on pasta in film.'"

I'd been leaning against the Outback's front fender. Now I pushed off and strolled away from the grimy brick apartment buildings and stunted trees, contaminated by decades of pollution from bumper-to-bumper cars waiting to get onto the Triborough Bridge. It was livelier around the corner—shops with their names in Greek and English, a gyro place with a glistening chunk of lamb rotating in the window. I regretted being full from my half of the Connecticut raccoon sandwich. "Did you think he'd been following you?"

"No. Definitely not. In fact, he made some reference to a British literary critic who wrote that one coincidence in a work of art is permissible only if it is weightless. I guess I must have blinked, not knowing the reference or why it was apt. Andre explained that I'd been on his mind, and it was such an incredible coincidence, seeing me at Trader Joe's. He'd thought about emailing me but was worried I'd think it was creepy for him to be contacting me after all this time, especially since he switched his major from cinema studies to English."

"But you were all-forgiving," I said.

"Almost," April said. "So this was his story. He said there had been a used-book sale in front of a church not far from the house he shares. He had found a few books he wanted to buy, and he was looking around to see if anyone was taking money, because no one was at the table. Then he noticed a woman in jeans coming down the street. He said at first he was sure it was me, but when she got close, he realized she was older."

"Did you ask—"

"Of course. Oh, sorry to interrupt, Corie. He said probably in her thirties or forties. Maybe fifties. A little depressing! It made me see how I'll be regarded soon. Anyway, he said her hair was longer than mine and dark. Dark brown or black. It was pushed up under a Rutgers baseball cap, except a strand was hanging down in the back. What really startled him was that her eyes were the exact same color blue as mine."

"Interesting," I told April. Across the street from where I was standing was a cute stucco house squeezed between two stores; its sign said ELIAS MANDRAPILIAS, DDS, PRACTICE LIMITED TO ENDODONTICS. "You must be used to people reacting to your eyes."

"Sort of. But this is the kicker, the reason Andre wanted to email me." She paused, so I made an encouraging go-ahead sound. "My earrings. You know they're all film-themed."

"You've got great ones," I said.

"I started collecting them in graduate school. My first pair were green glass emeralds with ruby slippers dangling down. Blame it on my youth. Anyway, as the woman walked by, he realized she was wearing *Gone with the Wind* earrings. Two little movie posters with Rhett kissing Scarlett! Andre—he's Black—said he did a double take because he'd just been associating her with me. But there she was, wearing my signature weirdness, except from such a racist film. He said it reminded him of the Freud essay he'd read in English class, on the uncanny: when you see something that's a very familiar thing, but just a little different in a bad way. You know, like all the horror movies where what's scary is a normally not-scary thing, like a doll or a car or a pet or a house . . . or whatever."

"Those are the scariest," I commented, dreading even more the moment when I'd have to tell her a person in her life who should normally be non-scary—a mother—was very scary. April agreed, and I added, "Okay, she had your eyes"—I spoke slowly. I knew who it was, but I was trying to figure out Kim's game—"and your very particular kind of earrings."

"Can you hold for a second while I put my salmon away?" April said.

"Sure." I closed my eyes, even though I was still facing the rotating lamb. Too much for one day. I wanted to get home, take a bath. Then have my mom make grilled cheese and tomato sandwiches. No reading or TV afterward. I wanted to be lying next to Josh, with Lulu occasionally poking one of us with her nose to remind us that pets have an inalienable right to be petted. No conversation, just loving having the window open so we could overhear the endless business being conducted by cicadas and the cooing of a mourning dove. Most of all, I wanted not to have to tell April what I knew I had to tell her.

"Corie?" April finally came back. "Sorry, I knocked over a box of blueberries."

"No problem."

"Do you think she could be a stalker of some kind? Someone who sees me around or maybe on some video talk on YouTube? Could it be some kind of con game being set up? Or are there mentally ill people who don't commit identity theft for profit, but try to become the person they're obsessed with? I'm sounding like the one who's crazy. She's probably some older transfer student who likes movie jewelry."

"With your turquoise-blue eyes."

"But that has to be a coincidence. You can't just get the exact same eye color with contacts," April said. She chuckled. "I just realized how narcissistic that sounded. 'You can't *possibly* re-create my *extraordinary* eye color with contacts.'" I heard a brief *pshhht* of April opening what I guessed was a bottle of beer and setting down the metal opener. I wished my dad were dealing with this, the breaking of awful news. He'd had years' more experience. He'd had to present the particulars of homicide all too often. He'd had to speak of deaths so horrific you'd hardly believe another human being could have imagined it, much less carried it out. I had done some of those disclosures in the Bureau when bad news had to be broken to someone who spoke only Arabic, but most of my work was focused on the future—uncovering plots, busting cells, trying to stop what had not yet happened by getting people to open up about what they knew.

I took such a deep breath I got dizzy for a second. "Tell me something. Think about the family members you met when you were growing up in Kentucky. Did anyone have eyes like yours?"

"Actually, a cousin of mine did. Luddy Gallagher. Ludlow."

"Last names are first names now and gender-neutral, so Ludlow is a . . ."

"Cisgender man. He's about twenty-one. Just got a job at a hospital in Cincinnati. He does sonography."

"From the way Andre described the woman who passed him, do you think it could be Cousin Luddy?"

"No way! Luddy is at least six feet tall," April said. "He also has one of those heavy beards, so he gets a five-o'clock shadow by noon."

"So your answer is an unqualified no."

After a long swig of her drink, she added, "Totally correct. And as far as the eyes go, it's just me and Luddy."

"And your mom, of course."

"Well yes, but . . ." April was such an easygoing person that I was taken aback by the edge in her voice. "Corie, my mom's been dead for over twenty years."

I left the lamb carousel and walked farther down the block, passing two bodegas right next to each other. I wondered how vicious their competition was, then forced myself to refocus on the task at hand. "April, your mother is alive and—as far as I know—quite well."

I wasn't surprised that there was no response. I heard only what sounded like the pulling out of a kitchen chair and April sitting down. She finally spoke, her usual even tone giving way to harshness. "What the hell are you talking about?" Before I could respond, she kept going. "Usually people say something like, 'I'm sorry, but I have some bad news for you.' I'm not accusing you of doing the wrong thing, sharing something huge like that. But—God—you just hit me with it."

I blinked at her reproachful tone, not because I blamed her for it, but because I hadn't heard it from her before. "I did blurt it out. I'm really sorry; I should have handled it better." I paused to let her sit with what I'd told her for a moment before I gave her the really bad news. "There's more. It's not good. Are you ready to hear it?"

"Yes," she said steadily.

"Okay. I'm worried about your immediate safety. For instance, if you go to the front of your house, you may see a patrol car outside."

From the scraping sound of a chair against the floor I knew she was up again. It took several seconds, but then I heard her footsteps as she walked hurriedly. "There are two police cars." Her voice wasn't hushed. She came off as matter-of-fact, like someone saying *Looks like it might rain*.

"My dad spoke with Detective Ricardo Jones of the New Brunswick Police Department. You met him. Remember? He said they will keep you under watch. To protect you."

"From?" April asked. She knew. Yet sometimes even the most strong-minded people hope for a little wiggle room. Anything less than a blunt comeback can free them to doubt or reinterpret the facts.

"From your mother. We think she's out to get you."

I gave April the barest outline of what had happened—*faked her own death, got Toddy the driver to be her accomplice, skipped town.* April seemed even-keeled, but had no questions except about the other woman Kim had killed. I had few answers for that, and I understood that April's reticence meant she was still absorbing the news. I told her to check in with Detective Jones, who was expecting her call, and that she should give him whatever information he asked for. I wondered whether I should give her any advice on coping skills I'd learned from my PTSD therapy, but she seemed to want to be left alone with her thoughts.

When I got back to the car, my dad was in the driver's seat. "How'd it go?"

"Okay. Calm. Calmer than I'd be if you told me my mom had faked her own death and was trying to kill me."

"Your mom would never try to run you over with an SUV. Too conventional," he said.

I agreed. "She'd probably try searching for hemlock or something to place in a chalice."

He smiled wryly at the thought of her theatricality. "Anyway, okay if I drive?" I didn't answer, but got in on the passenger side. "What's up on your end?" I asked.

"Jones isn't biting his fingernails, but that doesn't mean he's relaxed. Just hoping Kim can be found soon. If something big breaks, his department doesn't have the resources to keep up twenty-four-hour surveillance of April beyond a few days."

"Is he trying to wiggle out?"

"No, not at all. He didn't mean it as a threat. It's just the truth."

I brought him up to date on what Andre had reported to April: a woman with April's eyes wearing "April-style" earrings—obviously someone who didn't know April enough to know she'd never wear *Gone with the Wind* jewelry. Dad and I agreed I'd made a mistake not getting Andre's last name and contact info to see if he could ID any of the shots of Kim from King Sean's, and, as much as we'd like to give her the head-space to recover, we should get it from her today.

All those thousands of articles about diet tell you that food really doesn't make you feel better. And if it does, it's only for that first gluttonous moment. Primo bullshit. In times of trouble, a grilled cheese and tomato sandwich was an effective homemade antianxiety medication. (A baked potato would do in a pinch, though it wasn't quite as potent.) When my dad and I got home, I ate one and a half grilled cheese sandwiches and washed it all down with a glass of pinot noir.

Taking the final half sandwich upstairs to the office, I uploaded all the pictures I had of Kim, including the one of her in her senior year of high school that April had just texted to me. I paused frequently to take bites and each time had to wipe my greasy fingers on a paper towel before using the keyboard.

A minute passed. My dad was downstairs having a drink and what my mom called a "proper dinner"—protein, veggie, starch—three separate globs on a plate. Josh was in Tribeca having dinner with a bunch of his old friends from the US Attorney's Office. Eliza was in her bedroom, packing for a month of volunteer work at a dog sanctuary in Costa Rica, agonizing over what clothes to take. She had already rejected all my suggestions.

And then *boom!* as if God were going for a partial do-over of the sixth day. A woman's face materialized on the monitor. On a Nevada driver's license. White skin with blushing pink cheeks, shoulder-length blond hair, and—as the data beneath the photo noted—Eyes BLU. To be precise, turquoise. An official document, so last name on top, BLAKE, and underneath

VANESSA LEIGH. From Las Vegas. DOB was listed as 09/26/1985, which would have made April Brown's mother nine years old when she gave birth. That didn't mean she wasn't Kim: people who fake their identities aren't fastidious about giving false ages along with made-up names.

But to my (less spectacular blue) eyes, Vanessa Leigh Blake, millennial Las Vegan, was also the woman behind the red cat-eye glasses on the far side of the bar at King Sean's who failed to grab April's backpack. Change her hair, swap her look from Louise Brooks in a business suit in the bar to—on her first driver's license—overage ingenue in a sleeveless blouse with a ruffled bib, and she was still the same person.

Artificial intelligence can sometimes be stupid. Algorithms used for facial recognition are less accurate when trying to distinguish among Black faces, particularly those that are younger and female. But Vanessa Blake was whiter than Disney's Cinderella. The program backed up its conclusion with 99.1 percent certainty. I texted both my parentals to come upstairs so my mom could have a look, too. She had a sharp eye for the telling detail, not just in matters of style but also of character. She could interpret an arched eyebrow ten different ways, and one of them could be useful.

When they finished their dinner and opened the door to the office, both gasped at the profusion of photo IDs that now filled the screen. Driver's licenses—first California, in Los Angeles; that first one was issued just six weeks after the crime in Brooklyn. Kim had remained in LA for almost three years before moving on to Las Vegas. More driver's licenses over the years, pin-on laminated employee IDs, clearances filed with the state of Nevada to work in a gambling venue, although she only had a job for four months at the reception desk of the Flamingo Hotel at the beginning of her stay.

"You know what I sense her problem is?" my mom asked. "She's only pretty—very pretty in this one"—she pointed to a resident card for the Las Palmas apartments on Paradise Road in Las Vegas—"but even though she thinks she's beautiful, she's not. I'll bet she feels she never got what the world owes her—money, paparazzi, powerful men made weak by her beauty. By her perfection. She wants a perpetual celebration in her honor."

"That sounds right," I told her. "In high school, she kept hooking up with older guys. Maybe she thought that was glamour. When she left, she never made contact with anyone in her family again."

"And she wound up with Seymour Brown," my dad noted.

"If she were just a run-of-the-mill narcissist, she'd feel perpetually screwed. Take it out on someone close to her," Mom went on. "But she's also a psychopath, or maybe a sociopath. There's some distinction, but I forget what it is. In any case, instead of simply feeling screwed or angry, she's lashing out. The world's most perfect person, and no one is willing to give her all she deserves."

Some of the other driver's licenses had the same face, but in those she was Vanessa Dudley and Vanessa Blake Schroeder. Well, if the first marriage doesn't succeed, try again. The links to the Dudley name showed several photos of the couple in the out-and-about sections of Las Vegas newspapers and social media.

Ron Dudley owned gyms all around Nevada, which made him rich and fit, if not young. He and Vanessa, along with their son, Remington, lived in a house on a golf course. I checked the place out on Zillow, and it was estimated to be worth seven and a half mil. When I showed it to my mom, she murmured, "Bookmark it," and I nodded eagerly. Apparently Mr. Dudley was still alive, which was a plus. We checked a copy of their divorce decree. When sixty-eight-year-old Mr. D. and Vanessa divorced, he got full custody of little Remington.

But Vanessa had nowhere to go but up. Unfortunately, she married Wesley Schroeder, who had founded a tech company called flUX; at the time, it was on its way to becoming a household name in the field of UX design—if you lived in a household in which someone knew what UX was. The firm never got there. She must have sensed that Wesley wasn't a winner, because the name on her marriage license was Vanessa Blake

Schroeder. Even as newlyweds, they didn't often show up in media coverage of social events. Adding insult to injury, their high-rise condo in Las Vegas was worth only slightly more than three mil.

flUX began its descent not more than a year after their wedding. A couple of months after that, Vanessa dropped the Schroeder and the husband, kept the condo, and went back to being Vanessa Blake.

After walking Lulu and spending a few minutes with Eliza showing her what I said were CIA packing tips, I called April. If I sensed that she could handle it tonight, I would send her the pictures of the one California and several Nevada driver's licenses under Vanessa's various surnames. "I'm so sorry I didn't call you back," April said. "I was on the phone with Misaki—she wants to come home and be with me. She doesn't care what happens with her postdoc."

"That's wonderful," I said. "Selfless, too. But I would discourage it, unless Misaki happens to be a trained sniper." I explained as gently as I could that her fiancée in the house with her meant that Kim would have not one potential victim, but two.

"What's the next step then?" April asked.

"I'm going to send you some pictures of driver's licenses with what looks like your mother's photo on them. We used an advanced facial recognition program. The degree of certainty that this woman is Kim Brown is ninety-nine point one percent. It would be great if you could look at them on a laptop or an iPad rather than your phone so you can see her closer to life-size."

"When are you sending them?"

"In a couple of minutes. First, though, I would like you to call or text your former student, Andre, and ask if he'd speak with an investigator you hired. We can show him some of the pictures. Is that okay with you?"

"Yes. Fine."

"Good. Call me back after you reach out to him."

April got back to me in less than five minutes. She'd even bcc'd me on the email she'd sent, and he'd already replied saying he was willing to help.

I forwarded it to my dad, telling him to follow up, and called April back. "That was awesome," I said to her. "And fast. Now, is it all right if I text those driver's licenses to you right now? I'll hold while you study them. But if you've had too much turmoil today, I can do it tomorrow."

"Right now works," April said. "I'm upset, to say the least, but I'm not scared. The police cars are outside my house, and one of the cops is staying in the backyard. Ready when you are."

Now and then I could hear her breathing as she studied what I sent her. *Ding*—a text from my dad: "Andre says it's 'probably' her." I replied with a thumbs-up emoji.

I gave April nearly ten minutes, then asked her gently for her thoughts. "I do think she looks like . . . I don't know how to say it, but my memory of my mother. Especially that early driver's license, the California one. I was expecting a more visceral reaction, looking at a picture taken within a year of the last time I saw her. But no. It did make me think how sometimes I would sit on the floor and look up at her putting on her makeup. Essentially, I was seeing her reflection in a big mirror. I feel like I've always been a visual person, but it's almost as if I never really saw her."

"Did the more recent pictures remind you at all of the woman in the bar? At one point she was right beside you."

"I wish I could be of more help," April said. "I think what happened in the bar is that I got stuck on my Louise Brooks comparison, so that's all I could see."

"No problem."

"I know ninety-nine point one is a very high probability," she said. She was looking for a .9 percent hook to hang the hope on that her mother had perished in the fire, that Kim really was the mom she always thought she'd had: a victim and not a monster.

"It is very high," I said.

"But if it's her, then she killed my dad, right?"

"Looks that way. April, God knows you need solace, so think about this. If it is her—and I want to be clear with you that it's my professional opinion that it is—you might want to remember that whatever else she may have done, she gave you one free pass, pantomiming for you to jump." It wasn't the time to add, *But she didn't hang around to see whether you made it to safety.*

"The angel?" she asked carefully.

"That's my guess."

April paused. "Why did she try to steal my backpack?"

"I'm not sure. My guess is that she wants to use your ID. Maybe assume your identity."

"For what reason?"

"I don't know yet." Actually, I did.

CHAPTER TWENTY-FOUR

It was almost midnight on that incredibly long day. Josh, home after a night of what was surely high hilarity with his old gang from the Public Corruption Unit of SDNY, was in the fidgety sleep of the soon-to-be hung over. For a while, his arm was draped over me. From the depths of my dreams I sensed him giving my hip a reassuring pat, not knowing whether the recipient was me or Lulu. He needed sleep. He was leaving early the next morning, skipping a couple of hours of work to take Eliza to JFK to see her off on a plane to Costa Rica for her four weeks of working with the formerly feral.

At 2:14, a knock on the bedroom door woke me up. I smiled in the dark thinking, *Hey, this is really touching! Eliza needs reassurance that she will meet wonderful, animal-loving people and fantastic dogs on her trip.* I called out, "Come in!"

It was my dad, still tying the sash on his bathrobe. His whisper was as loud as whispers get: "Everything's fine." I was relieved to realize that he hadn't run down the hall to get help because my mother was mid-coronary—though his dropping by the bedroom at that hour did put me on alert. Something was not fine.

"Everything's fine," I murmured sweetly to Josh. He said "Good" with remarkable clarity considering he was still asleep. I didn't do bathrobes, but I went into my closet and grabbed a sweater in case my T-shirt and pajama bottoms weren't enough to keep me from shivering while my dad told me—I pictured us racing down the hall—what was going on.

Lulu showed that she remembered I was the one who had brought her home from the animal shelter: she jumped off the bed and followed me. Admittedly, she could have been thinking, *Early breakfast!*

"Ricardo Jones just texted, twice in a row," my dad said. "Wants to speak to us ASAP." My heartbeat went from the perceptible throb that comes from being woken at an odd hour straight to hard pounding. We hurried to the end of the long hallway, into the office.

I grabbed my notebook from the desk while my dad called Ricardo and put him on speaker. "You both there?" he asked us.

"Yes," I said.

"What do you want first? The bad news or the good news?"

This was not an after-two-a.m. question. Actually, not a question for any time. The answer ought to be axiomatic. What kind of asshole would want the good news first? So they could feel upbeat when punched in the gut with the bad? I said, "The bad news."

"The bad news is there were two attempted robberies in New Brunswick. Not that they have anything to do with your case." Jones had a show business baritone that gave much of what he said an air of consequence. "A convenience store and a liquor store. Meanwhile, we got a couple of patrol cars sitting at the professor's house. We got jurisdiction because she was attacked on the Rutgers campus. But we need to move on."

"When?" My dad asked.

Jones also turned out to be adept at doing sad and weary simultaneously. "Now would be about right." He must have heard our *Oh shit* mumblings because he added, "Hey, I told you there's good news, too."

"Can't wait," Dad replied.

"Hang on," Jones said, clearly annoyed at my dad's lack of upbeat anticipation. "The good news is that the Rutgers PD is going to take over when New Brunswick leaves." I jotted down the names and numbers of the people to liaise with at Rutgers PD. "We work with the Rutgers force all the time. Listen, this is the flagship state university, not some chickenshit college patrol with two guys and a siren. They can go over there now. So your client April will be getting excellent protection for another couple of days."

"I assume you'll be giving Rutgers—as well as your own officers—the photos of Kim we sent, especially the most recent one on her Nevada license," I said.

"Of course."

"Also, it's the middle of the night."

"You think I didn't notice?" Jones asked sourly.

"I'm making the point that we can't reach out to our technical people now," I said. My dad smiled at the idea of minions awaiting our direction, but he also shifted in embarrassment at what he knew was coming next: chutzpah. Mine, not his, so hopefully his budding friendship with Ric Jones wouldn't be jeopardized. I went out of my way to sound respectful. "New Brunswick is a twenty-four-seven operation." I hoped that connoted awed respect, like I was equating New Brunswick with MI5. "Can you get someone to image-edit the pics so whoever is guarding April can see Kim/Vanessa in dark hair as well as the blond? Also with some kind of a head covering. A baseball cap would be fine." Before he could get out a bitter laugh along with the word "No," I added, "I understand this is a big ask, but the clock is ticking, and our client's life may depend upon it." It was refreshing to see I could still squish three clichés into one sentence.

"I'll see what I can do," Ricardo intoned. "And while we're at it, I'll tell you what you can do."

"I'm listening," my dad said.

"I've got too many violent, crazy people to deal with. Death threats are a dime a dozen. We can respond to a crisis, but we are not equipped to provide full-time long-term protection. Understand, we are really stretching it here. What we're doing for her is major. Rutgers can't swing it for too long either."

"Ric," my dad said, "she's a professor there. It would be a shit show if something bad happens to her."

"Dan, I'm bending over backwards to help you here. Nothing material has happened after the SUV attack. I can't justify it. Your April needs to get private security if her psycho bitch mother manages to slip away. She's got to be willing to write the check for it . . . unless the two of you want to volunteer taking turns rocking on her front porch with a rifle on your lap. Anyway, from what we've been hearing, she's not living on just a professor's salary. She can afford to buy some protection."

"Do you have anyone in private security to recommend?" I asked.

"Yeah," Jones said. "There's a firm up in Newark. Their people know the difference between their ass and a hole in the ground." He took a breath and added in his sonorous voice, "If you reach out to them, you can say I told you to call."

I stood at the end of the driveway waving as Josh drove Eliza to the airport, like I was one of those people in a black-and-white historical photograph, standing on a dock and blowing kisses to a departing ocean liner. Meanwhile, my dad was inside trying to locate the woman who died so that Kim Brown could live and become Vanessa Blake.

Since Kim had stipulated back then that she wanted someone who spoke English, Tasha and her friends had suggested putting a help wanted ad in an Irish newspaper. There were several in New York, but the *Irish Eye* had been known for its listings for domestics since the 1920s. Naturally, my dad didn't bother looking for a digitized version of the newspaper. He called the *Eye*'s corporate office on a number from his burner app, said he was Lieutenant Michael Fogarty, Sixty-Second Precinct, and he needed someone to look up a classified ad to help in solving a historical homicide—now, because the case had once again become active.

Within fifteen minutes someone texted him the Household Help Wanted ads for the three Wednesday issues before the fire at the Browns'. It was a long list, and if Kim had placed an ad, he knew it might be hard to distinguish from all the others. Most prospective employers did not use their phone numbers; each ad had its own box number. But the *Eye* contact had resourcefully sent along a PDF with all the information on all their boxholders for that year—name, address for billing, box number, and phone number.

My dad later told me he gave God a shout-out: "I owe you one!" He was at the kitchen table with a cup of coffee and the Schottland & Geller laptop. He pointed to the screen. "Here's Kim!"

> Live-in housekeeper, babysitter for family with one school-age child, lovely home in Brooklyn near exclusive beach. No pets. Must have experience, fluent English. Own room with TV and private bath. Sunday and one other weekday (your choice) off. $350/week salary + generous Christmas bonus. Two weeks paid vacation.

I took over the laptop, checked a couple of charts from the Bureau of Labor Statistics, then did some arithmetic. "Hey, Dad. That $350 per week was average for a household worker at the time who wasn't getting room and board. But this one was, so it must have been top of the scale, which probably made it close to irresistible. It looks way better than the other ads."

I pulled over a chair to sit beside him. "I bet she got a ton of responses," he said. His scrolling was maddeningly slow, but it gave me time to see what an appealing offer Kim's ad was. "Good money, flexible day off. It sounds like an employer determined to please." We both sat back, struck by the seemingly endless listings. "Why would Kim want to be the highest bidder in the housekeeper sweepstakes? A hundred bucks lower, people would still be interested. This way, she must have had so many applicants."

"Because then she could pick one who physically resembled her the most," I said. "Don't forget, we're not talking hairdo, or even features, and as Toddy told us, she figured out she needed the same height, same body type. If the fire investigators and your people had been able to find usable remains, they would have noticed that the length of a femur of someone who was five foot seven wasn't likely to have been Kim.

"Let's check with Interpol. Find out if some woman from Ireland who came to the US was reported missing within, say, six months, a year of the date of the fire. If there is any family left, it might give them clo—"

He cut me off. "Not you too, with 'closure'? How about, 'It might give them screaming fucking nightmares for the rest of their lives'?"

* * *

With merely hideous traffic, I might have gotten to New Brunswick by five in the evening. But it was catastrophic. By the time I crossed the Hudson, my audiobook was finished, so for the rest of the way it was Mozart's oboe concertos and *Red* by Taylor Swift. I didn't get to April's house until seven.

For someone who loved noir films, she showed no interest in the specifics of the security arrangements. Ricardo Jones and the Rutgers PD agreed on two cops, three shifts a day. "Tell me which you prefer," I said. "I can stay at that DoubleTree that's not too far, or you can put me up for a couple of nights."

"I'd like you to stay," April said. "As long as you don't mind that the guest room isn't as elegant as yours is."

"That was my husband's first wife's decorator. I don't do elegance. Once in a while I accidently lapse into good taste."

"Me too," April said. "Which means you'll probably be okay with my guest room."

"Thanks. I just want to be clear that I'm not here to guard you. I'll be out and about. But at least when I'm here, there'll be an extra weapon."

The police had come through with photoshopped pictures of Kim, blond and dark-haired, baseball capped and bareheaded; there were even ponytailed and type 3B curly hair versions. They'd dropped off extra sets of the shots that I could show around, hand out if I had to.

I gave a set to April. I wanted her ready to size up anyone on her street, a shambling dog walker or a runner in total Lululemon, and know immediately: that is my mother.

Dad and I had become more convinced that Kim's plan was to pass as April. Obviously she wasn't intending to take over teaching American Film Directors. But she wanted the money that she'd told Toddy she should inherit—Seymour's money, which, since no one knew that Kim was alive, had gone to April. We agreed that this was likely the reason she'd made a grab for April's backpack—to get hold of April's ID. She wanted to withdraw money from bank and brokerage accounts, to access safe-deposit boxes.

My phone buzzed again and again as my dad updated me every time he wangled an update on the search from Salazar or Jones. Nothing. Nada. Rien. Bupkes. Zilch.

I had worried that I wouldn't sleep well in April's house. I always missed my bed and reading lamp when I was away from home. The murderer on the loose didn't help. But the abundance of plump, friendly pillows in the guest room and the bubbly elegance of the posters from thirties and forties rom-coms framed on the walls put me at ease. I surprised myself the three times I woke up by calmly assessing that all was well, touching the light around my neck, and falling right back to sleep.

The next morning, I chatted with the cop on the day shift. Nothing suspicious on the night shift, but word had spread from the swing shift guy that April's knowledge of the *John Wick* movies and *Blood and Bone* was encyclopedic. They seemed honored by their assignment.

A little before ten I made a quick call to Wynne, bringing her up to speed on Kim. Thankfully, she understood that she would eventually get the whole story, and she pressed pause on the bazillion questions she surely had. "Say you are trying to copy a person's looks and you're close to twenty years older than she is—so figure some loss of dewiness. What do you do?" I asked.

"You know, you can add back some dew with the right makeup."

"Good. What else? Kim has dark hair while April's is light brown with blond streaks. Kim's taller, but they both have the same standout turquoise-blue eyes—"

"Gotcha. Okay, here's what I'd do. If Kim's skin is getting crepey and textured, then Botox and fillers first, because they take a couple of weeks to settle in and take effect. Fillers can change your looks dramatically." I had called Wynne while in the car on my way to the hair salons of greater New Brunswick, and I hadn't even considered that. "Is Kim a planner?" she asked.

"I don't know whether she goes for plans or just gets a bug up her butt and acts on it," I said. "If we're right about her, she's committed one complicated crime very successfully and screwed up two very simple ones. But she's had more than twenty years to consider what to do if she thought people might be onto her."

"Fine. So, after a great dermatologist, hair. Hair is crucial. Not that you actually have to wait two weeks to do that, but you want to see how your face comes out before you do the final color and cut. Now . . ." She grunted. "I'm doing soleus stretches. Foam roller. Anyway, if they both have the same drop-dead turquoise eyes, then hair would be the next most defining feature. Its color and, to a degree, its style. If it were I—doesn't correct grammar sound wrong sometimes?—I'd get my hair very light brown with highlights and then see what else needs doing in terms of makeup."

"Would you consider a wig?"

"Probably not. A believable one would cost a few thou. It's a bigger deal than you'd think."

I was relieved that my instincts agreed with Wynne's knowledge. Another thing: I didn't think most people would attempt a multiprocess hair dye job in the sink of a motel bathroom. I thanked Wynne, promised the full story as soon as I could, and, continuing to follow Google Maps, headed to the first hairdresser on my list.

At each salon I showed my PI credentials and explained that the woman in the photos was wanted for questioning by the police. Yes, there was a possibility she might be dangerous, but all she would want from them was a change of color or a cut—like any client. She might even show them a picture of someone whose hair was just what she was looking for.

I hoped they'd consider texting or calling the New Brunswick police, I told them, pointing to the tip number for the case on the bottom left of the flyer. They could also call me, Corie, at the number on the bottom right. "If you do call or text me or the cops, and she's here," I added, "I'll be glad to give you two hundred dollars in cash."

After the tenth salon, I checked in with my dad. The police still hadn't found Kim. He'd spent the morning speaking with the successor of the successor of the guy at Interpol he'd worked with in the past. That guy got him a contact at An Garda Síochána, Ireland's national police force.

Inspector Catherine Shields. My dad said she sounded as if she had her wits about her; she promised she would get back to him by nine in the morning—New York morning! He must have been charmed because his usual rough laugh was closer to an *Erin go bragh* chortle. "New York morning. Hrr, hrr." Any minute he might develop a brogue, so I told him I still had more hairdressers.

"No" was the answer I kept getting. The people I saw said no one like that had shown up at their shops. One of them, holding the reasonably clear photo on Kim's latest Nevada driver's license up to the morning light streaming through the shop's window, suspected that Kim had had work done—as in plastic surgery. "Cheek implants at least and possibly an eyelift." Another shop owner complimented my highlights and said honey blonde was almost always a better choice than ash blonde on white people.

I headed back to April's. She'd contacted the security company that would take over for the Rutgers PD if necessary, and they'd already installed motion- and heat-detecting lights and cameras on the exterior of the house and all around the interior. The guy in charge of the team setting it up gave me a tour of what they'd done. He was about my age, with golden skin and eyes the color of coffee with a splash of milk framed by bristly black lashes. He would have been devastatingly handsome if it weren't for a jutting chin. I tried not to lock my eyes on his while he pointed out a vulnerability—the grilles were rotting in the basement windows on the north side of the house, so they couldn't arm the detectors there. But it should be okay as long as the security people posted outside were aware. In the meantime, I should arrange for someone to repair the windows ASAP. I thanked him and promised I would, stifling the urge to add that a beard would change his life.

I had April contact the window repair company while I ordered dinner for us. When the Uber Eats driver arrived from a Moroccan restaurant, so many powerful lights came on that he dropped the food on the porch and ran. Whatever was going on, he didn't like it.

* * *

Interpol came through for my dad. Inspector Shields in Dublin agreed that the woman who died in the fire probably had been killed soon before the crime. Assuming that poison caused her death, Kim couldn't have kept the body around for long. In a competition between something even as tiny as a dead mouse and air freshener, the mouse always won. A human being would start releasing gases and noxious smells almost immediately.

Kim needed to find someone to lie on the bed beside Seymour, wearing Kim's wedding and engagement rings. Heavy on the gasoline, Kim had instructed Toddy. My dad and the inspector were guessing that Kim's hope was that the couple in the bed would be unidentifiable yet manifest enough so the firefighters could look at two skeletons and think, *Mr. and Mrs. Brown*. She certainly hadn't planned for both corpses to be completely vaporized.

"Kim was looking for a loner," my dad suggested to Inspector Shields. "She wasn't going to take some woman who'd already made friends in New York, people who might have pointed out the ad in the *Irish Eye* and told her, 'The money is amazing. Hope the kid isn't a monster.'"

"That's classic," Catherine Shields said. "And your lady Kim had all the instincts for this sort of scheme: prey on the lonely. She probably all but said to the victim, 'You have a home here.' If that Toddy fellow is telling the truth, the girl who drank the cup of tea with poison was likely grateful for Kim's kindness for helping her upstairs, telling her she must lie down."

Inspector Shields gave my dad two names from missing persons cases on the national police's digitized records. Maeve O'Boyle, age twenty-two, from Galway. Anna Queally, age thirty-five, from Sligo. Both had been reported missing within eight months after the crime in Brooklyn. The inspector and my dad agreed to read through the case files, reach out to their sources at the NYPD, then speak in a couple of days.

April and I were sitting companionably at her dining room table, each working on laptops, when my phone buzzed at 1:12 p.m. Thinking it was Dad telling me, for the forty-seventh time, that Salazar had no evidence of Kim's whereabouts, I emitted a huff that abruptly ended when I saw where the call was coming from. Hair by Nikki O'. I almost gasped, "Hello."

A cigarette voice came from between clenched teeth. "She was here! At least I think it was her, except she was wearing sunglasses. You said she had like blue-blue eyes. Turquoise? So I couldn't be a hundred percent. And she asked if I could copy a certain look, and I said, 'You have a picture or something?' So she said, 'Yeah, but I can't believe I left the best one home. What time are you open till?' I said, 'Usually six on Saturdays,' and she said, 'Fine. I'll be back.'"

CHAPTER TWENTY-FIVE

Nikki O' was one of the farthest salons in the radius I'd searched, maybe half an hour away. I extracted a solemn oath from Nikki that she'd text me immediately if she saw Kim, and I began to prepare. Getting changed out of my shorts and tank top took under five minutes. Jeans with enough spandex so I could perform any act of derring-do of which I was capable. A black T-shirt. Mascara. My weapon, bellyband holster, and a black cotton jacket to hide it. Leather booties that were much more comfortable and flexible than they looked.

The second I'd hung up with Nikki, I let April know, in my calmest voice, what was going on. She thanked me and, to my surprise, went back to looking at her laptop screen, though now she was chewing her cuticles.

I knew I needed my partner in this. When I tracked his location, I saw that he was at the hardware store in Shorehaven. I called him.

"What's up, kiddo?" my dad asked.

I told him about the call from Nikki.

"Okay. So what are you doing now?"

"I'm here at April's. I've gotten ready. I'll head over to the salon soon."

"Excuse me. I thought this was a 'we' operation."

I mindlessly turned away from the dining room table and paced into April's living room. "Of course it is," I told him. "I want you to come out here. How long will it take you to get going?"

"Half hour to an hour."

"Okay."

Next, I called the police, conferencing Ricardo Jones with my liaison at Rutgers PD, Captain Happy—I had checked on the PD's website so

I knew it was actually the guy's last name. While not overtly miserable, Happy had probably spent his post-schoolyard life growing more and more snappish in reaction to being asked *Are you really?*

"Who gave you permission to go around to beauty parlors asking all sorts of questions?" Happy challenged.

"No one," I said. Often, the best way to defuse a provocative question is to be direct and brief.

"So what are you asking the department to do?" he asked. "Keep an officer in every beauty parlor around the city?"

"No."

"Then what?"

"I'm letting you know so you can be ready."

"Ready for what, specifically?" His voice came out so flat that I almost didn't realize I'd been asked a question.

"I'm guessing Kim won't show up at Nikki O' again," I told him. "Her saying 'I'll be back' without making an appointment probably means there's something about the salon that didn't please her."

"So?" Happy asked.

Jones, whom I'd half forgotten about, spoke up before I could. "So we're doing the same thing. Protecting Professor Brown, bringing Kim Brown in if we can. Just now we know she's in New Jersey and on the move."

The instant I hung up and turned around, April's phone rang. Although it was awkward, I kept my eyes on her as she murmured responses. In less than a minute, she was done.

"That was Detective Jones," she said. "He said you told him what happened, and he just wanted to warn me."

"Did he say anything else?" I asked.

"Just what you already told me. He all but ordered me to stay in the house, keep off the porch, and think twice about the backyard." She stretched, seemingly nonchalant, but I knew she was on edge. "Do you think she can shoot?" April asked. "If she can, why would she try to run me down with an SUV?"

"Good questions, but I can only speculate. Nevada is one of those friendly-to-firearms states, pretty much open carry, so she might have learned to shoot at some point."

April put her elbows on the table and rested her head in her hands. Then, apparently realizing she was in a posture of despair, she sat up straight. "Sometimes I wonder if all that happened hadn't happened . . . If she'd raised me, I wonder whether I'd have turned out like her."

"You wouldn't. Are you going to ask me how I know that? Because you don't have her rage. You don't have her narcissism—with a trail of broken relationships behind you. You have a moral compass. You have the capacity to love."

"And she didn't?"

"No, not apart from herself. As for your father, the only humane quality he demonstrated was his love for you. Sorry to say it, but everything else I learned about him showed that he was bad through and through."

"He did have some strengths," she countered.

"What were they?"

April laughed. "Devotion to his craft. All right, he was bad. To the bone and beyond. He just never showed that part of himself to me."

I sensed that April needed to hear something—anything—positive about her birth family. "Whatever part of him was decent—you inherited it. Along with some of his strengths. His intelligence. His work ethic, too. To his credit, he did what he could to mold you into someone worthy. He wasn't teaching you to play Wash the Money."

"That's true."

"He showed you the world's better side. He took you to the movies and to the library. He wanted you to be better than your mother. Better than he was."

A less ruminative, more immediate topic was needed. "I want to stress that you can't let normal, everyday feelings come into play if by some chance you come face-to-face with your mother. Don't expect her heart to melt when she sees her long-lost daughter who has her eyes. Don't think she'll get all teary remembering three- or four-year-old April running on the beach. She cares only about her needs. She probably thinks she deserves some major Humanitarian of the Year award for gesturing to you to open a window. That was probably her last act of beneficence."

April's breathing was shaky. But she looked at me levelly. "This whole thing is so crazy." She cleared her throat. "Is your dad headed here?"

"Yes."

"Great."

Nikki's hair—dark and shiny with a lively bounce—was a great advertisement for her salon. Also, while her voice was all vaping and whiskey, the rest of her appeared to be flourishing. I gave her two hundred-dollar bills and she gave me the premier-class tour. Which wasn't exactly exhausting, as all we did was stand by a mid-century style reception counter shaped like a boomerang.

"She showed me a couple of pictures," Nikki said, "but they weren't all that great. She said she had a good one at home, but she forgot it." She pulled at the neckline of what she was wearing, a cross between a smock and a tunic that had slits up the side—in the style of a Chinese cheongsam dress. An unusual choice, what with her black tights and black platform sneakers, but she stood with the confidence of someone who believed they'd achieved the quintessence of cool. I told her how much I liked her monogrammed logo—NIKKI O'—along with a tiny pair of scissors in brilliant red thread writ large just to the left of her breastbone.

"I designed it myself."

"You've got a gift. The pictures she shared with you: Were they cut out or did they look as if they were printed?" I asked.

"Printed. Both were the same girl. Pretty. Light brown hair, and I'm almost positive her sun streaks were the real thing. No makeup." She closed her eyes for a minute, conjuring up the likenesses. "Stronger features, the girl. Maybe she had an Italian on the family tree. You never know, right?"

"Absolutely," I said.

"Even though it wasn't the world's greatest print job, it was amazing with their eyes. Jennifer Aniston kind of eyes that make you want to keep looking at them. Except like a Southwest version. You know that turquoise they have on everything that's not orange? That color, exactly alike."

"Did she say why she wanted to copy that look?"

"Something about the girl being her niece. She hadn't seen her for years, but—I didn't totally get what she was saying—she wanted to show how they were family, because the girl was insecure. She wanted to make her feel like she belonged."

"And the woman who was here. Did she mention her name?"

Nikki shook her head, and her hair did a little dance. "No, not even when I said, 'Hi. I'm Nikki.' Just down to business. Took the two pages out of her bag. A Prada nylon bag. Beige, a big hobo—they're not cheap, let me tell you that. Anyway, she said she wanted to look like this girl. Then she said about her being her niece and blah-blah. So I looked at the pictures, then at her. I wanted to say, *In your dreams, sweetie,* but I just said, 'Sure, but first we have to strip that mahogany brown dye out of your hair.' Maybe I came on a little strong, because she looked insulted that I knew right away the color wasn't natural. It wasn't a home dye job, it was professional, but not by a great colorist. I tried to make it up to her by saying she's going to look fabulous in lighter hair. I actually said, 'You'd look great in any color because of the clarity of your skin. No reds, no yellows. That's very rare.'"

"Did she believe you?"

Nikki sighed. "No. I could see she was already on her way out even though she was still standing there."

There were no CCTV cameras in the salon, so I asked Nikki to describe Kim. "She was petite. Maybe size two or four. Most likely was once a zero, but once you get to be her age, the muscles can't hold it in. Shortish, like around five three. Really took care of herself. Lash extensions. Probably designer clothes, because there were no bumps on any seam. That's how you can tell."

I nodded my respect for her wisdom or her utter confidence in her misinformation. "After she left and you called me, did you get a moment to call the police?"

"Sure. Right away. Two cops came in. Then someone like CSI. I'm not sure what they call it in New Jersey, but it wasn't a team. Just one woman with thin hair. It's called female pattern baldness. My heart went out to her."

"The cops were from the New Brunswick Police Department?"

She nodded.

"Did the woman say anything about finding fingerprints, DNA samples?"

Definite no, with Nikki shaking her head. "She took back the pictures. Not that it would make a difference. The lady you're looking for didn't lean on the counter, not even once. Everyone leans or puts an elbow down. That's human nature. But I don't think she touched a single thing. I didn't pick that up when she was here, but I've been going over it in my head. She managed to walk out without leaving a trace."

Just as I stepped outside, my phone rang. The readout said "Mane Event."

I hurried down the sidewalk and answered. An androgynous voice spoke. "She's here. The one you were asking about. Shit, I'm the only one in the shop, and she's been watching me the whole time. Where's her phone? She never heard of Facebook? Her hair's in foils, so finally I get to go the bathroom. A second before I shut the door, she called out, 'Don't forget to wash your hands.' Rude enough for you? Whatever you think she did, you're probably right."

I'd been thumbing through my notes. The name of the Mane Event person I had was G. Risley. I double-checked the salon's address with G. and said, "An extra hundred if you can keep her there. But if she wants out, don't try to stop her."

CHAPTER TWENTY-SIX

At least I didn't have to circle around for ten minutes to find a parking space near the Mane Event. The parking lot for a small group of stores—a Spanish deli, a dry cleaner—was half empty. On the way over, I'd called Ricardo Jones with the update. He said he'd send someone over when he could, and to let him know if I confirmed that the woman in the salon was really Kim Brown/Vanessa Blake. It didn't sound like the cops would be there before I could be.

"It's not your job to worry," he said.

I wanted to say, *It's not your job to be a fatuous ass*, but I went with, "April Brown is our client, and it is our job to worry whether she's getting enough protection."

"There are cars in the area. Take it easy. Call my cell if you need to." He gave me a number I already had. "You don't have to say a word. I'll see your ID and my people will be there in seconds."

"More likely minutes," I said sourly, and hung up before he could tell me again how many resources he was already devoting to the case.

To be fair, Jones was under too much pressure, a good detective stuck with too much administrative work and too little time to think. Now here was an NYPD cold case brought back to life in New Jersey—with its former investigator, now a PI, aching to take charge. If Kim got caught, Ricardo Jones would get little credit. If she got away—or worse, got to April—his higher-ups, Rutgers, the mayor, the governor, the victim's family in Kentucky, and the media would be looking to him to take the blame.

The parking lot was a long strip behind the stores. Instead of walking into the salon through the back and risking unsettling Kim, I cut between the dry cleaner and a liquor store so I could come in through the front entrance, an ordinary customer. I caught myself combing back my hair with my fingers. I didn't see Kim at all. Or anyone else.

Even though I guessed that it was a small place, I couldn't judge the extent of it once I got in. The white, modern chairs on shiny brass pedestals at each station were placed in front of large rectangular mirrors. Between each mirror were floor-to-ceiling slats of bamboo. As I stood at the raised desk in front, it was up to my peripheral vision to take in the place, and it wasn't going well.

I was standing in front of a small computer terminal and a barstool-height white chair where in busier times a receptionist would sit. A partial wall separated the reception area from the getting-gorgeous work going on behind it.

Since I was trying to appear like a regular customer, I stood patiently—for a minute—waiting to be checked in, despite there being no one there to do it. I glanced up at the lighting situation: bulbs shaped like inadequate penises descending from the ceiling in bronze chains.

I called out, "Hello," in what I hoped was a mellifluous, nonthreatening voice.

"Be there in a minute . . ." The voice I'd heard on the phone. Now that I'd broadcasted my presence, I walked past the reception area. Mirrors facing mirrors, reflecting empty chairs and unused blow-dryers. Image upon image. The effect was disorienting. Well, I wasn't about to lose it just because I was faced with an infinity of Sebastian Gel Forte tubes.

I sensed the hint of a PTSD episode, the mildest vibration rising from my feet, then getting stronger as it rose throughout my body up to my head. All I could think to do was another of Dr. Greenblatt's calming tricks, the 5-5-5 of deep inhale, holding my breath, then exhaling slowly. I did a few of those and was encouraged when I started getting bored. For reassurance, I did another three, and my heart was steady and my mind clear. I gave myself a silent congrats, then called out, "Hi. I'm a little late for my two o'clock blowout, but there doesn't seem to be anyone around." My voice sounded just right—steady, pissed mixed with concern.

A "Hi" came from the back of the shop. It was not the androgynous voice. It was female, almost girlish, except with that slightly lower pitch that comes as estrogen begins to ebb. And there I was, face-to-face with Kimberly Brown. No black Dutch-boy wig, no cat glasses to obscure her looks. Actually, not face-to-face. I was standing, while she was sitting in one of those chairs that lean back to a sink. At the moment it was straight up, and she was not at her loveliest. Folded foil strips covered a third of her locks, starting at the top of her head and descending in a neat pattern, like roofing shingles.

She was wrapped in one of those black shrouds they give you to protect your clothes, a waterproof thing that may have been shaken out now and then but probably hadn't been washed since the Great Recession of 2008. She'd gotten a mani-pedi and was wearing tan paper sandals. Both her toenails and fingernails were painted a pale, frosted lavender, which was slightly disappointing as I would have imagined a killer as having bloodred nails. She held her fingers straight out in that après-manicure immobility—when you know that with one false move, your week will be marred by having to hide your left thumb and its thick, rippled smudge.

I sensed by her lingering, unashamed stare that Kim had looked past my simple jeans, T-shirt, and jacket and was scoping out my high-end booties as well as my engagement and wedding rings. While she was eyeing my accessories, I had a couple of nanoseconds to look at the sheet of paper she was holding between the knuckles of her index and middle fingers so as not to damage her nail polish. It was a printed-out screenshot from a YouTube video of Professor April Brown giving her lecture on *Stella Dallas*. April's sun-streaked hair was shorter back then. I thought I noticed some lip color and—I didn't want to ogle the photo—maybe some mascara and blush. April would have realized that her usual clean-faced look might not be vivid enough for video.

"Sorry to come barging back here like this," I told her with a regretful smile. I kept it subdued, echoing her manner with me. I guessed that all those years ago, when she saw her house and husband (and an unknown woman) being consumed by flames, she would more likely have said *Oh, wow* than shrieked and sobbed.

Kim smiled back at me. A pleasant smile, though she'd gone overboard on the Whitestrips. Up close—and without the wig and glasses she'd worn to obscure herself at King Sean's—she struck me as *pretty, not beautiful*—as she'd been described. Even with the whoo-hoo eyes.

For the first time, I noted that her upturned nose and rosebud of a mouth were overly close together, giving her a rat-faced aspect I hadn't observed in her photo ID. I guessed the ultrarich and persnickety men of Las Vegas wouldn't be lining up at her door without an extra dollop of charm or encouragement. At eighteen she'd been a trophy to Seymour, and maybe to others when she was twenty-five or thirty. But now the older guys she preferred would call her "nice-looking" or "well put together." No more *I gotta get a piece of that.*

"He said the foil had to stay on for another fifteen minutes," she told me, "and he was just going out to get a breath of fresh air. But you know what I think?"

A slight heart thud, but I did want to know what she thought. "What?" I asked.

"I think he wanted a cigarette." So the voice was a guy. "He's a smoker. I can smell it on him." Kim scrunched up her nose and mouth, but they were so near each other it barely altered her appearance. I mirrored her *Ooh, pew!* expression.

If she was trying to look exactly like April, she had hard labor ahead. Like spreading out her facial features. Growing three or four inches would be a challenge. She was slim, but didn't match April's small-boned but sturdy build. April didn't look like an ultramarathoner, but she had the wholesome look of a weekend athlete. Kim, on the other hand, seemed more buffed than buff.

I glanced at my watch and tried to look annoyed, but in a nonthreatening manner. Not for anything specifically to do with Kim. She sat silently, April's picture between her knuckles. Shiny foil rectangles made a slight *swish* sound whenever she moved her head.

I said, "I think I'll go outside to peek, see what's going on."

I moved past the sink beside hers, out of her line of vision, with the hope that not seeing me would make her forget I existed. I opened the back door and stuck my head into the warm air calling, "Hello?" No answer, so I repeated it louder. Nothing. I stepped outside but held the door ajar with my left hand so Kim could still hear me. "It's me!" I called out. Pulling my phone from my bag, I pressed Jones's mobile number while shouting across the pavement, "I'm here for my blowout."

I had no doubt that G. Risley, the owner of Mane Event, had scooted out the back door, got into his car, and was out of there. Whatever was going to happen in his shop, he didn't want to witness it, even if it meant giving up his fifteen minutes of fame. He wanted no part of the lady in foils or me.

Jones had promised that his people would arrive at the salon in seconds. My only question was how many minutes it would take. Two? Twenty-five?

Just then I heard the unwelcome shuffling sound of paper pedicure slippers. I pulled open the door I'd been holding open just a bit, and there was Kim, befoiled and berobed in the threshold, staring at my phone.

I bounced slightly on the balls of my feet to be ready for anything. At the moment, she was unpredictable. She could grab me and start sobbing—*Where is he? My hair is going to burn.* Or she might conceivably have a weapon—meant for April—though she wasn't displaying any of the characteristics of someone about to pull a knife or gun or even grab a pair of scissors: frequent weight shifts, glancing eyes, rapid breathing, panic, rage, swagger. I prayed silently that the missing hairdresser didn't set off any alarm bells.

"You were making a call?" Kim inquired. She still had the screenshot of April between her knuckles, but she carried it casually—as if it were something she'd put on when she got dressed and then forgotten about.

"Yes. I have his mobile number." No reaction, and she was still looking at the phone, not me. What I'd learned from my dad years before I learned it again at Quantico was that when you were uncomfortable, you shouldn't fake being cool. Just be you in your most simple form—no embellishment. Short, direct answers, whether they are lies or the truth. No sarcasm. I was uneasy right now, and there was no need to stifle it. Anyone would be a little uneasy if a stranger came over to them and peered at their phone.

She looked up from the phone to me. The hair on the top of her head and sticking out between the aluminum strips had been stripped of the dark color and now was a weaselly light brown.

"He gave you his private number?" she asked. I couldn't read anything from her expression, like whether she was surprised or huffy.

"Oh yeah. I'm here at least twice a week for a blowout. If I'm desperate and I call him, he always tries to squeeze me in." She lifted the hem of the black cover-up, draped it over her pinky to protect it from the hair dye, and scratched her scalp behind her ear. A gesture like that could be an involuntary signal of some alteration in her mood or an itch. I allowed myself to look a little put off at her nosiness.

She glanced down at her pinky nail. Clearly she saw no damage, because she looked right back at me. "Did he answer?"

"No."

Since Kim was still standing in the threshold, I found myself holding the door open. If it slammed in her face, she might get irritable. I kept straining to hear trucks rumbling, construction sounds, and of course sirens—anything predictable from a small city in the Northeast. But there was only bucolic quiet. A moo wouldn't have surprised me.

"If he didn't answer, why didn't you leave a message?" Her tongue flicked out, almost like a lizard's. I thought she was going to lick her lips, but she didn't. "You were holding the door open a little. I got up. I saw you make the call."

"You saw me?"

"You were holding the door open. Just a little," she said, holding her thumb and index finger a couple of inches apart. "I could see. You made the call, but then you hung up right away."

"It went straight to voicemail," I told her, scrunching my forehead at all her questions because that would be what she'd expect.

Kim gave an "Oh" of comprehension: like *Now I get it.* I felt relieved and opened the door wider so I could get back inside.

Her hand slid into the back pocket of her jeans, and I prepared myself for a weapon. I heard one of the cars near us unlock. To me it was as loud as a sonic boom, but I made myself keep my eyes on Kim. She withdrew her hand and flew past me, flat foil rectangles flapping up and down on her head. Right inside the door were the paper sandals she'd slipped off her pedicured feet.

I cursed myself for not being as prepared as I should have been. She was much faster than I thought. Part of me also didn't think that a narcissist like Kim could leave with her hair like that, and wearing that hideous black witch robe. No shoes, no purse. She'd barely looked at me earlier, but perhaps at the moment of that primitive flick of her tongue, she'd realized I was the person in the bar with April.

I swiveled and in a couple of steps was close enough to her that I was reaching under her armpit and pulling up for a side clinch, bending the wrist of my other arm to go behind the back of her neck, like the curve of an umbrella handle. She opened the door of the car nearest us and bulleted into the driver's seat. It was pure luck that I yanked my arm away before she slammed the door. The car might have been rented, but she knew precisely where the lock control was. Almost instantly, all four locks retracted. Then she turned on the ignition.

A car, not an SUV, which is what I'd associated with her. I had disregarded the midsize Acura sedan sitting right there, practically snuggling up to the salon. It also didn't register because she'd parked it in a handicapped-accessible space. The blue lines on the pavement were somewhat faded, but nobody could miss the big sign with the wheelchair symbol. *It figures that's where she'd park,* I thought.

Kim shifted into reverse and practically floored the accelerator. I barely avoided getting sideswiped, practically flopping onto the hood of the car parked next to hers. The Volkswagen directly across the narrow parking lot from her car was lucky, too, because all it got was a smashed headlight right before she shifted from reverse into drive.

I started to scramble across the hood to shelter myself between two cars before she tried to ram me. But she wanted out of there. I rolled back off the hood, running after her car, without a doubt looking like a madwoman. It wasn't that I expected to catch up. What could I do? Punch out a fender? My chase was fueled purely by high-octane adrenaline. At last I stopped. I knew precisely where Kim was headed.

April's house, about ten minutes away.

I ran back to my car and headed toward April's. On the way, I called Ricardo Jones. "I swear to God," he said, "they're seconds away." He was referring to his no-shows. "They—"

I cut him off. "Forget that. I'm in my car on my way to April's. Kim is going there too, and she's ahead of me. She's driving an Acura ILX, white. Better call the officers near April's house. And send your other people over there." I heard a sputter, which I assumed was a prelude to *Don't you dare give me orders,* so I hung up first and said "Fuck off" second.

A couple of blocks from the bridge that linked New Brunswick and Highland Park, I realized I was going almost twice the speed limit as some primitive survival instinct—for April's survival—kicked in. I forced myself to slow down. Also, I had to decide whom to call first, April or my dad, and I was paralyzed with indecision. Dad could be minutes away from her house. He could arrive at the same moment Kim did, practically colliding on the stairs up to the front porch. The image of that made me carsick, which isn't supposed to happen when you're the one driving. Still, a mixture of training and whatever sense of fairness I possessed made me decide: April. She was in imminent danger.

My dad could take care of himself. Couldn't he? Considering that he was also my partner, I had to hope so. And I had to hope he could also take care of April if he got there first.

"April, it's Corie. I'm on my way to your house, but so is Kim, and she's probably ahead of me." Much honking. The drivers were leaning on the horns, so I guessed I'd done something illegal or obnoxious. "Jones is letting the cops in unmarked cars know also."

"I have the doors locked." Her voice was shaking. "The alarm . . . I'm almost positive it's on. I took out my recyclables . . . Do you think she wants to kill me?"

"I don't know. Maybe she was trying to—with the SUV—then something changed. She wanted your identity. But you have to prepare as if she might try to kill you. She may be getting desperate."

"What should I do?"

"I should be there in a few minutes. I want you to hide. Not like under a bed or anything. Too obvious, too vulnerable." I paused for a few seconds to think. "Okay, remember when you showed me around the house? You pointed out where you keep your reels of movies and the projector for the screening room? That would be good because no one expects another room behind the screening room."

"Should I—" she began.

"Unless your question is life or death, get going and hide. If she finds you, try to keep her talking, but from her point of view. That's the only one narcissists are interested in. Not *What was my father like?* but *Tell me what things are like for you.* Okay?" I heard her walking from the hardwood floor to the rug. "Good," I said. "Turn off the sound on your phone so it doesn't give away your location."

"Okay, but the projection room is soundproofed. Because the equipment in there is very noisy."

"Good. But just in case, keep it on you at all times—don't lean against a hard surface with it!—so you can feel the vibration, but she can't hear it. If she attacks you physically and you can see her hands are empty, try to run. If you can't, push her away with all your might. It could get her off-balance, make her fall down. Is this too much for you?"

"No. I'm in the living room now."

"Your skull is hard. It's a weapon you have. Headbutt her nose or slam her face against something if you can. Poke her eyes with your fingers.

You don't have to bother with both eyes. One's enough. I think I'm about three minutes away now."

"I'm in the screening room."

"Great!"

"I couldn't lock the door." Fear must have constricted her throat. Her next words were fainter, as if they'd exhausted themselves pushing through a tight space to emerge. "It has the old-fashioned thing you turn. It gets stuck. Even with pliers—"

"Get into the projection room."

I could hear glass shatter though the phone. Then more. I said, "Quick. Give me the combo to the keypad lock you have to the projection room. We always like a backup. You can change it tomorrow."

She hesitated a second more than I would have liked. Finally, she said, "Nine-three-nine-one."

"Got it. Now get in that room and don't make a sound."

"But where is the cop who is guarding me?"

"April," I barked. "Quiet!"

A car that I guessed was an unmarked police car in front of April's was still there, and from halfway down the block I saw the driver's-side door open. A hopeful sign: the cop was in pursuit of Kim; her white Acura was pulled up behind it. She'd parked it so its rear wheels were so far from the curb, it would have failed parallel parking in a road test. No sign of Kim, not even a flash of foil.

But as I drove past the unmarked car, I spotted legs dangling out of the vehicle. I pulled ahead of it and ran back. The officer was still in the driver's seat, though his body was angled toward the middle of the car. His head had fallen forward so his double chin rested on an insignia on his shirt collar. He appeared to be eyeballing something on his dashboard laptop.

The bad news was that his eyes were closed. He responded to my trying to rouse him with a groan just a notch above inaudible. The good news was that he was breathing, though slowly. No signs of blood or trauma. Also good was that his weapon was still holstered. I unfastened his Icom and radioed in, "Your officer down." I gave the address as quickly as I could. Recalling how Kim had gotten Seymour and the Irishwoman into the same bed, I added, "Alive but unconscious. Possible poisoning or drug overdose administered by suspect in this case. I believe the suspect broke into the house. The homeowner is in there, too."

A voice cut in. "Who is—"

"This is PI Corie Geller. I'm going in now."

If Kim had entered April's house—and I would have put money on it after the crash of glass I'd heard on the phone—it hadn't been through the front. The tall Victorian entrance door was shut, and as I glanced at the windows facing the street, each one appeared intact. Closed, too, because it was a sticky day and the AC would be on.

I knew how elaborate the house's alarm setup was. As I turned the key and let myself in, it was all I could do to keep calm enough not to clap my hands over my ears in dread of what was coming. With expensive systems like this one, the layers of excruciating noise could be so horrific that it went from an attention-grabbing assault of sound waves to causing actual pain. Your entire body became destabilized. Guts banged against ribs, as if the latter were iron prison bars. Joints grew weak.

The impending scream of the alarm had me in such a heightened state of defensiveness that when my elbow touched something, I jerked it toward me, then rammed it back hard.

It was my dad. Luckily, his footwork was still nimble enough that he avoided a broken rib.

"Are you nuts or something?" he demanded in a whisper.

"Sorry." If not for the need for silence, I would have said, *Yeah, definitely nuts*. I might have owned up to *humiliated,* since it was solely years of training that had kept me from screeching. What made it worse was realizing that there were no lights, no ear-searing sounds. The alarms hadn't been triggered.

In fact, the silence in the house was itself frightening. For a second, we didn't look at each other. Maybe because we'd spot fear—or even defeat—in each other's faces. Where was Kim? Then, as if she were magically aware of our confusion and sympathetic to it, we heard her yelling, "You coward, come out and face me! Look me in the eye and dare to tell me I'm not the rightful"—a fraction of a second's pause until the word she wanted arrived—"heir."

Had I heard her right? She sounded less like a murderer on the loose in New Jersey and more like she was in one of my mother's roles in an Edwardian melodrama. I refocused my mind on the present: breath in my nose, feet squarely on the floor. Touching my gun in its holster to reassure myself I still had it, I took my first step into the front hallway. Kim chose that instant to stop for a breath—just as one of the floorboards squeaked under my bootie. It was a sound that could be missed only by someone in a full-tilt frenzy. "I am his next of kin, not you. What is there not to understand, Professor?"

My dad pulled his phone from his pants pocket, turned on the voice recorder, and stuck it into the pocket of his shirt.

"I'm sure it's easy for you to tell yourself, 'Daddy left me everything.'" Kim broke the word "Daddy" into two distinct syllables, heavily emphasizing the *d*'s. Then, in awful mimicry of a child, she squealed, "Daaa-dee, I drew a flower for you in school."

Kim's voice was loud, as if she were calling into another room. Good. We knew for the moment, at least, that April was not directly in front of her. My booties and Dad's shoes both had rubber soles, so we couldn't slide along the bare wood floor and maybe avoid setting off the old floorboards. We both knew what we were supposed to do in this situation—wait for backup unless the threat was immediate. But another part of me wanted us—my dad and me—to wrap it up on our own. We had some understanding of Kim. We had a better chance of handling her. The combined PDs of Rutgers and New Brunswick could set her off.

"Do you want to know something?" Kim blared. "Whenever you said 'Daddy,' I hated, hated, hated it. And lucky me, you said it all the time, even when he wasn't there. 'When is Daddy coming home?' 'Can we make thumbprint cookies for Daddy?'"

There in the hallway her voice was so loud it seemed amplified. Now she interrupted herself with an unnerving sound, somewhere between a hiccup and a gasp. Possibly it was her way of downshifting. Her next words were "I was his wife, and legally I am the one who inherits." Probably not the time to tip her off that her murder of Seymour and her legal death meant she wouldn't get two cents.

I guessed that April had gone into the projection room and kept the lights off. Otherwise Kim would have noticed the opening in the antireflective glass window through which the images were projected. She might have figured out that the small door along the back wall of the screening room wasn't just a cabinet. Somehow—maybe just after she broke in—she saw or sensed April heading toward the living room. Yet April wasn't there.

So Kim had turned the old glass knob on that wood door—odd for the outer wall of the living room—and discovered the screening room. Was the light switch in some weird place? Or did April, in the projection room, have control of the lights in the screening room? That made sense to me, thinking of how the lights fade into darkness in movie theaters when a film begins.

"Let me explain to you," Kim said. Although she wasn't shouting, her voice rang out like someone addressing an audience without a mic. "Your daddy . . . I can't bring myself to tell you what happened to him. All that really matters is that he is dead."

If I were April, I thought, I would be almost willing to let her know my location in exchange for being able to scream, *You monster!* Which may have been what Kim was going for.

"I managed to jump out of the window," Kim said, sounding stirred by her own valor.

Meanwhile, my dad flapped his fingers together, the common signal for talking. Then he sent two fingers of his right hand walking along his left forearm. Finally, he added *you and me* with his index finger. *While she's talking, you and I should start moving, get in a better position so we can intervene in case we need to before the backup arrives.* We began a slow sidle toward the screening room.

"I got hurt so bad. Burns. And when I jumped, I fell on my side. Later, do you know what I found out? I cracked my hip bone. But I got up—excruciating pain—and managed to get to your window. Remember? I know you remember. I heard your talk on YouTube before I went to hear you in person. You said the same thing both times, about the mother standing outside looking at her daughter. How she loved her."

My dad and I discovered that if we each stepped on the same board at the same time, a few feet apart, it cut down on the noise. Now we saw that the door to the screening room was wide open.

"I know I must have been crazy. But what I saw . . . and all the pain I was in—agony—I ran away. My only thought was that I had to get out of there. So I kept going and didn't stop."

It sounded like a performance, but I knew just enough about acting to know it wasn't acting. Whatever she was—narcissist, sociopath, psychopath—Kim was more than a first-class liar. She could fashion on-the-spot alternative realities and inhabit them as needed.

We inched around the perimeter of the room until we got to the door. I crouched, and so did my dad. I worried about his knees, but he didn't make a peep. I poked my head around the door. There was Kim, still in the black robe from the salon. I uttered a prayer of thanks that her back was to us. I couldn't make out the details, but I thought I saw something in her hand. I was pretty sure it wasn't a gun. I had to assume it was a weapon.

I drew my gun.

"I had to leave that suffering behind. I couldn't bear to be Kim Brown anymore. But know that it didn't just break my heart to have to give you up. It tore it up." A sob would have been cheap. There was only silence.

CHAPTER TWENTY-SEVEN

When you're wrapped in silence, you feel like you'll never escape it. There will never be a sound again. We stood against the stately wood door to the screening room that Kim had left open. The atmosphere from inside that room wafted past us—cold, conditioned air that seemed to hold several days of coffee molecules in suspension. My dad took his phone from his shirt pocket to text April, probably with a query like "can u see her?" but slipped it back in. When someone in distress is told to silence their phone, there's no guarantee that even a minute later they will remember to do it.

I heard sirens from far away, both police and ambulance. I was relieved, but they lasted only seconds—they had turned off the sirens. I mouthed "siren" to my dad, and he shrugged: *Didn't hear a thing.* He turned his head slowly, listening, then shrugged again.

Kim switched to growling: "What the hell is wrong with you, not saying a goddamn word?" The growl was menacing, more what you'd expect from a bear. "No matter what happened between me and your father, I'm still your mother. I deserve a certain respect." April wasn't convinced, or at least she didn't respond.

Dad and I both knew that Kim was never not dangerous. At this moment I knew she was more dangerous than she'd ever been. Shallow, rapid breathing served as punctuation between her sentences. I'd heard the same type of breathing from others just a couple of times before, someone revving up before one final, huge inhale and then *Attack.* I kept my focus on whatever was in her hand.

"I want the account number and the name you use for the offshore bank."

Loud again, she was no longer growling, but her voice had the sound of finality. She was letting April know this was her nonnegotiable demand, her last ask.

Could Kim honestly believe that money launderers, like the late Seymour, picked the Cayman Islands National Bank's George Town branch, opened an account, and got to choose a seashell or fish design for his checks? Money laundering was money in motion. With every stopover it moved farther away from its tainted origin and became cleaner and cleaner. Could she really have imagined that for all those years, millions of dollars or euros or rubles that was rightfully hers had been sitting in a bank's vault three blocks from a beach on a foreign island?

"It should be very clear by now. I'll do whatever I have to do to get what should have been mine."

I hated working in darkness. No facial expressions or tics to interpret, no body language. All I had was her silhouette and her voice. Where the hell were the cops? They knew they had an officer down and a probable hostage situation, or worse. By now they should have heard that their drugged colleague was in an ambulance, or had already gotten to the ER. Were they having a jurisdictional brawl over methods or gear for the SWAT team? Knowing that Kim was both a murderer and an arsonist, they should be busting down the door. They knew she was after her daughter, and if she hadn't yet gotten to her, April could wind up being her hostage.

Or did they believe they were being cagey, silently observing until they knew what they were dealing with? Were they already inside, as we were, or surrounding the house, beyond our awareness?

After all the righteous horror and fury over police violence, many in law enforcement have rethought the practice of "dynamic entry." That phrase was the euphemism for no-knock police invasions as well as for barely audible "Police-open-the-door!" bust-ins or SWAT teams who said good morning by using battering rams to open a door and then tossing in concussion grenades. Kim might be dangerous, but she wasn't an active shooter. They didn't have to storm in, but they should be making themselves evident—at least to me and Dad. And evident to Kim as well. Simply seeing five geared-up, helmeted cops wielding assault rifles could be all it took to make her surrender.

I could tell, wordlessly, that my dad agreed with me that we should wait to make a move until we knew we had backup—unless a perfect opportunity presented itself. Or April was in imminent danger.

With her next words, Kim's volume turned down again. She sounded regretful. "Do you know what my big mistake was? I shouldn't have changed my name. How can I go into the bank and say, *You have my money*, when my name is Vanessa Blake? They'd look at my identification and say, *Who the hell is Vanessa Blake and why should she get Seymour Brown's money?*—that disgusting, hairy fuck. So I need your ID. I need the account number."

Her voice fell even more, and I wondered whether April could hear her. Kim was speaking as much to herself as to anyone else. "Do offshore accounts have passwords?" She sounded as if she were winding down. My dad breathed a slow sigh of relief. Too soon. For a moment she fell back into silence, but that was only a chance to recoup. Her voice not only got louder but increased in resonance, as if she herself had magically doubled in size in the dark. "Listen to me when I'm talking to you!"

If the waiting was rough on me, I could only imagine how shattering it was for April. Sitting in that small, dark room, breathing in the dust from cans of film reels, listening to the outrageous fabrication spun by the maniac who was her mother. Unless she couldn't hear a thing because of the soundproofing. But I guessed April had an intercom in there. She operated the projector herself, so while she was in there, she'd expect anyone watching with her—Misaki, a group of friends—to let her know if something wasn't right.

"Listen to me, Little Miss Sunshine. I don't make empty threats."

And that's when the light went on in the projection room. *What the fuck, no!* I shouted in my head. But April didn't know where we were, didn't know the cops were on the way. April had clearly decided it was time to show herself, and there she was, framed in the window, unmoving. For an instant I thought she might be in dissociative shock—the kind that comes with trauma—like when terrorism victims cut away from reality and walk around unseeing.

Kim snapped her head up and stared at her daughter. Enough light was spilling out that I could see that all the foil rectangles were gone from her hair except one toward the back that she'd missed.

The sight of Kim made April recoil. Mostly, I guessed, at how bizarre Kim's appearance was. All her life she'd been hearing recollections of the allegedly dead woman as *pretty* and *blond* and *petite,* and here was this slattern in a hideous black muumuu.

Kim's hair now stuck to itself, tress by tress, clumped together by the remains of the chemical paste. She looked like Medusa in Greek mythology, except the Gorgon's hair was made of snakes and one glance at her could turn men into stone. Kim just looked like someone men would avert their eyes from in pity.

I didn't take my own eyes off her, and I still couldn't make out what was in her hand. Her movements were bizarre and alarming—they would make it hard to get a clean shot. Kim was staring at April, yet her hips were moving up and down as if she were involved in some warm-up exercise. Even though I'd studied body language, I hadn't seen this before. I tried not to think of how many months it had been since I'd practiced at the shooting range.

"Well," Kim said impatiently, as if the daughter she hadn't spoken with in twenty-three years was an obstacle in her way. "Let's move it along. I want the name of the bank and the account number and whatever name it's under. Is there a password? Because if there is, obviously I'll need that too."

No answer. April did tilt her head slightly, but it was as if she were about to answer a *Jeopardy* query: *This element forms the largest percentage of the Earth's atmosphere.* All she showed was dismay at her mess of a mother. "Facts are facts," Kim said impatiently. "I loved you much more than you ever loved me. You were daddy's girl the whole time. I gave you the chance to escape. Daa-dee would have turned on you one day, just like he turned on me. Calling me a whore when I wore anything fun. Crappy presents. And, you better believe this, he smacked me around. But upstairs, never downstairs where you could hear it. He was a pig. Not even that upscale. When he heard I was pregnant, he dug his hands into my shoulders and shook me. That's how mad he was. And then he fell in love with you. It was sickening. Bent, I think."

April opened her mouth to speak. Whether she was going to say how shocked she was, how she hadn't known that—or that Kim was a liar . . . Again, no clue in her expression. And then she closed her mouth.

It was time. My dad and I, perfectly in sync, nodded at each other, and he was off, slinking around the three chairs in the back row, heading toward the front. I was right behind. We moved together intuitively.

The thing that wasn't a gun in Kim's hand glinted. I thought I had seen something like it before, though I couldn't remember where. I wasn't up on new weaponry. It was gunlike anyway, with a high polish to its oddly long barrel, as if it were made from stainless steel. Not that there weren't guns made from that, like some Smith & Wesson revolvers the cops used to extol, thinking them infinitely cool. But what she was holding seemed to have a weird angle to it. I stopped and aimed my weapon as my dad reached her.

In his day, he hadn't been first-rate enough in martial arts to be a Krav Maga instructor, though he had been proficient enough to be called on to be the opponent in a demo. He would move against the instructor and—*whomp!*—the instructor would execute a kick or a grab; my dad, knowing what would happen in a real-life situation, would feign getting brought down. All in slow motion, all without injury, and always with the warning, *Don't try this at home.*

He was older now. He'd been depressed for years. He'd lost muscle tone, energy, and swiftness. I thought, *Crazy Kim is about five foot three inches, and who knows what her weight is, but she's not made out of lead. I believe he can do it.*

I heard a plastic-sounding click, and a white flame shot out of the thing she was carrying. That's when it hit me that the object in her hand was a kitchen blowtorch. A friend of mine from college, Xavier, had one. He had some job with Facebook in the city, but he was a great cook, always making dinner for friends. I watched him using one of those things to turn the top of crème brûlées crunchy. He said I should feel free to borrow it to put beautiful brown peaks on my lemon meringue pie.

"For someone who's supposed to be smart, you are so stupid," Kim called out. "Why would you live in a wood house?" At that moment, April turned and Kim screamed, "Where are you going? Do you think you can escape?"

"I'm just going to get all the information for you. Everything." April's voice had such a tremor it was hard to understand her. "It's all written down. I'm getting it for you. Just give me a minute to pull it out. Please."

"You're shitting me."

"I swear to you, I'm not. Please give me a minute."

"Sure," Kim said, extending the word. Now she was sounding like the mellowest psychopath east of the Mississippi. "Not a problem."

She turned and aimed the blowtorch at the seat of the chair and started to ignite it. I kept my trigger finger loose. I knew my dad was ready, and I was correct. With his right hand, he grabbed her wrist from behind and bent it up. She screeched, shocked by his presence and her pain. "Stop! You're hurting me!" she shouted. As he turned her wrist and hand upward and away from the chair, he grabbed the blowtorch with his left hand and gave it to me. The chair cushion didn't burn. It did stink, but it must have had a fire-retardant fabric over fire-retardant stuffing. It smoldered a lot and made thick, nasty, low-rise smoke.

I reluctantly reholstered my gun and found a small wheel on the side of the blowtorch, which lowered the gas. I couldn't find the switch, so I turned it more, and it clicked off. It took another minute to figure out how to eject the small butane cartridge, while Kim tried to get out of my dad's grip by biting his arm.

Krav Maga is basically an aggressive martial art based on street fighting. It isn't beautiful, like aikido—just jabbing here-there-everywhere close to the face to confuse. At times there may be grace, but no elegance. He hit her with the heel of his hand halfway between her jaw and her nose. Kim's legs wobbled, and she crumpled to the ground.

The seat was still smoking, and the stink was dreadful. I looked up at the lighted projection booth window, expecting to see April there, watching us take Kim down. Had she passed out from the terror? Was she lying on the floor of the projection room?

"April!" I called.

My dad yanked some zip ties out of his pocket to secure Kim's hands behind her back before dragging her out of the room. I really didn't want to see him do it, because that was how I was held during the days I was kidnapped.

I called out more forcefully this time. "April! It's me, Corie. It's okay. We've got her and it's okay. Please come out." I had never had a sweet valentine of a voice. If she were able to be roused by hearing her name called, she would be standing up by the window again, albeit a little unsteady on her feet. But there was no one. I glanced over at my dad, who was dragging Kim's motionless body over the threshold into the living room.

That's when the crush came. The front door flew open with a giant crack, and I heard glass shattering to my right. The house became a river of helmets and black uniforms and Kevlar as cop after cop swarmed in, a hundred feet pounding on the old wood floorboards. I threw my hands in the air, and so did my dad, letting Kim drop to the floor like a sack of flour, with a *thunk* so loud I could still hear it over all the noise.

My heart was thudding against my rib cage, but thankfully they seemed well-briefed enough to know that Dad and I were harmless and that Kim was the perpetrator. I watched Kim and my dad get enveloped by cops and separated. Within seconds I was surrounded, and before I could blink, one of them had patted me down and taken my weapon.

As they began searching every nook and cranny of the screening room, I stepped into the living room to get away from the acrid chemical smell. I leaned against the doorjamb, watching the throng of cops and fingering my flashlight. Breathe in for five, hold for five, exhale for five. I pursed my lips to slow my breathing, sipping at the air as if through a straw.

I was terrified that my dad was in shock—or worse. He didn't have any heart problems I was aware of, but at his age, who knew? I spotted him across the room.

He was better than I was. Completely normal, as if nothing had happened, as if he hadn't just disarmed a psychopath with greater physical expenditure than he'd made in forever and then faced a mass of people all pointing guns at him. Better than normal, I realized. He looked energized.

He was standing behind a tall chair in deep conversation with someone. The guy he was talking to was about fifty, Black, and so tapered that if he'd worn a leotard, he could have passed as a classical ballet dancer. But he was wearing detective clothes—white shirt, unmemorable tie, and bland pants.

"Hey," my dad said. "You two haven't met in person. This is Ricardo Jones." His voice was as smooth as if we were at a cocktail party, but his hand found my upper arm and gave it a squeeze to let me know how relieved he was that I was safe.

I swallowed and gathered myself. "Good to finally meet you," I said to Jones. Surprisingly, my voice sounded normal. "Did you call the fire department? The film reels are flammable."

He smiled slightly. "They're coming," he said. "You're okay now. We're here. You'll be safe."

At another time I would have found his reassurance patronizing, but just at this moment it was exactly what I needed to hear. "Good. Now we just have to find April."

As if I'd summoned her, April emerged from a knot of cops who were standing on the other side of the living room. I was confused—how had she gotten there without coming through the screening room door? Her face was calm but stony, and I realized how infrequently I'd seen her when she wasn't smiling.

"Thank God. How are you?" I asked, embarrassed by the inadequacy of the question, given everything she'd just been through. I covered up for it by throwing my arms around her.

She seemed surprised for a second but then embraced me too and held on, resting her head on my shoulder. After a moment she pulled away gently and looked at me. "I'm . . . okay, I think? Actually, probably I'm not okay, but . . . I'm here." She drew in a shaky breath.

"I was so worried. I didn't see where you'd gone, and I knew we had your mom but . . ."

She nodded. "Sorry. I was in the bathroom," she said, as if that were a perfectly normal place to go right after your mom threatens to burn you alive.

Well, I thought. *For all I know, that is a perfectly normal place to go right after your mom threatens to burn you alive.*

The fire department and an ambulance for Kim came simultaneously. She was handcuffed to a gurney, still out of it, though no longer unconscious. The left side of her face was swollen, and I hoped my dad had knocked out a couple of her teeth. Difficult to get good dental implants in prison.

I kept thinking about that cop she'd drugged, the one with the double chin. He was still in the emergency room, and the doctors were working on him. And the Irishwoman who'd been brave enough to come to America alone, live in a stranger's house, care for their child, who never got a chance to decide if she wanted one of her own. And even Seymour, who may have been a shitty person but loved his kid and deserved to live to see how she turned out.

As they wheeled her past me, Kim turned, looked me over, and managed to mutter, "Who the hell are you, anyway?" It did sound as if she were down one or two teeth. Her hair looked like a chemical dump that could be declared a Superfund site. They'd surely have to shave it off, and a weird, tiny part of me actually felt bad for her, since I knew how much that would upset her.

Behind them, firefighters carried out the chair Kim had tried to ignite.

I turned back to the living room. April was sitting in a tufted armchair, feet tucked under her. Her entire body was curling into itself, as if she wanted to become a ball. Earlier, I'd seen her explaining what happened to two attentive, nodding cops. One of them took notes while the other asked what looked like gentle questions. I'd been pleased to see that someone had draped a blanket around her and brought her a glass of ice water.

Now she was sitting alone. I walked over. When our eyes met, she shook her head ever so slightly: *I don't want to talk*. She tried to curl more, but I put my hand on her shoulder and said, "I need to speak to you. Come on, walk over to the couch with me." I would have knelt beside her, but my bad leg was bothering me.

"Not yet. Please, give me a little time."

I needed to know how she had gone from a sealed room behind the screening room to the living room without my seeing her. I could still feel the last of the cold fear that had turned my bones to ice in that moment.

"I'd love to give you all the time you need," I said softly. "But we need to talk for a few minutes. Then I promise to do everything I can to control everyone coming at you, asking questions." I cupped her elbow and lifted her slowly. She didn't resist, and when a fire inspector came toward us, I waved him away. Politely, gently. I figured that he had the chair and the blowtorch—and he could start with that. He backed off, probably thinking April would be more approachable after some girl talk.

We sat on her couch, a flawless white linen, incredibly comfortable. It was a blissful spot for conversation: also perfect for stretching out on to read or relax. We were a couple of feet away from each other, with enough space between us for her to sense that this was business. It struck me that only an impeccable person would buy a major piece of furniture on which you couldn't risk a spilled cup of coffee or a day-early period.

"I'm sorry you had to go through all this today," I told her. "There should be a weight limit to how much one person can bear. Please know that we will continue to be around as long as you need us. We'll see you through all the questioning and help you in whatever way we can."

"Thank you, Corie." I was about to go on, but she asked me if it was safe for Misaki to come home for a week or two. I told her it was, and in fact it was an excellent idea to ensure that she had a strong support system. "I guess I'm a little paranoid. What if my mom gets off?"

"She won't. There's not a shot. Listen, April, they have so much evidence against her. We recorded that long, incredibly detailed confession from Toddy. Even if he doesn't decide to cooperate—which he will—the details of her planning, conniving, and abandoning you are devastating. We're witnesses. We even recorded her rant at you in the screening room."

"But is it enough?"

"Yes, it is enough. And the prosecutor will have DNA linking her directly to you. So they can prove she didn't die along with your father and that other woman."

"At least she tried to save me." I wasn't sure whether Kim had tried to save April because she had a pang of conscience or because she wanted to prove to Toddy how compassionate she was, but I decided now wasn't the time to say that. April went on, "That poor housekeeper."

"We're working with Interpol now to find out who she was."

"You'll let me know, so I can write to the family?"

"Absolutely." Just before I got to April's house, I'd been telling Josh how that murder seemed particularly cruel to me. Not just because it involved the awful death of a young woman finding her place in the world, but because it was unnecessary. "And just know you can call either of us at any time if you have more questions. Is there a friend who can stay here until Misaki gets here? Otherwise, my dad or I would be glad to stay. You shouldn't be alone."

April gave me a wan smile. "I have a friend in the Sociology Department," she said. "She's compassionate, but doesn't ooze it, if you know what I mean."

"She sounds perfect. I have one more question, if you're okay to answer. About what just happened." April nodded, and I went on. "Once my dad was able to take Kim down and the blowtorch was turned off, I called to you that it was all right for you to come out. And if you had looked out the projection room window, you would have seen that we had her. But you didn't. How come?" I asked it lightly, as if inquiring about her choice of lip gloss.

"I guess I was traumatized. I'm so sorry. You must have been scared."

"Well, scared enough," I said. She looked embarrassed. I truly did want to leave her alone. But I had to ask. "How did you get out?"

"I told you about how the projector gets so hot, right? Even in a home theater, if you have an old reel-to-reel, you need to have a vent in the wall. Right between the two shelves of the films I've collected, there is a three-by-five vent—feet, not inches. Obviously, I have a thing about fire. I had it designed so I can pull it down from the top pretty easily if I have to."

"And you had to." April nodded. "Where does the vent let out?"

"On the side of the house." She swallowed. "All the upholstery and curtains in the house are fire retardant . . . All of it. It's not something I talk about a lot." She shuddered, but low-key. "I didn't know how awful the upholstery would smell. I don't remember that from the first fire, when I was a kid."

I nodded in agreement, then thanked her for talking to me even though she wanted solitude. I squeezed her hand and said I was going to hang around for a while to go over the events with Jones's detectives. Then my dad and I would probably go to headquarters to give a videoed statement.

April's feet were back under her, and she was curling into a ball again. I told her that if she felt up to it, there was some research showing that playing a simple phone game—Tetris or Candy Crush or whatever—reduced the impact of a traumatic event. She looked dubious, but shrugged and took out her phone.

I stood up and pinched the bridge of my nose, rubbing in small circles. She'd been lying when she said she'd gone to the bathroom after my dad took Kim down. That was one thing: there were so many other people around at that moment, and maybe she'd been self-conscious. But she was still lying to me now about the vent. I needed to know why.

There was crime scene tape around the basement area where Kim had broken in, and a few cops milling around. I'd been wondering how she'd known that was the one spot that wasn't connected to the alarm. Kim had committed many crimes in her life, but she did not seem to be an expert on breaking and entering, able to tell from the outside which windows would not set it off. Now that I was outside, I saw from some scuff marks on the panes that she'd first tried the kitchen door that led to the patio, but it was some sort of shatterproof glass. Only then had she gone to the basement, and I guessed it was because the windows looked easy to break.

I went around the corner to check out the projection room vent from the outside. The slats were slanting only slightly, like pulled Venetian blinds. I opened my magnifier app and studied the top of the vent. Whoever painted the house had used not only the same color white, but also the same brushstroke for the vent's slats and the house's horizontal clapboards. No doubt it wasn't just fitted into the side of the house, jigsaw style. The security guy with the gorgeous lashes had not mentioned it as a vulnerability, and he would have if you could simply pry it out of the wall from the outside. It had to be latched or locked on the inside. If someone had unfastened the latch and pushed open the vent from the inside, the thin layer of paint on the outside would have split. Now, even magnified, the perfect paint job was unmarred. No one had shoved that vent open.

Not that I was surprised. The cops were already surrounding the house at that point. They'd burst in seconds later. I knew right away that there was no way they missed an adult woman climbing out of the house through a three-by-five-foot hole.

Why would April lie like that? She was hiding something—most important, the answer to the question of how she got out of the projection room when one exit, the door, was being watched and remained closed, and the other, the large vent, hadn't been opened.

I came back into the house. My dad was on the phone, standing next to the door. He pulled it away from his ear and told me, "I just let April know, and I don't have to tell you, but I'm going to tell you anyway. Forensics is almost here, and they're going to clear us out. Don't mess around with too much stuff." I said okay, I was just going to use the bathroom.

"Just checking that I didn't already forget," I said to April when I got back inside. She was still on the couch in the living room. "The combo to the projection room? Nine-three-nine-one? I just want to make sure Kim didn't manage to lob something through that hole in the glass. Chances are next to zero, but just to be safe."

"Right," she said. I was counting on her exhaustion to keep her from seeing through my bullshit excuse, and it paid off.

I pictured 9/3/91, but that was before she was born, so not her birthday. Not her parents' anniversary either, which I had memorized after staring at their marriage certificate. It could be anything: an old address, Misaki's birthdate. I asked, "Wasn't 1939 a major year in movies?"

"The most major," April said, managing a benevolent smile. "I didn't think it was that obvious."

"At some point you might want to switch it to the last four digits of someone else's phone number. Something really randomized. Just not from your own life—like the year you got your PhD."

I stepped into the bathroom. It had a closet on the side that abutted the projection room. Like the doors in many of the other rooms, including the one upstairs I'd slept in for a night, this closet door was painted white and had four panels. Like the others, too, it had a round glass door handle set in a brass plate with a scalloped edge—pretty, though not overly elaborate—and a keyhole. The key was in it, and though I turned it backward and forward, the closet door wouldn't budge. It seemed held in place. I tried three times, no doubt turning red-faced, but no matter how hard I pulled, the closet stayed shut.

I pictured one of the cops or the fire inspector waiting outside the bathroom and getting curious as to who would be in there so long. I washed my hands with much running of water, then opened the door to the hall. No one was there.

I would try the screening room one more time. The space still had an acrid smell; no one would want to stay, even to watch a movie's opening credits. I walked to the rear of the room and pressed the combination. The projection room door opened easily.

I took note of where the light switch was, but I didn't turn it on. If Jones or one of the cops came into the screening room, there was no need to advertise where I was. I was concerned that the flashlight on my phone might be too bright, so for the first time, I actually used the one that had been dangling above my cleavage for almost two years. LED, the website had said. Ten years of use!

The projector was larger than I thought it would be, the room smaller. There were dozens of reels lined up on shelves, the names and dates of the films written in neat letters with a black marker. Very systematic, but these were April's cherished possessions. The shelves slid from side to side on a track, so that she could retrieve reels from behind the ones in front. Very cool and well thought out.

I checked behind the shelves, and there was nothing there. I stepped up on a lower shelf—very sturdy construction—and knocked quietly on the ceiling. It was solid, probably plaster. There was no crawl space up there to access from the screening room.

All that was left to check out was the back wall. I walked over to it—three steps—and turned off the narrowed beam of my flashlight so I would stop seeing. I was nervous. The whole reason I wore the flashlight in the first place was because I was frightened of being in the dark. But since the wall was painted a matte black, touch might reveal more than sight—as I had unfortunately learned during my kidnapping.

If the panic didn't come out from wherever it was hiding in my body and brain, feeling blindly was actually a cool way to search. The only downside was that I had no idea what I was searching for. A secret button? A flat-to-the-surface handle? A simple door?

After taking a moment to picture the location of the no-access closet in the bathroom so I could find the same area in the projection room, I sat on the floor and did much wall-feeling, patiently and thoroughly, though less so toward the end because the whole endeavor began to embarrass me. I felt bad for the forensics team about to arrive who would be forced to contend with my hairs and fibers, but at least I wasn't worried about damaging evidence we'd need to convict Kim.

While I was sitting there on the floor, I texted my dad, giving him my location. I wasn't sure if the audio system was on anymore, so if he called my name from the screening room, I might not hear. He texted back, "Why u there?" I answered, "Crazy theory. 5 min more."

I got up from my cross-legged position on the floor without using my hands, a nice fillip when a Krav Maga class began, but now it was a schlep and a half, and I'm sure I looked graceless; my legs and core needed serious remedial work. I switched my flashlight back on, then turned and rested my back against the wall.

I hadn't noticed while I'd been palming and tapping the wall, but now, with my full weight against it, it didn't feel as solid as it should. Okay, Victorians did not build projection rooms, though the occasional stereopticon was not out of the question. But this felt like wobbly plywood—not even drywall. Even a contemporary architect, given the job of creating a screening room and a projection room by taking space from a living room, would—as Wynne would say—honor the materials. What kind of designer would choose wobbly plywood or whatever for such a solid house? Maybe April was saving her seven-million-dollar inheritance for a rainy day, but I couldn't see her being cheap when it came to anything connected with film.

I faced the wall and knocked on it. Then I pushed against it with the heels of my hands. The left side of the wall felt sturdier. The less rigid right side was where the unopenable bathroom closet would be.

Was. Though the little flashlight was still on the chain around my neck, I'd held it with its beam now more spread out, hoping I could spot a push button, a seam, an inset handle. I put the flashlight in my mouth so I could use both hands. Until that moment I'd been thinking up/down or in/out. Now, sideways came to mind. I braced myself against the sturdier left side of the wall, pressed my hands against the wall where it seemed less stable, and pushed at it with all my might. It slid so easily I had to do a little jump-sidestep to keep up.

A pocket door! Not the high-end kind, where an entire door slides into a wall, but a flat piece of black-painted plywood that slid—I was never any good at measurements—about three feet before butting up against the exterior wall. I crawled in and realized I'd solved the Mystery of the Closed Bathroom Closet: two large sliding bolts kept the door permanently shut from the inside. April could have slipped into the closet, unlocked the bolts, and stepped into the bathroom—with access to the rest of the house.

The fact that they were locked again told me that at some point after I'd seen her in the living room coming through all the cops, April must have excused herself—*I need a few minutes by myself, okay?*—and slipped back into the screening room. She'd keyed in her passcode to get into the projection room, then slid back the rear wall and bolted the closet again. My guess was she didn't even need a flashlight. She'd done it so often, she could do it with her eyes closed. She could be in and out in only a couple of minutes. Her secret was safe.

But what secret? The closet itself was empty of everything except a card table and a chair. But when you slipped in and moved the other way—and it was a relatively tight space—past the first two-by-four wood stud, the opposite wall had two rows of small doors, three doors each. They went from my shoulders to the top of my head. They looked like the doors you see in banks where the safe-deposit boxes are kept. But instead of a double-key arrangement on the front, these were biometric, also double entry. They looked as if they required not only an iris scan, but fingerprint recognition as well. Probably from the same person, April Brown, PhD.

CHAPTER TWENTY-EIGHT

Before leaving April's secret room, I took pictures of the setup—with flash—and a thirty-second video of how the back wall worked from both sides. When I returned to the living room, I saw Dad and April on the white couch. She had a different blanket wrapped around her now, one of those ubiquitous throws with nubs and loops that show up in folk-craft shops from Finland to Maryland. I saw a cushioned footstool in a corner and carried it over.

"I'm making a checklist," my dad said. His small spiral-bound notebook was resting on his knee. "Jones and I talked. The police officer she drugged is in the hospital, but he's going to be fine. They may even be able to release him today, tomorrow at the latest."

"Thank goodness," April murmured.

"Also, he said the forensics team won't need more than a couple of hours. You can stay here tonight. If you want to, of course. You've got to decide what works for you."

"Good," April said. "I want to stay." The house exuded serenity, as if it were thankful to be rid of the lawless and the law.

"Someone should come today to board up the windows she broke," I said to April. "A few other details, but they can wait for tomorrow."

"I'm going to call the insurance company," April said as she stood. "One of the detectives wrote down a case number to give them. It's in the kitchen."

I was thinking that the insurance company could probably wait a day or two, when the forensics team arrived and shooed us out of the house. They gave us permission to sit on the front porch, which they'd already cleared before coming in. Dad and I settled into the love seat while April, still wearing shorts and a T-shirt, swaddled herself with that hideous throw and settled into a wicker rocker.

She squinted, as if staring into the sun, even though the porch was shaded. Abruptly, she asked, "Do you think they'd let me go change into long sleeves or something?"

"Couldn't hurt to ask," I said.

She nodded, slapped her hands on her knees, and got up slowly, as if she were twenty years older than she actually was. She murmured something to a cop near the door. Apparently the answer was yes, because he ushered her inside.

The instant she left, I told my dad about my discovery of the hiding place.

"That's crazy!" he said. "You must have misunderstood what it was."

I seethed at his condescension but held my temper. Instead, I showed him the photos on my phone. His jaw literally dropped.

"What the fuck?" he said.

"Hell if I know," I replied.

"I think you should be the one to ask her," he told me. "Gently. I'm going to head out to my car. Tell her I'm working on Jones to get more information."

"Sure. But don't you think you should do it, considering your relationship with her? You go way back. She views you as a paternal figure."

"Right, so if she's up to some sneaky shit, she'll be reluctant to confide in me. My good opinion matters to her. Not that yours doesn't, but she sees you as more of a contemporary who can understand her thinking."

I agreed, though I decided that if she wasn't responding well to me, I wouldn't hesitate to head out to his car and ask him to take over.

April came back outside carrying a water bottle and wearing jeans, a long-sleeved T, and sock slippers with pride stripes. She said she'd ordered soup and sandwiches.

I took out my phone and placed it on the small table in front of us. "Did you call your sociologist friend?"

"Yes. Thanks for suggesting it. She's coming over at about nine."

"Oh!" I said, as if suddenly struck by the thought. "I have some pictures I want to show you. And a short video, less than a minute."

Her eyes were still somewhat glazed, but whose wouldn't be after the nightmare of the day she had. For all she knew, I was about to show her pictures of Eliza at the Costa Rican dog sanctuary.

I inched a little closer and held the phone so that she could get a full view. She glanced at it, then looked up at me, her color draining before my eyes. Dots of sweat appeared on her upper lip. I sensed where this could go. I'd dealt with fainters before.

"Put your head between your knees for a second, April. You're going to be okay. Actually, wait a second." I got up and went behind her to pull back her rocker so she had room to fold herself over her lap. She was lighter than I expected, and the rocker jerked back quickly with a loud *BRRRAAAAAAAP* against the floorboards. I guided her head down gently between her knees and reminded her to breathe. After a moment, she started to sit up. "Slowly," I said reassuringly. She raised herself more slowly and took a hesitant breath. I was surprised to see her look back at me steadily. "I'm going to continue," I said. She nodded, resigned.

I flipped through the pictures of small doors, biometric locks, and the bolted interior closet. "Not great lighting in there," I commented, mindful that I was making her very bad day that much worse.

April was subdued to the point of being nearly inaudible "It's recessed, so you can't see any fixtures," she said. Her eyes were on my phone.

"I'm not trying to invade your privacy," I said. "I gather that's even more important to you than I'd realized. But we're just trying to figure out everything that happened here, and this seems important." She tried to meet my eye, but couldn't. We both needed a time-out, so I massaged my jaw. She rubbed her eyes and took a sip of water.

I continued. "You stood there listening to her, not sneaking out. Why? To prove she couldn't cow you? Or because you didn't want to give away the fact that you have an elaborate system to protect whatever it is you're protecting."

"Both, I guess," April finally said.

"Those must be some pretty important possessions you're protecting."

She rubbed the palms of her hands together very hard, as if trying to generate all the heat she could. "Do I have to tell you?"

"No." I gave it a minute. She did a lot of hard swallowing. "You don't have to tell the cops either."

"Will you tell them?"

"No. But I can't lie if they ask me. Private investigator–client isn't a privileged relationship the way a lawyer-client is. To put you at ease, they didn't imply that they suspected anything wrong with either you or your projection room. So I don't expect them to ask at the moment." She pulled up the neckline of her T and this time dabbed her eyes with it. "So keep to yourself what you want to keep. In general, the more we know, the more we can help you as we wrap all this up. But that will be up to you."

"How do you know it's not"—she gazed at a pepper-and-salt mill on the table—"the 1938 version of *A Christmas Carol* in there?"

I offered her a wry half smile.

The sandwiches came. I brought my dad's over to him and asked if he would eat his separately from us—maybe in the backyard—and he said sure, but I'd better remember every fucking word. I returned with her turkey club and my tuna on toast, which I knew was an iffy choice because of the chance of sog, but I had felt daring. April was still seated, which I took as a sign that she was willing to stay on the path we'd been on. I was also encouraged that we were sharing not only my untruffled french fries but also her coleslaw.

"So?" I asked.

She exhaled and looked right at me. "The day after I turned twenty-one, I was still at UC—University of Cincinnati—I got a registered letter from a lawyer in New York. He was in a big law firm."

"Do you remember the name of it?"

"Yes. White Voss Singer," she said. I nodded. "No commas."

"Arrogant putzes," I told her. "Too big to punctuate." White Voss had offices all over the world. "And do you remember the lawyer's name?"

"Leonard Diehl." I waited. "He was a partner in the trusts and estates department. He asked me to call him. I Googled him. He was what he said he was, so I called. He said my father had made arrangements with him when I was four years old. He had given Diehl some cartons and a letter that was sealed with actual sealing wax. Diehl's firm was supposed to have it warehoused, and if anything happened to my dad, they should hand it over to me when I was twenty-one. Their job was to keep track of me. Some women get married while they're still in their teens, so they'd had to keep up with my last name and where I lived and all that, until I attained majority."

"So Diehl was the one who met with your father and arranged for this?"

"He said they did most of it over the phone, but they met briefly when my dad came in to sign all the paperwork."

"Did you ask him if he knew what was in the cartons?"

"Sure. He said he'd been legally obliged to check the contents, so he knew—some antique boxes my dad had collected to store the valuables. The boxes themselves were worth a lot. He didn't go into any more detail."

"Did you go to New York?"

"It was right around finals. I'd been accepted at NYU for my master's, but I didn't want to wait until then. I said I'd pay to have them shipped to my house in Kentucky. He sort of laughed, as if I were being droll. He said all those expenses had been taken care of in their fee, that it might be better for me to—some legal word—get them at a bank because there were valuable items—I could put them in a safety-deposit box. He would make the arrangements if I'd like, so I said okay. I was really curious, but I had already gotten money and some unset jewels when I turned eighteen."

"Right," I said. "I remember. Your aunt Patty's bandmate from high school was your lawyer's father, right?"

April tried a smile, but couldn't make it. "I didn't think this would be a big deal," she said. "Possibly an emotional big deal, but I was thinking more along the lines of love letters between him and my mother. Maybe a picture of him and me when I was little: that's what I was really hoping for."

"You wouldn't need cartons for that," I observed.

"That's true."

"What were they?"

"They looked like regular document boxes or those cartons for hanging files. I thought of the ending of *Citizen Kane*, when they're boxing up all his belongings. But anyway. That was a kind of camouflage, I guess. The antique boxes were inside, and they were much smaller, surrounded by padding."

"Did your father explain to Mr. Diehl why he didn't just specify this stuff in his will?"

"He told the lawyer that the Browns were an old family. Unfortunately, some of them could hold grudges for generations. My dad said he knew that handling it this way was a cumbersome and expensive process, but it would be easier on me in the long run."

"White Voss Singer is one of those old-line Wall Street law firms," I told her. A couple of Josh's law school classmates were partners there. "A firm like that almost always has a stick up its butt, but it can be a pliable stick. Mr. Diehl was going to check the contents, and your father probably had a well-researched explanation that would pass the White Voss sniff test. He got his venerable institution—no sleaze attached. What the law firm wanted, and I'm sure they got, was a humongous fee."

I paused. April was wolfing down the fries, but if she looked down at them, she would probably be amazed that there were only seven left. I took three and left the rest for her. Anyway, my tuna on toast was amazing and sog less, so I was content.

But not completely. "Do you have the letter from the envelope that was sealed with wax?"

"The seal was blue, not red, and debossed. You know what the design was? Thirteen stars in a circle, like the Betsy Ross flag."

"I'd like to see the letter, April, and to have my dad look at it too." To call her disinclined would have been an understatement. While she didn't move her chair, she crossed her arms, though there was a small chance that was because there were no more fries. "This is the closest I can come to hearing your father's voice," I told her. "I want to get to know him, and I know my dad will, too."

In another twenty minutes, April had given the okay for my dad to join us and had gotten permission for us to go back into the house.

Dearest April,

A funny thing happened to me today. Remember I told you there are two kinds of funny? Funny peculiar and funny ha-ha. Well this was peculiar. I was having a hamburger at a very famous restaurant in Brooklyn with an important client Ivan. Ivan has a steak and a salad for lunch there every single day! Well I just had the burger and I thought "this is the best burger I ever had." But around 4 o'clock I didn't feel so good. A bad pain in my chest and it went under my arm. I went to the emergency room at Coney Island Hospital. A woman doctor took care of me. She said it was not a heart attack, it was a hamburger attack. That was funny ha-ha.

But it made me think. If something bad ever happened to me, I wanted my girl to know how much I love her. April you brought sunshine into my life. Everyone says April is a rainy month, but I know it is 100% sunshine. My best times are taking you to the movies and the library and reading to you. I love how we talk things over. It makes me laugh inside when you tell me to be quiet because you have an important idea to tell me.

If I'm still around, and I expect to be when you turn twenty-one, you will never get this letter. I will tell you in person how much I love you and how much you changed my life. But if for some reason I am not around, please know the things in these boxes are important to me. Valuable things, at least now they are worth a lot. I want you to have them. You can do whatever you want with them but you should speak to a topnotch lawyer first. There is plenty of money in there for his fee.

I know what a good heart you have, but I ask you not to share this stuff with Mommy. I have already taken care of her extremely generously in my will (I hope you know what a will is, but grown-ups know and can explain). Mommy is great and loves you, but she might not know what to do with all the valuable things. She could talk about them and that would not be safe. I hope this can be our secret. Remember how we put our finger against our lip and said shhh when we swept up the pieces of the bowl you broke? Our secret forever we said. And we never told.

You are the best child in the world and I know you will grow up to be a great woman.

SWAK which means sealed with a kiss,
Daddy

April needed my dad and me to say something. I said, "You can really tell how much he loved you. Believed in you, adored you." Her head went up and down, up and down, as if she couldn't agree with me more, but maybe wanted a little extra. My dad was taking a while to chime in, so I added, "All through the letter I sensed an undertone of gratitude."

"What do you mean by gratitude?"

"I think he believed that you redeemed him," I said. "Before you, he knew he was brilliant in two areas—accounting and corruption. But when you came along, this amazing relationship began between the two of you, and he discovered that he was a loving man."

It was tight in that room, even with the closet door open, so only two drawers at a time could be opened and pulled out to examine their contents. I stepped back into the bathroom so my dad could take my place, and he looked down into the drawer where she kept the letter.

April wore white cotton gloves and a mask; she had been told that the oil in a person's hands and the heat and gases from their exhalations could degrade paper. She returned the letter to its drawer and closed the biometrically operated door. "I feel stupid doing this every time, but I contacted someone at the New Jersey State Archives, and this is what they said to do."

"No one screws with the New Jersey State Archives," my dad said. "Listen, April, it was a beautiful letter. He put great thought into it, along with great feelings."

"Do you think he had any inkling that my mother was homicidal?" she asked. "I mean, it wasn't just the letter. Think about all the trouble and expense to make those arrangements. It sounds to me that he had a lot more incentive than heartburn."

"Who knows, but I think it was probably the heartburn," he said directly, with no sense of *I'm sorry to be saying this* regret. "He'd led a charmed life and was near the top of his game. He could have gone further—money laundering for the top oligarchs, dictators. This was the first time it hit him that he was mortal. If he had been worried about his wife, there were many steps he could have taken to protect himself."

"Do you think he was going to leave her for Luisa?" April asked.

"No clue. My guess is he was hoping that Luisa wouldn't insist on it and force him to make a choice. Kim was acceptable in his world—pretty enough to show around, and she didn't threaten to call the police or leave him when he abused her. He wasn't a guy to rock boats."

I was standing behind him, so I couldn't throw him a look or even give him an elbow. On the other hand, I might not have, because he was telling April the truth as he saw it. She was no longer a child he had to protect.

He kept going. "Possibly he would have dumped your mother eventually . . . as long as he got custody of you. But if Seymour had any idea that she was dangerous, he would've put any thought of divorce out of his head." He sensed that more clarity was necessary. "He would've had her killed. By a pro. No one would have suspected that her death wasn't an accident. No one."

The other drawers contained treasure—literally. Within lacquered antique boxes were lovely black and dark green velvet bags. Inside each bag, wrapped in something akin to tissue paper, but softer, were jewels. Giant emeralds, rubies, and medium-size stones as well in colors so rich it was as if I were seeing that shade of purple or blue or yellow for the first time. April put each back into its bag before opening another.

I finally comprehended why *Thou shalt not covet* had been included in the Big Ten.

"Do you know any details about the stones, where they come from?" I asked.

April pointed to the bottom of the drawer where, under the dividers, there were a couple of sheets of paper in a clear plastic folder. "The numbers on the pages correspond to numbers on tags that are sewn into the bags." She shook her head in the manner of somebody trying to get their thoughts into order. "I was so blown away at the precision of the system. The descriptions of each stone—the weight, its provenance—were so meticulous."

"Do you think your father did that?" I asked.

"I think he came up with the system and had it done for him, and then had it checked. Probably double-checked. I learned a lot about him just by going through this stuff."

"Where did he get the jewels from? One person—or was it the thing to give Seymour Brown a jewel as a kind of thank-you?"

"There was a tag inside one of the velvet bags that held the Burmese stones. It had a name on it: M. Roland Paulu. I researched the name. He was a Corsican arms dealer. Apparently some arms dealers were paid in gems when they had dealings with unstable countries. Like Afghanistan could pay in emeralds and tanzanite because of its mineral deposits. Colombia is famous for emeralds. That guy Paulu was linked to the Colombians, and I wondered about why they needed arms, but—"

"Major drug trafficking," my dad said.

"Cocaine especially," I added. "The Medellin and Cali cartels ran most of that. And they had major guerrilla insurgencies, though that situation has improved. But I guess one side or another needed arms."

"The rubies are mostly from Myanmar," April said. "That used to be Burma. Violence between Muslims and Buddhists, human trafficking, and they needed arms either to kill each other or stay in business.

"Did you ever sell any of the jewels?" I asked.

"Just one. A ruby. I couldn't believe I was getting into this, but I found a guy who sent me to another guy and he led me to someone else who bought it. I wanted to give Misaki an engagement ring, but I didn't want to give her one from Burma—I felt they were tainted. Anyway, I used the money to buy a ruby from Thailand. I'm sure an ethicist would find that discouraging." She started to put them away. "I want you to understand why I kept these," she said quietly. "I assumed that because they were part of a criminal enterprise, the police would take them. It's not so much the money. As you know, I have more than enough for the way I live. But *he* gave me these. They're from him. That means something." She looked up at us, her eyes shining. "I mean, if there were a family out there mourning their lost treasures and they'd get the jewels back, that would be one thing. But this way, they'd just be auctioned off by the government."

As she put away the last Afghani aquamarine, I felt sad to see them go. I imagined April saying *Feel free to come back and visit them anytime*, but that didn't happen.

"Wait a minute," my dad said. "Can you bring out the box before this one? It was black with blue things on it." April nodded and stood taller to go iris-to-electronic eye of the detector of the door above. She drew out the box fast, as if it had grown hot at her touch.

Dad gently took the box from her, handing her each of the four wrapped jewels, one at a time. He knocked on the bottom, then pressed down, leaning his weight into his thumb. Nothing. Frowning—unsettled, maybe fearing humiliation—he slowly slid his fingers around the seam where the edge met the sides. Suddenly one corner of the bottom lifted, just a little, as if it were being coy. He put his pinkie finger under it and carefully worked it off. Underneath was a pile of papers in a clear folder.

April looked stunned. "What are those?" she asked. I wondered if we should get the archival gloves, but my father started rifling through and she didn't object.

We both stood and looked over his shoulder. They were pages of tables in tiny, meticulous handwriting, like some brand-new font. Name after name, with long strings of numbers, dates, and cryptic notes. At least half of the papers had a ragged side, as if they'd been torn out of a notebook.

We stared at them. Stared some more. Finally I said, "Let's get some air." April put the jewels back into the box and locked it away.

We sat in the living room, my dad and I on the white couch, April in a leather chair adjacent to us. The forensics techs had finally packed up and gone. Silence in the house, except for the occasional loudmouth cicada. Dad spent almost an hour going over the pages, making a few notes. When he finished, he said he wanted to take a drive while there was still some daylight. He and April hugged each other, and he ruffled her hair. Then he left.

I said no to April's offer of a drink, but she opened a bottle of Malbec for herself and a San Pellegrino for me. "Thank you for showing us what your father left you," I said. "Beyond that letter, it's an insight into what he was. Meticulous—"

April interrupted. "He was bad. I know that. Laundering money for someone who sells arms to child-trafficking gangs? That makes the people he dealt with in Brooklyn seem morally impeccable."

"Other than you, I'm not sure Seymour knew anyone who was morally impeccable. He was a bad guy. Very bad. But he loved you. He looked at that love as redeeming him: *No matter what terrible things I've done, hurting people physically, emotionally, economically, I love April, want to make her someone good, someone of consequence.*"

"Thank you."

"You have . . . I'm so tired, and I forget what you call it," I said. "The result of his endeavors, the fruit of the loom—wait, that's underwear. Anyway, you have something of enormous value in that room over there."

She set down her glass and waited.

"And I'm not talking about the jewels," I went on. "There is no evidence that they were stolen. That lawyer, Mr. Diehl, looked at them and believed it was okay to hold them for you. They had been your father's property, and they were his to give you. Let's talk about the papers."

"His letter?"

"That's yours. From him to you. Heart to heart." I wished she were still wearing her mask. I wanted to slip off my booties and feel cool air between my overheated toes.

"You mean the papers your dad found?"

"Yes. Even now they could give the authorities an insight into the workings of global criminal activity. They could aid in the arrest of drug traffickers, sex traffickers, extortionists, murderers for hire, pornographers who specialize in children."

"Maybe he meant for me to have them," April said hesitantly. She added more wine to her glass even though it was still pretty full.

"I don't think he meant for you to use the information in those papers to access the money he'd been in the process of laundering. That would make you a coconspirator. My guess? He hid the papers because he knew the lawyer wouldn't accept them. A lawyer would be obligated to disclose their existence to the authorities right away, otherwise the lawyer would be an accessory. No, I think he meant for you to disclose it after he was gone. He didn't want the Vory to get that money. While his love for you didn't make him a good guy—far from it—maybe it made him want to see the other bad guys get what was coming to them . . . though not when he was around."

She hesitated. "The Vory . . . They're ruthless."

"They are. But how would they know? Why would they possibly think that after all these years, Seymour Brown's little kid who grew up to be a college professor suddenly has access to papers they stopped looking for at least fifteen years ago?"

"But couldn't they find out if all of a sudden their people are getting arrested and accused of all sorts of crimes—especially money laundering? Because they were involved in my dad's criminal activities. What happened today with my mom will be in the news. It will bring him to the forefront of their minds." She took a long sip of wine and then said, "Remember we ordered vegetable soup? I forgot to serve it."

I laughed. "You'll have the soup tomorrow." I wanted to urge her to do what her father wanted her to do and use that information to put away the bad guys. The worst guys. But I couldn't pretend it wasn't a risk. We could take steps to keep her anonymous, but the Vory might guess who turned them in, and they wouldn't need much evidence to come after her. There was also a chance that the information was too outdated to do much damage.

"Your father left you a moral choice. It was obviously one he wasn't brave enough or good enough to make on his own. You've been through so much. It's up to you whether you can bring yourself to go through more." She was silent. "If you do decide to go through with it, my dad and I would support you every step of the way. We would need a lawyer, but Josh knows a million of them. He can't get involved at all, but he can give me a list of A-plus people. We could arrange a way for you to hand over the papers to the authorities."

"Couldn't they charge me with aiding and abetting a felony?" she asked.

"A lawyer can advise us about that. But my dad just found the papers today. We could testify to that. And you'd have been the one to offer to turn them over."

"Let me think about it," April said.

"Sure."

"Do you want me to warm up the soup for you?" she asked.

"No thanks, but I wouldn't mind a cookie."

She flashed into the kitchen and came back with a plate of two different chocolate cookies and an oatmeal raisin. As I bit into my second cookie, she said, "If I were to say yes, could I make copies of them to keep?"

"They're yours now. Why not?" The oatmeal cookie was crunchy, but the raisins were soft.

"Would I have to testify in any trial?"

"That would be part of the deal the lawyer would work out for you."

"Okay," she said.

"April. I can't advise you whether it's worth it. But I will tell you this: your dad trusted you to make such a weighty decision, and so do I. In the meantime, Misaki's coming home, you're going to get married, and I hope you will have a loving, steady life after so much trauma."

She had a tiny bathroom off the kitchen, just big enough for a poster from *A League of Their Own*. I missed the bathroom on the other side of the secret vault, with its framed old movie scene pictures and unopenable closet. When I came out, she had wrapped some cookies for me for the road.

"Please be in touch if you decide to turn the papers in," I said. "Actually, please be in touch either way. It's been great getting to know you."

"For me too with you. And I will be in touch. One more thing."

I nodded.

"I want you to do some more detective work for me."

I sensed my eyebrows drawing together as I asked, "What?"

"I want to know who my dad was. I don't mean just his money laundering, although that was definitely part of him. When you were checking out his history, it stopped. Remember? Everything before he became an accountant is a mystery. He said he went to Pace, but there's no record of him there. No birth certificate. No sign at all that he ever existed before he took his exam to be a CPA."

I paused, considering.

"I'm not asking you to produce a documentary. I'm not asking for a family tree, although actually, that would be interesting. But only his side of the tree, because I know where my mother comes from." I pictured the rotten apple falling off a branch in Northern Kentucky, but I kept quiet. "What I want is what the two of you have. Knowledge of the steps criminals take to hide their identities. Intense curiosity and a great ability to get people to talk to you. Also, you both have a strong work ethic and you're honest. I admire how the two of you work. You have a synergistic effect on each other, so I'd be getting more than two specialists."

"April, if we were to do it, you'd have to be prepared for the fact that a lot of it's going to be ugly. You know he was a bad guy—sometimes a violent guy—so I know you're expecting that. But there are other things you could find out that might do even more damage to your opinion of him. You may feel you were his only loving relationship, and from his letter, you would be right. But it's possible he was a bigamist, with a family in the Bronx and five kids he adored. Or maybe he had plans with his girlfriend Luisa to ditch you and Kim and run off with her. You would also have to deal with that. Do you want that at a time when you and Misaki are starting a life of your own?"

"I want his story. No, not his story. His life. I want to know where he came from, what made him who he was, and what he did."

I thought about it for a minute. "We'll have to charge you our full fee this time. We'll discuss a retainer, but it's going to be costly. You would have to pay for any outsourcing. I mean, like, I don't know, off the top of my head, maybe a specialist in Eastern European languages for documents."

"Any one of those emeralds," April said, "would take care of you and the lawyer if I decide to turn over the papers."

Maybe two of the emeralds, I thought. But then again, I didn't know about gems. What I knew about, what my dad knew about, was getting the bad guy before the bad guy did any more damage. Bad Seymour Brown was long past hurting anyone, except his good daughter. No matter how he had loved her in life, he was hurting her from the grave.

We shook hands, then hugged. We seemed to get teary at the same moment.

I walked out to my car, one shoulder aching from my holster, the other numb from my cross-body bag. But Schottland & Geller had its first client on retainer. Actual income, maybe even enough to pay the rent on a second-floor office in town instead of holing up in Dawn's exercise room. It might be energizing to get out of the house. Find eight hundred square feet above a shop on Main Street that had a view of the bay that led to the Long Island Sound and the Atlantic.

When we started investigating who tried to kill April Brown, I thought I was doing it for my dad: Corie Geller, the human antidepressant. And then I thought no, I was doing it because sitting alone in a room reading a novel in Arabic about a private investigator in Amman wasn't keeping me engaged with other people, and the fictional Jordanian PI was having a far more intriguing life than I was.

But now I knew why I had done it. I needed the search, I needed the chase, I needed to keep asking the right questions. I did it because I loved it.

Acknowledgments

Bad, Bad Seymour Brown is fiction. Though I had a visceral feel for each of my characters—that happens with all my books—I needed facts and the texture of each one's world. Normally it would have meant an informative lunch with a detective or a south Brooklyn real estate agent, a trim at a salon in New Brunswick, a stroll and store-hopping afternoon to get a feel for an area's style. This time, my research was limited by pandemic lockdowns and pandemic restrictions. So thank you, Internet. I am also beholden to the librarians at the Port Washington (New York) Public Library and the Brooklyn Public Library.

Thanks to the following forthcoming individuals who answered my (many) questions about money laundering and arson investigation via phone or teleconference, or who gave me video tours of their blocks. When their facts did not fit my fiction, I went for the story: Molly Abramowitz, Nathan Abramowitz, Paul Cirone, Antonio Del Valle, Dan Farrar, Mary FitzPatrick, Gregory Gavarian, Frederick P. Hafetz, Brian A. Jacobs, Susan Lawton, John S. Martin Jr., Robert J. McGuire, Robert M. Radick, Chris Sanborn, Margarita Sandoval, and Janis Traven.

Thanks to Hiroshi Yamauchi for his contribution to the Liz Smith Center for Adult & Family Literacy; his generosity gave him the right to become a character in this novel.

My BFF, Susan Zises, artist and designer, has advised me on my characters' living spaces and their clothes since *Compromising Positions*. This time around, she actually drew up the plans for a small Victorian house not far from Rutgers University that existed only in my mind. Her contribution made it so much easier for me to find my way around in the book's second draft. I treasure her devotion as well as her knowledge of plinth block moldings.

I am delighted to have my second book in the Corie Geller series published by Grove Atlantic. Morgan Entrekin, publisher and editor, is brilliant, courteous, and patient. I am blessed to have him in my corner. I also want to thank Ian Dreiblatt, Chad Felix, Gretchen Mergenthaler, Deb Seager, John Mark Boling, Sara Vitale, Zoe Harris, Alicia Burns, and Julia Berner-Tobin.

My assistant Ronnie Gavarian has (as always) been a great help.

I am so grateful to my agent, Richard Pine. Besides being wise, he is honorable, loyal, and hardworking. I couldn't ask for better representation.

My favorite corporate lawyer, my son Andrew Abramowitz, answered my "what if" questions with clarity and grace many times during the three years it took to write this book. My daughter-in-law, Leslie Stern Abramowitz, is a woman for all seasons . . . far more than any year can hold. She shared her understanding on subjects from publishing to dog behaviors to suburban sociology.

My daughter, Elizabeth Picciuto, whom I lauded in my dedication, was my go-to on all matters cinematic. Since a professor of film looms large in this book, it couldn't have been written without her insight and knowledge. My son-in-law, Vincent Picciuto, patiently explained the rules of good behavior in finance so I would understand how to make Seymour Brown *Bad, Bad*.

Lastly, if someone should ask you, "Who is the best person in the world?" feel free to use the answer I always give: Elkan Abramowitz.